Books by *April Alisa Marquette*:

Fiction

~The Cohort Trilogy
Absolution
Progression
Iniquities

~The Cohorts, Generation Next
Improbable

~The Sea Isles Series - A Trilogy
Exodus
Affinity
To Be Announced

Turnabout

~A Tranquility Tale
Rebuke

*

Non-Fiction
Co-Authored with Jessica Janna

~The Relinquish & Reap Series
Seedling
Sowing
Yielding

**Ask for them … at your local Barnes & Noble,
or Books-A-Million bookstore!**

Progression

Progression

Movement, a new position; a succession…

The Cohort Trilogy

Book II

by

April Alisa Marquette

Books that captivate

Visit the author at www.aprilalisamarquette.net
Library of Congress Catalog Card No.: On File

Publisher's note:

The novel **Progression** is a work of fiction – for adults, only.

Though I walk through the valley of the shadow of death, I will fear no evil...
Psalms 23:4

Chapter 1

AS she drove, she felt upset. Actually, 'upset' was too mild a word. She was *pissed the eff off*! However, the funny part was she didn't actually know why. Oh, she knew she needed more time; there weren't enough hours in the day to do everything she needed to. She also felt guilty, because she never spent enough time with the wee ones, the two little people she loved most, the two who needed her the most.

Nevertheless, she had to work. She had to be bothered with people who sometimes made her sick so she could make paper. She needed the money that putting up with crap provided.

Kismet had bills. There was the light bill, the gas bill, the car note, car insurance, and groceries cost a bit. There was the property tax bill, and the cable bill. The list was endless, really.

On top of all of that, the new mother sighed, here she was, stuck in Mid-Manhattan traffic. Just sometimes, she hated the city that never slept, primarily after she'd worked a nearly fourteen-hour day.

Uh-oh... Darn. She glanced from the dashboard clock back to the parkway. She was supposed to have been there half an hour ago! Kismet Staar slammed a hand onto her steering wheel. She also eased her foot off the brake. Hurriedly, she'd had to pump it. She inhaled then exhaled, numerous times. It was what she did when she sought calm. Somehow, the exercise didn't seem to help, because all she could think was dag-blame-it, if another yellow cabbie cut her off...

IN the Port Authority, *she* watched the last of the passengers file off the big Greyhound bus. Looking at her watch, Nell realized. She had been in the station for nearly twenty minutes. For all of that time, the wind had angrily raced off the Hudson River. It had snatched people's hats and flurried their scarves. Nell frowned. She wondered if she was ready for this kind of cold, again. It had been so long since she had lived in New York.

Oh, she had been back, occasionally, but rarely when it was cold. Her bones could no longer take it.

Nell forgot herself. She realized she had been observing those who had ridden with her. She had done so for as long as she had been in the station. First, she had eyed passengers who had briskly disembarked, to hail yellow cabs. Those less hurried had simply walked away. Nell had seen others. Stepping down from the big coach, these people had stood beneath the sullen gray of the New York sky. Surrounded by luggage, they seemingly took no notice of the whipping wind. Leisurely, they'd greeted family and friends, people who had appeared at their journey's end.

Still seated on the bus and watching a toddler, Nell had laughed out loud. Wearing a bulky, red, hand-knit hat and sweater, little Mr. Rambunctious had run complete circles—first one way, and then the other—around his parents, an enchanted striking twosome.

Then Nell had felt her brow furrow as she'd watched her seatmate, the *muy* sexy, petite *chica*. That child's lovely raven hair hid the purple and blue of a bruise. Nell watched as little *mami* offered her un-bruised, rosy cheek to her vast mountain of a boyfriend. Turning away to check on others, Nell had not failed to say a prayer for the petite flower.

Then... the woman in the belted all-weather coat caught Nell's eye. With her hair attractively cut, this sleek New Yorker stood, seemingly awaiting her own passenger.

It was that woman's lopsided grin that Nell Moore saw when she stepped off the bus. "What, might I ask," Nell inquired, "Are you smiling at?"

Nell found herself caught up. The woman, whose skin was the color of a biscuit that had just begun to brown, embraced her. Displayed were lovely white teeth. "I'm smiling, Miz Nellie, because you're here!"

With a good-natured scoff, Nell eyed a throng of people. Hurrying across a wide mid-Manhattan street, all seemingly took no notice of blaring angry traffic. Nell re-focused on the curvaceous New Yorker. Nell grinned and waved. "Girl, you've seen me all your life."

"So I have," Nell's daughter stated. "But not lately," the daughter said and bent to inspect her mother's luggage.

6

Nell lifted her nose and clearly identified the smell of 'real' New York pizza. She wanted some, soon. On the crisp of a northeasterly wind, the dark, inviting scent of freshly ground coffee reached Nell's nostrils. Inwardly, she vowed to partake of that too, before she returned home to California.

"Now Mama," Nell tuned in, just in time to hear her daughter say, "I know you've got more than these two bags."

"You could be wrong," Nell quipped, her eyes twinkling.

Thirty-eight years young, Kismet slung the strap of her mother's carry-on over a shoulder. Grasping the handle of Nell's roller bag, Kismet's lips wryly twisted. "Mama, if you only had two bags, I'd be surprised. However, I know you, and I knew something else, too."

Retired from Juvenile Corrections, Nell pulled at her jacket. "What's that, honeybunch?"

"I knew you'd be the last person off that bus."

Up and out, Nell's laughter bubbled. "You did?"

Kismet nodded. "I knew you'd wait until the 'traffic flow' let up."

"Don't use my words, girl, to poke fun at me. You know your old Mama's hips ain't as strong, or as young as they used to be."

Kismet chuckled. "I knew you'd say that, too. Hey, to prove I know you, let's see..." She released the handle of her mother's roller-bag. The attractive brown woman forgot the glowering, gray, near-evening sky. She ignored blaring traffic and bright streetlights. She forgot the warm glow spilling out of stores, some already decorated for the Advent season. Kismet no longer noticed hordes of people bustling about. "I'll bet," Kismet slowly began, as though she and her mother were the only two in a peaceful world, "You packed a few pieces of fried chicken. Yep, and homemade potato salad. Oh, you've got chocolate chip cookies, too. In your purse—Right?"

"Well, actually..." Nell felt around in her oversized leather handbag. "I ate an apple, so I could keep the cookies. For you."

With a girlish squeal, Kismet accepted the small package pressed into her hand.

"Don't ask me one question, KissGirl" Nell ordered. "I knew to make those with unbleached flour and raw sugar. So, you see Missy, Mama knows you too."

Kismet smiled as Nell pulled her wool jacket close. Indeed the older woman had known that New York would be gray and cold. She wasn't even surprised at it being so soggy, but what Nell hadn't been prepared for was the bone-chilling wind. Frenzying her hair, it dried her lips and angrily crept between her layered clothing. It caused her to shiver, just like it had years ago. She had lived a stone's throw away from where her daughter now resided.

"Kiss, honey," Nell began, forgetting the cold for a moment, because in a way, it was almost refreshing, after that stuffy ride. "Mama needs you to know something."

"What's that?"

"I was *second* to last off my bus."

Kismet chuckled as slowly she and her mom walked. "Okay. Well, how was your trip? On the bus that you were second-to-last off."

WHEN Kismet Staar pulled up before her tidy, three-bedroom ranch home in suburban Elmont, New York, she sighed.

"You sound tired," Nell remarked, and took in her surroundings. She noted beautiful shrubbery. It hugged her daughter's picturesque home. It was set back among trees on a cul-de-sac. With its two and a half baths and remodeled kitchen, Nell recalled, the house was just darling.

Peering across the street, she noticed other homes, some of which boasted Christmas lights. One had a group of teenaged girls clustered before it. All wore flimsy jackets, but none appeared cold. Youth.

"Some days I'm so tired, Mama," Kismet began, unaware of her neighbors. "Until if I didn't have Lyle, I don't know what I'd do."

"Then pray you don't soon find out," Nell sagely advised.

Kismet removed her car key, and Nell unlatched her seatbelt. Kismet placed a hand on her mother's arm. It caused Nell to halt. "What is it, baby?" she asked. Turning, Nell saw the wistful look.

Although Kismet wanted to speak, she could not.

Seeing the struggle, Nell gently coaxed, "Tell Mama about it."

Swallowing the lump in her throat, Kismet could not say all she felt. Therefore, she simply took comfort in her mother's presence. Nodding, she whispered, "You're really here..."

"I am, sugar."

Kismet squeezed her mother's arm. No longer was Nell a figment of her imagination, "You're not out in Cali, Mama," where Nell had moved many moons ago.

8

"No, baby, I'm here, with you." She was there, Nell recalled because her baby needed her, although her adult baby would never admit it, outright. However, Nell silently thanked God for letting her safely make it, another year, to be with her daughter.

Kismet's voice drifted through the cold. It had begun to creep into the car the moment the ignition had been shut off.

Despite it, Nell's eyes widened. Had her daughter really said she was grateful, every single day, *for her*? Surprised, the five foot three, hippy, buxom woman gaped at the person she remembered pushing forth. "KissGirl, why would you be grateful for me?"

Noting her mother's mostly gray hair, brushed back from her forehead, and the currently deeper grooves around her mouth, Kismet sighed. "I'm grateful, because your being 'Mama' wasn't easy." Kismet touched a tendril that curled over Nell's collar. "I know that now. Before, I didn't give it much thought, probably because you had everybody fooled."

Nell frowned. "Explain, sugar."

"Well, Mama, you made things look easy, even though being responsible for everything and everybody is darn hard. You did it for years. You held us all together, even when we lost Daddy..."

Bittersweet that it was, for Nell, it was nice to know that her sacrifices and her labors of love had not gone unnoticed. Just like her daughter's being overwhelmed and stressed had not gone unnoticed, by her.

It was natural, Nell thought with a sigh, for any mother to feel besieged, especially a new one, but being proud and stubborn to a fault, Kismet would never admit that, outright, either. So here they were.

Reassuringly, Nell patted her daughter's hand; she also admonished the younger woman to remember that sometimes motherhood was tough. It could leave a woman feeling guilty and worried, "But, if it doesn't, I was once told, you're not doing it right. Oh, and it does have its joys."

The daughter, hippy and buxom as well, agreed.

"Ahhh... there's the smile I love," Nell crowed. Then she motioned for Kismet to exit the car. With a shiver, Nell called, "Help me out, KissGirl. When these old bones get cold, they get stiff, sho nuff!"

Hurriedly rounding her vehicle, Kismet gently aided her mother. Suddenly she couldn't wait to show off her babies. Kismet smiled wide because boy, would Miz Nellie be surprised. Just wait until she saw how the wee ones had grown.

NATIVE of Belize, Lyle Manfred met both women at the door. Happy to see Nell, the woman he thought of as his second mother, Lyle kissed Nell's cheek. Exchanging pleasantries, he took her coat, and Kismet's. He hung both and disappeared with Nell's luggage.

When Kismet disappeared, older Nell took the liberty to stretch out on the sofa. Vigorously, she rubbed her stiffened hands. Nell thought, boy, was it good to be warm again. Looking from a toy tucked into a chair, she noted the décor, Afro-centric, as before, with walls the color of a cantaloupe-inside. There was plush, cocoa-colored furniture, and as was often the case, Kismet's home was tranquil.

This evening there was a delicious aroma wafting from the kitchen. Hopefully, it was some kind of stew, Nell mused. Her mouth watered at the thought of crisp vegetables, new potatoes, and tender meat, all in a savory broth. She hoped for fresh bread and soft butter. While they were at it, Nell thought, she wanted to round out her meal with dessert.

Forgetting food, Nell's mind went back to the man who was going to be her son-in-law, although her independent and stubborn daughter didn't know it yet. Lyle Manfred, the tall, milk chocolate man, had neat, long, locked hair, that he often pulled into a ponytail, one that hung down his back. Thinking about Lyle, Nell smiled, because he was a smart, successful, software engineer. He had also been perceptive enough to begin a prospering business with two of his college chums.

Looking at his picture, on her daughter's coffee table, Nell realized. She could not have been prouder of the man if he had been her own son.

Suddenly, Nell saw why other women were attracted to Lyle, the man who had asked her daughter to marry him, several times. With his broad-shouldered rugby players' build, large neat hands, and warm brown eyes, he was a head-turner.

Uh-oh. Hearing voices, Nell pulled herself up and into a sitting position. She laughed, as a three-year-old streaked by.

"Come on, Pumpkin," Kismet coaxed. She asked didn't her child want to give Nannie some sugar.

Reappearing as well, tall, milk chocolate colored Lyle reclaimed Nell's attention. He said, "Nannie, look. Over here." In his arms, he held a chubby, manila envelope-brown baby.

10

"Oh my," Nell exclaimed. Reaching for the six-month-old, whose name was Chance, she marveled. "Look how my boy has grown!"

Standing back, Lyle smiled as Nell kissed the pudgy cheeks. Lyle also laughed when Nell held the baby away, to ogle him. Broad-shouldered Lyle proudly chuckled when Nell mentioned the baby's inquisitive stare. "You were toothpick thin, lil' sugar," Nell stated, "and all bunched up with the colic. Yes you were, the last time your Nannie saw you. Now, look at you! My boy."

Beaming, Kismet managed to plant her daughter before her mother. "Say hi, Nannie," Kismet prodded, only to receive a shy wave.

"Well, hello to you too," Nell cooed. She fingered the long, thick ponytail twist atop the little girl's head. With a nod, Nell said, "That's a pretty dress, beautiful girl. Did Momma pick that?"

With a hand atop her daughter's head, Kismet chuckled. "Déja wants to pick her own clothes. Right, Miss Pumpkin?"

Shyly the three-year-old nodded. Then she quickly turned, to hide her face between her mother's navy slacks-clad thighs.

THAT evening, Lyle Manfred bid Nell good night. Then in the front hallway, out of view, he kissed curvaceous Kismet, lasting and sweet.

On locking her front door, Kismet returned to the oak and white kitchen. She joined Nell, who sat with a coffee cup and saucer before her.

"That Lyle sho' is a sweetie."

Kismet waved a manicured hand. "Mama, you always say that."

"You never disagree. Oh, and wasn't this sweet of Valeria René?" Nell asked, changing subjects. "Baking this raspberry swirl for me."

"Ma!"

"Huh?" Nell looked down at the cheesecake on her plate. She quickly swallowed. "Oh, talking with my mouth full. Again. I'm old, KissGirl." Nell near whined, "But, I do apologize. Still, this was nice of Val, especially since she's a busy optician, and since…well, you know."

Kismet knew. The young woman, the family friend suddenly passed. It had been a shock to everyone.

Placing her cup on its saucer, Nell spoke. "You know, KissGirl, there was a time when mostly only older folk went on. Nowadays, though, it seems as if more young people are leaving here."

Kismet agreed. She thought of the young woman who had recently passed. Kismet acknowledged that it was good that the family friend had lived. "I mean, that girl squeezed all she could out of her time. That was great because who knew she'd be gone, so soon?"

With a frown, Nell asked if the young woman had been ill.

"No," the daughter shook her head. "It baffles. One day she complained. A few days later, she went to the doctor, received a diagnosis, and then in under a month, she was gone." Kismet snapped her fingers, "Just like that."

"I suspected as much," Nell revealed. "KissGirl, the truth is, it almost always seems sudden when anyone goes, young or old. I know, well, from my ordeal with your father..."

As a young married woman, buxom Nell Moore had desperately wanted to believe that sweet Brantley would always be with her, despite the disparaging diagnoses of three different doctors. Back then, Nell had armed herself with prayer. She'd had a host of supportive friends and family, but her husband Brantley had given up.

One evening he'd begged his young wife to let him go.

Crying, young Nell had taken Brantley's face in her hands. While leaning over his recliner, gently, she'd kissed his eyelids. Nell kissed Brantley's cheeks, his nose, and mouth. She had also whispered—she couldn't recall how many times—that she loved him. The man she'd promised to forever love was worn from his battle with cancer. Aware of it, Nell sighed, and gingerly, she'd tucked Brantley's blanket around him.

Moments later, Nell heard him expel a breath. Again, she placed her arms around Brantley. She had been unaware that it was for the last time.

Cancer-thin, when before he had been all brawn, Brantley Moore slipped quietly away. However, for him, Nell's love remained, all these years later.

Seated, she sighed as her coffee cup was re-filled. She also called out, "KissGirl, this life is uncertain. That is why every woman should live each moment as though it were her last."

Replacing her mother's cup and saucer, Kismet nodded. She knew that indeed her mother Nell attempted to live life just as she had said.

12

Chapter 2

"**I** told you he was greedy, Ma," Kismet Staar Moore announced, having noticed the struggle between her infant son and his grandmother.

Wearing an old, burgundy, velour jogging suit, Kismet stood in her oak and white kitchen. The room, the busiest in her home, contained an array of leafy green plants. Kismet eyed the one on the windowsill at the sink. She recalled that the space was often inviting. When her small son wasn't screaming his head off.

"I'm thinking Mama," she smoothly began, "if you let Chance hold his own bottle, he'll stop hollering. He can drink at his own pace."

"Fast is his pace," Nell complained, trying, and failing to wrench the bottle from her grandson's chubby hand.

Mindful of her son's frustrated wails, Kismet nodded. "You're right, Ma, but he's hungry."

Pulling the bottle free and shifting her wailing grandson, Nell scoffed. Gently she patted the baby's back to induce a burp. However, she was caught off guard. Clad in a fleece one-piece sleep-suit, the squalling baby lurched forward. Nell managed to dodge his chubby open hands. She did not miss her daughter's stilted laughter, either.

"No, no," Nell scolded and managed to hold her grandson away, in case he swung again. "Little boys should not hit."

Sick of the 'newness,' Kismet's son continued to wail. He also tossed himself backward in his grandmother's arms.

With a sigh, his mother crossed the room. Gently she rescued both her son and his bottle. "There now," she cooed as the baby settled himself in the crook between her arm and ample breast. She watched as greedily he drank. "It's okay, Momma's boy."

"There, nothing," Nell harrumphed as her grandson's wet lashes touched his cheeks. "Hmmph. Y'all new parents..."

Ignoring the verbal jibe, Kismet called to her small daughter. "Déja. Déja Neeva. You're not going to eat again this morning?"

Seated opposite her grandmother at the oak table, the child stared at the bowl before her.

Fully disapproving, Nell shook her head. Never would she understand new parenting. In her day, you just told a child what to do, and they did it—or else. It was that simple. Yet Nell kept her mouth shut. To say anything would spark a fuss. Therefore, she rose and began clearing breakfast dishes.

"Guess I'll take this here bowl," she mumbled, eyeing soggy cereal, a waste. The Momma really should have made the child eat, Nell thought.

"I suppose *your* kids did everything you wanted," Kismet huffed. Dang, moments prior, she'd told herself to disregard the insinuation that she wasn't rearing her children right, but she couldn't.

"KissGirl," Nell called from the sink, "I ain't said a word."

Keeping her eyes on her rapidly gulping son, Kismet snapped, "You didn't have to. You implied you're a better mother."

"I did not." Nell faced her daughter. "I know that look, young lady."

Kismet tried not to cut her eyes. She felt exasperated because her mother often made her feel like a ten-year-old. "What look, Ma?"

"The one that says you're geared up for a fight," albeit verbal.

Kismet inhaled, and exhaled. Indeed, she felt like a good spar, but, she reminded herself, it would serve no purpose. Again, she exhaled and spoke. "Ma, I only want peace, and calm, for my babies."

Nell rolled her eyes. She wanted to tell her daughter that the *world* wasn't calm. Yet she remembered...

She actually needed to respect that her once high-strung daughter was not so anymore. Kismet now sought peace. In the past, she had often attempted to resolve matters with her fists. Kismet had started the quest years prior. First, in her Long Island City apartment, she'd lit candles. She'd progressed to meditating. The younger woman had garnered a collection of positive energy crystals. Further enhancing body and mind; she consumed more fresh fruit and vegetables. After she'd progressed to this her current home, she had started limiting her processed sugar, starch, and meat intake.

Batting her eyes, Nell felt it was all pretty 'new age,' but so be it. It seemed to help. Running hot sudsy water, Nell remembered that her daughter had visualized the child she wanted. Then Nell's granddaughter Déja had arrived, via a child welfare agency.

Splashing around in hot soapy water, Nell recalled the whispering caseworker, Macy. The woman informed Kismet that the then-three-month-old had been abandoned. Déja's mother had left her at the utility

14

company, in the payment office. Macy had also said the infant's biological mother, Contessa, was addicted to the drug crack. According to records, before 'the abandonment,' Contessa had been seen wrapping the baby in a blanket.

On hearing it, Kismet had diligently refused to judge Déja's mother. Instead, she had been grateful for the seemingly careless act—until caseworker Macy mentioned a series of visits. During these, which were necessary, Kismet's toddler was expected to interact with her biological mother. The very woman who had marched away from her baby, despite the shouts of bewildered onlookers.

Then, try as she might, Kismet could not erase the conjured image of Contessa clomping off without a backward glance.

Kismet wound up telling Nell that despite all her praying and meditating, each moment of each visit was torture. "I just can't see why," the daughter moaned, "I have to take my toddler to see a woman who should, but doesn't, give a good gotdurn about her."

As she washed breakfast dishes, Nell glanced out the window. With her eyes on a bare tree swaying in the wind, she recalled having heard, for the umpteenth time, what caseworker Macy had said. All visits were designed to help a child transition back to the biological parent(s).

"But I don't *want* a transition!" Kismet had yelled. On the phone, she'd broken down enough to tell the truth. "Mama, for me, and Déja, these visits aren't working! How can they?" Kismet had howled, "Most of the time, Contessa doesn't show up!"

Kismet admitted that, in a way, the no-shows were sources of relief. She claimed Déja was relieved too.

"She's only a year old, KissGirl," Nell softly stated, aware that her daughter's nerves were frayed. "Our little bugaboo's too young to know, one way or the other."

"Oh no," Kismet insisted, "Always, on our way home, Déja is a chatterbox when *before* these 'visits', she acts withdrawn."

Nell hadn't pressed the issue, although she'd wanted to say that before each appointment, the baby likely felt Kismet's anxiety.

Yet Nell had prayed. Each day she'd beseeched her Savior, her trusted friend, to turn Contessa's attentions elsewhere, if she would not be a good mother to Déja. Nevertheless, Nell had added, if Contessa *could* get it together, Kismet had to accept it. She needed to do so with minimal hurt.

Nell had also prayed that if Déja was to be adopted by Kismet, then KissGirl had to comply with the Child Care Agency's rules.

As she stood washing the hot cereal pot, Nell recalled one visit. It had severely broken her daughter's heart...

Contessa showed up for her appointment. She was neat, clean, and bearing a red teddy bear, along with a game.

Knowing this was out of character for Contessa, Kismet stood in the hallway. In hushed tones, she spoke into her cell phone. "Mama, the stupid game is for an older child. But I guess if you're trying to bribe a toddler, you figure, what does *she* know." Kismet forced herself to head inside. She whispered that she would call Nell later. Inside, she grudgingly acknowledged the visit was going well, until Déja stepped out of hearing range.

"I'm getting her back," wafer-thin Contessa smugly proclaimed.

Kismet eyed the woman who had sounded a bit too haughty for her liking. Kismet also felt like all the air had left her lungs, so quickly, she turned her palms face-up. She willed herself to breathe, slowly. She cautioned herself not to swing her big fists into the other woman's face.

Watching the strange lady who did some wild yoga shit, Contessa spoke. "I know you heard me. What you got to say?"

Kismet convincingly suppressed advancing hysteria. She sounded calm as she replied, "I wasn't told that, *by the agency.*"

"Well," Contessa waved, "you being told, by *me*—the baby mama. I want my chile back."

Kismet watched the puppet girl whose speech was slightly slurred, like she was on something. Through jumbled emotions that threatened to turn into full-blown panic, Kismet heard Contessa. The woman mentioned having had a nice job.

"I worked in Maa-hat'an. *I* was a supervisor. Before..."

Contessa might have said she'd tried crack too. Kismet didn't know. She only felt unnerved, listening to the disjointed speech.

"Then, I was craving it. Bet you didn't know," Contessa seemingly digressed, "I had a son. He's eleven, but he ain't mine no mo.' They took him, but when I was carrying Déja, I started getting clean. I named her for *déjà vu* because I had been there before. Yup, when I had my son.

Now I'm getting my self togeva." Contessa wound down. "That's why I'm getting' my baby back."

Kismet remained quiet. Baffled, Contessa asked, "You still ain't got nuthin to say?" Indeed, she had expected an angry word, or two. She had even pictured a wild screaming match. Contessa had imagined hair pulling, on her part, and punching the baby stealer in the face.

Unaware of Contessa's musings, Kismet was not about to let the scrawny marionette get to her. Well, not any more than she already had. Therefore, Kismet agreed, she had no words. She shrugged, "But then again, you seem to have enough for both of us."

Tired of playing with the make-believe stove with its real pots, Déja toddled over. Sleepily, she climbed up and laid her little head on Kismet.

With narrowed eyes and a constricting heart, loudly, Contessa announced that soon *she* would hug Déja that way. "When I have her back," Contessa continued, inexorably angry, "I'ma make sure she forgets yo' fat ass because she'll be with her *real* Mama! I'm gon erase you! Like you was pencil lines on a piece of paper."

Fat? Kismet was stuck on that. It stung. Gently, however, she turned Déja. Kismet attempted to forget the bony woman who had angered her. Buttoning her toddler's coat, Kismet asked, "You ready, Pumpkin?"

"Yo, you'll see," Contessa loudly predicted, bolting up. With bare legs, she forced her chair back. "I'm gittin' her!" A tear escaped as Contessa also thought, the nerve of that big chick, calling *her* daughter pumpkin!'

"They *want* us to be togeva," Contessa hissed, fighting the desire to jump-kick Kismet. "They told you, fat girl. These people don't keep muvas n children apart." With one hand, Contessa indicated the Child Care Agency workers who all but blended into the drab gray walls. "You gotta get you anuva person's kid. You greedy child wolf!"

Kismet had had enough. She swung around. "Contessa," she called. "Take your own advice. Get your*self* another child, because I will never let this child, *my* child, go."

Caught off guard, Contessa claimed she hadn't heard correctly.

"Oh, but you did," Kismet stated, seemingly unperturbed as she settled her toddler on her hip. Angling the child away from Contessa, Kismet snarled. "Look, puppet girl, you would *want* to believe me when I say I will move heaven 'n earth to keep this baby. So, do—not—fuck with me!"

Contessa flinched, as though she had been struck. She also blinked, then she hollered, "You ain't *birth* her!" As she watched the woman carry her daughter away she screamed, "I want my baby!"

Kismet did not look back or respond, which made Contessa angrier. The thin woman drew herself up to mirror a barnyard rooster. Violently she shook, while feeling unbelievably angry. Contessa shouted an epithet as the cords in her neck stood out. "That's right, you fat cow, I said that! I'm telling you: you did not *birth* that baby! *I* did!"

"Doesn't matter," Kismet coolly called while she faced the elevator. From her peripheral, she watched Contessa, who just might run up. Perversely, Kismet wished Contessa would. Kismet ached to knock the wind out of the woman. Firstly, because Contessa had cursed her. Then secondly, because Contessa had reawakened the fighting demon. Long and hard, Kismet had meditated and prayed to subdue it. Now here she was, back at square one, because of Contessa.

Standing near her chair, Contessa swiped at tears. She desperately wanted to ignore the strong, familiar pang...of need. Turning one way, then the other, she wanted to scream. No! She wanted to best the ache that rose. Shoot! It surged forth any time she felt ill at ease, and dang, she was trying to get clean!

Using both her thin arms, Contessa hugged herself. She wondered, why now? Why was the crack pipe calling? Doubling over in agony, she again raised herself, and her two middle fingers. She wanted to use them to pick out Kismet's eyes. Contessa kicked the teddy bear that she'd brought. She watched the baby-stealer step onto the dusty elevator. Contessa could not refrain from letting loose a blood curdling scream. Then she fell onto her chair. She shook and cried, and hated that those still in the room with her appeared unfazed, while she was so unhappy.

Outside, driving away, Kismet played soothing jazz. She tried not to allow upset to claim her.

When she put her car in park, Déja excitedly whooped. Dazed, Kismet gazed up. There was her longtime sista-friend's lovely gray-brick home. It sat on a perch atop a winding stone staircase and sloping lawn. *How* had they gotten there, without incident? Kismet wondered. She did not remember the drive over. Getting her baby out of the car, she recalled something. Her mom often said it. When a woman couldn't carry herself, the angels did.

Valeria René opened her front door. She ushered her sista-friend and toddler into the two-story home that she shared with her husband, Fabian. As Valeria's fluffy, plumed-tail gray cat, Mystical, tiptoed around her, the homeowner bent. She cooed at Kismet's baby. "Hi, God-mommy's girl."

Entering the den, adjacent to the kitchen, Kismet plopped onto a comfy chair. Fatigued, she watched her friend remove Déja's outerwear. She watched Mystical the cat too, as daintily he sat beside his mistress.

In silence, Kismet's eyes wandered. Again, she saw her friend's home, in hues of white and tan. Vaguely, Kismet realized why she and others loved the place. It was the right mix of modern with traditional. There were older, creaky, polished wood floors and banisters. Overhead there were hand-hewn beams. There was a small powder room boasting original fixtures. The kitchen had been updated, and an excellent job Valeria had done decorating. The space was often flooded with natural light. More importantly, though, Kismet mused; Valeria's home resonated peace.

It seemed as the house had taken on the persona of the woman whose voice was always soft, her mannerisms gentle. Actually, when Kismet thought about it, she remembered that her male first cousin had once described Val, her sista-friend, to a tee. Now, what had Beau said?

Oh, yes. Beau said Val was a mocha color, with big, fluffy, natural curls. First cousin said Val's eyes were almond-shaped. They were some color, grey, green-flecked, or like liquid honey; it depended on her mood. Beau felt Valeria was too thin, though, for a sister. In Hollywood, however, and Canada, and Tribeca where he made a living as an actor, she would have been gold; she was top-heavy, God's gift. She had a slight lisp, garnered from her mother, a native of India. Little Val also had a picture-perfect doll-face, replete with her African-American father's snub nose and lush lips. However, Valeria's *inner* beauty was magnetic. It was what drew people to her.

Unaware that she was thought so highly of, the homeowner gently inquired, "Kiss, what happened?" Kismet looked beat.

"That woman—"

"Wait." Valeria turned to the toddler. "You and I should find Godfather. He's got cookies." Moments later, Valeria returned, followed by her ever-present pet with the plumed tail. Putting her feet up, Valeria knowingly stated, "We're talking 'bout Déja's mother, right? What'd she do now?"

Kismet moaned that Contessa intended to take her baby back.

"No!" Valeria gasped, as Mystical hopped onto her lap.

"Yes, and that crack addict said it like I'm powerless to stop her."

Valeria's eyebrow shot up.

"I'll go to court if I have to," Kismet divulged. "Up in that office today, I almost strangled her. She was so haughty and rude. Get this, when I stepped onto the elevator to leave, she yelled *eff* me, in front of all these people. Oh, but that was *after* she had called me *fat*."

"You're curvy. Anybody can see that" Valeria stated. She recalled that while attending Georgia's Clark-Atlanta University, Kismet Staar, her dorm mate, had often been referred to as 'healthy,' and 'stacked' like a 'brick house.' Kismet had always been called some version of curvaceous, or a bad mamajama. Never had she been called fat.

Absently Valeria stroked her cat. "Kiss, can't that woman see your flat stomach and teensy waist? Sure, you've got a big ba-donk-a-donk and fluffy bazooms, but you're so shapely."

"I'm surprised puppet girl can see anything—other than the crack pipe," Kismet quipped. "Listen. She told me a sob story. She has a son, who was removed." Kismet held her head. She hadn't meant to spill her beans. Yet something about the comfy chair and her friend's willingness to listen prompted her to tell all.

"Well," Valeria said afterward, "Contessa will have to tell the next person about the *daughter* she lost. We're not letting Déja go," not so that unstable woman could run off from her again.

Once more, Kismet became livid. "You should see her, Val! She's back on that stuff, if she was ever off it. Oh, and I have a question. If she wanted my baby back so badly, why didn't she turn up before now? If she loves my baby so much, why does she shirk visits? Wait." Kismet's eyes widened. "She has never mentioned loving Déja."

Suddenly Kismet wondered, aloud, if Contessa was simply on a power trip. "Ooh, I pray not, because..." Kismet shook her head, "I can't stomach the notion that I might actually have to give up this baby."

Suddenly Kismet gasped and her eyes filled. "Val, I can't breathe..."

Leaning forward, and unsettling her pet, Valeria grasped her friend's nape. "Head down, honey. Stay there."

Moments later, Kismet sat up. Her face was a dull red as she asked, "Val, if you gave birth, could you leave your baby? Or if you and your baby were separated, God forbid, wouldn't you try to re-connect?"

Valeria was aware. The questions were rhetorical. Her friend was simply trying to make sense of Contessa's actions, so she kept silent.

Wringing her hands, aloud, Kismet asked all the questions that she could never have asked Contessa. "Why have a baby when you know you can't care for her? Why allow *me* to get intertwined? I've fallen in love with her! Val, that woman can't possibly love that baby as much as I do. She don't know Déja! She doesn't know what my baby eats, or what toys she likes. That woman hasn't spent *half an hour* with my child since she was months old! My baby is walking and talking now. She knows her ABC's. She can sing '*Yes, Jesus Loves Me.*' *I* taught her those things!" Kismet tapped her own chest. "I feed and bathe Déja. *I* take her to the doctor. I sit up with her at night. *I* am the Momma. I am. Now."

As cold fear raced through Kismet, she wheezed. "Val, my baby's *little*. You've seen her big trusting eyes. Oh, my God!" Kismet yowled, because it broke her heart to think that her child might one day roam the halls of a crack house. Covering her eyes, Kismet fought the notion that Déja could wind up surrounded by addicts and pedophiles.

"Val," Kismet called, trying to erase ugly thoughts. "My baby is *defenseless*..." Kismet's face crumpled. She began to keen from deep within. With her hands at her face, the Momma rocked. She announced that she would become a fugitive. "You will see my car and plates on Amber Alert, because I *cannot* let Déja go, not to her." If Contessa was another sort, Kismet Staar blubbered, maybe she could see it.

Quite maternal as well, Valeria understood.

"Oh, Val," Kismet moaned. "I could *not* have left this baby, not until somebody found me. Then I never could have said that I left because my baby bothered me!" Kismet suddenly rose and swung at air because Contessa was not there for her to pummel.

"Hohneee, don't." Valeria got up and placed her arms around her friend. "Let's go get you cleaned up. Lil Mama doesn't need to see you like this." Valeria also said, as she often did, that she would brew a pot of coffee. "Then, you and I will pray. Oh, and I'll call Donovan," their lawyer friend. "I'll find out what leverage we have, if any. Okay?"

Kismet nodded, grateful for a friend who cared.

As Valeria led the way to the powder room, her feline followed. As she ran water, Valeria internally acknowledged that *spiritually* Déja belonged to her friend. Actually, the child belonged to everyone in their family of friends. That was the reason Déja had to remain with Kismet.

Sagely, Valeria said, "Kiss, it may not seem like it now, but we *will* watch this child grow up. One day, we will grandmother *her* kids, even if," Valeria winked, "we have to do it while walking with canes."

Despite niggling doubts, Kismet chuckled.

Standing in her daughter's kitchen, Nell sighed, because that day and others like it seemed a lifetime ago. Turning from the sink, Nell forgot memories. She gazed at her daughter. Kismet now sat feeding her son a jar of baby fruit. As she watched, Nell remembered another morning…

Kismet picked up the phone. "Hi Macy." With a hammering heart, Kismet wondered why the caseworker called. Yet Kismet's voice was steady when she asked, "What's up?" She prayed for no negative news. She wanted to hear nothing that pertained to her small daughter.

"Well, this involves you and Déja—but it's *not* bad," Macy quickly clarified. Taking a breath, Macy asked, "Kismet, do you love Déja enough to give her a sibling?"

Bewildered, Kismet narrowed her eyes, "Pardon me?"

"Déja's got a brother."

"I know. The boy should be thirteen or fourteen now."

"You're right," Macy admitted. "But—"

"Oh, hell no," Kismet Staar blurted. "Macy, don't you dare."

The caseworker sounded confused. "Don't I dare what?"

"Don't you ask me to take in her brother; I will not."

"Not even if we'll pay you, until you adopt him as well?"

"Macy, I'm not equipped to handle teenagers that I didn't raise."

"Wait, Kismet, this brother is only a few days old."

Kismet blinked. "Come again?"

"Contessa had another baby," Macy explained. "He's just days old, and he may be addicted to crack, like we thought Déja might have been." Macy expounded, "Contessa is in jail. Her mother is too frail and old to help, so we thought of you. You know we aim to keep families together, so, since you adopted Contessa's other child…"

"A boy baby," Kismet mused aloud.

"Cutest thing too," Macy put in, hoping Kismet would agree to give him a home. "He has Déja's father. We could have this baby to you within a few days. So, what do you think?"

With the phone wedged between her ear and shoulder, Kismet continued combing her daughter's hair. She remembered that Macy had said infant placements often ended in reunification with birth parents.

"Look, Kismet, this baby needs to be with family," Macy pleaded. "We want him with someone who will love him, too."

"Will I be able to adopt him?" Kismet inquired.

"I'm sorry. Um, backing up. I couldn't answer just then. Someone was in my office, but… Hmmm." Macy rifled through papers. "Adoption is possible."

"How?" Kismet asked, remembering that Contessa had never gotten clean, but repeatedly, she'd balked at Déja's adoption.

"Well, for one thing," Macy explained. "As I said, Contessa is behind bars. She'll be there for five years or more. And she asked for you."

"No!" Kismet gasped. "She hates me."

"She hates herself, what she's become, but she specifically asked for *you*. She said you love the best part of her, her daughter. She hopes you'll love this baby too."

Kismet was stunned. "No way…"

"Believe it. Oh, and another thing," Macy continued, "Contessa has a day or two left, but she's decided on a name, if you approve. Want to hear it?"

Kismet chuckled because life sure was strange. "Tell me."

"She likes *Chance*. She said with you, her son will have that."

Wow. Kismet told herself to stop grinning because she had to discuss things with Lyle, the only father that Déja had ever known. Holding the phone, Kismet cringed. The inclusion of another child would re-fuel Lyle's argument. He'd say that Kismet Staar should become his wife.

He would say, once more, that he *got* her. Before they met, Kismet had been independent. Nearing thirty, she'd wanted to make her life count. Therefore, weary of waiting for a man, she'd bought a house. She had also purchased beautiful diamonds, among other things. Then when none of that had satisfied, she'd fostered a child, so she could lavish love on someone other than herself. Lyle Manfred would remind Kismet that he, the software engineer, had come along. He wanted to buy a bigger house, and a significant diamond. He would reiterate that for a while now, he had wanted to adopt Déja, but Kismet Staar kept balking... Like Contessa had.

Now, Kismet realized, she pondered rearing another child. Ms. Self-sufficient forgot her man. She would cross that bridge when it was time.

Stacking now-clean breakfast dishes, Nell smiled. Four years of events. Some she had seen firsthand. Others she had re-lived through the telling. Turning from the cupboard, Nell's gaze fell on her adult baby. Kismet now had her own babies. The younger woman was doing a commendable job. Nell squeezed her daughter's shoulder.

"Kismet Staar, you are a good mother."

Kismet looked up, surprised. "I thought you were washing dishes."

"You're really special, Kiss." Nell nodded. "Mama's proud of you."

Sheepishly, Kismet nodded. "I'm only doing what you did."

"No, baby," Nell shook her head. "You are doing more."

"How so?" Kismet queried as her son scooted over clean tiles. She pontificated that Nell Moore had reared both her and her male first cousin. Calling Beau by his nickname, Kismet said, "Diddley was your brother's child, but you took him in. You did the same for Fah-WRY," Farai. Kismet's half-sister was older. Her South African name meant *rejoice* in Shona. Kismet raised three fingers. "The way I figure, Mama, I still have some going to do if I'm going to catch up with you."

Nell scoffed. "I did what any mother would. You would do the same."

"I don't know, Ma. Let's hope I never have to disappoint you."

Nell grinned. "I hope *I* never have to wash another sticky fry pan."

Kismet watched the woman who quickly ambled from the kitchen. Laughing, the daughter called out, "Miz Nellie, you didn't wash that one!"

24

Chapter 3

VALERIA René sat on the side of her down-covered bed. Wearily, she gazed through sheer panels. Out of doors, it was gray and cold. Turning away, she greeted her furry pet, "Hello, Mysti."

She knew she should shower and get to her kitchen, but she couldn't move. Valeria thought about lying back down because on this Thanksgiving morning, she felt exhausted. Perhaps a cup of coffee would jump-start her. Her husband had brewed a pot just minutes earlier.

In her warm bedroom, Valeria used her toes to feel around for her slippers. While pulling on a plush robe, she vowed not to be sad. On this holiday, she needed to be thankful. She had an attentive, attractive husband, who made coffee—when *before*, she had always had to make it, even when she'd lived with capable roommates, Ronni and Beau. Valeria reminded herself, she had a beautiful home, and heaps of friends and family, for which she was grateful. Yeah, she cryptically thought, swiping at a tear, but her family was missing a member, or two.

Father in Heaven, Valeria prayed, *please* help. She didn't want to start the holiday thinking negatively; but darn if she didn't miss that girl! Over the years, she'd watched the girl grow and mature. Then she'd watched her die. Valeria swiped another tear and wondered again. Where were her slippers? She sighed when her toe struck a worn bunny-head. Her husband hated the ratty footwear, but later, she'd wear a new pair.

Wearing the hideous things, she went to bathe. Valeria vowed to think happy thoughts. She would concentrate on the food she had yet to prepare. She would contemplate all who would appear at her home in the early afternoon. Doing those things would keep the tears at bay. Then, just maybe, she would get through this holiday, without incident.

BEAU and Sandal stood in an archway, beneath a hanging glass and brass fixture. It illuminated the round-top heavy wooden door of the Sinclair home. However, impatient because it was cold out, Beau could have cared less. With puffs of breath visible, he groaned. "Where *are* they?"

Then Valeria appeared. She opened the door and said, "Welcome."

Standing in the doorway, her onetime roommate introduced his guest. Sandal Foxworth. Crossing into her foyer, Beau handed his host a bottle of wine, exquisitely wrapped. "Yo, you 'n your girls need to get it together." Beau announced it and unwound his cashmere scarf.

Valeria gazed up at the man with whom she had lived for three years. She used his nickname. "Diddley, why not just say hi? Why not ask how I'm doing, instead of starting off with complaints."

"I could," Beau informed the small-boned buxom woman whose cat tiptoed around her feet. "That is, if I didn't wind up lurking outside, in the cold, every time I visit you 'n your girls."

"That's twice that you've mentioned them," Valeria pointed out. "Now, I have to ask. Who are my girls?"

The tall, well-built man removed his coat. "You know, your mother, Kismet Staar, and A'nt Nell."

"I guess *they* don't let you in either, the moment you ring," Valeria smiled. "Well, your complaint has been duly noted. Now, if you're going to eat in this house, you had better give me some sugar."

"Oh, I'm going to eat." Beau pulled his host into an embrace. "I didn't trek this far out, just to bond with you and the husband. Heck, if you want, I'll even hug your cat." He bent. "Commeere Mysti."

Valeria grinned. Her friend lived to eat. Turning, she advised her visitors to follow.

Beau's guest, Sandal, took a seat in the spacious den adjacent to Valeria's kitchen. Looking around, the redhead became impressed. Beau's former roommate's place was warm and festive. Spicy smells wafted from her kitchen. Not bad, Sandal ruminated, and glanced at his sizeable phony Cartier watch. He could get used to living like this. Then he could have real jewelry, among other things.

The only thing was, Sandal told himself, if he lived here, that furry monster would have to go. Heck, who did the cat think it was, eyeing him? The feline did so while wearing a rhinestone collar.

Hearing an unfamiliar male voice, Sandal forgot the cat. He put his mental 'home inspection' on hold. Turning, he watched his friend, his lover—what did he call Beau? The truth was, Sandal did not know. So far, he and Beau had just been kicking it, getting to know each other, Sandal guessed. Watching Beau grasp the hand of a good-looking bald man, Sandal became fascinated. Mmm, Sandal mused, *this* man was tastefully dressed, as was Beau.

When Beau motioned, Sandal stood. He found himself introduced to Bald 'n Beautiful. What a firm handshake, oh my. The man's name was Fabian. Sinclair. That meant he was... Valeria's *husband*. She had opened the door. Forgetting the woman, the cat-fish, Sandal eyed the dark-skinned man. He was five-ten, maybe, and good-looking. His solid build suggested a physical strength to match that in his eyes. The man was obviously successful, Sandal wickedly contemplated, while trying to make prolonged eye contact. Damn, and he was disappointingly heterosexual. Oh well, Sandal sighed. He reclaimed his seat and forgot the *bor*-ing opposite-sex couple.

Sandal got the life nearly scared out of him when the furry monster jumped him. The cat dug its claws into his leg. Man, that hurt!

With a yowl, the cat launched away, and Valeria appeared. She looked stunned as she spoke. "I'm sorry. Mystical never does that."

The doorbell chimed, and forgetting Cujo, the cat, Sandal sighed when Nell Moore, strode into the room. Try as he might, Sandal could not figure it out. Beau's aunt seemed more like a mother to him. When Sandal mentioned it, Beau evaded. Therefore, Sandal thought, who cared?

Oh phooey! Beau's cousin, named Kizzie—or some slave shit—followed. Fresh horrors, she had her brood with her. There was also a man. Broad-shouldered, he was tall, and a milk chocolate color. Wow, Sandal liked. The man's long, locked hair hung in a thick ponytail down his back. The Caribbean god looked like he always had money.

That was probably why 'cousin' was with him, Sandal sourly cogitated. Cousin probably wanted the dinero as well as the dick.

Sandal listened as the man spoke. He had a slight accent. It was apparent when he said something smelled delicious. Sandal wanted to wave and call out, "Yoo-hoo, big man. Come see if it's me!"

"Hey fam," Beau's cousin, the young mother called, with her snow-suit-wearing small son on a hip.

"Hey-aay," the family of friends chorused. Wryly, Sandal thought, 'Oh Gawd. These people are the Brady Bunch, Black.' Turning away, he wondered if he would hurl. Gazing at the flat-screen television, hung like artwork on one of the den walls, Sandal pretended to be engrossed in the game. Really, he hated sports. However, what he could get into were the players. All them big fine men, with big parts, big homes, big cars, big willies, and big wallets.

Sandal noticed when Beau stepped away from unconcealed windows. Sandal watched Beau bend, just in time to catch a little girl. With abandon, she'd flung herself up and into his arms.

"Lord, Diddley," the aunt, Nell, called, "I pray you and Déja never miss."

Now that would be a blast, Sandal wryly thought. He'd have loved it if the kid had gone splat!—the attention-stealing little brat.

"Ask Buncle to take off your coat," Nell advised her granddaughter. Shed of her outerwear, the older woman asked if Valeria needed help.

"Buncle." Sandal frowned. "Why'd your aunt call you that?" Sandal watched the kid snatch off her woolen hat and run to Fabian, Val's husband, her Godfather. Sandal nearly hated the kid then. She got to run into the arms of all the men, while he was expected to behave, like someone's puppy. He plugged back in, just in time to hear Beau say that when the running kid had started talking, 'Buncoo' was the best she could do with 'Uncle Beau.' "Now," Beau shrugged, "All the kids call me that."

"Cute," Sandal replied and appeared very un-amused.

Noting the dour reaction, Fabian turned from Valeria. His lips barely moved as he inquired of Kismet. "What is Opie's story?"

Removing her son's outerwear, Kismet laughed, aware that Fabian referred to light-skinned Sandal's red hair and freckles. "I don't know, but I'll bet it's really sad because he is one sour little man."

The doorbell chimed, and Valeria's father joined the informal gathering. The older, dignified African-American man carried large foil-covered dishes. His wife, a native of India, followed, ferrying smaller parcels.

Valeria's three sisters, their husbands, and families arrived shortly after that. Within minutes of the last arrivals, Valeria announced, "Looks like we're all here. Dinner is served."

"Alright!" Beau headed for the washroom. "A'nt Nell, a seat?"

Pulling herself up from a sofa, the older woman called, "I got you, Puppy. I'll save two."

DURING the sumptuous and spicy meal, Valeria's father, Horace Thompson, remained silent. He simply enjoyed all that was set before

28

him. Near the end of the meal, the older man with the hooded eyes put his fork down. He motioned to Beau's guest.

"Well, young man," Horace began. "We've about finished breaking bread together, and I realized. I did not make your acquaintance."

The uneasiness of others in the room became palpable. Noticing it, Horace surveyed everyone seated. Turning to Valeria's mother, he asked, "Chee, did I overstep some invisible boundary?"

Chitra daintily tucked a lengthy wisp of hair behind an ear. Although her voice was naturally soft, she replied loud enough for all to hear. Her husband had committed no wrong in making an observation.

"Sandal," Nell called, taking the situation in hand. "I'd like you to meet Mr. Thompson. He is our hostess, Valeria's dad." Nell nodded at the imposing, older, mahogany-skinned man. "Hor'ce, do meet Sandal; what's your last name, honey?"

"Foxworth."

"Hor'ce, meet Sandal Foxworth." Nell noticed that the younger man rose only slightly. He thought it appeared as though he attempted to stand—shame on him. Sandal did so while extending a slender manicured hand to the head of the table.

Horace extended his own hand. "Nice to meet you, Sandal."

"Pardon me, Hor'ce," Nell seamlessly continued. "I should have introduced you first, as age permits. Sandal here is a pal of Beau's."

"Oh, so you're an entertainer too?" Horace inquired with nothing short of admiration for Beau. Years back, Horace would have advised Beau, or even his own son to get a job as an actuary or to enter the export business with him. However, Horace's son was gone. Beau's film career was booming, so there was no need. Therefore, Horace thought, perhaps by association, Sandal was also to be admired.

With his choirboy high voice, Sandal said, "No, sir, I am nobody's entertain-ter."

To Kismet, who had also noticed the mispronunciation, Fabian whispered. "This twerp's nobody's reader either."

Unaware, Sandal admitted he couldn't carry a tune if it had handles. Glad to have all eyes on him, he offered, "I'm just an accountant, sir. Nothing glamorous about what I do."

Well, at least he got the last part right, Beau thought while reaching for his glass. Lord, what a liar this Sandal was turning out to be! For crying aloud, he was no accountant! He was the *errand boy*, at the Hair

Castle! He swept up fallen, cut-off hair at the frou-frou salon. In addition to hair duty, on Saturdays, Sandal picked up chicken dinners for patrons. He ferried them from the church fund-raising drive. Sandal also ran those same people's digits to the numbers joint.

Accountant, Beau thought, with disgust. Sandal ran numbers. He didn't actually work with them. Why hadn't he said he was a simple working man, instead of flat-out lying? Of what was he ashamed?

Fabian, Valeria's husband, wondered why Beau refused to look at his effeminate guest. Why did Beau finger the dog tags ever on a chain around his neck? That was the surest sign that Beau was upset. Suddenly Fabian wondered, was there trouble in paradise?

"Oh, you're all right too, then feller," Horace said, approving of Sandal's phony line of work. "Hey, without accountants," Horace chuckled, "the IRS would run over us hard-working businessmen."

"You can say that again," Nell chimed, as others inaudibly breathed.

One person who especially exhaled was Valeria's mother, caramel brown Chitra Thompson. With Horace, she owned a thriving export business. It serviced the Caribbean, as well as third world countries. Chitra knew her husband loved their daughter's former roommate, Beau. Since Chitra and Horace had lost their son years prior, she knew Horace took a particular interest in Beau. However, she felt Beau's little friend there was dubious.

Forgetting red-haired Sandal, Chitra thought about her son. Horace Jr. had been the only male child in a family boasting five girls. However, at eighteen, he had been gunned down.

One warm evening, Junie, as they'd called him, had stood on a street corner, joking with neighborhood acquaintances. He hadn't seen death coming. Yet the intended victim, an avaricious young male, had escaped, while Horace Jr. and others had lost their lives.

If only, Chitra thought, as she had countless times, if Junie had been at work. If he had not had that evening off, had he not been aimlessly hanging about, he would be alive. Junie would have gone on to finish college. He might have gotten married, and perhaps become a dad...

Imperceptibly, Chitra shrugged out of the painful past. Again, she cogitated on Kismet's first cousin. She knew Horace believed Beau was misguided because the actor was homosexual. His sexual preference, however, Beau never flaunted. For that, Chitra admired Beau. She even recalled speaking with him. At the time, Beau revealed that the only place he desired recognition was in his career, as a multi-talented entertainer.

Desiring to understand, Chitra had said, "So, you're saying you'd never be a queen?" A flirtatious, oft times overly effeminate male.

"You got it," Beau nodded.

"But why not?" Chitra had asked. "What's the difference?"

Patiently Beau explained. *He felt* that particular homosexual male was sometimes flamboyant. "Perhaps he wants to be seen, or validated by others," Beau quantified. "I'm not sure, but I don't have those desires. So, like you, Ms. Chitra, I don't always overtly flaunt my sexuality."

"Okay, if I'm wrong, correct me," Valeria's mom had advised, needing clarity. "Beau, if your personal preference was questioned, you would tell the truth?"

"I might," Beau shrugged. "It depends on the situation." Beau said he had nothing to hide. "Still, I won't knowingly allow anyone to use my sexuality against me. Just like you, a heterosexual, would not allow it either."

Valeria's mother thanked Beau for being candid. "Now I'll be frank with you, my son. Due to your preference, you and Horace will forever split hairs."

"That's fine;" Beau revealed that he liked verbally sparring with Mr. Thompson. "That ol' guy's tough, and bouts with him sharpen the mind."

Chitra chuckled. "Call my darling that to his face, Beau, and you might wind up physically sparring with him."

Released from the reverie, Chitra gazed at those seated at her eldest daughter and son-in-law's table. Her eyes landed on Nell. At sixty-something, Kismet Staar's mother could smooth any problematic situation. When everyone started moving about, Chitra intended to tell Nell so. Tuning back in to the talk at the table, Chitra wound up having to excuse herself. Forcing herself not to run, she exited the dining room.

With eyes on her back, Beau apologized. "I didn't mean to cause pain..."

"Ma will be okay." While speaking of his mother-in-law, Fabian took his wife's hand. "Val's okay too." He eyed her. "Right, babe?"

Red-haired Sandal stared down as Valeria tearfully nodded. How he hated public displays of affection, between opposite-sex couples.

"I'm okay," Valeria told Beau. "I just miss her. This morning really wasn't a good one because I couldn't stop thinking about her."

"I believe we all miss our dear girl," Nell offered. "Kiss and I happened to speak of her the other evening. Ain't that, right, sugar?"

Kismet nodded while watching her daughter, who heartily ate.

"We were saying," Nell reminisced, "that our dear girl was so full of life. Oh, and I'll bet none of you knew. She took *me* dancing."

Every adult, but Sandal Foxworth, the newcomer, chuckled. Once more, Sandal recalled why he abhorred family gatherings. Well, other peoples' gatherings, because his family never gathered. Still, when others united, Sandal loathed that they always tried to make him feel left out. They did so by discussing things of which he had no knowledge. Just like Beau's chunky little aunt was doing at present. Butterball delved into the past, which Sandal also hated.

Gleefully clapping rose nail-polished hands, Nell again snagged Sandal's attention. It seemed she and dear girl, whoever that was, had gone to the Hullabaloo. "Can y'all believe it?" Nell inquired, "Me, at a club—and on *gay* night too?"

Oh, Gawd, Sandal sardonically thought, and the old hag was telling people?

"Whoo-hooo!" Horace guffawed, despite the tug of loss.

"It was incredible," Nell hooted. "Listen, you guys, our girl told me she chose gay night because we could stick together. She said if we'd gone on a regular night, we'd have looked silly dancing together. Wasn't that sweet? She said her kickboxing classmates had told her about it."

A likely story, Sandal wryly mused.

"Anyway, she and I strutted up in that club," Nell continued, "And my dear girl and I danced. Honies, I got to swanging these old hips, and 'fore long people were ambling to buy me *and* 'my date' drinks."

Looking sheepish then, Nell admitted that two young women wanted to buy her companion drinks. "But guess what?" Nell whispered. "Lil honey said people thought we were lezbeen—oh, it was the most fun!"

Nell went on to speak of an altogether different occasion. Then too, she and dear girl had hung out. Laughter rose, but stoic, Sandal found nothing funny.

However, Horace, Valeria's father, chortled, "Lord, Lord!" Wiping wiped his eyes, he said, "Nellie, you sure can tell a story. So you're saying on this other night people thought you two pretty girls were men, huh?"

Nell spoke slightly louder. "Yes, and imagine *me* a man." She placed a hand at her ample chest. "Me, with this big bosom." Nell grinned widely as her family of friends guffawed. "We all know," she called out, "Our dear girl could not have been anybody's man either, with that angel face 'n figure."

"Oh, I don't know," Sandal sing-sang, his voice soprano high. "I've seen she-men who look better than every woman at this table."

In the stunned silence, Beau scrubbed a hand over his face.

"He can't take Opie anywhere," Fabian again whispered to Kismet.

She agreed, "Not with that mouth."

Dreadlocked Lyle nearly caused both his lady and Valeria's husband to keel over with stilted laughter. Using Beau's nickname, Lyle quietly advised, "Diddley, dawg, lose the bitter-ass homo."

In the ensuing silence, Sandal felt stupid, but smoothly again, Nell piped up. Then Sandal remembered the second reason he hated family gatherings. Somebody always tried to make him look stupid, he felt.

Nell didn't miss a beat. Steering attention away from Beau's silly young male friend, she caused everyone to laugh at another tale.

Chitra, hearing all from the hallway, returned to her seat. Faintly she smiled as Horace whispered, "Chee, Nellie was talking about our baby."

"I know." Chitra squeezed her husband's hand before she turned to Nell. In the beauteous smile that Nell offered, Valeria's mom saw something. She had never noticed it before...*pain.* Kismet's mother had known love, as well as loss.

Patting Chitra's hand, stocky Nell nodded. "I'm done honeybunch, but you go on," Nell coaxed. "Talk about our dear girl, if you want to."

Chitra felt shocked, because she had been so grieved, unable to even *breathe* her son's name following his passing. Years later, she had lost her daughter. Now Nellie was saying she should speak aloud of her baby. Chitra did not know if she could...

Taking a breath, however, she breached the silence. "Nellie was speaking of my Lovey, "Chitra began. "LorRen was her given name. She is—I mean she was—Horace, and my last baby." Chitra explained that Valeria's youngest sister had been twenty-three. "She was stolen by

Lupus. It is not contagious, or even a form of cancer, but its victims are usually women, of childbearing age. That is why I ask you ladies to get medical check-ups." Chitra looked, beseechingly each young woman at the table.

Afterward, as most everyone began to move about, Nell nodded at Chitra, Valeria's mother, who was slightly younger. "You did good, girl," Nell announced.

Kismet's mother also said she would reveal what a friend had, back when she had lost Brantley. Nell said her friend had admonished her to *celebrate* her husband's life. "I was told; don't dwell on your person's passing."

Nell reassuringly squeezed Chitra's hand. "*Speak* of LorRen, Chee. Then, I promise you, our dear girl will live on...in you."

Chapter 4

PUTTERING around in her daughter's kitchen one December evening, Nell spoke of her sister-in-law. "Given the life Ophelia led, I'd have thought she was long gone."

Anticipating the meal that her mother currently prepared, Kismet didn't know what to think. Her first cousin Beau's mother had been missing for more than two decades. However, the woman had recently contacted him.

"Why?" Kismet asked. "Why turn up now? I mean, what's she going to gain by doing so now?"

Wearing a denim tunic and matching drawstring pants, her mother Nell sounded argumentative. "Why're you asking *me*?" Dismissively waving, Nell apologized. "KissGirl, I'm sorry, but no one's ever known why that woman did any of what she did." Checking on broiling fish, Nell re-closed the oven. "Guess we can ask that simple 'Phelia though, when she finally shows up – if she does."

Quickly Nell whisked together a sauce for the meatloaf that she'd made especially for Lyle, her unofficial son-in-law. While whisking, Nell revealed, "My mama never liked that girl. Your gran called Ophelia," Beau's mother, "fast. Your gran said 'Phelia had ugly ways."

Kismet nodded. "Well, Grandma Lacey was right."

"You know," Nell pensively began. "I can't remember a time when that old lady was wrong." Wistfully Nell smiled. "KissGirl, your grandmamma sure loved your daddy; from day one. Despite the glitch in his and my courtship, she rooted for him. Brantley and I worked things out."

"Yep," Kismet grinned "and look what you got."

Nell nodded. "Almost twenty years of wedded bliss."

"I was talking about *me*," the daughter pouted. "You got me."

"Oh, yeah," Nell tried to sound unfazed. "We got you in there too." Unable to keep up the charade, Nell chuckled, as did her daughter.

"A few times, I've felt sorry for Diddley," Kismet admitted.

"I did too," Nell divulged. She said that she had often wished that instead of Beau being her brother's child, he had been hers.

Kismet looked up from the for-four-year-olds puzzle that her daughter would gladly disassemble. "You did?"

"Yes, because like you, I always felt a little hurt for Beauregard. I loved my brother, don't get me wrong, but with him not being able to see his son, because Beau's crazy mama was on the run; then with my brother dying of cancer, it was all so unfortunate. I felt if *I* had been Beau's mama, his youngest years would have been stable."

"Why'd Ophelia keep Beau away from your brother—Beau's father?" Kismet asked because she had always wondered.

"The woman was a bitch," Nell offered plain and simple.

"Ma! She was your sister-in-law."

"That may be, but, ain't another way to describe Ophelia." Washing her hands, Nell painted a picture with words. "Say you birthed a child, KissGirl. Then say you ran off with that child. Say you did so because your husband didn't want you doing drugs. He didn't want you sleeping with other men in his bed, either. Now say you mistreated your child. You caused him to be frightened of everything. Then say yo' husband's people wanted to help, but you pushed them away. Say you believed you were making them pay, but really, your child was the one paying. Then," Nell huffed, "What if you kept a nasty place and barely fed that child? What if you didn't care if he went to school or not? What would all of that make you?"

Kismet stared at the puzzle that she had so easily put together.

"Tell me," Nell demanded.

"You told *me* already," her daughter said. Aware that Nell was perturbed, the younger woman stood. "Mama sit, lemme make you a drink."

"No. I'on't want one of your sugarless green gag-me concoctions." Nell griped, "What I want is to pound the daylights out of Ophelia!"

Kismet was amused as she said, "Well, Miz Nellie, next week, you might get that chance, but tonight you need to relax."

"KissGirl, I'm sorry." Nell lowered herself to a kitchen chair. She shook her head. "All I know of that woman suggests one thing. Ophelia contacted my boy with a motive –and it's more than likely *money*."

36

Kismet admitted that when she thought about what had been done to Beau when he was little, she too wanted to beat Ophelia down. "Still, mama, we've got to let anger go, because what if she's changed?"

"Oh, you think that heifer done found religion?"

"Be nice, Mama," Kismet beseeched, filling the kettle.

"Kismet," Nell moaned, "I'm a good Christian, but that woman dogged my brother. While he suffered from prostate cancer, *he still* made a home for her. What did she do? She catted around on him."

Nell sighed, and told the truth, "I really don't want to be angry anymore, sugar." It had been too long, "But it just seems like I don't know any other way, not when it comes to Ophelia."

Nell's daughter understood.

"KissGirl," gray-haired Nell struggled to rise from her chair. "Ain't you got a fifth of gin 'round here? Pour me two fingers of that, or I know you got some Tennessee whiskey, pour that up and forget that kettle."

With a laugh, Kismet Staar gently pushed her mother back down. Getting a cup and saucer, she said she was going to teach Nell to meditate. "Then you can leave the bottle alone." Kismet was teasing the woman who drank socially a few times a year,

"Girl, you talking like I'm an ah-ca-holic. Look," Nell huffed. "Just get me my gin. Then tomorra you can teach me your mediation mess."

"It's med-dit-*tay-shun*," Kismet corrected, "meditation, Ma, and it's not mess. It helps. You'll become more centered and calm."

"Okay, KissGirl. Whatever." Nell waved, "Teach it to me tomorra. Then hope it sticks. Or after I lay eyes on the whore that my brother married, just pull me off her."

Chapter 5

LIGHT-SKINNED Ronni Brown with the short, naturally wavy, blue-black hair placed the last folder in her large leather carryall. Looking up, she noticed a young woman.

Approaching, the blonde with steel-blue eyes, carried a large tote.

Ronni noted the shoulder-grazing hair, a coarse sunflower yellow. She saw pale skin not hidden beneath a mask of makeup. All of this, Ronni glimpsed in the few seconds it took for the woman to walk up.

The University's lecture hall suddenly seemed hot and stuffy. However, Ronni forgot the endless rows of chairs and the painted-shut windows. Breathing in, and out, she focused on the Jenny-come-lately.

"I was impressed with your presentation on HIV/AIDS prevention, treatment, and counseling," Ms. Blue Eyes offered without preamble.

Fatigued, and ravenously hungry, Ronni was polite, "Were you?"

The blonde that Ronni suddenly thought of as 'nature girl' nodded. Blondie also announced, "I liked the *feeling* with which you delivered your lecture."

Ronni was compelled to meet the younger woman's riveting steel-blue gaze. "What feeling was that?"

"Well, I got a distinct impression that you weren't up there faking it. It seemed as though you *knew* someone, a friend, or a lover, who was an HIV sufferer. Or maybe you know someone who has full-blown AIDS."

"Bingo." Ronni slung the strap of her carryall over a shoulder. Immediately, she felt more at ease with Ms. Blue Eyes than she'd felt with anyone new in a while. Therefore, she said, "Walk with me? I ask because the chalk dust in here is about to choke me."

"Well, yea-ah..." Quickly the young blonde fell in step with the shorter bright-skinned African-American woman. "You were up there for what? Nearly an hour and a half –not that it seemed so," blue-eyes hastily added. "But after that, I'd want to choke too."

Abruptly, Blondie stopped walking.

Halting as well, Ronni was surprised when she was offered a black nail-polished hand.

"I'm sorry. My name is Keesa. Keesa Louise Foster. I know you're Ronni M. Brown because you wrote it on the board. I remembered your name from when I registered for this lecture." Closing her introduction, Keesa revealed, "Ms. Brown, I am an HIV sufferer, but *not* a victim."

SEATED in her living room, Ronni recalled Keesa's 'sufferer' statement, made months ago. The young one hadn't prefaced it with excuses, nor had she begged for understanding.

Ronni thought it strange, as she lay listlessly on her ivory, camelback sofa; the way a person could remember so many little things.

Now, why had Beau crossed her mind?

Perhaps because five years prior, she and he had lived together. Val had also lived in their large three-bedroom apartment. They'd called it The Cohort Quarters, The Quarters for short. Perhaps, Ronni mused, she even thought of Beau because while living at The Quarters, he'd loved to lounge on the sofa upon which she now sat.

Wow. Ronni couldn't believe how time had flown. Not long ago, she and her roommates had lived in Astoria, New York, in this very apartment. They had almost believed they would be together forever. Silly. Sillier still was the fact that they and Kismet Staar, Beau's first cousin, had called themselves Cohorts. Back then, though, Kiss had lived in Long Island City, alone. She'd progressed to her current home in suburban Elmont, New York.

With a sigh, Ronni realized how young and misguided she and The Cohorts had been. Ronni's mind drifted back to Keesa. What a shock it had been to see Keesa lying in the hospital. She'd had tubes everywhere. Despite that, Ronni had taken Keesa's frail hand. She had tried to offer what small measure of comfort she could.

Swiping at fresh tears, Ronni remembered Keesa's eyes. While in the hospital, the blonde had barely been able to speak. Her *eyes* had spoken volumes however. They had silently conveyed that for Ronni's presence, Keesa was grateful.

Lying in her home, on her sofa, Ronni reached out to stroke her mostly black cat. Her cat had milk-white paws, and its underside was the same color. The cat stepped around on Ronni's lap.

Ronni stared out of a window. Dismissing the gray afternoon, she remembered. Keesa had been back on her feet. Profusely, Keesa had thanked Ronni for being there for her. "You know," Keesa had said, minus malice, "I'm alone in the world, now. So your concern means more than I can say."

Oh, and then over Cappuccino in a cutesy lower Manhattan coffee bar, Ronni recalled how her own brow had furrowed. She had listened to Keesa speak of her family, the Fosters. Keesa said her father, a brilliant surgeon, had no time for her. Dr. Foster's schedule simply didn't permit.

Keesa shrugged, "But Dad's reaction is a typical result of my illness." Keesa said her father had written her off like so many sufferers' families had done them. "He figures I'm going to die anyway, so why prolong the agony? This way," Keesa stated, "when I'm gone, he won't miss me."

"How awful," Ronni remembered blurting, horrified.

"It is," Keesa had agreed, "but that's my dad's rationale."

Ronni recalled Keesa's mother, Amy. Keesa said Amy couldn't bear to look at her. Amy hated knowing that her baby was being 'consumed.'

"That's her reason for never being around?" Ronni inquired.

With tears shimmering in her steel-blue eyes, Keesa had shrugged and said she didn't fault Amy. Her mother, a socialite, just couldn't face that this 'thing' had happened to her baby. "I love my mom and she calls, but it's not the same as seeing her or getting a hug from her." Therefore, Keesa reiterated; she really had no one, other than Ezmerelda. Keesa also said that unlike her debutante friends, tuxedo kitty hadn't deserted her.

Lying on her sofa, Ronni also remembered how Keesa had switched gears to break up with laughter. "When we met—oh Ron," the blonde gasped, "the look on your face when I said my name!"

Ronni grinned. "I thought you were being facetious, for me."

"I know," Keesa guffawed. "You felt my name was strange, for *me*."

Keesa then tried to mimic Ronni. "Ron, I know you were thinking, 'Now what is this skinny-behind white girl doing with that name?'"

Bright-skinned Ronni remembered shaking with laughter because, indeed, she had thought that. To Keesa, she'd admitted the belief that only people of color had 'different' sounding names.

"Shame on you, Veronica. Now you sound European."

"You know Keesa," butter-yellow Ronni remembered saying. "For a vanilla child, you are mad cool."

As she lay on her sofa, stroking her cat, Ronni remembered that she hadn't meant to become fast friends with Dr. Foster's daughter. Actually, Ronni's co-workers at the Gay Men's Help Center in Manhattan had dissuaded it. At GMHC, they'd admonished Ronni not to become too involved, personally, with any of her clients.

"Losing your professional distance," one man had knowingly offered, "will only be the catalyst for heartbreak in the days to come."

Lord, had he been right. Ronni had tried to back off, especially when Keesa's condition worsened at an alarming rate. With fear and horror, she'd watched Keesa rapidly deteriorate, despite administered miracles of medical science. Ronni found herself reaching for professional distance. Alternatively, she had also wondered, how could she step back? She'd felt guilty for even pondering doing so. Keesa had no one, outside of Ronni. Oh, and Ezmerelda, the black and white cat.

During the times when sleep eluded Ronni, as it often did, the big question plagued her. What if *she* had no one? Swiping tears, Ronni probed her cat's shiny coat as loudly the creature purred. Then Ronni noted the silken fur, the warmth, and the *life*. She realized that was what she'd have lost if she'd had no one.

Suddenly Ronni knew. She had done right. She had befriended Keesa Foster without boundaries, the same way her Cohorts befriended her.

Even when they'd found out she was an HIV sufferer, Kismet Staar, Valeria René, and Beau had stuck close. It hadn't been easy either, because, at the time, Ronni had been quite a jagged little pill. She'd tried to get shed of her friends. Ronni had done so in an attempt to protect them. She'd wanted to shield them from the hurtful knowledge.

However, nosey Val had squeezed too much information out of her. No, that wasn't true. Valeria had simply called, and called, even after Ronni had told her to piss off. Val had called again, and apologized, *again*, for her wedding fiasco. Sick of the other woman, Ronni had said, "Val, forget it. I deserved it."

Thinking back, Ronni knew she had acted ugly, but she'd really wanted her friends to leave her alone, with her illness. Yet Ronni had been unable to disappoint Valeria. Ronni, Kismet, and Valeria had always been there for one another. Heck, the three of them had attended and graduated from Georgia's Clark-Atlanta University together. Now those had been the days!

Therefore, Ronni had appeared at Val's wedding, but Ronni had acted like a heel. Catching Ronni off guard, Val's baby sister, 'the assassin' had done Ronni some severe damage. Therefore, Val had kept calling.

Hey, Ronni thought, lying on her sofa with her black and white cat on her lap, hadn't that sister of Val's recently passed? She'd had Lupus.

Ronni remembered that she and Val had made up, eventually. They'd claimed all was in the past, just water under a bridge. That had been when Ronni revealed her secret. She'd just had to tell someone.

To Valeria, Ronni revealed that she had the HIV virus. No, it was worse, Ronni truthfully stated. She suffered from full-blown AIDS.

That, Val had run and told. Then the Cohorts had been galvanized. Valeria, Kismet Staar, and Beau had forged past all of Ronni's defenses. They'd met her at the hospital. They appeared at her apartment and at her job. They'd prayed, and Aunt Nell, who'd been out in California where she lived, had prayed too. The Cohorts had cooked, cleaned, and shopped for Ronni. Kismet had even given Ronni a considerable gift, when in the past; Ronni had poked fun at it. Yeah, when Kiss had owned it.

Back then, Ronni remembered, Beau had visited her too, since he had at last been a BMW, a black man working. In Hollywood, he did his thing. The actor had been generous with money too. Beau had also made Ronni cry. In the past, she'd called him cheap, among other derogatory things, but Beau had proved Ronni wrong.

In short, Ronni's family of friends had helped her to see that when someone was loved, they were not deserted. That was why she had not abandoned Keesa. She'd loved Keesa, like her Cohorts loved her, still.

Keesa had been Ronni's younger white sister. The only thing was: the slender blonde had been too smart. She had gotten ahead of herself. At seventeen, she had already been in college. She was a political science major who'd met some wannabe poet in a trendy Soho café. Had she still been in high school, she would not have met the man! Sure, Ronni might not have met her either, but Keesa would yet be alive.

Ronni screamed inside because why had that corny man wooed Keesa? He'd taken her virtue. Then later, with no feeling, he told her that she, like he, would die of a disease that would break her heart and dull her drive before it sapped her spirit.

Yet precious Keesa had been a trooper. Not once had she complained. She'd uttered no unkind words about anyone who was supposed to love her. On the day that had been her last, she hadn't moaned. She had simply thanked Ronni for becoming her mentor. Despite Ronni's tearful scoffs, Keesa had lain abed in her tiny apartment. She'd thanked Ronni for being her one true friend, her sister, her angel.

Then, before Ronni could swallow the screaming ache, before she could blink past the sea of salty tears swimming in her eyes, Keesa was gone. At twenty-something, Keesa hadn't struggled. She had just closed her eyes, and too young, she had slipped, whisper-quiet, away.

As she lay on her sofa, Ronni remembered holding the thin, warm hands in her own. She'd stared into the emaciated, once cherubic face. Ronni whispered a prayer requesting safe passage. Ronni had asked that Keesa's new existence be peaceful. She had also prayed that Keesa would not forget her because they were destined to meet again. Soon.

That horrible day had been ten workdays ago. Ronni remembered going to her supervisor. Everyone knew the man didn't say much but he was always willing to listen. For privacy, Curtis Hurst had pushed his office door to, but he had not closed it. Ronni's Gay Men's Help Center supervisor hadn't stared as she spoke in a voice shattered with grief.

"I feel so disconnected, Curtis, like nothing belongs to me anymore," Ronni had divulged.

Quietly Curtis d suggested downtime, "So you can get composed."

Ronni had agreed. Woodenly, she'd nodded, like she was in a trance.

Now here it was, the end of her second week, and still, she was an emotional wreck. How could she return to her counseling position at Gay Men's in two days?

Oh, and there was something else. Ronni had a longstanding engagement with Kiss and Val. Perhaps she could get through it if she stopped thinking about the gaping hole that Keesa had left in her heart. Maybe, Ronni thought, she should just pick up the phone and beg off. Although when Ronni thought of it, Kismet and Valeria had been her strength on numerous occasions.

Ronni sat up. Tired of the moving about, the cat jumped to the floor. Oh well. To the feline she'd inherited, Ronni spoke. "I believe I need to see my ladies tonight." She eyed the black and white cat given to her by a sweet blond, blue-eyed friend. "You think so too. Don't you...*Ezmerelda?*"

Chapter 6

CAUTIOUSLY, butter-yellow, naturally wavy-haired Ronni Brown opened her apartment door.

"Hey Boo," mocha-skinned Valeria cooed and threw an arm around Ronni. "You've been crying..." Rubbing Ronni's arm, Valeria asked, "Kiss here yet?"

"Soon," Ronni replied, feeling those darn tears again. She forgot them to say, "These days, Kiss has three people to contend with. She has her self and two babies. Count Lyle and daddy makes four."

Valeria nodded and handed over a beribboned box. She also stated that not long ago, people could have set their watches by Kismet.

"Not anymore, but remember how she used to barge into The Quarters on weekends?" Valeria asked. Entering Ronni's living room, she said, "Kiss would bam on the door before any of us were up."

"Val, I hated that, *and* those lectures she gave, about us being lazy."

"Yeah..." Valeria remembered. "Kismet Staar said she got more done on a Sunday morning than you, Beau, and I, did all day."

Ronni waved. "Kiss was a cocky thing." With a weary sigh, Ronni added, "But so many things change, if you keep living."

Valeria softly revealed she'd heard the fatigue and sadness in her friend's voice. "So, Ron, if you want quiet, we'll understand."

Headed to the kitchen to open her gift, Ronni internally acknowledged that she did feel worn. Yet, no one understood better than Valeria. She'd had significant losses. Therefore, as Ronni handled her new wine, Val's understanding meant a lot. Ronni set the bottle—good stuff—on the table. She also recalled what Val had once said, that after a loss, even *breathing* felt like a chore. How right Val had been.

"Ron, I'll light some candles," Valeria called from the sparsely furnished living room. "Then we'll relax, okay?"

"I thought," Ronni began as the buzzer sounded; "tell you in a sec."

Curvaceous Kismet stood across the threshold. "Hey-aay," she sang out before folding Ronni into an embrace. Kismet felt Ronni lean in. Kismet also felt the sobs, as forcefully, they gurgled up and out of Ronni.

Kismet rubbed Ronni's back. The curvier woman staggered as she attempted to keep her near-limp friend upright. Yet Kismet whispered into Ronni's short, dark, waves, "That's it, baby. Let it go. Cry it out."

In empathy, Valeria softly moaned as Ronni came undone in Kismet's arms. It was not the first time. "Aw hohneee..." Valeria cooed.

Yet sobbing, Ronni realized that had she wanted to, she could not have explained how she felt. For months, she had tried to keep it together. It had started in the hard months before Keesa passed. Oh God, Ronni heaved. She also wondered, why did Kismet Staar have to be so motherly? Kiss was like her own mother, sweet Nell.

As Ronni cried on, Kismet murmured, "It's okay, Brownie. You don't have to be a rock." As she rubbed her friend's back, Kismet knew Ronni Brown wanted to be strong. Ronni wanted to go on as though the loss of Keesa hadn't taken a bite out of her. However, Kismet said, "These things hurt." She continued to rub Ronni's back. Having lost her father as a youngster, Kismet also intoned, "Crying's good; you loved that girl."

Holding the little yellow woman who nearly laid in her arms, Kismet thought *poor thing*, because Ronni Brown believed she always had to be strong. Kismet guessed because lil Brownie's life had been tumultuous. Ronni had been a runaway, one who'd not had loving parents. Ronni's father had been abusive. She'd watched as the man had systematically demeaned and destroyed her mother. Then Ronni's beloved brother had voluntarily disappeared. While growing up, he had been her only friend.

The list went on; Ronni had had unspeakable run-ins with men and sore catfights with women. She'd had miscarriages and abortions, and scrapes with venereal diseases. Ronni had been told she would never bear children. Then she found out she was HIV positive, yet she'd kept it moving. If Ronni hadn't toughened up, Veronica Marie Brown would never have survived or thrived.

"You're gonna be all right," Kismet whispered, holding her little yellow friend. She didn't mind that with tears, Ronni wet her denim shirt. The way Kismet saw it, her babies did worse.

At last, Ronni composed herself, but she would not; could not, leave the comfort of Kismet's arms. Something about Kismet Staar's earthy embrace always felt like home, especially when it crossed Ronni's mind that her own mother, no longer living, would never again embrace her.

Not that while she lived Minerva Brown had done so more than a handful of times, anyway.

Suddenly Valeria's bell-like laughter rang out. "Boy, is Ronni holding tightly to you, Kiss!"

Kismet chuckled, content to hold Ronni for as long as Ronni wanted.

Mocha-skinned Valeria called out, "I guess now you know how little Déja feels when she doesn't want anybody but her Momma to hold her."

Ronni half-smiled through waning tears. With her voice muffled, she predicted, "Well, your Goddaughter is gonna have to learn to share."

When she released puffy-eyed Ronni, Kismet watched the thin bright-skinned woman turn in a disoriented semi-circle.

With a finger at her temple, Ronni was aware that curiously, her guests eyed her. "Oh," she mumbled. "I was about to say, before you got here, Kiss, that we could have Chinese." Ronni wasn't hungry though. She hadn't been for days. "Oh, and I already ordered."

Kismet shrugged. "You know what we like." She hung her coat, and spoke to Ezmerelda, who brushed against her legs. "Hey, Kitty."

"Ladies," Valeria called from the kitchen. "Saavion said Beau *must* go out with him." Valeria uncorked the bottle she'd brought over. "This time, I don't believe Saavion will take 'no' for an answer."

"Well," Kismet said, stroking feline Ezmerelda, "Saav will have to wrestle Diddley," her cousin Beau, "away from Sandal."

Relaxing on her sofa, butter-yellow Ronni plaintively announced, "I hate that guy."

Valeria grinned and peered from the kitchen. "Why, Ron?"

"First of all," Ronni looked down, grateful for the wool throw that Kismet placed over her; "his name is stupid, like he is—lil red-haired, freckled-faced queen."

"Okay," curvaceous Kismet sarcastically quipped, "hate on 'Opie', as Val's husband calls him, just because Opie is simple."

"Hush, Kiss," curly-locked Valeria gleefully scolded. "Ron, tell us the *real* reason you don't like Sandal."

Ronni pulled the wool throw up to her neck. "Be funny, Val, but..." the sickly, wavy-haired woman ran her words together. "That guy's-a-liar-and-a-little-turd. Oh, and he's not good enough for Beau."

With her head thrown back, Kismet roared with laughter. Valeria chuckled too. "Now Ron, explain why you feel that way."

"What is this, Val?" Kismet asked, "Twenty questions?"

"Another thing," butter-yellow Ronni pouted out, comfy and warm under her blanket. "Even that kid's last name is wrong. Foxworth. He *thinks* he's sly like a fox, but he ain't worth squat. Sandal thinks he got game, too. That's a shame because Diddley is so open. He's not pretentious or arrogant, although though as an actor he could be. I say he needs to lose the spotted red fraud, and get a real man."

Kismet howled with laughter.

Sounding argumentative, Ronni asked, "You feel like Sandal's a fraud too, right Val? I know you do."

"Well..." Valeria frowned. "I think Sandal is a gold digger."

Ronni watched curvaceous Kismet walk toward the door. "See, Kiss? Val feels like Scandal is skanky, too. Val knows Red is with Beau for what his skanky ass can get."

"*Scandal!*" Valeria yowled. "You didn't just call him that."

Kismet returned with the food delivery. "The boy's name is Sandal."

Butter-yellow Ronni faced Valeria, who poured amber liquid into wine glasses. "Sandal or Scandal, both names are stupid." Ronni said it as she lay sprawled on the sofa as the ladies spooned up food.

Moments after biting into a spring roll, Kismet seemingly digressed. "You two know I pray for Diddley, right? I do because he needs somebody who'll be good for him, but—"

"That red switchie, Juwanna Man," Ronni interjected, "is not it."

Spooning up fried rice for Ronni who needed to eat, Valeria laughed. The curly-locked one reminded her sista-friends that she didn't often judge. "But I do feel like you, Ron. That's why we should talk Diddley into going out with Saavion."

"Now him..." sickly Ronni accepted a plate. "Refresh me. He is?"

"He works with me. He was at my wedding," some five years prior.

"Ohhh." Now Ronni remembered. Saavion Kennings, "He's primo."

Like Valeria, the man was an optician, Ronni recalled. That meant he had his own loot, unlike Sandal, who seemed poor as a mouse. Val's associate also owned property. The man was a mentor for underprivileged children. Eating, Ronni realized; she'd been famished. Wow. "Val, I didn't know Saavion was gay. The only reason I didn't push up on him at your wedding was because I was keeping a low profile." Yeah, before disaster struck. "But if he's interested in Diddley, then we should—"

"Quit talking with your mouth full," Kismet interjected.

"Yo, your kids are at home!" Ronni yowled. Her thick dark eyebrows knit together. In conspiring mode, Ronni spoke sweetly. "Ladies, if Val's co-worker is serious, let's get Red kicked to the curb."

"It's not *our* affair," curvy Kismet chirped.

"Oh, Kill-joy Kismet," Ronni waved, "you never let us have any fun."

"That's not true," Kismet blurted. "And before you started talking—with your mouth full—I was going to say it'd be nice to lose Sandal. Yet the choice will ultimately have to be Beau's."

"Okay," Ronni waved. "Now, you're only *half* Kill-Joy Kismet." Ronni turned to Valeria. "Forget Kiss. You and I have work to do."

Mocha-skinned Valeria agreed because she and Ronni loved Beau in a way that Kismet would never understand. As Beau's first cousin, Kismet had known Beau since he was a gangly shy boy. She didn't see him as her girlfriends did. Valeria and Ronni had met Beau later in life. He had been grown, well built, and more genuine than many men.

Pushing her curls back, Valeria remembered even wishing, on occasion, that her then-roommate wasn't gay. She'd have stopped her search for Mister Right because Beau, whom she often called Boyfriend, would have been perfect. Indirectly, however, he had led her to Fabian, her husband. Therefore, in her heart, every day, she thanked Boyfriend. Valeria remembered that back in the day, Ronni, who'd worn skin-tight clothing, had been similarly infatuated with Beau. On a few occasions, Ronni had even tried to seduce him. She'd mistakenly believed she could 'turn' Beau; get him on the straight 'n narrow.

Blinking back into the present, Valeria winked at Ronni. "We'll hook Boyfriend up. Forget Kiss; because Saavion will be good for Beau."

"Yeah," Ronni muttered, "unlike *the shoe.*"

Kismet guffawed. "You did not just call Sandal that!"

Valeria feigned innocence, "Well, if it fits...right, Ronni?"

Chapter 7

IN her cozy boudoir, Kismet sharpened pencils. "Ma, I don't need the grief I'm sure to get from her."

"What makes you think she wants anything other than to talk?" This Nell asked, as she eyed her feet. Man, did the masses of tiny bubbles in her daughter's foot-soak machine feel good. "Maybe your sister just wants to ask how you're doing."

Seated at her desk, erasing names from a list, Kismet became sarcastic. "Yeah, and Ophelia just wants to see *Diddley* to find out how *he's* doing, too."

"We're not talking 'bout Beau's mama and her mess," short stocky Nell huffed. "Your sister probably needs you."

Kismet sighed. When had her half-sister ever needed her? More than likely, Farai just wanted to complain. The high-profile fashion magazine editor probably wanted to vent. Maybe this time it would be about her housekeeper, or her husband, the African Diplomat. Or perhaps she'd moan about her thirteen-year-old son.

Since Kismet's nephew had been three, Farai had shipped the kid off to fancy boarding schools. The current one was a prep school. A *preparatory* learning institute, Farai insisted, for gifted children. Kismet shook her head; poor kiddo. The boy's mother had no time for him, but she jetted everywhere to make sure her magazine covers were perfect. She oversaw layouts and maintained a rigorous schedule. She also found time to keep her Mani/Pedi and her coiffure perfect.

Therefore, Kismet announced, "Ma, I know you'd like me to call Farai, but I happen to be busy right 'long in here."

Kismet was planning Ronni's thirty-ninth birthday bash, despite her own full life. Therefore, Kismet figured, her father's older daughter needed to be grateful, for a change. Anyway, Kismet heard enough moaning from her first cousin Beau, these days.

"Why," she suddenly blurted, "did Diddley tell his long lost mother that he would see her? Again."

Scratching one foot with the big toe of the other, Nell didn't reply.

50

"I don't understand." Kismet revealed, "Especially when she didn't show up the last time Diddley agreed to meet her. That little stunt broke his heart. Doesn't he know she'll keep hurting him as long as he keeps opening himself to her?"

Nell feigned interest in her feet.

"Okay, I'll leave that alone." Kismet leaned over. "Uh, Ma, if you don't take your feet out of there soon, they're gonna prune."

"I don't care." Nell folded her arms over her ample bosom. "This is the best my dogs have felt in a while. And Beau's got to make his own choices."

"But Ophelia will hurt him," Kismet near whined.

Stocky Nell pointed out that the woman *was* Beau's mother. He'd lived with her for most of his pre-teen years. "So we can't expect him to just forget her," although Nell had often wished for precisely that.

"I just meant," Kismet began, "that—"

Nell cut her daughter off. "Look, KissGirl, I'd like it if my puppy stayed away from 'Phelia too. Nell sighed and placed a wet foot on her towel. "The truth is he might *need* to see her. If that's the case, we shouldn't make him feel bad about it."

Softly Nell advised, "Kismet Staar, be understanding. One day Déja and Chance just might want to see Contessa," their biological mother.

Disturbed, Kismet waved, "That'll be different."

Now how will it be different? Nell wanted to ask, but she changed the subject. "KissGirl, tell me again, what're we supposed to do for Ronni?" Reluctantly, Nell lifted her other foot from the soaker.

"Next year, we surprise her, since this year we're taking her out."

"You really think we can catch her off-guard?"

"No," Kismet admitted. "Ronni always expects *some*thing, but my ace in the hole is that she usually doesn't know what to expect."

Nell rubbed a gob of petroleum jelly on her right foot. "So, what should *we* expect?"

"A huge birthday bash." Kismet appeared pensive. "Mama, you remember me telling you, a few years back, that Ronni wanted a party?"

"One where she'd be the Nile Queen?" Nell interjected. "Of course."

Back then, Ronni Brown had announced her desire to have a lavish birthday fête. She said she would be Cleopatra, and her Nile Soiree attendees needed to don ancient Egyptian attire. Ronni had suggested that her Cohorts throw the affair. However, their attendance would be unnecessary, since the guest list would be comprised of eligible men.

How Kismet Staar, Valeria René, and Beau had laughed! Upon realizing that Ronni was serious, they'd laughed even harder.

Seated at her boudoir desk, Kismet smiled, thinking about Ronni's outrageous demand. Ronni made it before her family of friends learned she was HIV positive. Kismet also remembered that for the past four years, the Cohorts had indeed celebrated Ronni's birthday, but never as she'd requested. Next spring, Kismet vowed, Veronica Marie Brown would get her Queen of the Nile soiree.

Ronni would be thirty-nine, and who knew how much longer she would be with them? Who knew how much longer any of them had, Kismet mused. Life was so if-y. It was not promised.

Watching her daughter, Nell knew Kismet had big plans. They were in her eyes. Still, Nell had a question. "How you gonna get Ronni to whatever place this thing is to be held at, and in costume? I ask," Nell revealed, "because if she has to get dressed, she'll know."

"There'll be no getting dressed," Kismet Staar winked. "Not before she arrives."

Nell rubbed her greasy hands together. "I can't wait!"

"Me either," the daughter grinned.

"Stop a minute." Nell's smile faded. "If this thing's got an all-male guest list, where do *we* fit in? Because you know, I ain't nobody's man."

"We don't," Kismet admitted with averted eyes.

Nell sounded crestfallen, like a child, "But I want to go."

Kismet felt her mother's gaze bore into her. "You will."

"I ain't gon be no server Kismet Staar," Nell sullenly announced. On her daughter's bed, she lowered herself into a half-lying position. Heck, she could see it now. Her girl ordering her, the mama, little Val, and Beau, to stand around wearing aprons. Holding big spoons, they would have to ask people if they preferred fish or chicken. Nell frowned. Attempting not to wake her napping grandbabies, she hissed. "KissGirl, I hope you're not planning on me cooking—*or* serving anything, for anybody, on that evening."

Kismet chuckled because, indeed, Ronni loved her mother's cooking. However, Kismet would not ask the older woman to lift a finger.

"I'm telling you KissGirl," Nell whispered and crossed her shiny ankles. "Me 'n these ol' hips are going to be at that party. I am going to have fun. You will not have me slaving away like some pack mule. I'm telling you now, in your planning stage, so you will know."

Kismet shrugged. "So be it."

"What does that mean?" Nell probed.

When Kismet remained silent, fretfully, her mother folded her arms. "Well, smart girl, since you aren't about to tell me any more of your lil covert plans, you need to come paint my toenails."

Curvaceous Kismet stared at her mother. She also whined as though she might have been ten-years-old. "Do I have to?"

Nell appeared smug as she wiggled her sausage-like toes. "It all depends…"

Kismet appeared skeptical. "On what?"

"Whether or not you want peace."

Resigned, the younger woman groaned and heaved herself up. "Mama, didn't you teach me that blackmail isn't pretty?"

Wiggling her chubby stubs in anticipation, stocky Nell grinned. "Kismet Staar, sugar, yo' mama has no such word in her vocabulary."

Chapter 8

SCHEDULED to meet his mother at an eatery in busy downtown Brooklyn, Beau felt nervous. Seated in his posh Manhattan apartment, he realized. Each time he pondered seeing her, he felt sick. Therein lay the truth. He hadn't seen Ophelia DeVeaux in nearly three decades, because she had upped and walked away, without a backward glance.

In his cozy home, Beau ruminated. As a child, rarely had he spoken of his mother. As an adult, he had spoken even less. Actually, once, he'd told his then-roommates Valeria and Ronni about Ophelia. Kismet had been there. Beau had said his mother's name was the same as a character in *Hamlet*. Shakespeare's Ophelia, however, went mad and drowned herself. Perhaps, Beau had said, his mother should have done the same.

He remembered mentioning that his mother hadn't truly loved his father. "I guess because to start with, she didn't love her*self*."

Beau's father had been a tailor. Emmett had abhorred that Ophelia, a stay-at-home mom, sought trouble. Often claiming boredom, Ophelia begged Emmett to take her on lavish trips like those she'd seen on TV; The *Love Boat* and stuff, but Emmett didn't have boat money.

Therefore, Ophelia took trips of her own, forays away from her and Emmett's charming home to the crime-infested bottoms. There, she spent her grocery money on drugs. Then when her cash ran out, to get more drugs, Ophelia sold her body.

Beau recalled telling his Cohorts that his father's sister, Nell, had come to get him. His cousins Kiss and Farai had appeared too. A fight ensued, "Because my father called his sister. He'd called my Grandma Lacey too, God rest her soul." Beau told his Cohorts that Emmett had done so because he had to work, and his small son needed looking after.

At the time, Ophelia pitched a fit. She also vowed to quit getting high, if only she could get her little boy back.

Against her better judgment, Beau's Aunt returned him to his mother. "Then all hell broke loose," Beau told his Cohorts. His mother became abusive. Angry with his father and the family, Ophelia punched and kicked her small son. She made him keep it a secret.

She also began allowing men to frequent Emmett's home.

Beau's Grandma Lacey who had nicknamed him Diddley, after a rock 'n roll guitarist, began to visit. The older woman did so to keep an eye on things. Beau's Aunt showed up, too. Those times, Nell wound up literally fighting Ophelia to get the small boy out of the filthy house. When Beau's Aunt reluctantly took him back to his mother, Ophelia left Emmett. Ophelia didn't care that Beau's father had just learned he had cancer. Beau's life then became hell. To keep Emmett from catching her, Ophelia moved numerous times. Each place was worse than the one prior was. However, one day she decided to travel light.

She left her eight-year-old. Days passed before Beau realized Ophelia was gone. Then the small boy crawled out of the closet. He thought about the older man who lived in the apartment below. To Beau, that man seemed different. He didn't look terrifying. The ones who'd paid Beau's mother for the use of his small body had scared him. So, Beau thought, just *maybe*...

Sure, the child was fearful, hungry, and smelly, after having been locked away. Yet when he heard no fighting or sex noises, he stepped over drug paraphernalia and an empty pizza box. Pulling open the apartment door, he saw no one, so he ran to the steps.

On the floor below, shakily he knocked on the old man's door.

Opening it, Mr. Fulton asked where Beau's mother was. Noticing that the kid was famished, the man offered homemade soup, in the clean apartment that reminded Beau of his Aunt's home. When the kid was full, Mr. Fulton sent him back upstairs, saying he didn't want trouble.

Beau kept showing up, and the older man, whom Beau had begun to call Pa, wondered why no school. Pa also wondered, again, where Beau's mama was; as did the landlord.

Beau wound up staying with Pa Fulton until the older man broke Beau's heart.

Suddenly, in his spacious, nineteenth-floor apartment, Beau, the adult, jumped up from his cushy sofa. He threw aside the binder from which he should have been studying. He would star in a cable TV original movie. However, he couldn't focus on the character. Beau's mind kept drifting back to Ophelia, and to Pa Fulton. Why hadn't Ophelia been more like the old man, or more like his Aunt—who was a real mother?

Turning from the stupendous view of Central Park, Beau retrieved his binder. Beau tried not to think about the day that Pa had brokenheartedly announced that the boy needed to go live with his daddy's people.

Standing in his sumptuous living room, Beau again opened his binder. On the stark first page, he 'saw' the first real father he had ever known. He saw himself, the boy, claim, "I ain't *had* no daddy, Pa—except you!" In the eye of his mind, Beau saw the old man nervously pull his suspender straps. He'd always worn them over button-front shirts.

Beau saw the boy plead to stay but the old man shook his head. The boy did as he'd been taught. Small Beau remained respectful, but inside he'd died.

In his sumptuous living room, Beau the adult leaned against the large window frame. Now, he realized. It had taken an untold depth of love on Pa Fulton's part to give that shy boy back to his father's family.

Huge-hearted, Nell Moore had then, in exchange, given Alphonso Fulton, a family. She had done so by incorporating her nephew's rescuer into all three of her children's lives. Beau, Kismet, and Farai, had loved their 'grandfather,' until the last, a year ago.

In his sumptuous Manhattan apartment, with his head pressed to the cool window, tall, buff, and brown, Beau fingered his beloved dog tags. His Aunt had given them to him when she'd started calling him 'Puppy.' She had even presented him with him a live dog. Nell said Pal from the pound was skittish. Like Beau, little Pal had been abused. However, Nell espoused; Beau, Kismet Staar, Farai, and the little dog Pal, never had to worry, because now they were all Nell's pups.

"That," Nell said, "makes *me* the mama dog—the bitch—and I protect my own." Nell had promised to protect Beau, even from Ophelia. Beau, the man, stared into oncoming dark. It glowed with golden light thrown from many windows. Indeed, Nell had kept her word. For many years, the stocky woman had protected him.

Turning from watching a couple climb up into a horse-drawn carriage, Beau wondered about Ophelia. Was she still painting herself up to appear attractive? Did she still meet men everywhere, at liquor stores and at bus stops? Did those men, when angered, still trash her living spaces? Did Ophelia still lay on a filthy plaid couch, nursing a black eye or a cut lip, while between her teeth, a bent and ebbing cigarette dropped ashes on a floor that she had never swept?

Beau wondered if Ophelia had other unfortunate children. With all the men she'd slept with, it was possible. Beau suddenly hoped she hadn't sold her other children to sweaty naked alcoholics, like she had done him! He prayed that vile men hadn't held Ophelia's other children on hairy thighs like they'd kept him, against his will, before they tore into his small body. He hoped Ophelia's men hadn't caused other children to feel aflame with fright and pain. The way he'd felt.

Beau wondered. If he saw Ophelia again, and soon, would he get the big question answered—*why*?

Oh no, there it was again. The *fear* that ever plagued him when he thought of Ophelia. Therefore, reaching over, he picked up his cordless.

She answered.

"You *are* going with me, right?" Beau asked, just to be sure. He didn't know what he would do if she changed her mind.

"Diddley, I said I would, twenty times," Kismet reminded him, sick of the same inquiry, repeatedly. Yet gentling, she sighed. Kismet apologized. "I should not have snapped at you, honey." Kismet said she knew her cousin was nervous. She said he had every right to be.

Beau loved that about Kiss, she cared for others. Mother-ish, she cared about their feelings. She even tried to fix the un-fixable.

"You know," the younger cousin began. "Even though I'm a man—"

"A big strong one," Beau's first cousin interjected.

"Yeah, well, this big strong man doesn't know what that woman wants." Beau could not say his mother's name. "Kiss, I wonder what I'll say to her. Afterward, I feel like…crying. Isn't that weird?"

"No, it's not," Beau's confidante soothingly stated. "It's natural." Although she understood, Kismet felt hurt for Beau. "Diddley, listen, that bitch should wonder what to say to you. *She* was the dag-blame adult. She's the one who abused and abandoned *you* as a *child*!"

Fiercely protective and maternal, Kismet took a deep breath. "Forget what I just said." Soothingly she spoke. "Diddle-Diddle, I know she your mama 'n all, so I'm trying not to make things worse. I mean, I know you've got tons of emotions right now, all churning inside you."

Remaining silent, Beau wondered, how did his cousin know?

Kismet breathed deeply. "I know you want to see that woman, for a lot of reasons. But there's one thing I detest." Softly Kismet admitted, "I hate that she still has the power to make you feel small. Thoughts of her nearly reduce you to the eight-year-old you were when she left."

Breathing deeply, Beau felt better, because although candid, his cousin really did understand. "Kiss, I know, and...thanks."

"No, save that for we return from seeing her. Thank me when I manage to keep myself in check. Maybe I'll manage to *not* beat her old ass down."

Beau's laughter boomed like a shot out of a cannon. "Kiss," he called, knowing his cousin meant every word, "you are too funny."

Suddenly Kismet shook her head. "Damn if I didn't sound like Mama. Oh Lord," the younger woman groaned. "I do not want to turn into Miz Nellie."

Roaring with laughter, Beau felt even better. "Kiss, go cook, or bathe the kids." The actor said it because he knew she had things to do, always, in that inviting home of hers. "Uh, and cuz?"

"Yeah, Diddley."

"Thanks," for being there.

Chapter 9

ABOUT to enter their bedroom, he saw her. On their king-sized bed, she sat in a pool of late afternoon sunshine. Her legs were folded beneath her, yoga-style. Standing quietly behind her, Fabian took the liberty to study her. He also wondered where was her cat, her ever-present shadow. Mystical was probably outside in the snow, torturing some small creature.

Forgetting the cat, Fabian noted Valeria's satiny, fawn-colored camisole and matching lingerie pants. He saw that she had caught her long curly locks atop her head in a flyaway ponytail. That genie look, he loved on her. He liked that it showcased her dark, graceful neck.

Voluminously drinking her in with his eyes, Fabian became cognizant of something. He had always believed Val a rapturous vision. It could be early morning, or late at night when she appeared dewy because they had just made love. To him, she was always exquisite.

However, never had Valeria been more beautiful than the night they'd met. She'd worn red, high heels, and her toenails were red. What had had him gaping was the wicked little red number she'd poured herself into.

Ah, wait. Fabian recalled another night when Valeria had appeared almost as lovely. On that full moon evening, he'd proposed. At a renowned eatery boasting two on-site clubs, he'd done the fanciful, to get her to marry him.

Then there had come a day, one where she had been incomparably beautiful. On that Indian summer's eve, they'd both worn white silk. Fabian had hardly been able to take his eyes off her. They'd traded matching diamond rings and sugar-sweet kisses. Then they'd hopped the broom.

In February, on this brisk cold day, he realized. This vision he would also keep. Today, again, she was the most beautiful thing he had ever seen.

Unable to continue to stand away from her, soon to be forty, Fabian approached, on silent cat feet. Unaware, Valeria sat without moving. Her husband's heartbeat quickened as stealthily, he crept toward her. Inhaling the jasmine scent ever about her, Fabian reached out.

Valeria shifted and turned. "Hey, you."

"Hey, *you*," Fabian said. He leaned to reverently kiss her mocha-hued cheek, her earlobe, and her neck. Allowing his eyes to hungrily dip to the valley between her breasts, he sat. He asked what she thought.

With downcast eyes, Valeria's lashes swept the apples of her cheeks. Watching, Fabian recalled that he and she had been married for nearly six years. And here he was, still infatuated with her. He wondered, did other men feel the same way about their wives?

Inhaling deeply, Fabian tried, as he had many times prior, to release himself from the cloying, sweet, and suffocating power that this woman wielded over him. He also noticed she appeared sad.

"I love you," she said.

"But?" he inquired, feeling chilled, although he too sat in her pool of late afternoon sunlight.

"*But,* I want a child." She tried not to moan; as relieved that it wasn't something else, something worse, Fabian took his wife in his arms. "I know we've tried," she said with tears filling her honey-hued eyes. "I know we've lost too," horribly. "We've seen doctors, and spent loads of money, but I can't help *wanting*, Fabe. I do try not to think about it..."

"But you really want this," he acknowledged. Fabian said he had a secret. "I want this too, Ms. Vee Ree-nay, in a way that scares me."

"Do you?" Valeria asked, her eyes widening.

"I do," her husband nodded. "I thought you knew."

"I do," Fabian's wife admitted, "sort of, but sometimes I need to hear you say it. Again." Mocha-skinned Valeria gestured with elegant hands. "Sometimes I feel like I'm in this by myself, you know? Because it's *my* body that isn't cooperating."

Resting her head on her raised knees, Valeria said she wanted to forget the whole baby thing. It had caused them immeasurable pain. "I'd love to say it, and mean, if this never happens, I'd be okay, but somehow, I know I'd be lying. I was born to be somebody's mother."

The cocoa-skinned bald man licked his full lower lip. "I know." Staring at leafless trees beyond their bedroom window, he tried to see past how frightened he had been, *that* time. The time the doctor told him that he could lose Valeria René, his wife. Pushing the horrible incident from mind, Fabian focused on making his bride understand that he wanted to be a father. He wanted it as much as she wanted to be a mother. Fabian admitted he wanted an infant girl, one who would look immensely like her. "Baby could be the second love of my life."

With a smile, Valeria pictured Fabian's daughter. Gingerly, placing herself within the circle of his arms and thighs, she leaned back, against him. Listening as Fabian spoke, Valeria felt his words reverberate through his chest, and her back.

Fabian said he would love to watch his baby daughter sleep. "I'd touch her little head. I have even imagined our baby's glossy black hair. It would be like yours, but not long. It would be a little cap. Or," he revealed, giving it more thought, "she might have a small 'fro."

Valeria chuckled, "Like her daddy had, when he had hair." Fabian's wife reached up and back to stroke his shiny dome.

"You know what I want most, though?" Fabian asked, loving the feel of Valeria's slender fingers tripping over him.

"What?"

"I want people see my baby and know *I* was the man. I was the one who made love to you. I helped bring that baby into being."

That, Fabian really wanted, although what they had been through sometimes caused him angst. There were times when he almost feared physically loving his wife, because there had been bleeding, and cramps. Those things were never far from mind. Therefore, sometimes, as Fabian and his wife were about to swerve, he felt guilty. Really, he felt akin to a murderer, because if one of these pregnancies-gone-wrong took his wife's life, wouldn't he would be to blame?

But how could he not love her? How could he not show her love, by lying intimately with her? This, he asked himself, as he closed his eyes, because he felt torn, again.

"You *are* the man," Valeria whispered. "Even if a baby never comes for us. For me, you will always be the man."

Boy, did she know what to say to pump him up! Suddenly, back in imagine-mode, Fabian nodded. "When we give baby VerRia a bath, I'll nibble on her tiny fingers and toes."

"Wait." Valeria René turned. "Where'd you get that name?"

"You don't like it?" Fabian asked, hope suspended by a thread.

"I do, but where'd you see it? I missed that one."

"It's not in one of your name books." Fabian pulled his wife back against him. "It happens to be your name, shortened, with a twist."

"So it *is*!" Valeria laughed. She was intrigued. She liked that Fabian had cared enough to conjure the name, "Ver Ria. I love it!"

"Wait now," Fabian cautioned, "because to get this baby…" His pulse quickened, "You, Mrs. Sinclair, and I, have work to do."

Clasping her hands over his that were protectively folded across her midsection, Valeria saucily inquired, "Do we now?"

"Oh yeah." Fabian rose and pulled her across their bedroom.

With incredulity in her voice, Valeria revealed that she hadn't known, fully, that Fabian felt as he did.

"Well, now you know. I'll tell you how else I feel."

Fabian's voice held that lilt, and suddenly feeling tingly, as her nipples pearled, Valeria wantonly breathed, "Tell me."

"Well," Fabian licked his lips. "I feel…like laying you down, in front of that fireplace." Gently he guided her toward it. Then clasping the remote, he pressed. A cozy fire roared to life. "Now that we're down here," he said, moments later, "I want to remove your bottoms."

"I want you to remove mine," he directed, placing her hands on him.

She tossed his garment aside. Then she massaged his jutting shaft. Nevertheless, as hard as it was to stop her, he did, to kneel between her knees. He announced, "Now, I want to pull this little top over your head."

With lust-filled eyes, he watched as her full, nude breasts spilled forth. Feeling pulsation in his loins, Fabian whispered, "I want you to lean back…as I lick you. Here." He placed his mouth over a taut nipple, "And here," he said and transferred to its mate.

"Then, as you stay back," he intoned, "I want to push these sexy thighs of yours farther apart." Desire-ridden, he rasped, "Because I want to see you open, just like…that."

Bending, he fondled her, inched fingers inside, where they became moist. "I want to stick my tongue…" His mouth covered her, "Here. Deep, inside you, and I want…to lap – up – your…"

"Ohhh," his wife moaned, arching to give him easier access.

"Then," Fabian lifted his head, "when you're ready, I want to give you…this." He raised himself.

Anticipating the hardness, eagerly, Valeria slid her hands around to Fabian's backside. She pulled, as he pushed.

Content, she sighed, as enraptured, he groaned. He retreated, only to glide back in, and felt moist warmth, again and again. Feeling his wife vise blissfully around him, he said, "I want you to—oh yeah, do that."

"Oooh, and I want you to...do that," Valeria panted. "Keep it there. Right there. Harder. Yes," she moaned as he withdrew, only to drive deeper. "Mmm, right there," she advised. "Again."

Wrapping her husband with her legs, Valeria kept pace with him, until Fabian abruptly ordered her to turn. From behind, he panted, "I want you to ...take this."

Avariciously, she hoisted herself backward, onto him. "Oh Jeeee..." She nearly screamed, because things were so different this time, so unlike any time they had done it before. Then again, it was almost the same; slippery, wet, hard, fast, then slow. It was soft, warm, and long.

With one last slap of slick skin against the same, both husband and wife collapsed.

"So, Mister," the mocha-skinned woman called when she could again breathe. "Got anything else you want?"

"I'll show you," Fabian promised and squeezed Valeria tightly. "In a minute, or two. I just need to catch my breath."

Chapter 10

HEARING the knock on her small office door, Ronni looked up. A woman she had never seen, who was well off, waited in the hallway. "Yes?" Ronni surmised that the average height woman in the high-heeled gray pumps had most likely not found her party in the large building.

"I'd like to see..." the woman looked down at a slip of paper. "Ronni? Ronni M. Brown?"

Ronni's mind matriculated, as her eyes darted to her desk. She hadn't penciled in a ten o'clock. Oh well. She admitted, "I'm Ms. Brown."

Just beyond the threshold, wearing a gray wool cape, the woman gestured. "May I?"

Ronni nodded. "Come in and tell me how I can help."

The woman hesitated. She eyed fresh flowers in a cut-glass vase. "There's no way to preface this, so I'll just say it. You may remember my daughter..."

Ronni noted the brown curly hair, stylishly cut. She noticed the pink cheeks, the brown eyes, and the charm school poise, as the woman cleared her throat. "I am Amy. My daughter is—well, she was—Keesa. Last name—"

"I know her name." Ronni appeared shaken, and took her seat. Indiscernibly, she attempted to catch her breath. Her eyes narrowed. Keesa had mentioned her mother, Amy. Amy hadn't been around, not that much, while Keesa lived. So, what could she possibly want? Now.

Timidly, Amy smiled. "May I call you Ronni?"

You may not, you're no friend of mine, Ronni thought as she stated aloud, "I'd prefer Ms. Brown."

Nervously, Amy nodded. She began rummaging through a handbag the same color and high-end leather as her shoes. "Well, Ms. Brown," Amy began, "I gathered from *these* that you and my daughter shared something." Mrs. Foster placed a Manila envelope on Ronni's desk. "It appears you and my daughter were friends."

Ronni stared at the woman, the envelope between them.

"Oh, I do hope that was the case," Amy continued. "You see, Ms. Brown, I know you were my daughter's counselor, but I hope you were more—Oh Heavens, I'm babbling."

Not caring that Amy Foster had stopped speaking, Ronni removed photos. There *she* was, with Keesa, and with Ezmerelda, the cat.

Suddenly, Ronni felt miserable. She ached for her lovely young friend, and tears stung her eyes. Ronni dropped the envelope on her desk. Snatching up a tissue, wearily she asked, "Mrs. Foster, what do you want, with me?" *Now that Keesa is gone.*

The unsaid words hung in the air.

Keesa's mother, her sorrow visible, watched the younger, attractive, bright-skinned African-American woman. With her short wavy hair, the woman was saddened, but boy did she also fume! Not wanting to see the anger, Keesa's mother chose to look at the slender woman's flattering olive green sweater dress, instead of into Ronni's eyes.

Amy forced herself to speak. "Ms. Brown, I know you loved my daughter." With tears dropping from her eyes, Amy sighed and explained. She had been removing Keesa's belongings from her tiny apartment when she'd happened upon the photos and Keesa's journal.

"I felt like a cad," Amy revealed, yet unable to meet Ronni's eyes. "Going through my baby's things, but it had to be done. Harvey, my husband, Keesa's dad, hasn't the time or the inclination, so it fell to me."

Ronni listened and still couldn't ascertain why this polished woman had come *to her.* Now. This woman who hadn't wanted to face that her daughter had AIDS.

"You were good to my baby," Amy Foster stated. "Unlike my husband and me, you were physically there. Oh, I spoke with her, often, but it's not the same as being there." Tossing her head, Amy spilled out that when she'd learned of her daughter's illness, she'd been fearful, and had no clue what to do.

Curiously, Ronni watched as Keesa's mother tumbled headlong into telling her that Keesa Louise Foster had been sickly from the day she had been born, prematurely. Amy enumerated one health issue after another that Keesa had faced in her short life. Amy divulged that her 'baby' had lived her last twelve years with one kidney.

Again, Ronni marveled at Keesa's tenacity, and unbeknownst, Amy continued. She said oh, she'd forgotten, but at a few months old, her daughter had battled pneumonia. Keesa also had a heart murmur. "My

Keesa, though?" Amy chuckled as she removed her outerwear. "She took everything in stride. Never was she without joy."

Semi-stunned, Ronni watched, recalling that she hadn't asked Amy to stay or get comfortable. Settled, Keesa's mother placed an emerald and diamond bejeweled hand at her chest. "I haven't mentioned the surgery!"

Noticing Ronni's horrified look, Amy caught herself. "Ms. Brown, suffice it to say, my baby overcame many things, without complaint."

"Knowing that," Ronni began, feeling the heat of anger, "Why'd you leave her, when she needed you the most?"

Amy looked down to softly admit, "I'm ashamed of that. I've continuously asked myself that question, too. Perhaps I was tired. I *had* been through so many things with my baby. Ms. Brown, if you don't have a sickly child, then you honestly don't know—"

Not paying attention, Ronni now understood a few things. Now she knew why latter treatments administered while Keesa had lain dying had aggravated her condition. Those marvels of medical science had offset the fragile ecology that Keesa had striven to maintain within her body. Now Ronni knew why Keesa had not eaten flesh foods and had only bought organic. She had been trying to preserve herself.

Ronni glanced at Amy, who gazed at a framed black and white by the African-American photographer Thomas Askew. "Ms. Brown, Harvey, Keesa's father, and I, would like to do something for *you*." Amy droned, "In a way, we'll be making up to our baby for not being there. We want to thank *you* for being with her when we were too simple-minded to do so, ourselves." Amy pushed a check forward.

Ronni politely refused, although the figure was astronomical. Sure, she had pressing financial needs, but she would not become indebted to Mrs. Foster. Moreover, Ronni was definitely not about to assuage some socialite's guilt by accepting blood money. Not when absentee mom Amy could have done right by her daughter.

Attempting to pass the check back to Ronni, Amy insisted.

Then Ronni became adamant. "Mrs. Foster, I can*not* take your money, although I do thank you for the gesture."

"You don't seem to understand," Amy began.

"No, *you* don't understand," outspoken Ronni opined. "I feel like you're trying to buy me. No," Ronni amended, "Allow me to more aptly say, I feel like you and your husband are probably consumed with guilt. So that check is supposed to parallel penance. Mrs. Foster; you probably pored over those photos of Keesa and me. Then you got the notion that *I* could help alleviate your guilt, because what better way to attain *absolution* than to hand some 'little black chick' an exorbitant sum of money?" Ronni's eyes held Amy's. "*Or*," Ronni continued, despite Amy's stunned look, "Maybe you're offering that check because for you, attaining, multiplying, and retaining money is not an issue.

"Whatever, the case, Mrs. Foster, money will not make up for what you did *not* do for your daughter. Giving *me* money will not erase the fact that your daughter wanted *you*." Ronni was resolute. "Keesa told me. She wanted so few things from you, yet where were you? Keesa only wanted to hear that you loved her, although she knew you did, albeit in your strange way. Keesa said she just wanted to hear it, *in person*."

With a sigh, Ronni walked around her desk with one thing on her mind. She would get rid of the woman whose presence dredged up unpleasant emotions. "Look, I should not have told you that last part." At her office door, Ronni admitted, "But you need to know. You also seem strange to me. I mean, why would you visit *me*, someone you don't know, when you could have visited *your daughter*?" Ronni did not await an answer. "Whatever. Good day, Mrs. Foster."

"Amy."

"Amy, then," Ronni opened her office door. "Please go."

Amy Foster placed the unwanted check back on Ronni's desk. Softly, she spoke, feeling chastised. "It has your name on it, Ms. Brown." Gracefully, Amy collected her things. "Since you're adamant about not receiving our offering, would you give it to charity?"

Utterly worn, Ronni stared at the woman. "I could." Ronni didn't know why the sudden change.

"Good," Amy nodded while adjusting her magnificent cape.

Ronni walked back. She leaned over her desk. Sounding pre-occupied, she wrote while saying, "I am endorsing this right now."

"For whom—or for what organization?" Amy Foster asked. Quickly, however, she deferred, realizing the money was no longer hers. "If you don't mind my asking." Amy appeared sheepish. "I'd just like to know."

"Oh, and you should," Ronni nodded. "I've endorsed the check for here, the Gay Men's Help Center." Ronni felt dazed, even as she said in unison with Amy Foster, "Keesa would have liked that."

Briskly, Amy nodded because that had been surreal. "I'm aware that you have things to attend to Ms. Brown. Therefore, I will go, but I must ask, is there something we can do for *you*?"

Veronica Marie Brown assured Amy Foster there was not. Ronni simply wished Amy would go, then perhaps she could compose herself. However, Ronni suggested an Evening Intensive. "Why not attend one, Mrs. Foster? You can listen and even ask questions. At one of my seminars you may even learn how to be of service to young suffering people, young women like Keesa."

Tears shimmered in Amy's eyes. "I'd like that."

Something about Mrs. Foster's tears softened Ronni's heart. Ronni realized. The woman had to be hurting. Sure, Amy hadn't done all she could have for Keesa, but who was Ronni to judge? "Call me," Ronni admonished, handing over her business card.

"May I?" Retrieving her card, Ronni hurriedly scribbled her cell number on the back. Really, she couldn't hate on Keesa's mom. Ronni also heard herself say, "We'll talk, Mrs. Foster."

"Call me Amy, dear." The woman almost sounded refreshed. "Now, I shall depart, for real."

Both women chuckled, and Ronni escorted Amy to the exit. There, they awkwardly embraced.

Stepping back, Ronni and Amy both felt strange, almost as if they'd known each other long before the memory of a sweet young woman brought them together.

Wow, Ronni thought as she strolled back to her office. "Keesa-little-girl, I can feel you right here with me..." It was the first time since Ronni had lost her friend that she didn't feel piercing sorrow. Aloud Ronni spoke to Keesa. "Girlfriend, this is not a bad thing, at all."

Chapter 11

BEAU lifted the jacket sleeve to better see the price tag. Sandal turned away. That piece was not his style, and Beau was not going to purchase it for *him*. Bored, Sandal shifted and wondered. Why had he accompanied Beau on this little shopping jaunt? It felt like they had been standing in the exclusive men's boutique for hours. That was getting on Sandal's nerves.

Now, if this had been *his* proposed outing, Sandal mused, things would have shaped up differently. He would not have hobbled to one store and spent way too much time inside.

A zipper caught his eye, and quickly Sandal stepped around Beau. "Oh!" he gasped, "look at this."

Beau raised his eyes. He sounded preoccupied, "Nice."

"You don't love it?" Sandal inquired, as he imagined himself the proud owner of the exorbitantly expensive piece. He pressed it to his chest, and whirled in search of a mirror.

Beau did not reply. He simply pored over an array of foil print tees.

Before a full-length mirror, Sandal called out, "This jacket is fierce." Mood clearly changed, Sandal preened. "This baby is extra."

"If you say so," Beau mumbled and headed toward the register. He wondered. Why had he even mentioned this outing to Sandal? Deftly he had avoided the slim red-haired young man ever since Thanksgiving, when Sandal had lied to Valeria's father. Actually, whenever one of his phones rang, Beau thanked Heaven for caller I.D. It had saved him many times. Yet he'd heard Sandal moan, in lots of messages, that he didn't understand; Red claimed he hadn't done anything wrong, so why was he being treated like an outcast? Sandal had also demanded, each time, that Beau call him back.

What a pain, Beau thought, a melodramatic pain. Then yesterday, he'd grumpily answered his cell. That had been when Beau said he and Sandal needed a break. The truth was the actor was tired of the drama.

Sandal had kicked his hurt into high gear, and Beau had said he had to go. Sandal had called *wait*, and Beau wound up listening. Now he realized, he'd mentioned a shopping trip before he would head out of town. As was Sandal's way, the redhead had wheedled his way in.

Next in line at the register, Beau forgot Red. He watched as the man before him took the store name-emblazoned bag. Placing his articles on the marble countertop, Beau pulled out his wallet. Hopefully, he thought, when he left this store, he and Sandal could part ways, for*ever*. The actor had grown tired of being the only one with something to do. He was tired of feeling as though he was Sandal's sole reason for living.

The cashier quoted Beau's total, just as Sandal dashed up, out of breath. "Don't you just love this jacket?" he dreamily inquired.

Bagging the customer's items, the cashier glanced at the guy with the customer. Cashier had one thought. Red mirrored an infatuated girl.

"I said it was okay, over there," Beau reminded Sandal.

"Wait." Sandal stepped before Beau, with his back to the cashier.

Holding his credit card, Beau became aggravated. "Wait for what?"

"If you hate my jacket, just say so," Sandal ferociously whispered.

Your jacket? The cashier rolled his eyes. There had been no transaction for that piece.

Looking up at Beau, Sandal injected a good dose of hurt into his voice. "I'll have you know, this jacket is a *Jon*—"

"We know," the cashier interrupted. "If you're buying, rear of the line. Please." Annoyed because customers were waiting, the clerk simply wanted to get to them, and then to his packing lists in the back.

Flippantly, Sandal told the clerk, "Speak…when you're spoken to."

"Well, I am *speak*ing to *you*," the cashier retorted. "Quit holding up the line," *queen*.

Still facing Beau, Sandal raised a hand to dismiss the boy. "Aaahk!"

Utterly aggravated, Beau recalled why he wanted to get rid of the character whose name should have been *Scandal*. He was a trickster; he wanted the jacket. The one that looked like the flamboyant pianist Liberace had worn it. Sandal wanted Beau to pay for it. Therefore, to be on his way, through clenched teeth, Beau ordered, "Put it up there."

"If you don't wanna get it," Mr. Melodramatic moaned, "just say so."

When Sandal stamped his foot, Beau caught himself. He realized the red-haired man brought out the worst in him. Handing over his credit card, Beau levelly spoke. "Step aside, Sandal."

"Yeah, blazing, what's the hold-up?" someone bellowed.

Signing his name, Beau took his receipt copy. He nearly laughed at the cashier who wore a magnified scowl as he handled the gaudy jacket. Again, Beau understood how one could be driven to beat another, especially when the other person attempted to be manipulative.

"Should've got you nothing," the cashier mumbled, nearly balling up Sandal's ill-gotten gain. He shoved it in the bag with Beau's neatly folded purchases.

"No." Sandal shook his head. "No. That goes in a separate bag."

"No—to you." Sick of the flaming fag, self-satisfied, the cashier announced, "Same purchase, same bag."

"Put the jacket in another bag, boy," Sandal commanded, "or we'll stand here all day."

"*You* can stand here," Beau advised taking the bag, "but I'm out."

"Have a nice day, sir," the cashier politely offered. With a smirk for Red, whom he had outmaneuvered, the clerk called, "Next, please."

Sandal was furious.

Experiencing his own share of fury, Beau stepped out of doors. In the hustle and bustle of lower Manhattan, he noted it was unseasonably warm for February.

Catching up with him, Sandal whined, "You're no real man."

As though he hadn't heard, Beau strode down Broadway. As one who had boxed for many years, he thought about making Sandal his personal punching bag. Hurriedly, the tall man sidestepped a group who'd stopped to gawk at a jeweler's wares. Beau remembered seeing Ronni, down near Columbus Circle, a few evenings prior. Happy to see his former roommate, he'd asked her out to dinner. As he circumvented an olive-skinned nanny pushing a blond toddler, Beau recalled Ronni mentioning Sandal. While eating, she'd admitted she didn't like Red, at all, for Beau. Beau had laughed, but come to think of it, *he* didn't like Sandal either.

"You'd have stood up for me back there," Sandal huffed. He ran alongside, and pulled Beau from his reverie, "if you were a real man."

"That kid was doing his job." Beau snorted. "Please."

"See?"

There Sandal went, stomping again, Beau thought, moving quickly.

"Rod-*reego*," Sandal whined, "would never have let that little smart-ass talk to me that way. And in front of people, too."

Furious, Beau pivoted. He faced Sandal; and surprised, Red realized he'd pushed the wrong button. "Since you wanna make comparisons..." Beau pulled the outlandish jacket. "Why don't you," he tossed it over Sandal's head, "take this shit—and go find ghetto-assed *Roderick*! Wear that for him, because I'm done."

Sandal managed to untangle himself. As curious New Yorkers dodged him, he wondered. Why would Beau make such a scene?

Suddenly, for tall and buff, something took shape. If indeed he and simple Sandal were finished, then red-hair shouldn't get the over-priced jacket. If Slipper wanted something, he needed to buy it, with his Hair Castle earnings. Or let that Roderick character, the one that Sandal always mentioned, let him buy it. That guy could use whatever money he could scrape up. Beau thought it and snatched the garish looking piece.

"This mess goes back."

Quickly Beau re-trod the way he'd come. He nearly laughed too as he realized it was the first time all day—since he'd laid eyes on Sandal—that he'd felt any joy. Beau bet the kid at the store would be amused too, when he reappeared to make the return.

Dumbfounded, Sandal stared after Beau. He wondered, *what* was wrong with the actor? Beau seemed so angry. Shaking his head, Sandal knew it wasn't him, or anything he had done. It could not have been. Therefore, Sandal guessed, Beau was having a bad day. Oh well.

A man passed. Sandal eyed him, noting the magnificent male form. It suggested the man spent a great deal of time in the gym. Sensing interest, the man slowed. Prolonged eye contact ensued. Suddenly, Sandal realized, he wouldn't go after Beau, not right now. He would hang out with body-builder, sort of get to know him.

Beau would cool down.

Then, Sandal mused, while exaggeratedly licking his lips, for body-builder's benefit, in a few days, he and Beau could pick up, right where they'd left off.

Chapter 12

AMY Foster had seriously pondered the card. Repeatedly, she'd pictured the bright-skinned African-American woman who worked at Gay Men's in Manhattan. Following a deep breath, Amy picked up the telephone, before she lost her nerve.

Ronni answered. She and Amy spoke for far longer than either would have expected. Afterward, again, both women felt, strange, as if they'd known each other for the longest time; perhaps it was because they had both known Keesa.

Now here Amy was, about to attend church with Ronni. It was strange. Amy thought it because Ronni admitted that only recently had she started attending services again as an adult. She'd done so after the loss of Keesa. Although she hadn't said so, such was the case for Amy.

"Don't you look nice," Keesa's mom marveled as Ronni approached.

"You do too." Wearing winter white from head to toe, on stylish boots, Ronni stepped inside the wrought iron gates of Mount Hebron. As people passed, she asked, "You had no trouble finding it?"

"Goodness, no, your directions were specific." Amy's eyes roved the massive, gray, stone building. "Like you said, I followed the steeple."

Feeling the biting cold despite the brilliant winter sun, Ronni suggested they enter. Inside the cavernous sanctuary, she and Amy followed a white-gloved usher down a quiet aisle. Spotting Nell Moore, Ronni stepped past people while whispering, "Excuse me." When seated, she kissed her friend's mother. Then quickly and quietly, Ronni introduced Amy, just as a solo was announced.

All eyes followed a woman with a shock of auburn hair. Tipping in high heels, Shanrae Price-Owens took the microphone. Slowly and softly, she sang '*Somebody prayed for me...*' The words magnificently trilled as with her head back, the soloist's voice grew. --*Had me on their mind. Took the time --I'm so glad they prayed...*

Melodically also, the African Methodist Episcopal choir, as well as the congregation, joined in. Listening and feeling enthralled, Ronni stood, as did others. Feeling inexplicable warmth, Ronni turned to see if Amy fared as well.

Ever polished, Amy sat, silently dabbing tears. Reaching to reassuringly squeeze Amy's hand, Ronni recalled crying in the House of the Lord many times. Turning, Ronni rejoined the swaying congregation. *Hallelujah.* She raised both hands. She was grateful for life because due to illness and other things, she should have been long dead. Nevertheless, she was still in the land of the living, as her grandmother would have said.

When Ronni checked on Amy again, Keesa's mom had shifted. She was behind Ronni, *and* she held hands with Nell. Ronni didn't know who had taken whose hand first. Nevertheless, the brown and beige hands were intertwined. Then Amy tumbled over, and for a moment, Ronni felt panicked.

Quickly though, motherly Nell embraced Amy. As Amy sobbed, unruffled, Nell patted her as if to say 'There, there baby, go on and cry.'

The soloist and choir wound down, and loath to let the song go, the congregation sat. Smoothing her skirt, Ronni wondered if Amy thought of Keesa. During their phone conversation, Amy had admitted to wishing she could do many things over. She especially wanted to right the wrong she had done her daughter. Scooting down to give Amy more room, Ronni prayed. She requested peace and forgiveness. The kind that only Amy could offer herself. Ronni also prayed that inside Mt Hebron's hallowed halls, Amy would start afresh.

FOLLOWING the benediction, Nell gathered her bible and wool scarf. Kismet's mother also suggested, "After that lovely service, we should all have Sunday supper at my daughter's house."

"Oh, I don't know," Amy said, not wanting to intrude. She had a funny feeling Nell was just being polite because she'd cried. For help, Amy looked to Ronni. "What about you, dear?"

Ronni grinned. "Amy, if you don't need to be anywhere..." The younger woman placed an arm around her adopted aunt. "Then agree because this lady is one great cook." Ronni looked at Nell. "You did cook, right? I mean, Kiss cooks well 'n all, but *you...*"

Nell laughed and squeezed the younger woman tightly. "I cooked honey; as a matter of fact, I started the meat off last night."

"Then, we'll join you," Ronni crowed. "I speak for Amy as well."

Buttoning her coat, Nell nodded. "Well, good. You two, and me and my brood, for dinner." Nell spoke as fighting chill winds; she and Ronni approached old Betsy. At the car that had originally belonged to her mother, Nell spoke. "Veronica, even if I hadn't mentioned dinner, you would have still offered me a ride, right honeybunch?"

SEATED at the laden table in Kismet's home, Amy Foster pushed her chair back. "Ms. Nell," she called with a hand on her stomach, "I haven't had hoppin' john and cornbread, or yams, *or* ham that good since I was a child! And chow-chow! Most Northerners aren't even aware of our southern, sweet, hot pepper relish, so thank you."

"You are welcome," Nell smiled, rocking her grandson. "Sit down, Ronni. You too, Lyle." Nell told the pair that the dishes could wait. "Right now, we just wanna relax; enjoy one 'nother's company."

"You sound just like someone I knew years ago," Amy exclaimed, recalling another round, brown woman.

Comfortable, shoeless, and in her stockings, Amy mentioned her experience that morning. "I felt like I was home. With all that beautiful singing, the warm church, and the bright sunshine pouring in, I could've been back in Alabama." Amy admitted that sitting beside Nell had caused memories to flood back. "I'd forgotten dirt roads, the smell of gardenia, honeysuckle, and oh so many things." Amy revealed she had also thought of her daughter, "While that woman sang. What a voice! The woman's I mean; I hoped too, that wherever my baby is, she is praying for me."

With her napkin, Amy dabbed her eyes and said she would leave that alone. Sounding stronger, she said that because of Nell, she'd recalled another woman she'd loved. "Her name was Zola Mae, and Ms. Nell, you remind me of her."

"She black?" Nell asked, bouncing her near-sleeping grandson.

"Matter of fact she was." Amy mentioned that while growing up in the south, Zola Mae had been "What people today would call a nanny. Except," Amy swallowed, "to me, she was so much more." Amy said African-American Zola Mae had shown her so much love until, as a small Caucasian child, Amy had wished to be Zola Mae's child. "She was warm and caring, and she always hummed a little tune about her Jesus."

Vigorously, Nell nodded, and chuckling, Kismet addressed her mother's guest. "Please, Mrs. Foster, do *not* get my mama started. If she talks about her Jesus, she just might get to preaching."

"You hush," Nell smiled. She implored Amy to continue.

"Well, sitting there," Amy resumed, "When sister Shanrae sang, I realized. With my baby, I didn't do everything right." Amy peeked at Ronni. Then she gazed at Nell for understanding. "But I can say I did what I knew to do. I did what I could manage."

"Well, honey," Nell hugged her chubby grandson, "you couldn't do anymore. Amy, lamb, you gotta leave the rest in the hands of the Lord."

Amy chuckled, despite tears, and with bejeweled fingers clasped, she said, "Ms. Nell, you really do remind me of Zola Mae!"

"Glad you ain't said we look alike," Nell teased.

"Oh pshaw," Amy winced, knowing that Nell had cleverly mentioned an age-old stereotype. "No, Ms. Nell, all black people do not look alike. I simply think you're such a mother, just like my Zola Mae was."

Nell admired her own image in a teaspoon. "I am precious, aren't I?"

Suppressing mirth, Kismet asked Amy to tell them more.

Pleased to share, while Ronni spooned up another helping of black-eyed peas 'n rice, Amy Foster said Zola Mae had taken care of her from the time she was just months old, a curly-haired girl in the Jim Crow south. Amy said her father, a doctor, like her husband, and her mother, a socialite, hadn't much time for her. Her father had often claimed more patients than he actually had. "Other times, Father tucked himself away at his gentlemen's club. Mother was no different. She spent her time shopping. She always needed something to wear to the next Pink Tea, Ladies Luncheon, or upcoming charity ball."

Therefore, small Amy had often wound up spending even weekends with Zola Mae and her daughter. "Then I'd love church!" Amy revealed. In the summer, she announced, the little clapboard building was stifling hot, despite every window being open, "But Gini, Zola Mae's daughter, and I would fan with our hands. Back then," Amy nodded. "I would feel the Spirit." She admitted, "At the time, my heart would beat so fast, and I'd feel like warm honey had been poured over me. So I jumped and cried out like the people around me."

"Didn't you feel strange," Ronni had to ask, "with all those African-Americans surrounding you?"

"No dear," Amy replied, "perhaps because Zola Mae and Gini—who is actually named Virginia—were all I had ever known. To me, it made sense that everyone around us would be black, I mean African-American."

Amy said after church, the threesome would walk the dirt roads back to Zola Mae's house. "Sometimes, on a rainy summer Sunday, Gini and I would cover our heads with small starched hankies." Closing her eyes, Amy wistfully intoned, "Ah, the scent of summer showers..."

"Oh, I know," Nell agreed. "There's nothing like it, but go on, Amy."

With crinkled eyes, Amy gushed, "I am so loving you, Ms. Nell!"

"That Zola Mae stuff again. Right?"

"Oh, talk to the hand," Amy tossed back, between chuckles.

"No you didn't!" Kismet squealed and turned to Ronni. "I see you're corrupting Mrs. Foster, already."

"Dear," Amy smiled. "I have been hip to the jive a long time."

Those at the table could not contain their laughter, even as Amy called out, "You all must know, I am nobody's square."

Nell struggled up to go lay her grandson down. "Lyle, sit. Amy, wait until I return; I don't want to miss any of your story."

Upon re-entering, Nell saw that her daughter had offered dessert and coffee.

Over warm berry cobbler and ice cream, Amy Foster resumed her stroll down memory lane. She told of how back at Zola Mae's small, neat wrap-around porch home, flowers grew in a profusion of color. "I was awed by Gini's dad, too," Amy admitted. "Gini explained he was called Coffey because of his dark skin. That big beautiful man," Amy recalled aloud, "he had a booming voice, but he was so gentle with Gini, and me, and Zola Mae. Oh, and listen! He made us girls a swing, with rope and an old rubber tire." Amy said she'd been fascinated watching Coffey's powerful hands pull knots in the thick rope that she and Gini had had trouble fetching from the shed. "It was amazing how that man had so much power, but *never* did he use it to do harm."

Amy looked miserable as she admitted, "Mind you now, during that time, Mr. Coffey was provoked, daily, by 'good Christian' whites."

"We lived through it," Nell sighed, "and we thank God for now."

"Yes, we do," Amy agreed. She also revealed that she and Gini, who was an educator at an HBCU, were yet friends.

"Well bless y'all hearts," Nell announced, "because my KissGirl *and* Ronni both graduated from a historically black university."

That Amy acknowledged before she said Zola Mae wore white gloves each Sunday because she ushered. "How I longed to have a pair of those gloves too." Visibly proud, Amy revealed that as a young woman, she, a CORE—Congress of Racial Equity member—had gone on Civil Rights marches alongside Gini, two years her senior. Looking at Nell, Amy whispered, "I was scared as the Dickens, too."

Nell nodded. "We all were, but as Dr. King said, it had to be done."

"God bless that man," Amy reverently whispered. "If not for him and others, my Keesa and Ronni might not have been friends without fear."

"We mustn't forget our shining Prince Malcolm," Nell added. "Often, the militant is as important as the one who advocates peace."

Amy agreed, stating that due to the Movement of the 1960s, Americans *of all nationalities* benefit. They enjoy freedoms today that they might not otherwise have, "Although most are unaware of it."

Nell nodded. "Yes, most newcomers to America are not aware of the vast African-American contribution to this country."

"That's because the negative actions of some are always highlighted on the evening news," Ronni put forth. "Even though, all over this country, there are communities of productive black people just like us."

"In every society," Lyle responded, "there are scapegoats for all that is wrong. Those people get the blame." He shrugged. "In North America, the black race is 'it' because we are visible."

Suddenly Amy felt herself becoming emotionally overwrought. Although her new friends could not know it, as they shared in seconds of dessert and coffee, she thought of Keesa.

Again, Amy felt the up creeping of grief. It laid low until the most inopportune time. Then it would spring, along with crushing guilt. Amy was aware that both plagued her because here she was, talking about her lifelong friend Gini. Nevertheless, she hadn't even told Virginia that Keesa was gone! Amy had not been *able* to; had she, then Gini would have learned of Amy's deplorable near-inaction during Keesa's last year.

Amy didn't want Gini to think she hadn't loved her daughter half as much as Gini and Zola Mae had loved *her*.

In hindsight, Amy could see how much like her socialite mother she had become. Like Mother, Amy had hidden from her own daughter. Amy had allowed Women's Teas, bridge club, and other inconsequential things to keep her from Keesa. The one person who had needed her most.

Oh God! Amy fought not to cry, but here she was, conversing with people she barely knew; Amy had been enjoying herself too, but *why* hadn't she done the same with Keesa Louise, her only child?

With guilt gnawing huge chunks out of her, Amy asked herself what kind of mother—rather, what kind of *monster*—was she? With her eyes smarting and her nose and cheeks aflame, she blurted, "I lost my baby!" She looked down. It was the wrong time and place for grief and self-pity.

However, privy to the workings of grief, Nell called out, "That's all right, Amy honey." She instructed Ronni to pass Amy another napkin. "Pour a little of that cold water on it, too, so she can dab her eyes."

Nell then spoke comfortingly. "You did lose your baby, Ames. That will always hurt, so if you want to cry, you go right ahead. We all know how it feels to lose someone we loved. If you don't want to cry, then Amy, honey lamb, look around you, at the *family* you've gained, *because of* your baby."

Through tears, Amy managed to smile, even as her daughter's bright-skinned friend pressed a cold-water soaked napkin into her hand.

"It gets easier," Ronni whispered because she too had loved and lost Keesa. "The pain lessens. It becomes bearable. Most of the time."

With a nod, Keesa's mother dabbed her face. She surely hoped so.

Chapter 13

WEARING a plush bathrobe, Kismet rummaged; while lying atop her bed in the cozy Afro-centric motif bedroom, Lyle watched. With baby Chance sprawled across his chest, Lyle ignored the baby's light snores to better hear Kismet, who said, "I don't know what to wear."

"Why not something you'd normally wear," Lyle suggested. Clothing would be the last thing on *his* mind if Ophelia were his long lost aunt. Lyle would have questions for the woman, and lots of them.

Pulling out a pair of pinstriped wool trousers, Kismet murmured, "You're right." Rhetorically she also asked, "Why am I getting worked up? Over somebody I don't even care to see."

Lyle patted his son's back when the baby whined.

Pulling out a beloved cardigan and its matching shell, Kismet sat on the roll-arm bench at the foot of her bed.

Aware that she needed to be alone with her thoughts, Lyle slowly eased up. He intended to go to the den, get comfortable, and channel surf for a basketball game. He walked past Nell's bedroom.

Déja called out. "Daddy..." She peeked at him, "Comineer."

Lyle rubbed Chance's back. "Is Nannie dressed?"

Nell spoke up. "Nannie is dressed. Come on in, honey."

Obliging, Lyle eased into a comfortable chair.

"See," Nell said, "you and KissGirl have spoiled that baby. Now y'all can't lay him down without him hollering."

It was true, Lyle thought, noting his pajama-clad daughter. She and her Nannie were thrown raggedly across a patchwork quilt. Eyeing their checkerboard, he asked why Nell wasn't getting dressed.

"To meet 'Phelia?" Nell frowned. Clad in a corduroy skirt and a cable knit sweater and socks, the grandmother watched Déja contemplate a move. "I save my finery for special occasions." Nell wagged a finger at her granddaughter while speaking to her would-be son-in-law. "That's one good thing about being old. I know what's important; being present for Puppy is. Clothing? Not. My young man won't care that I ran errands in this outfit."

Nell spoke to Déja. "You know that red game piece belongs to your Nannie; moving it is cheating. That is not nice." Nell struggled up. "Game's over, sugar pie. Let's tidy up." At the bureau, brushing her gray mane, Nell remarked that Beau would appear in a bit, "And since he hates to wait, I had better pull my boots on."

Seated with the baby blissfully asleep on him, Lyle wondered what it would be like to meet *his* mother again, after being abandoned for more than twenty years. Lyle could not imagine. His mother, Collette, had always been there for him, his three brothers, and his father. She had even become a 'girl' type friend when her boys were in college. A great listener, Mama Manfred, had given them great 'girl perspective' advice.

Lyle rubbed Chance's back and thought it was a shame that Beau hadn't had a loving mother. Well, Beau had, Lyle recanted, but that mother had been his aunt, Nell. Lyle wondered what had Beau felt when Ophelia had called, out of the blue. Had he been angry? Had Kiss's cousin agreed to see O out of deference because she was his mother? Or was Beau genuinely curious to know her, after all these years? Hopefully, Ophelia had morphed for the better, for Beau's sake. But what if she was worse? Watching Nell apply moisturizer, Lyle knew Beau had to have questions for the abusive woman.

Hearing the doorbell, Déja dashed into the hallway, as if she was ever allowed to answer the door.

"You come back here!" Nell called as Lyle rose. "Dé, stop," he calmly commanded, and the child waited to walk with him. Carrying her clunky, rubber-soled boots, Nell heard, "Hi Buncoo!" In the living room, she also saw pajama-clad Déja fling herself up into Beau's arms.

Nell greeted the tall, handsome man who hugged her. She could tell from the darkness beneath his eyes that he hadn't been sleeping, but he didn't like her to fuss. Therefore, she bent to pull on her boots. "You ready, Puppy?"

Beau offered to help because he couldn't say he was ready to meet Ophelia again, although part of him had always wanted that. Beau turned because Déja whined. His smile appeared strained, but he was glad to ponder something trivial, if only for a moment. Done with Nell's boots, he asked his small cousin, "What's the matter, sweet-cake?"

"Want to go," she moaned and rubbed an eye. "I go too…right?"

"No, pumpkin," Kismet appeared. "You're staying with daddy, and no crying."

With her coat on, the momma kissed Lyle and their sleeping toddler. Beau and Nell exited as Kismet kissed her whimpering daughter. "Be good." She used Nell's words from long ago, "Remember, hardheads make soft behinds." Getting in her car, the Momma laughed.

"What's funny?" Nell inquired as in the rear, Beau remained silent.

Kismet smirked. "I'm turning into *you*, Mama."

As her daughter backed onto the tree-lined street, Nell became smug. "Well *I* am turning into Halle Berry," the movie star.

Kismet roared with laughter.

In the rear, noting the wintry, late-February evening, Beau felt like abandoning Ophelia, like she had done him, so long ago.

Through her rearview mirror, Kismet eyed her cousin, "You nervous, Diddley?"

When he didn't reply, gingerly Nell reminded him that they didn't have to do this. She pointed out, if they didn't, though, he might always wonder.

As the family neared the restaurant, Beau finally admitted to being a bundle of nerves. Clucking softly as they stood outside the car, Nell rubbed her nephew's back. She did so again inside the eatery.

Noticing his cousin and aunt who sat on either side of him, Beau thought of them as protection. But from what? He recalled suggesting Ophelia meet him at this eatery. During their phone call, his palms had dampened; it was why he'd figured meeting out was best. He hadn't wanted the woman in his home, and who knew if she even had a home. Seated with his family, Beau felt silly, because he was an adult now. Vivid memories of Ophelia were not supposed to unnerve him. Glancing at the menu, he guessed all them hours in therapy and boxing had been for naught, if he still felt this way.

Beau remembered the call... He had known Ophelia's voice immediately. He'd felt hollow inside. Hearing her voice had made him wish he'd requested an unlisted number from the phone company.

During that call, Ophelia had demanded that Beau see her. He'd remained silent. Then she'd yelled, as she had years prior. Perhaps she'd forgotten, or maybe she didn't care that he was no longer a child. Right then, he had known. *She was still the same*. Now Beau wished he'd hung up. If he had, he would be home now, not waiting for the unwanted.

82

Putting his menu aside, he pondered why he'd brought *them*, as vaguely his aunt and cousin discussed meal choices. It was unfair, Beau thought, to have dragged the women out in the cold. Really, what kind of man was he, to have solicited the 'protection' of two mothers, to protect him from his mother?

Kismet noticed Beau's hand. It shook when he reached for his glass. She tried not to think about how nervous he had to be. Kismet also tamped down bitterness. If she didn't, heavy-handed, she would slap the crap out of Ophelia when the woman appeared.

Beau wondered if he was still slightly frightened that Ophelia might attempt to smack him. She often had, when he was a boy. Did he fear obscene words from her, like those she'd hurled during her eight-year reign of terror? Suddenly, Beau stiffened because he sensed movement. Poised to pounce, he focused, not on Ophelia, but on a man in an apron.

Okay. Beau exhaled. He eyed the shot glass set before him. Inwardly he also asked why he hyperventilated. It wasn't like the woman could pose a threat to him. Now. Beau reminded himself that Ophelia could not hurt him anymore. He was a big strapping man. And she would be? He blinked to think clearly. Many years had passed, but he recalled, Ophelia had been small-boned. Sure, she'd been vicious, but she had only pulled off that strong-arm shit because *he* had been little. Now, he was a towering six foot three, a good two hundred and twenty pounds. He was toned and slender, but muscular. He could bench press two hundred and fifty-five, sizably more than the average Joe, and boxing had long been his hobby. He had knocked many a sparring partner to the mat. Therefore, the mean little woman could not do him damage. This he reasoned, as he gulped the fire hot shot.

Vaguely, Beau heard his aunt, who had mothered him so different from the way Ophelia had. He heard music and voices in the cozily lit eatery. Yet what he heard the most was blood, his own, rushing, in his ears. Looking around, Beau commanded himself to come together.

Food was set before him. His aunt had probably ordered it because his menu was gone. Beau only hoped his family didn't realize what an emotional wreck he was. Looking at his plate, he wondered, did he still love her? He wondered if she wanted to see him again because she was penitent now. Unable to eat a morsel, Beau forgot his plate. Fingering his dog tags, he realized.

Tonight had been a mistake. He should not have agreed to it.

Looking around, Beau noticed. Ophelia was not present, and he and the fam had been seated for a while. No, the mean little broad who'd beaten him with her fist, and with a stick another time had not shown, again. Embittered, Beau wondered if Ophelia was the reason he could not trust women. There were only *three* with whom he fully let his guard down. His aunt, his cousin, and his former roommate Valeria. Ah, and his middle school friend Mireya. She made four. Oh, Farai made five.

Was Ophelia the reason he was homosexual? Again, Beau wondered. He had often pondered his preference in sexual partners. Was it psychological, a manifestation of his inherent female distrust? God knew he would never have *chosen* a life of near secrecy. He was honest and open by nature, but maybe the witch had emasculated him.

Beau had a recurring thought. A woman with the same name populated Shakespeare's *Hamlet*. That Ophelia had done in Polonius, her father. She had even driven another character mad. Now, because of *his* Ophelia, Beau thought, he could join the Shakespearian crew.

No. Stop, Beau told himself. Ophelia wasn't his. She never had been.

The thespian realized he was ready to leave. He didn't want to think anymore, not about that woman. He opened his mouth to tell his family. However, they all heard another's voice.

"You're not pleased with your meal?"

Beau looked up at the puzzled waiter.

"Oh, he'll eat later," Nell intervened. She asked the man who'd said he was a new grandfather to bring to-go containers. "Just set them down, sir, and I'll do the rest." She then turned to the man she'd reared as her own son. "You're not here, Puppy."

"I am," Beau argued.

"You're not, and that's to be expected." Nell buttered a few soft rolls. "You'll want these, so we'll wrap them up with everything else."

Beau really looked at his aunt then. Her thick hair was longer and grayer. She was heavier than in years past. The grooves around her mouth had deepened, yet she was the most beautiful woman he had ever seen. Suddenly Beau realized. Arnell Moore's beauty was *character*. It shone from the inside right out. Beau also realized something more. *He* was as important to Nell as the daughter to whom she had given birth. It was why Beau could not help but ask, "Why wasn't she like you?"

84

"Oh, sugar," Nell cooed because each time it was asked, it stung.

Listening, Kismet knew her cousin was hurt. She despised Ophelia for causing it. That bitch had called, then she hadn't shown up, but she'd dredged up all Beau's old hurts. For that, Kismet could have beaten the woman down. Kismet thought it as she watched her mother, who was never at a loss in any situation.

Taking Beau's big hand, Nell kissed it. "Puppy, I have always wanted you." Nell said had there been a way, "Any way…to make you totally mine, I'd have done it. I would still do it."

Beau caressed his aunt's cheek because she *had to know*. He loved her, *so much*…even as the words stuck in his aching throat.

Looking up, Nell received her to-go plates. Thanking the server, she requested the bill. "If you don't mind, Puppy," she said when the waiter pivoted. "We've given this here, enough time and energy."

Kismet agreed. "We should go."

Beau laughed despite his sorrow. He spoke to the woman he sometimes called Mama. "I used to wish she cared, like you do."

Nell sighed while pushing untouched food from Beau's plate. "Puppy, that heifer ain't like me, and you wishing keeps you hurting."

"I know, but letting go isn't easy."

Nell patted Beau's hand. The pats were non-injuring slap-slaps. "You don't have to be over her, sweet pea. I mean, like it or not, she's part of you. She's your Mama. Part of you will always want her."

Tears suddenly assailed Beau. "But, I hate her, most of the time."

Embracing her nephew, Nell murmured, "That's okay."

"It's not." Beau sat ramrod straight. He couldn't snivel like a girl. He was in movies, and on a top-rated crime scene cable drama. Someone could recognize him and take photos. Those would grace the pages of the tabloids. Yet he divulged, "I don't feel like anything is okay."

"You are okay, most of the time," Nell pointed out. "Right now though, you're hurting. If I had my way, I'd fix things for you. I'd do it by damning that 'Phelia bitch to a burning hell, right away!"

Kismet had to laugh at her mother's vehemence.

"Puppy, I'd do so," Nell stated, calmer, "because that woman makes you feel less than you are. She is so not worthy of you, or your love."

Kismet did not want to place a hand at her head. She hated that 'this' was happening now.

Beau noticed, as did her mother. They knew she would have a vision. Lasting only seconds, and often unclear, Kismet's visions came true. Therefore, her family knew that while she trusted them, she dreaded them. It had been the same for her mother and grandmother.

"What did you see, baby?" Nell asked.

Kismet sighed. "There was a woman, vaguely familiar, with wild hair. There was *a clown* too, of all things, with this woman. He had the classic red hair, red nose, and a big fake pocket watch. He and the woman had their heads together like they were plotting..."

Nell nodded. "Well, we know one thing. The truth will come to light soon enough." The older woman spoke of the server and settling the bill. "KissGirl, give him your card."

The younger mother balked. "You give him your card, Diddley."

"KissGirl, I told *you* to do it."

"I've got this," Beau said to avert an argument between the women. They could so quickly get started. He sighed. "This was my stupid outing. Neither of you should pay."

Nell nodded. "Well Puppy, let's move on then. You're a fine young man, and you're doing fine. If your Mama shows up, next time, if there is one, then she does. If not, you'll always have your cute cousin Kiss there—who is being cheap—and you'll have broken down ol' me."

Kismet ignored her mother, who sometimes got on her nerves, treating her like a child. Taking deep breaths, to remain calm, she pulled her car keys.

While Beau placed his card for payment, Nell considered the woman with the wild hair and the clown. *What*, she wondered, did Kismet Staar's vision mean? And who were those two people, the woman and the clown?

Nell sighed because time sure would tell.

Chapter 14

KISMET was lying beside Lyle. He stared at the television. The ESPN commentator spoke, but Lyle couldn't hear. He'd pressed mute when Kiss picked up the phone. Listening to the river dance on the roof, he knew she spoke with Valeria. It seemed as if Val had asked to keep their small Déja for the weekend.

"Kira could bring her child too," Kismet suggested of Valeria's sister. Then someone Déja's age would be at her godparents' home as well.

Valeria chuckled. "She's getting too grown, huh?"

"She's three, going on four—teen," Kismet acknowledged.

"I'll call Kira and Magi, get my nieces over." Valeria offered. Suddenly she yelled. "I gotta go—I'm burning something!"

Chuckling, Kismet hung up. "Lyle, how am I gonna tell her?"

Switching the television off, Lyle sighed. "Kiss, if you *don't*, soon, you won't have to."

Aware that he was right, Kismet put her bare leg over Lyle's. Lyle was right. If she didn't inform her sister-friend that she was going to have a baby, Valeria would see the inevitable rounding. Then she would know. Val would be happy for her friend, but sad for herself.

"It's all so unfair," Kismet moaned because for a few years, Valeria had been trying to conceive. Kismet had two babies, and without trying, she was about to have another.

Privy to her thoughts, Lyle rubbed her bare thigh.

"Stop it," she told him, feeling frustrated as well as aroused. "That's how we got in this mess, to begin with."

"Mess?" Lyle rose slightly to look into his woman's eyes.

"You know what I mean," Kismet recanted. "Your touching and getting me heated started this predicament."

Lyle didn't like the connotation. "So, our having a baby is a predicament?"

Kismet attempted to soothe his ruffled feathers. "I didn't mean that."

"You did," Lyle informed his longtime lady. "Kiss," frustration emitted in his voice, "You won't marry me, or take my ring. We can't move in together. You won't think about us buying a bigger house together—although God knows we need it. Yet I am the only father your children have ever known, and you won't let me give them my name. Now, my baby's inside you, and, you're willing to continue as we have." Lyle shook his head. "Lady, you are contradictions personified."

He sat up, and forced her to face his back. "You say it's not me, but I'm starting to think differently." Lyle acknowledged that he was supposed to understand, "But I don't."

His feelings were hurt. Aware of it, Kismet sighed and tried to explain. She had only meant Valeria would be hurt.

"Yeah, but what about *me*?" Lyle inquired.

"I just meant this should be her, rather than me," Kismet tossed back.

Lyle's face registered incredulity. "You know, Kiss, it's always about you, or somebody else."

Kismet appeared shocked. "What do you mean?"

"Everything is about you, the babies, or somebody other than me."

Kismet felt hurt and moved her leg. "You can't mean that."

"I do. You get most of what you want, but when do *I* get something?"

Kismet could not speak but she'd known Lyle felt that way. He wanted to be married to her. Lyle wanted to give her children his name, thereby giving them a loving and present father. Lyle wanted their family to mirror the family he'd had while growing up.

Angrily, he said his father would never have heard of abiding elsewhere, "But not being married, it appears I've got no choice."

Kismet knew that Lyle wanted to love her, without obstructions. In silence, she watched him walk to the window. In her Afro-Centric motif bedroom, he stared at March rain. With his long neat locs hanging down his broad back, Lyle appeared disheartened. Kismet knew he was a good, faithful man. He loved her. Yet for years, she had held him off.

She knew women who wanted to crawl all over him. She had even been taunted by one of his admirers. "If he wanted to," the woman said, "Lyle can make *my* kids his own." The admirer had saucily revealed that *she* would turn herself out for Lyle. The woman said she'd do so to see a smidgen of love in his eyes; but alas, that was only for Kismet. The other woman further admitted she wanted what was in Lyle's pants, his fat paycheck, and his penis.

Kismet recalled barely managing to keep her fists unclenched. Looking at Lyle Manfred, she realized. The good-sized software engineer did not have to be so bothered, with her. For crying aloud, the man could have his pick of women. Why then, she inwardly asked, was she having the devil's time with his proposal?

The man was excellent husband material. Kismet loved him, in her way. Yet she could not understand the holdup. She watched as Lyle returned to sit bedside. He faced away and she reached out to touch his bare back. Kismet was aware that she should say something, but she couldn't come up with anything right. The notion made her want to cry.

Dang hormones, she thought. They and the baby had her all twisted up. Heck, she was independent and nobody's crybaby. Breathing deeply, she told herself she only had months left, then no more hormonal bawling. Deciding she would simply rub Lyle's back, she hoped he would remember that she cared. Perhaps he would remember that although she was a simpleton, she loved him.

Feeling her fingertips on his back, Lyle turned and pushed Kismet onto the pillows behind her. Rolling the straps of her nightie off her shoulders, he peeled the soft material down her body. He placed both hands on her expanding waistline and his open mouth over an areola. Gently he sucked, aware that her breasts were tender these days.

"I love you, Kismet Staar," Lyle said, lifting his head to look into her eyes. "You could love me, too, if you'd let yourself." Lyle knew she bought into all that super-woman stuff, the mess that her half-sister, a women's fashion magazine publisher and founding editor, propagated. Lyle knew Kiss wanted to be independent and capable, and she was, but she was carrying it a little far. If she would just tone things down a bit, Lyle thought and caressed a large breast, then her decisiveness would be just one of many things he loved about her.

As she placed her arms around Lyle's massive brown back and arched to more fully meet his mouth, Lyle wondered why Kiss couldn't see; intelligent woman that she was; he only wanted to enhance her life. They had been together for nearly six years. He knew he had proved he would be there for her, and that he would make life easier.

As he placed his lips over a nipple, he realized something that Kismet probably had not. All the things wives relied on husbands for, she relied on him for, but she was too afraid to commit. Her reason was lodged somewhere in his brain. If he could get her titty out of his greedy mouth. If he could get his ravenous hands off her warm, lush body, it would come to him. He knew she'd told him, in a few words, some time back.

Ah! Lyle's eyes widened as cognizance dawned. Kismet Staar Moore, the Client Managing Director of Global Accounts at an I.T. company, had seen her mother lose her father. Kiss said she never wanted to experience that kind of hurt or anguish. She had even asked if Lyle had imagined living with a woman and loving her so much until that woman became part of him. Kismet revealed she'd been privy to that kind of love. She had even imagined it for herself. However, she simply could not get past the knowledge that one day she could lose that person. Kismet said she would lose her mind.

That was why she didn't want them to live together! Lyle realized that was why Kismet kept him and his marriage certificate at bay. It was why she kept the adoption papers hidden. Those things were her last bastion, her fledgling attempts at protecting her heart.

Immediately, all the tenderness that Lyle had ever felt for Kismet rose. He poured it into their kiss. At that moment, although he didn't know how it was possible, he loved her more, for her illogical logic.

Holding her in his arms, softly Lyle stated—although he hadn't meant to—that he wasn't anybody's pretty boy. Sure, women found his rugby-player's build, his dark skin, and his height attractive. They found his long, locked hair and warm brown eyes intriguing. However, even in high school, he had known. He wasn't movie star dude.

"I'm no Denzel, Chestnut, or Shemar," he stated, figuring he might as well go on and speak his piece. "I'm no James Earl Jones either, to offer eloquent words, but Kiss, baby, I am what you need."

Kismet closed her eyes as she lay exposed beneath Lyle's amorous gaze. She realized he was what she needed and wanted. He was her best friend, the person she told most everything to, even the things she couldn't tell her longtime sista-friends. Kismet found Lyle amusing, and vice versa. He was her lover, her mechanic, her chauffeur, her chef, her babysitter, and lately, her baby-maker.

"Did you hear me?" Lyle asked because lost in thought, Kismet had not responded. "Kiss, I can be—"

"Whatever I need; I heard," Kismet acknowledged. With her eyes on the rain dashed window, she wanted to tell Lyle he already was everything to her, but the words wouldn't come. Why? Why did she have a hard time saying what she felt, to Lyle, when it pertained to them?

"Lyle," Kismet forced out because she had to get real, after six years, "You really are my everything, already. I don't need any more than you."

He was stunned to hear it. "Well, let's make it official." Although he felt light years from it, he appeared nonchalant. "Let's cement our deal, girl. Just say yes."

Kismet nodded and startled herself. "Yes," she said. "Okay?"

Lyle's heart pounded with exuberance, yet he forced himself to sound calm when he asked, "When?"

"*When*?" Kismet's eyes widened. She stammered. "Soon, I-I'd guess." She claimed they would know when the time was right. Quickly she looked away. She hoped Lyle wouldn't feel she was evasive again.

He knew she was stunned, but he wasn't going to cage her by pushing. He would get his date, later. He would again present his request, with a ring. Then Kismet Staar would answer, he knew. Lyle Manfred had one stipulation. Kismet Staar had to marry him before their baby was born. He'd told her before, and he would say it again. Not now, Lyle thought and felt himself swell, *there*, for the woman he would marry.

Between kisses, he told her, "Making love is great…" He placed his mouth over an expectant brown nipple, "when there's rain for background music."

Kismet sounded breathy as she spread her legs. "We should try it."

Lyle placed a hand beneath Kismet's bottom. Before he knew it, he was gliding, then inside her, giving her what he gave best.

When the pushing and pumping became nearly too good to stand, he slowed the pace. He also suggested, "You on top."

"Oooh," Kismet licked her lips and got into position. She eased herself down onto Lyle's substantial erection. "Oh my," she gasped, "I feel so full."

"You only think you do," Lyle said before informing her there was more. "I'll give it to you in a minute." Raising his upper body, he moved to again taste his betrothed's breasts.

Moaning and moving on him, Kismet bent to lick Lyle's lips.

Before they were done, pleasing and teasing, breathlessly, she whispered. They were going to need to do everything all over again.

Laughing, Lyle said, "Then it must be true," what he had heard about women and pregnancy.

"If you've heard we need it more, then that's true." The mother-to-be shrugged as she rode him, "At least in *my* case, it is."

Chapter 15

SHE had tried so many times, and nothing. There was no baby, no life growing inside her. This Valeria René realized as she pondered that for months she had been slowly pulling away from her loving husband.

She now avoided Fabian Sinclair. When they were home together, she would suddenly go out for groceries, or sort laundry. She had even shampooed the carpet in her car. She'd washed the upstairs windows of their home, all so she would not have to face Fabian.

How could she? How could she look in her husband's eyes and know she would never be able to give him his dream? Durn! It appeared she would never give birth. To know *she* couldn't do the one thing that careless teenagers did every day, hurt badly.

True enough, Valeria had become pregnant a few times; but nothing had been right. She'd miscarried. Therefore, she figured, she really wasn't much of a woman. *That* was the reason she couldn't stay with Fabian. He was loving, virile, and sexy. He was funny. To Valeria, the truth was clear, now. Fabian deserved so much more than her, or what she could give.

Therefore, Valeria could not go home again. She would just sit in her corner of the chain bookstore a little while longer. She would pretend to read until closing time. Then riding home, she would ponder getting a second job. When she got it, perhaps after she had been away for twelve or fourteen hours a day, Fabian would be asleep when she got home. Maybe he would stop waiting up for her. Maybe he would just…drift away. Then she wouldn't have to see the hurt in his eyes. It always reminded her. She was not getting pregnant, her wifely duty.

IN his and Valeria René's charming old home, the one that she had painstakingly decorated, Fabian wondered where his wife was. He didn't want to call her again. But heck, where was she? Fabian was tired of feeling like a heel just because he wanted to know why Val no longer wanted to be at home with him.

Feverishly, he hoped there wasn't another man. Fabian didn't know if he could take that. He wouldn't think about it. If there was though, whoever the dude was, Fabian would rush out and beat that home-wrecker's ass. He swore he would, and he would feel no remorse.

Vowing to get hold of himself, Fabian tried to stop thinking ill of his wife. Sure, she refused to discuss the increasing distance between them. She never had time. That was another thing that bugged him. Valeria René had time for everything *but* him.

Shoot! Fabian had invested his all in this relationship. He'd put in almost six years. So heck if he was going to lose, or let Val go now.

What to do? Fabian wondered. If only he and his wife could talk, they could make sense of things. Damn. It probably *was* another man. Yep, because Fabian had seen the wolves, everywhere. Those males hungrily ogled his pretty baby, wanting to snap her up.

Just pondering it, the cocoa-skinned man became short of breath, despite being physically fit. Irate, he realized, wherever his wife was, he would appear there, tonight. She would speak to him, or so help him…

Recalling a place he could go, the husband grabbed his keys. He thought of a person whose advice he trusted. He would attempt that, before he did something rash and unforgivable.

As he drove, in the spring evening, Fabian realized that for three days, he had hardly seen his wife. He ignored the new buds on trees. Forced tulips had their pretty heads up, but all he could think was that Val had been preoccupied. She filled out college re-enrollment applications. She stayed online. Well, he was unwilling to be put off any longer. She was going to un-busy her schedule and give him *his* moment.

He recalled how busy she'd become with their godchild. It seemed she enjoyed small Déja's company more than she enjoyed his. Val also spent inordinate amounts of time on the phone. That wasn't like her. In addition, she no longer wanted intimacy. It was like one day she'd just lost interest, in them, or perhaps *him*. Hurt, Fabian realized his wife didn't even want him to hold her. She avoided his kisses too, like he had halitosis, or like he'd maltreated her at some point.

Driving, Fabian wondered. What had transpired to turn his wife off? Where was the intimacy that had been their connubial joy? Turning his SUV onto a familiar street, he remembered. On this night, his wife would be at her parents' home. He had overheard her telling Kiss, a few nights back. Therefore, he would show up at the Thompson homestead. He wouldn't budge either, until sweet-sweet deigned to see him.

Fabian thought fast and drove furiously. He would never do anything to embarrass Val, not intentionally, but he was desperate. That was why he was about to enlist her father's aid. Wheeling onto his in-laws' lavish Lindenhurst township property, Fabian pulled up on the circular drive, behind his wife's car.

The side door of the house opened. His father-in-law, a mahogany skinned older man, stood guard as Fabian climbed from his SUV. Under an ominously darkening sky, the younger man proceeded up the drive lined by white rocks and manicured foliage. Why did Horace Thompson look disapproving? Had Val told her dad something untoward about him? Fabian wondered.

Horace, who could appear imposing, remained in the doorway, smoking his usual cheroot. Watching his eldest daughter's husband draw near, he spoke. "Been waiting on you, son."

"Have you?" Fabian wondered why. He had never known his wife to tell tales; yet, of what had she accused him? Moreover, how had her father known that he'd been en route?

Horace held the screen door wide. "I wondered," he said with smoke streaming from his nostrils, "*When* you'd come to claim your wife."

"Sir?" Fabian was baffled.

Horace closed the outer, as well as the inside, door. "I'm *saying*, son," he clarified, "If my Chitra went off, for one day, I'd go after her. And here you are," Horace sighed, "strolling up here, how many days late?"

Fabian felt relieved as he admitted, "I didn't know whether I was supposed to pursue. I guess I'm still a novice at this marriage thing."

"All men are," Horace divulged, his face showing no trace of the chuckle he felt. "But boy, do I feel sorry for your generation. This new breed of woman could even scare the cool out of Casanova."

Horace led the way through his dark, peaceful home. He cut through the dimly lit, multi-functional kitchen. He tossed over a shoulder, "I'm so glad I got my girl back when life was a helluva lot simpler." Back then, everybody knew the rules. Men and women had specific roles. "Now, who knows? It seems to be a free-for-all."

Fabian smiled as he recalled that his father-in-law was his favorite. The man spoke his mind. Fabian looked around the comfortable den. He took a seat, as puffing away, Horace exited.

When Valeria timidly entered, it was with downcast eyes.

"Hey," Fabian called, not knowing how to greet her.

"Hey, *you.*" She glanced at him. Then she went to the open patio doors. Feeling a breeze through the screen, she sighed.

Watching, Fabian longed to take her in his arms. Instead, he asked, "So, you been okay," because when had he seen her last?

Wearing a denim jacket, she nodded. "You?" With her back to him, she knew he had been as miserable as she had. Her eyes swept her parents' lush green lawn. She squinted up at the sky that threatened rain.

"Been missing you..." Fabian said, and startled her.

Yet facing away, Valeria stiffened. She whispered, "Fabe, don't."

"Don't what, babe?" He asked with his throat aching. Shit, he was sick of being strong amid what felt like he was losing, everything.

Valeria softly replied, "Don't do *that.*"

"What?" Fabian queried, feeling anger. "Are you saying *don't* love you, *don't* miss you, *don't* want you? Because if you are, it's a little late. Hell, you should've said that the night we met. You should never have let me see you again, either."

"Fabian!" Valeria hissed, her hand on the screen door.

"I'm here," he said and walked toward her, "Like I always have been, and like I always will be...if you let me."

"Why're you doing this?" she asked when her husband stood close. She felt his breath on her nape. Although she tried not to, Valeria inhaled Fabian's bewitching cologne and realized how much she loved him.

Yet attempting to remain rigid, she queried, "Why do this?"

"What?" Gently Fabian took her in his arms. Wrapped around her, in her ear he revealed, "I'm not doing any of what I really want to do."

Valeria longed to simply rest against him. She loved the feel of his cheek against her own; his hard body flush against hers.

Fabian's inquiry startled his wife. "Has your love for me died?"

Unable to breathe, she whirled to face the man she had vowed to forever cherish. "*Nooo...*" Although she'd wanted to lie, to make parting easier, Valeria couldn't. Unshed tears caused her eyes to shimmer. "Never." *I will always love you.*

Fabian swallowed, relieved to know love remained. Still, he knew little more than he had days ago. "Then, what's wrong, bae?"

In the space between Fabian and the screen door Valeria turned. Again, he faced her back. Softly, she said, "Our thing has run its course."

What the–? Fabian blinked, and could not comprehend. "What?"

"I'm letting you go." With a hand at her mouth, Valeria stifled a sob.

"You're...letting...me go," Fabian slowly articulated. Dazed, he turned away, only to turn back. "What does that mean? And *why*, Val?" Suddenly, the husband exploded. "What have I done—or not done, to make you want *this*?!"

Valeria muffled the sobs that threatened to erupt.

"Talk to me," Fabian ordered. He was owed at least that.

With a hand splayed across her mouth, wifey shook, unable to speak.

"*Why*, Valeria René," Fabian badgered, "Why would we be *over*?"

"It's what you'll want," she softly cried.

Dumbfounded, Fabian echoed her. Then, needing clarity, he bellowed, "Yo, what does that mean?"

"It means," Valeria sounded like she didn't care, "Just that."

"Stop it with the riddles," Fabian growled. He jerked his wife to face him. "I'm sick of them, and of you, staying away and being on the phone at all hours. I despise your college apps, and the time you spend with Déja. So before I really lose it, you'd better say how we can fix this shit."

Valeria struggled to release herself as she whined, "That hurts."

Fabian loosened his hold. He lowered his voice because they weren't in the privacy of their own home. "Babe, talk to me. I need you to say something that makes sense. You owe me that."

"You'll *want* to go," his wife predicted.

Icy horror danced up Fabian's spine. "What – did – you – do?" He asked with narrowed eyes. Indeed, they had discussed leaving, only if one of them cheated. Early in their marriage, they agreed; the cheat that would dismantle everything would have to be ongoing. It couldn't be merely a one-time thing. No one got a pass. However, from time to time, the marrieds would be attracted to others. It was a fact; yet to destroy all they had worked for? Both people vowed that before dissolution, they would carefully consider all possibilities.

Recalling those things, Fabian's voice became flat. "So, you cheated." Clenching his hands, he couldn't look at his wife. "Who is he?" Fabian's mind raced to pinpoint a culprit. "Who you crept with?" he asked, feeling as though he had been stabbed, and like life ebbed away.

"No one," Valeria claimed. "I don't creep." Hell, this new turn of events was worse than any of the leaving scenarios she had imagined.

"You said I'd want out," Fabian charged. "The only reason I'd want that is if you crept on me, repeatedly—and you been staying away..."

"You're wrong," Valeria hissed.

"You just *said* I'd want to go!" Fabian snarled. He tried not to picture some nameless, faceless man lapping at his honey. He tried to unclench his fists. "I know you remember our pact, so...who is the muthafucka?"

Nearly afraid to, Valeria pivoted. She had never seen Fabian so enraged. Still, she knew that he held himself in check, but barely.

Lethal and low, he barked, and caused her to jump. "Who is he?!"

Looking into Fabian's anger-reddened eyes, Valeria made her ordinarily soft voice hard. "I *said* there *is* no one. I *said* I haven't crept." At regular decibel, she explained, feeling somewhat heated herself. "There ain't nobody else. I don't wanna lie with any man but you." With her heart breaking, Valeria choked out she was giving Fabian license to walk because in a year or two he wouldn't want her. How that hurt.

"Fuc—*forget* next year," Fabian snapped, "talk to me about now, about this mess." He pointed. "Say why you been strange. And tell me why you're putting this all on me because I can't think about no future. Right now, from where I'm standing, don't even look like there is one."

"Fabian. I know how much you want a baby," Valeria softly disclosed. She opened the screen door and stepped out onto the covered patio. With March wind frenzying her long dark curls and tugging her voluminous georgette skirt, she nearly felt better. She felt like the oncoming dark and the impending spring torrent mirrored her emotions.

Dropping wearily onto a rattan sofa, she felt depleted. Closing her eyes, she leaned back into huge cushions. Not looking, she knew her husband was near. With her eyes shut, before he could start gnawing at her again, she mentioned their attempts at baby-making. Since it hadn't happened, she was giving up. "This way," she stated, over his attempt to interrupt, "You can go. Have a future. Posterity. With someone who can give that to you."

"Oh my God," Fabian moaned. Instinctively he grabbed his wife. Pulling her up, he held her tight. "I want *you*, babe." With evening stubble pressed roughly to her hair, and her cheek, he inhaled. He loved the jasmine cloud that ever surrounded her. "Without *you*, baby," the cocoa-skinned man lamented, "I've got no future. None at all."

"You deserve children." Valeria buried her face in her husband's shirtfront. "Who am I to stand in the way?"

She was his *wife*, the woman he loved. Fabian thought it as he forced out the words lodged hurtfully in his throat. "Val, honey, love..." he swallowed past the ache. "I can't go." Mournfully he shook his head. "Where *would* I go—Now that you've become my whole life?"

For the first time, in months, Valeria initiated a kiss. Opening her mouth, she pulled Fabian close, while feeling ravenous.

When released from the enveloping kiss, Fabian's voice was filled with hope. "Come home... Okay?"

"Fabe, I'm sorry," his wife apologized. As though she hadn't heard the suggestion, she blurted that had she known this baby thing would drive such a wedge between them, she'd have left it alone, "Long ago."

Fabian repeated himself. "Come home."

"You mean, after all this, you still want me there?"

"If you want to be there." He nodded. "It *is* your home."

Valeria's eyes were shyly downcast. "We'll do what we used to?"

"Stuff like this?" On his knees, in whistling wind and imminent rain, Fabian ran his hands up and under his wife's billowing skirt.

"Yes," she breathed. She widened her stance; while hooking a hand in her lace panties Fabian caressed her. Suddenly and powerfully, torrents of rain fell. Hearing and feeling them pummel and spatter, Valeria realized she wanted her husband with the same ferocity.

With fingers making their way inside her, hungrily, Fabian placed his mouth on that of his wife. "I can do better than this."

Sexily, crazily, Valeria's hair flew wildly about her head as she asked, "Oh, you can, huh?"

"I sure can, girl." Fabian placed his wife's small elegant hand on his erection. "Remember, I've got this."

Nightstick. "Why not use it?" she asked. With desire-glazed eyes and a leg encircling him, she drew Fabian close. Valeria gasped when she heard a zipper and felt the knob of his penis pressed to the apex between her thighs. "Do me," she whispered, biting Fabian's lush lower lip. Excited, she taunted him. "Get all up in me, big man."

"Here?" Incredibly aroused, he ground himself against her.

"Why not? You're here. I'm here. You're ready. I'm—feel that?"

Fabian indeed felt moist warmth. He licked the two fingers he'd used to explore, *but*, he articulated, this was not home. He said he wanted to be there, where they wouldn't worry about being discovered. There, he would lay it *down*. "I will work you over, girl," he growled.

"Hey." The thought quickly arose. "Ride back in my car, Val."

"But mine is here."

Insistently, Fabian fondled the ample breasts that he loved. "We can pick it up tomorrow."

Through his wife's blouse, he put his mouth on a nipple. "Ride with me, and strip, while I drive..."

Nearly liquefying with desire, Valeria could see herself doing just that. She could see them making love in Fabian's SUV, even before their automatic garage door fully closed.

It would be fantastic. His greedy mouth would be on her tits. His muscular thighs would rest in the cradle of hers, and his hands would be on her petite bottom. His engorged male member would surge into her.

"Come." Turning quickly, Valeria grabbed her husband's hand. Hurriedly, she stepped out of blowing rain, back into her parents' den. Hastening past the stairs, she called up to say she was leaving.

Her father, Horace's voice boomed back down. "You taking that man with you? You'd better..."

Valeria and Fabian both laughed before she admitted, "I fully intend to." With her smaller hand in his, she pulled her husband along.

At the side door, the wife lifted her skirt and pressed herself to her husband's throbbing erection. Ohhh. She couldn't wait to feel him, fully, to taste and enjoy.

With her mouth hot and sweet on his, Valeria Sinclair whispered that on this rainy evening, she would take Mr. F. A. Sinclair, the only man for her, to the crazy sexy moon.

Then they dashed out of doors, to get completely wet.

Chapter 16

AT the Gay Men's Help Center, where Ronni worked, she passed a doorway, and someone caught her arm.

Quickly, he had stepped from his office into the hallway. He'd done so upon seeing her. Preoccupied, she would never have noticed him. Therefore, Curtis Hurst reached out.

Startled, Ronni turned. "Oh—hi, Curt." She smiled up at the man with whom she had been on a few outings, not dates. Sure, they'd shared evening meals, but never would she admit that she'd wished those had been dates.

"Looks like you're on a mission." Curtis smiled down at the woman he could only admire. Once, she'd told him some of her story. Ronni had been a vibrant Production Head for a major publishing house, but she had become ill. Her employer had 'let her go' after it became known that she suffered from HIV. Veronica M. Brown could have sued. Instead, she'd moved on, choosing to help others. She had thereby become a darn good teacher/counselor for Gay Men's. Curtis remembered hiring the woman, and bonnie Miss Ronni had never looked back. Not even when those that she counseled and grew close to passed on. Man! Curtis hoped he didn't look like a dopey puppy, but she really was something.

Dressed as spiffily as ever, Ronni revealed she'd been headed back to her office. The butter-yellow woman didn't tell her supervisor that these days she was forgetful. Nor did she say she'd left a folder atop her desk.

Still, Curtis nodded and wondered why it seemed like the five foot four, light-skinned woman thwarted any honest attempt of his to get close to her. "Well," he said, because them standing idly around wouldn't do, "Just don't come around here smelling like that anymore."

Feeling alarmed, Ronni forced her eyes not to widen as she asked, "Like what?" Did she stink? Could her illness be smelled? Oh, Jeezis.

Curtis realized he'd startled Ronni, so smoothly, he said, "Don't keep smelling like Heaven. It's hell on us mere mortals."

Oh. Ronni didn't yet smell like an oozing, leprous exile. Her smile wavered. "Curt, for a minute, I wondered if I'd forgotten my deodorant."

When he seemed genuinely amused, Ronni turned to go. She had no business engaging in small talk with her supervisor, even though he had said she smelled like Heaven. He had probably only said it because she looked like hell. The truth was she didn't look anything like she once had. Back a few years, she had been a real hottie. Hers had been a body that wouldn't quit, and she'd worked it! Sadly, she thought, Curtis now threw her bones, because most likely, he felt sorry for her. The dilapidated poodle.

Yep, Ronni mused, that was probably the man's reason for being so nice, asking to take her here and there. Curtis knew her life was lonely. He knew things weren't like they had been when she was well.

"Curtis," Ronni made herself say, "I'll let you get back to work."

He hated that they both had to; it was why he said, "Let's do lunch. Let's make it one day this week, to discuss your new lecture series."

With a nod, Ronni resumed her purposeful stride. She knew Curtis watched her. Why? When her booty wasn't nearly as naturally padded or curvaceous as it had once been. She was no longer anything to look at. Walking, she almost wished Curtis had seen her back in the day. She had been a serious man-draw. Now, she Ronni Marie Brown just appeared skinny, tired 'n old, when she was only thirty-eight.

Tears of self-pity welled in Ronni's eyes. Again, she despised her plight. She recalled how stupid she'd been, too, back when life had been grand. Men had fallen over themselves for her. At the time, she'd taken her health for granted. Now, she strove to be grateful for every breath, because any day she could wake up...dead.

Watching as the thin but shapely Ronni hurried away, Curtis wanted to call after her. He actually wanted to run after her, so he could spill the contents of his heart. The average-height brown man would say he knew Ronni had been *thru*. He knew it was why she was cautious, but she didn't have to be, not with him. He was genuinely interested. Then after saying all that, Curtis would beg her to allow them to spend whatever time she had left, together.

Feeling like she needed a good cry, Ronni quickly detoured. Veering into the ladies' room, she leaned on the closed door. What if someone wanted in? Hurriedly entering a stall, Ronni felt she should have gone back to her office. There she could have locked her door. In her private space, she could have cried her eyes out.

In the stall, she unrolled tissue and pressed a wad to her eyes. Life was so unfair! Ronni pressed harder when tears came. She commanded her fleeting heart to regulate. She told herself, this was not happening. She ignored feeling strange. She felt that way every time she braved to think about that man, Curtis Hurst.

With his slim build, he wasn't anything spectacular. So why did thoughts of him cause her brain to shoot fireworks? Why did Ronni sit in her office or at home, or in her little old car, pondering what it would be like to lie naked beneath him? Why did she think of Curt licking her breasts and caressing her hips, just before he entered her?

She despised thinking about having his mouth on hers, or meeting him thrust for thrust while slicked with salty sweat. Heaven knew she didn't want to spend her little time thinking about stuff she couldn't have. She hated waking up nights with peaked nipples and a moist crotch. She despised opening her legs and pleasuring herself because he wasn't there. Ronni dabbed her eyes because if she hadn't been sick, she and Curtis could have enjoyed the sweetest taboo, him entering her anus.

Agh! Ronni sighed heavily. She told her stupid self to forget such things, because even now, at work, in a bathroom stall, she wanted that man so badly. She wanted to race down the hall. Ronni wanted to skid into Curtis' office and drop her dress. She would bend over his sofa with her legs parted—*but* she wanted him to want her, too. Wouldn't it be something if he could be as excited as she was? What if he locked his office door before he commenced to giving it to her good, like she had been used to getting it, in the past? That would be the best.

Oh, this was all wrong, Ronni told herself. If her dreams were to ever come true, it would be the end of Curtis. He was healthy. Ronni could not allow him to risk dying, even if he would, for a little coochie. Sick coochie. The crumpled tissue she again pressed to her eyes. Deep breath, she told herself. She even let herself wonder the very thing that she had refused to ponder in prior weeks.

Was she actually... falling in *love*? Shame on her for thinking such a thing. Falling in love? Please. Love was not for her. It never had been. Anyway, with her health and other issues, it was a bit late for love, lust, or anything that remotely resembled either.

102

Chapter 17

BEAU drove Kismet's car and wondered. How had he wound up with Sandal beside him? Beau had promised himself he was through with the red-haired greed-monger. Darn it, he had seen Sandal at the movies. Coincidence? Beau thought not. Sure, the actor's first thought was, hide! But he was too big.

Now he was driving Red home. Salacious Sandal wanted to Beau to stop for a lil something. Beau knew better. They'd wind up at a four or five-star hotel restaurant, ordering a few courses before they'd stay the night, if Beau wasn't careful. Nope, he would drop red hair off, forever.

"You know…" Sandal fished for words because Beau seemed lost in thought. "The lead in that movie reminded me of you."

At a light, Beau did not reply. He thought of his cousin, whom he would call. He would thank her for lending her car. He'd tell her that his Huntington, Long Island meeting with 'Indie' producers had gone well. When rid of Sandal, Beau would also approximate when he'd arrive. He'd ask Kiss to drop him at the Rail Road. The fast-moving Long Island train would get him to Manhattan quickly. In the a.m., he'd make his latest casting call.

"Beau, did you hear me?" Sandal's voice had been slightly shrill because he felt panicked. The feeling nearly choked him. He knew he was losing, and Sandal could not! It was why he'd called 24/7. He'd staked out the theater to which Beau had once taken him. Fear was also the reason that Sandal had spent coins he didn't have. Occasionally, he stopped by Beau's posh Manhattan apartment. It was on the same side of the street as the famed Pierre Hotel, a New York landmark. Sandal hated that the snooty Fifth Avenue doorman wouldn't give him the time of day. That uniformed clown knew he had seen Sandal with Beau, more than once! Sandal should have expected it, though, because people with money, or those who worked for them, always shunned him.

The same way Beau had shunned him, for weeks now.

Sandal didn't care, though, because he wanted his life to be different. Beau was his ticket; the actor just didn't know it yet.

Noticing that they neared his run down hood, in the shadow of the bridge, Sandal told himself it would be a little while longer. Then he would never again have to think about his current rat hole. He would have a new address, Beau's elegant address. Sandal would gaze out on Central Park every day. He would have spa days at the hotel. Sandal sighed. He just had to play his cards right, and reel Beau back in.

Sandal couldn't tip his hand where his 'friends' were concerned either. They were sweating him, when a few months ago they'd laughed and claimed he'd never be more than a little red queen.

Sandal forgot people he wanted to impress. Gazing out at the night, he realized he liked this car, even though it belonged to *her*, Beau's big-behind cousin. Red-hair was sure she didn't like him, but who cared? Heck, when he got his way, Sandal would talk Beau into getting a car. Then Beau could drive him, sweet Sandal, around all the time. Hey, forget that. Beau could buy Sandal a car. Red couldn't drive, but he'd look cute in a sporty something. It needed to be…red, to match his hair. Yeah, then his so-called friends could eat their jealous hearts out.

They thought he would never keep Beau. In recent weeks, since he hadn't blathered on about Beau, Sandal's 'friends' questioned him. He knew they'd secretly been gloating, and he'd felt the sting of embarrassment. Then he'd resorted to doing what he did best. Lying. He claimed that with Beau's gritty Crime Scene series, the actor was supremely busy. "He only has time to make love to me, then go back to work." Sandal recalled saying it, *and* that no one believed him.

As Beau pulled up to crumbly bricks, Sandal realized the actor hadn't said more than ten words to him all evening. Something was wrong, and that had to be fixed.

"How about," Sandal began, and placed a hand on Beau's thigh, "A good night treat?" He fully intended to unzip Beau's jeans. He would take Beau's member into his mouth. Sandal leaned over.

He was firmly pushed back. "I gotta get this car to Elmont, in Queens. Then I'll still be rolling," Beau stated, "Ain't got time."

What? Sandal's head swam, because what man didn't have time to get his dick slicked, especially by Sandal, the master sucker? Ooh lordy, Sandal thought, frightened, something had to be done, and fast, or he'd be out, and replaced by some French, Hollywood fag. "Well," Sandal said and tried to keep alarm from his voice, "Will I see you soon?"

"I'm busy these days," Beau remarked. He eyed the bums and winos that ever occupied the corner on which Sandal lived.

"I know that," slender Red snapped because what did Beau think he was, stupid, along with poor? "I'm just saying, we haven't seen much of each other lately and you don't seem to care. Haven't you missed me? You can do me; I've got warming jelly upstairs..."

Get out, Beau thought. "I've got an early call tomorrow."

"That's always the case, now," Sandal moaned. "No time for me."

"You know I have to work," Beau said tight-lipped. "Yo," he nearly yelled, just wanting Sandal out, "If one of us didn't have a real job, who would pay for the excursions you love, the dinners, and the shows?" This dude was starting to mirror Ophelia, and all her dreams of what Emmett should have done for her. The correlation Beau did not like.

Like tonight! Beau thought. He'd spotted Sandal in the theater lobby, but it had been too late to smoothly get away. Recalling that he had paid for them both still rankled, but Beau attempted to maintain calm. "I've said this before, Sandal, I don't have time—for a relationship," *with you*. "When I told you, you seemed to understand."

Oh, I understand, Sandal mentally fumed. He tried to appear unfazed as he stated, "You don't see it yet Beau, but I could make things easier for you. If I were at your place, you wouldn't have to drive me over here. I could clean and run errands for you, like an assistant."

"I pay a girl, through a service, for that," Beau stiffly stated. He just wished Sandal would get the devil out of his cousin's car.

However, the red-haired man had other ideas. He attempted to sound tough. "Yo, that was wrong, you talking about 'excursions' and who would pay, like I don't work. My work ain't like yours," Sandal wheezed, furious, "but that doesn't mean I'm nothing." Sandal's voice was startlingly high-pitched. "If you forgot, everybody ain't a celebrity!"

Man, was Beau sick of the drama. "Why are we discussing my work? Yo, why we gotta go there?" Beau asked. "Again."

"You started it," Sandal screeched, his voice high and cracking. "You spoke about my job, like it—and I—am nothing. I'm hurt!"

Hurt. Again. Overwrought. Always. "Why're you yelling?" Beau barked. "Why holler? I'm sitting right here. Calm down," *bitch, and for crying out loud, get out.*

"See? I hate that," Sandal shrieked. He was tired of being told what to do. He mocked Beau, "You're always saying: 'you really should blah

blah.' Gawd, am I sick of all your rules. 'That fork is for the shrimp; that one is for the salad'—and so what!"

Beau calmly replied. "I only tried to expand your horizons, but I see you're not appreciative. Well peep this; I'm sick of you, too."

With a mighty sigh, Beau glanced out of the window at the run-down tenement. "Uh, you're home now. Get out."

Sandal tried to tamp down surging fear because he had overdone it, as usual. He had never known when to clam up and leave well enough alone. Arrrgh! Why had he had that outburst? Now he'd received the level, pseudo-calm voice. The one Beau used when he was done. But oh-ho no! Sandal deviously thought, he would not so go smoothly or quietly. This was his time.

He pushed on the car door and thought about breaking the handle. That would be a nice present for Big-Titty Kizzie Brick House. Forgetting Beau's cousin, Sandal whined, "You'll call me?"

The tall, buff man laughed. He almost said, don't hold your breath. Summoning his acting skills, he showed no emotion.

Exiting the car with the plush leather interior, Sandal tried to be brave. Carefully, holding himself together, Sandal vowed not to allow Beau, or the neighborhood never-do-wells, to see him cry. He was perilously close. On stilettos, Sandal teetered toward the building, hating that for weeks, he'd felt a separation between him and Beau. Honestly, Sandal didn't know why. Feeling desperate, he screamed inside. He couldn't lose Beau! Wanting to sob, he watched Beau roll away.

Oh, man! Sandal thought. The actor was more than he had ever hoped to have. Beau also made Sandal look good. Sandal was aware that some people were born with less, but he knew they didn't have to stay that way. The lesser born just had to do what he had. The hair sweeper had found Beau. The slender man had slept with Beau. He'd sucked Beau's dick. He'd swallowed cum. Sandal had licked Beau's balls, literally. He'd let Beau be the top, so Sandal had done his part. He had paid his fare. It wasn't like he was asking for a free ride, so now he wanted more, and he deserved it.

As he neared his building, Sandal recalled that at the Mangrove Jungle, people had laughed at him, not long ago, before Beau. Now, club patrons laughed *with* him. The girlz now touched their fingertips to him and said, "Sss, Miz Thang, you are so hot!"

Sandal knew it was because of Beau, but he didn't care. Beau was Sandal's ticket to *more*. Something inside Red craved it. Sure, he would keep stocky, brooding Rodrigo as a sidepiece, but Beau would be the main because Beau could get Sandal where he wanted to go.

That reminded Sandal. Rodrigo—Roderick really —had an ol' blue-faced mama. She'd shaken her broom at Sandal. She'd shrieked that he should take his stank skinny self away from her Brooklyn home. She'd squawked, loud enough for passers-by to hear, 'Lea' my son alone! He ain't like you, ya low down, whoring faggot!'

That had hurt. Nevertheless, Sandal opined, Mama Rodrigo didn't know that her son was after Sandal! Sweet Sandal was the prom queen rising. Moreover, since he'd worked so hard to come up in the world, since he had endured so much, he would not be dethroned now!

Sandal entered the dimly lit hallway, putrid with piss, and Sandal knew one thing. He had to make things right between him and Beau. He had to keep getting the attention he'd always desired but had never received. Not before. Sandal wasn't stupid. He knew the focus was only because people thought he was in a relationship with Beau. Everybody knew Beau was on TV. Even the ol' biddies at the Hair Castle were aware. Now they treated him, *Mister* Sandal, with respect. Them old hags eyed him now, when before, they'd ignored him, or run him around until his bunions hurt. Now they knew he was somebody, because of Beau.

Outside his ramshackle apartment, Sandal passed a man who said lecherous things to him. Ignoring the man, Sandal crossed his heart and promised himself one thing. Since he desperately needed a new address, among other things, stuff that his Hair Castle earnings could never provide, Sandal would never let Beau go.

Now that he'd experienced a taste of fame's trappings, Sandal would have to prove to Beau they belonged together. Suddenly Red had a jarring thought. What if Beau refused to see? Well, Sandal decided, if that happened, he would just have to find a way…to make Beau pay.

Chapter 18

KISMET Staar made the mistake of picking up the phone. She asked herself why she hadn't let her mother get it. She could have scooted. Then Nell could have truthfully told Farai that Kiss wasn't present. Now Kismet was stuck, listening to her half sister's singsong. She had been avoiding just this. Kismet was also missing the fun in her kitchen. Dang, the ladies laughed without her.

Ronni had dropped by after work, and Amy Foster followed. They and Nell currently sat at the table, over coffee and warm apple streusel.

Tuning in to her sister, Kismet forgot the kitchen goings-on.

"You know, Kiss-met," the sophisticate said and sounded like a grown up Valley girl, "It is *so* ridiculously hard when you have children. They keep growing, and needing things. And it is reeeally hard for us right now; with my O-KAR-u still paying child support."

Kismet wondered why she had to hear about Farai's husband, the African diplomat, again. Farai should have been glad the man didn't shirk his responsibilities, and that he was a monogamist. She'd have been justified in crying if he had six or seven other wives.

Kismet halted the publisher and founding editor's diatribe. Hers was a world famous fashion magazine. It detailed the doings of the wealthy, famous, and glamorous, 'the cognoscenti.' Kismet forgot them to call her sister's name, "Fa-WRY Laura-LIE," Farai Lorelai.

"Yes, Kiss-met dear."

"I hate it when you say my name like that," Kismet announced for the thousandth time.

"But that is your name dahling, is it not?"

Kismet sighed. She was stuck on the phone with Ms. Bourgeoisie, while raucous genuine laughter wafted from her kitchen.

"Farai," Kismet began. "I agree. Rearing children can sometimes be a chore, but think about it this way—"

"Oh I'm glad you've admitted that," Farai cut in, "because I wanted to mention something. Sweetums, you're about to have your own

108

bambino. Why not get rid of those other children? The ones from that drug-addicted jailie."

"Did you say *those children*?" Kismet's blood pressure spiked. "I know you did not just call my Déja and Chance 'those children.'"

"Dahling, I'm just saying," Farai cooed while nodding at the manicurist in her office, "that—"

"You're not saying anything I want to hear," Kismet snapped. "Furthermore, since you don't realize, let me inform you. You were out of line." Perhaps the upper crust snobs with whom her half-sister often dealt had rubbed off on her. Like some of them, Farai might think she could say anything to someone of lesser stature. Well, the younger sister wasn't having it.

"Look," Kismet began, feeling more perturbed by the moment, "I need you to understand one thing. Déja and Chance *are my children*. If you can't accept that, then stop calling me."

"Settle down, Kiss-met," the surprised woman interjected. "I know your hormones are agog right now because you're expecting."

"You settle down," Kismet angrily advised. She informed her sister, that she had been a snob ever since that summer. Farai had descended from the home of her mother, a jet setter. Sullenly, she'd glided into the home of Nell and Brantley Moore, like she was Princess Somebody.

"Oh!" Farai gasped, taken aback at Kismet's outlandish behavior.

"Oh! To you too," Kismet retorted, knowing her sister wasn't used to getting as good as she gave. "And since you're finally listening, Farai, do not moan anymore about my nephew. You need to start mothering him and spend quality time with him. Talk to Brosnan. Then *listen*. It's not something you do well, although the minions in your employ would never say so. Then maybe after you've heard my nephew, you might be surprised. He may even stop doing things that you find appalling."

Farai waved to get the attention of the manicurist in her office. "Give me a moment. Please." Startling the retreating woman, she hissed at Kismet. "Are you saying I'm not a good mother, Kiss-met?"

The younger sister rolled her eyes. "Say my name right, and I said you need to become a *more attentive* mother. *Listen*. Listen."

"Now what would *you* know about mothering?" the magazine publisher shot back, a freshly polished hand at her chest. "I mean really?

What books have you written, or even read, you false Dr. Spock? Your children aren't even real. They're crying *babies;* my son is twelve—"

"Brosnan is *thirteen!*" Kismet yowled. She hadn't meant to, but occasionally her sister rattled her cage. "My nephew is thirteen, and he's acting out because he needs *his mother's* attention.

"Farai," Kismet sighed, because she was going to have to break it down. "You used the money you inherited, not to lie around in the sun, but to start your own wildly successful business. You fly to Milan, Budapest, and South Africa, for layouts. You teleconference and interact with people in Hong-Kong while seated behind your desk on Madison Avenue. You dine in Paris and play in Capri, but *when* do you take time for Brosnan? When do you simply listen to what he has to say?"

When the editor remained silent, Kismet asked, "Sis, when was the last time you did something he wanted, without interruptions?"

The boy was starved for attention. During summers spent with his aunt, she had seen it. She had also seen that Brosnan was a sweet, caring, adolescent. He had been so gentle when she'd brought her babies home. When he'd picked them up, he'd held their little heads. Eventually, when they began to toddle, patiently he'd walked round and round with them. Moreover, the boy had sat with his auntie, telling her things he had never thought to tell his mother. That was how Kismet knew. Her nephew needed his mother, and this she gently told her sister. Again.

With tears suddenly assailing her, Farai waved the tea service woman. "Go," she croaked, wanting none of the help privy to personal matters. "Sit in the outer office until I'm done with this. Please. Thank you." Into the phone Farai eked, "Kiss-met Staar, I try..."

"All I'm saying is try harder." The younger sister asked the elder to remember how good they'd both felt, back in the day. Each had had a designated Saturday with Nell. "If it was my turn she'd say, 'don't pout Farai, you had Saturday, last week.' Sis, Mama made us feel special."

"I recall," Farai admitted, her voice muffled by an embroidered hankie. "Mama did whatever *I* wanted, on my day. It wasn't even a big deal that she didn't have much money," unlike Farai's biological mother.

"It wasn't a big deal because Mama gave us *herself.*"

110

"Oh Kiss-met," Farai gushed. "I want to be angry with you, for speaking to me as you did, but Mama really was perrr-fect. She didn't schedule meetings or talk business on her cell phone as we played."

"No she didn't," Kismet agreed. Suddenly she laughed.

Fearing another of her sister's hormonal outbursts, Farai yet wanted to know, "What is so funny?"

"I just realized. Mama didn't have a cell phone. I don't think regular people had them. Not back then."

Farai chuckled too. "Mama would have left hers off during our time, don't you think? If she'd had one."

"She would have," the younger sister agreed. "You can do it, too."

"Oh Kiss-met, I am saddened."

"Why, honey?"

"Because I see I am not mother material, at all." Farai sighed, "Thirteen years, and I've focused on my career. I've made it, instead of Brosnan, my priority. The magazine and other ventures are my babies."

"Change that," Kismet gingerly suggested. "You can, you know."

"You say that like it is easy. I've got a schedule, one I'll need to adhere to, well into the next five years."

"Farai, I will tell Mama you're shirking responsibilities…" That, Kismet's over-achieving sister could not bear to have said of her.

"Don't you dare!" the magazine publisher hissed.

"Then try an experiment. Call my nephew, up at that fancy schmancy St. Lawrence Prep of the Redeemer school. Ask him how *he* feels."

Farai's heart raced, as she said she could not.

"Why can't you?" Kismet demanded.

"I haven't told you everything," Farai whispered. "It's the reason I've been calling."

"The child is still starting fires," Kismet knowingly stated, "At that *trés* expensive boarding school where you've got him stashed away. They told you to make him behave or he's out, right?"

With a lump in her throat, Farai blinked back tears. Though it was mortifying, it would never do to mess up her recently administered eyelash job. She had to make an appearance in an hour. However, forgetting appointments, she thought about her son. All the money she'd poured into that kid; he was not supposed to shame her this way.

"You think he's disgracing you," Kismet offered, knowing Ms. Idyllic all too well. "You're worried about what others will think."

"How do you read my mind, Kiss-met?"

"I don't. I just know you, babe," Kismet sagely stated. She acknowledged they would both have to go soon. "Still, Farai try my experiment. Spend time with Kiddo, without all your 'stuff.' Make him a priority, like Mama did us, and see if he doesn't come around."

"I've got so much on my plate right now, Kiss-met. You don't understand, and with my Okaru in Lagos—he *is* a diplomat you know."

"Ex-cu-ses," Kismet sang out. "Okay. Make my nephew a *project*. Have your assistant pencil him in. Then you'll give him the time he needs. Call me afterward and tell me how it went."

With a lump yet in her throat Farai said, "I'll try, but Kiss-met?"

"Yes?"

"I have to tell you... I am frightened."

Kismet sputtered with laughter. "Well you would be; you ain't spent a good half hour with the child since he was born." Kismet pointed out, "That's what's wrong with my poor nephew. He's been shifted from the *au pair*, to the day tutor, to the chauffeur, and now to the headmaster at this new school. So yes, you're frightened at the prospect of time alone with him, but remember, he's a little in awe of you, too."

Humor aside, Kismet told the woman who'd proved she could do anything, "Do it, or Kiddo's tap-ins to the school system won't be to simply change the grades of kids he doesn't like. His pranks will progress from making it appear that the tuitions of some haven't been paid. He'll use his creative genius for embezzlement—or worse."

"Thank you Kiss-met, for that hair-raising scenario." Although her sister's stinging commentary hurt, Farai vowed to do as bid. "Oh Kiss-met, do allow me to speak with Mama for just a moment."

"She's got company right now. I'll ask her to ring you tomorrow."

"Ask her to use my cell, Sweetums, because I'll be traveling." Big Sis made kissing noises.

"Bye, Farai."

"Cuddles, dahling."

Now, Kismet thought, if she hurried, she could have some fun. Headed toward merriment, she felt a pang of regret for her sister. Farai really didn't know how to mother. But how could she? Farai's mother had been the same as she was now.

112

Kismet recalled hearing that one summer; Farai's mother had flirted with Brantley, Kismet's father. He'd been a cabana boy then, at the club where Suzette's father—passing for white—had been a member.

Nearly white-skinned like her father, tall, willowy Suzette Harbrace had been used to getting her way, and she'd decided. She needed to have her way with young brown Brantley. However, his heart belonged to short, fiery, tart, Nell Lovington. Therefore, armed with family money, Suzette tried to buy Brantley. It didn't work, so she seduced him. She wound up pregnant. Suzette thought surely she had Brantley then. She didn't care that although in love with Nell, he still would have married Suzette, to give his baby his name. However, just that fast, flighty Suzette decided. She didn't want to be tied to 'Brantley's kind.'

An old aunt had spoken of Brantley, who'd progressed to becoming a 'lowly' clerk at a bureaucratic office. Old Auntie claimed he wasn't on Suzette's level. Auntie said Suzette needed someone educated, fine, and financially stable. Therefore, Suzette dumped Brantley. She even told him she *wanted* him to be with short, poor, Arnell Lovington. In addition, Suzette promised, Brantley would always have time with his daughter. She also informed Brantley that neither she nor six-month-old Farai Lorelai needed his trickles of money. The Harbraces had more than the gods. "The child just needs to know her father," Suzette had advised.

The baby grew, and one day Suzette and Brantley's cute-as-a-button became gangly and unruly. Farai, the long and lean teenager, had grown tired of being shuttled between the help. By that time, Farai's mother had married an Algerian businessman, one who did not fancy children. Therefore, Suzette called Brantley.

"You've got to take Farai Lorelai," she stated, her voice well modulated. "If not, I'll be forced to shut her away in an all girls pavilion, possibly in Switzerland. Then," Suzette voiced, knowing Brantley would not allow it, "You'll not see her until she turns twenty one."

Brantley discussed things with his wife and daughter, the then-twelve-year-old Kismet Staar. Nell didn't foresee a problem, as long as everyone understood; she had rules. Recently, Kismet had learned to share her parents with her cousin Beau, so she'd shrugged. Thereafter, Farai entered the Moore household. Nevertheless, she came with emotional baggage. Since the teenager had been allowed to do as she pleased, it took her nearly two years to get used to Nell, who did not believe in free reign for children. It took Farai another year to realize she loved her earthy outspoken step-mom.

Although *nowadays*, Kismet recalled as she stood watching the women in her kitchen, Farai often swore, even to her own mother Suzette, that she was Nell's daughter. Farai acknowledged Kismet as her sister; they weren't *half* anything.

Joining the chatty gathering, Kismet felt the same way as she realized one thing. Her sister had not yet grasped the fullness of having a child. Still, Kismet believed what Nell often said. It took some moms longer to adjust than others. Receiving only a spoonful of streusel and half a glass of soymilk, Kismet smiled. "Maybe you're right Mama," she whispered, mostly to herself. "My sister just might get motherhood right, after all." That, Kismet really wanted.

Scooping up sweet pastry, something she rarely ate, Kismet glanced at Amy Foster. The doctor's wife spoke to Ronni about a man with whom Ronni had gone out, a couple of times. "Don't keep pushing him away, dear."

With a scowl, Ronni griped that she wasn't about to get into a relationship with Curtis Hurst, or anyone. "He's my supervisor too—ew. How awkward would that be? Anyway, my time is short."

"Honeybunch," Nell nodded, "everybody's time is tantamount to that of cut flowers. All too soon, the beauty fades." Reassuringly Nell patted Ronni's thin yellow hand. "Just get you a piece of heaven, this side of Jordan, if you can."

Nell then addressed every woman at the table. "Take it from one who has lived, loved, *and* lost; make all your moments count."

With a nod, Amy Foster added. "Yes dear, if you and Curtis have only *ten minutes*, spend them together." Contrite, Amy continued, "Every single day, Ronni Marie, I wish someone had told *me* to do that...*with my baby*," the blue-eyed blond girl now gone. "Although parents should never have to bury children," Amy said sorrowfully, "I wish I'd understood that I wouldn't always have my Keesa."

114

Chapter 19

IN downtown Brooklyn, she stepped off the mall escalator and it didn't take her long to find her party. At the noisy, crowded food court, Kismet approached Beau and Ronni. On one side of a table they sat, while a woman and a man sat opposite. Kismet dragged a chair over.

"You gotta be Kismet," the woman in the leopard print, clingy shirt and pants offered, her eyes raking every inch of the younger woman.

Wearing high-heeled shooties, and a button-front shirt over denim, Kismet leaned back on her folded leather jacket. She thought nothing of her dangling freshwater pearl earrings, or her hair, stylishly cut and glossy. She simply appeared as she always did.

However, to Ophelia, who envied youth, Kismet appeared radiant, and hate-able. With narrowed eyes, Ophelia jeered, "I'd know *you* anywhere." Her voice was raspy from years of free-basing, "Ya look like when you was a kid—ya just bigger now."

"You haven't changed much either," the expectant mother retorted.

So, Beau's uppity cousin didn't want him meeting with his mother, Ophelia mused. Well, she didn't appreciate her son bringing his cousin along, like some kind of watchdog, so there.

Ophelia nodded at the man seated beside her. "My other son."

Ronni assessed him, before her gaze returned to the woman who'd packed on the makeup. Shades too light, it caused her to appear deceased. Noting bushy hair, Ronni facetiously wondered if the woman had spent the last twenty years swinging through the jungle. Forgetting red, haphazardly stuck on fingernails, Ronni looked at Beau's—*brother*?

Seated away from the table, nervously, he folded unnaturally fat hands that bespoke his drug use. How old was he? Ronni wondered because the man wore his weary years on his face. Undoubtedly, he was younger than he appeared. He was also unkempt, and for shame, Ronni thought, because he wasn't bad looking. That is, she further cogitated, if one peered past the rough-dry clothes, the dirty fingernails, and the lop-sided afro dotted with lint.

Ronni nearly shook her head as Ophelia advised her nervous son. "Tell your brother's cousin yo' name."

It was quickly mumbled, "Um, Thomas."

Tactless, Ophelia tossed out, "He's younger'n you, Beau." She crossed one animal print-clad thigh over the other.

Du-uh. Beau didn't care, and his voice emitted uncharacteristically hard. "You said you needed to see me."

"About what?" Kismet asked, her eyes holding Ophelia's.

Ignoring the cousin whom she couldn't stand, Ophelia shrugged and addressed Beau. "I ain't knowed where you was. Until he," she jerked her head at Thomas, "said he seent you."

Surprised, the younger man jerked to look at his mother.

"He saw Beau where?" Kismet sarcastically inquired, aware that the half-brother could not have known Beau before the present day.

"Talk, boy," Ophelia commanded.

"Um, I saw h-him on T-TV," Thomas mumbled with lowered eyes as nervously, he flipped his hands.

"How'd you know who he was?" Kismet probed. "When he was out of the picture, so to speak, before you were even a thought?"

Ophelia became defensive because who did Beau's cousin think she was, *Colombo*? "*I* told him the boy's name," she challenged.

Kismet felt fury. "Does this *man* look like anybody's *boy* to you?"

"Who is you?" Ophelia derisively inquired, wanting to knock the daylights out of bigmouth. "You here to be his bodyguard?"

"I'm here 'Ophy,' because I'm *family*," Kismet snapped. She ignored two small giggling girls racing past. "I care about him. I prove it, every day. Now let *him*," Kismet nodded at Thomas, "answer my question." Her voice softened. "Thomas, how'd you know my cousin?"

"I d-didn't," the younger man admitted, eyeing his hands. "N-Not until M-Muh saw him on T-TV. Then I read her the credits."

Oh. So, *the mother* had seen Beau. Kismet had thought as much; while within, Ronni inquired, Afro can read?

Feeling utterly exposed, Thomas refused to look at anyone. If he did, in his eyes they might have seen all that he had *not* said...

A few months back, Ophelia had been drinking her favorite cheap liquor, *Swig Up*. She'd been channel surfing too, when she'd seen a man interrogating another. Soon the interrogator began to resemble the son she'd once had. Fired up, Ophelia wasn't sure. When she'd last seen her son, he had been a boy. However, he could have grown up to look like

116

Mr. TV. Actually, she thought, excited, TV man resembled her dead husband! The one who'd tried to control her; so quite possibly, Mr. TV *was* her son, and if so...well, well!

With piqued interest, Ophelia watched the crime scene drama, until someone banged menacingly on her door. "Been out there messing with them hoodlums," she yelled as Thomas eased into the small hot room. "You was in that alley," back of their Brooklyn tenement, "doing drugs, again," Ophelia accused. Doggonit, her stupid son should have been selling, not using; she needed money.

Wordless, Thomas fell onto his 'bed.' The lumpy plaid sofa had come with the place. Closing his eyes, he hoped his high would last. This time.

Returning to the television, Ophelia was horrified. Her show was ending and she squawked. "Open yo' eyes! Read me dem names!"

Thomas was being pummeled. "Yo' druggin' behind," his mother screeched, "done made me miss somethin' important!"

Cowering from the blows, Thomas called "M-muh, s-stop!"

Wearied, because her son was an idiot, and because her life was in shambles, Ophelia glanced at the cheap clock left by the previous tenant. Eleven p.m. That meant the show had probably come on at ten. Okay, what was the show called? She yelled. "Git up! Thomas, git me a paper. I need the TV section." She said they'd watch the show when it aired again. "Then yo' dumb bahind gon find out who played that detective."

Seated in the noisy food court, Thomas eyed the hands he couldn't keep still. He wanted to spill the tea to his mother's older son, and to the two beautiful women with son. Thomas wanted to say that Ophelia had been obsessed with Mr. TV's identity. She had even recorded the show, and repeatedly watched it, after learning the man's real name.

Thomas wanted to tell the three strangers that his mother had crowed with delight, claiming she had found her son. She'd cackled that God sure worked in mysterious ways. Thomas had never heard the old crone mention God before, unless she'd been cussing. He wanted to blurt that his mother had said now she would get paid; now she would live in a big fine house, and go on the love boat— whatever that was. She said she would get her nails professionally done; no more corner store stick-ons, and now the landlord, and all them down at the county, could kiss her ass, because she no longer needed their checks! But she would take them. She said her TV actor son was going to take care of her, in high style!

Ophelia had whooped that she would drink champale, the good stuff, every day. His mother had said it, Thomas recalled with his eyes smarting all over again, like *he* was nothing. Ophelia had spoken of Mr. TV, like he, Thomas, didn't exist. Then her ol' haggard behind had taken to dancing around, as if Thomas hadn't taken her abuse and put up with her crap for far too long. As he'd watched the old hag sing and clap, like *he* had only been dirt under her shoes, and like he'd never had dreams, Thomas realized. *He* could become someone too, if he could get away from drunken, manipulative Ophelia, the way his brother had.

"So y'all saw my cousin on some show," Kismet surmised. "Then you both saw dollar signs, right?"

"No!" Thomas yelled. That was not the case, for him. "Not me..."

Ophelia wanted to slap him, and tell Ms. Nosey Butt-In-Skee to piss off, but she forced a smile. Flaky bits of makeup fell from around her mouth. "I jist hadn't seen the boy—I mean, *him*," she nodded at Beau, "in a long time."

"That's because you *abandoned* him," Kismet nearly growled, not about to let Ophelia pretend otherwise. "You *left* him, with nothing, and no one, when he was a child!"

The older woman cut her eyes, and hated the way her son, Mr. TV, put his hand on his cousin's arm, like he was trying to calm her down, and like Bigmouth meant more to him than his mama did.

"To finish what I was saying," Ophelia stridently responded. "Since I seent him, I mean you," she glanced at Beau. "I wanted to make uh attempt to mend our broke relayshaship."

Then Ophelia tried to appear sorrowful. Hating her act, Thomas nervously scratched his neck. Using an elbow, his mother nudged him. "Ain't dat right?" Needing Thomas to give her story credibility she hissed, "Din I say I jist wanted to see him, and have a relayshaship?"

Appearing puzzled, Thomas woodenly nodded. "Um...y-yeah?"

Kismet tsked. "I think you're a liar, Ophelia."

Feebly the older woman jumped up, as though she meant to do harm. "Who is you calling a *lah*?"

"Sit down," Beau cautioned and noted that Ronni and Kismet were also up, like he was. All three faced off with Ophelia who was disgusted that Thomas remained seated.

118

"I said," Kismet reiterated, "I think you're a liar, Ophelia, and I'll never walk that back. Really, I should beat you down. Hell, you can't even say my cousin's name. You need to move on." Kismet reached for her jacket. "Let's go, Diddley. Oh, and Momma Dearest? Forget you ever saw 'him' again."

"No! You shet your mouf, because you always would butt in—just like your fat little mutha." Ophelia angrily gestured at Beau. "We done heard from *her* all day. You my son. You speak for yo' sef."

"Ophelia," Beau began as Kismet shrugged into her spring jacket. "I'm glad I met with you—"

"Me too," she interrupted, noting that her son, the gentleman, gave his hateful cousin a hand. Well, she, the mama needed 'a hand' with a few things too.

"I'm glad," Beau added, as likewise, Ronni readied herself, "that we did this, because now I can stop wondering about you."

Ophelia's eyes narrowed, because that didn't sound right. And this was not how things were supposed to go! Them two tarts weren't supposed decide for *her son* that it was time to leave, not when she, Beau's *mother*, wasn't finished. Her big fine son wasn't supposed to say she was still the same, because even *she* knew that was a veiled insult.

Suddenly Ophelia felt confused, and angry. She should have bum rushed the trio—if she had more strength—because casually, they walked away. Inside, she howled. Things had gone all wrong! As Ophelia watched the threesome move farther away, her inner scream built, because there was *more*, and she wanted it!

Looking down at Thomas who remained seated, Ophelia felt overwhelming anger. Beau was not supposed to have been manipulated by his bigmouth cousin. He wasn't supposed to have walked away with her and that skinny yella girl. And not one looked back! Ophelia, the mama, was not supposed to have been left with—him, her other, good for nothing son.

Well...okay, Ophelia thought, as she slapped Thomas and told him to get up. Since Beau wanted to be stupid, he would now need to learn a lesson, *from his mother.*

WHAT a surprise! Sandal scurried through the food court, and spotted Beau. Oh. Sandal stopped short. That cousin of Beau's was there, and Beau's too thin, yellow, sista-girlfriend.

Ooh look, Sandal mused as he backed up and took a seat because he didn't want to be noticed. There were two others. Who were they?

Uh-oh! The older woman, someone Beau had never introduced Sandal to, jumped up. Well really, she struggled up. Sandal desperately wanted to hear, but he couldn't; the food court was too noisy, but Sandal guessed trouble brewed. He glanced at his oversized watch. Days ago, it had started to turn his skin green. Shoot! It was time. He needed to meet Rodrigo on the lower level. Well, Rodrigo would have to wait. Sure, he hit hard when things didn't go his way, but Sandal needed to see how things up here would play out. Now that Beau's trio faced off with the woman, while her man remained seated. Scuzzball.

Ooh! Sandal wished he were closer as Beau 'n them left. Rising, he wondered why hard-life woman and messed-up-man stayed. When neither Beau nor anyone else looked back, Sandal felt it safe to proceed.

Purposely, he circumvented people who ate and laughed. He *had* to get to the forgotten couple, before they too left. Again, he glanced at his large fake designer watch. Uh-oh. The woman slapped the man. Sandal wondered if he should forget it and skip on down the escalator. Stocky Rodrigo hated to be kept waiting, and it did hurt awful when Rodrigo didn't get his way. However, the split-second decision was made. Sandal neared the woman who collected her purse. Up close, Sandal thought, what a Gawd-awful animal outfit. And that face! She needed a serious makeover, and new teeth, to replace those broken brown ones. Summoning non-existent acting skills, Sandal wanted to appear puzzled. "Uh, excuse me..." His voice was choirboy high, "Did I just see Beau?"

The woman looked him over. Her shark-beady eyes expressed interest. Therefore, Sandal said, "Beau's my friend, you know..."

Ophelia's heart beat faster, as Thomas buried his chin in his chest. To the faggotty little stranger, she slowly stated, "He's my *son, you* know."

Mmm. Sandal was elated at his good fortune. Now he *had* to get to know the busted-looking woman, *if* she told the truth. "Is he now?"

Ophelia puffed up. "I gave birth to him thirty-some odd years ago."

Although reluctant to touch the old sea hag, Sandal extended his hand. "Nice to meet you," he said, because the crone could prove handy.

"Hmmph to you too," Ophelia mumbled, grasping the fairy's fingertip. Frowning, she'd have preferred not to touch at all. Heck, the

120

little fem-fem probably had germs; fags were notoriously nasty, she stereotypically remembered. For all she knew, this one was a carrier of the bird flu. However, a mental bell tolled and Ophelia's eyes narrowed. Nut-licker said he knew Beau, so maybe… Red could come in handy.

ANGERED, she looked over at her son. He was such an albatross about her neck. When Red had appeared, Thomas had buried his chin in his pseudo down jacket. Why the heck was he wearing that hot mess anyway? It was April, springtime; this day, it was near seventy degrees. And why was he shaking?

It took a moment before, horrified, Ophelia realized. Thomas was snickering, silently, violently away to himself. So, he was laughing, at her, huh? He thought the goings-on were funny, did he? Well, ugh! Ophelia threw up her hands, because neither of her sons was worth salt. However, that would change, and soon too.

Watching Thomas who continued to laugh, Ophelia banged a fist on the table, and lost a red plastic fingernail. Disgruntled, she wondered, could things get any worse? Then her stomach growled and she remembered. That older boy of hers had gotten away without even offering her a meal! Well, next time, she vowed, eyeing a man who gathered up his electronics purchases, that oldest boy of hers wouldn't be so lucky. Quickly scooting over because electronics man walked away, Ophelia snatched up the remains of his lunch. She picked through cold fries. With her mouth full, she moaned that she hated ketchup. And why were the sandwich leavings fish? She liked beef.

Staring at his mother who stuffed her mouth like a pointy-toothed prehistoric beast, Thomas realized what he had never before consciously considered. He *hated* her. Every single inch of her. He despised the way she currently resembled the scavengers he'd seen on TV. The cable TV she'd had hooked up so that without paying, she could 'piggyback' off an unsuspecting neighbor. "So m-much f-for your little *p-plan*," Thomas cantankerously spat.

He was ordered to shet the devil up.

"Yo, y-you s-shut up," he tossed back. Yeah, she thought he was nothing. Old hagarina thought he needed her. She thought he didn't know he could do better, *if* he got shed of her… Suddenly feeling empowered, for some unknown reason, Thomas spoke. His voice was filled with malice. "M-my bruva d-don't know how l-lucky he is. He din h-have to deal with y-yo' sh-shit all these years."

Ophelia raised her hand to slap Thomas, but the look he gave her stopped her hand, mid-air. Quickly she turned away from the man she no longer knew. From her peripheral, she watched as slowly he rose. She also wondered. What had that fool's look meant? Moreover, who did he think he was, saying that stuff to her, his mother?

With her eyes mere slits, she glanced around. She sure hoped stupid Thomas wasn't getting ideas, just because he had seen his brother, Mr. TV. If so, she would have to teach young buck a lesson.

Raising both hands, Ophelia lifted her wig in back. She didn't care that those nearby could see her furiously scratch beneath the synthetic hair. When she patted the dry mass back into place over her grays, she promised herself one thing. She would give her son, Mr. TV, one more chance. Then if he messed up... Heaven help him.

Chapter 20

WITH evening approaching, and the sun's rays diminishing, three of The Cohorts rode in silence.

At last, she turned onto her tree-lined street. There, gleefully squealing children flew past on colorful bikes. In the picturesque cul-de-sac, she pulled up before her garage, alongside Ronni's old car, Betsy, and Beau sighed.

At his cousin's front door, he inhaled. Ah, the aroma of fried chicken, and homemade bread. Those things had been made especially for him. This Beau knew, and mentally, he began to unfurl. Inside, he heard Johnny Mathis singing *Chances Are*. Beau's aunt loved that song.

Passing the Afro-centric motif living room, Beau noticed the bevy of burning candles. He smelled the mingling of sandalwood and patchouli. Taking a deep breath, the tall man whispered, "God love my auntie."

In the brighter, cozy kitchen, Nell instructed Ronni, who'd washed her hands, to butter hot bread. Ronni, who usually could care less about eating, couldn't wait to do so, as Kismet prepared coffee.

"So Lyle took Dé and Chance to the movies?" the momma asked.

Busy, Nell nodded. "KissGirl put that salad on the table."

As Beau retrieved mugs, his father's sweet sister turned to him. As she rubbed his back she asked, "How you feeling, Puppy?"

"I'm fine," Beau replied, and meant it.

"I'm glad." Nell pointed to a stack of plates. "You hungry?"

Beau watched as she handled a succulent chicken breast, just for him. He sampled crisp, savory, golden batter and his memory was jogged. "I gotta go!" He glanced at his cousin. "Kiss, run me to the Rail Road?" Beau admitted he'd completely forgotten a meeting with his manager.

"Well, we'll wrap this up." Beau's aunt pulled foil as he scrolled through his contacts. "Puppy, grab you one of them cold drinks."

As Beau rearranged things with his manager, Kismet seized her purse, and the soft hot bread that Ronni had just buttered and drizzled with honey. "I'm *starving* Brownie," she said by way of apology. "You get to stay, so...thanks."

Leaning to kiss his aunt, Beau said, "I sure hate to go." Holding her in his arms, he admitted, "I'd love to stay." Then he could have enjoyed the ambiance, the food, and the company, but it was not to be. He forgot putting his feet up, too. Headed out with food stuff in hand, he called. "You'll always be my favorite girl. You know that. Right, *Mama*?"

BENEATH the velvet night sky, pierced by shimmering stars, Beau's cousin returned. To her delight, her children and their father were home. After hugs and kisses, she was offered hot food, and fresh coffee.

Following a sip, she called out, "Ma, that woman was awful! Right?" Kismet looked to Ronni for confirmation.

"She was worse."

"I'm not surprised," Nell admitted.

"Mama, she's uglier than before—inside and out."

Ronni rubbed her full stomach.

"Did you see her hair?" Kismet inquired, gently tugging on her girlfriend's sweater.

"Hair, no. I saw a cheap, dry, wig."

Eating, Kismet tried not to laugh, as Nell smirked. Nevertheless, Nell cautioned the younger women not to speak ill of others.

"I'm talking 'bout your sister-in-law," Kismet clarified.

"She's your cousin's *mother*," Nell pointed out.

"Okay." Kismet requested forgiveness. "But Ma, she's got another son. That poor thing's beat down, like Diddley would have been..."

Nell appeared pained and placed a hand at her heart. Quietly, she reminded herself that she could not save every child, although not one deserved Ophelia.

Kismet admitted that on the drive home, she'd been thinking. "What if Beau hadn't had you mama, to rescue him? And what if Daddy hadn't taken an avid interest in him. Then I thought what if my babies didn't have me, or Lyle? What would *they* become, in a few years?"

Suddenly Kismet's eyes filled and she eked, "Mama, my *heart* went out to that young man..." The younger mother fought the need to bawl. "You should have seen him. He's...so *broken*. I didn't even want to leave him there with her."

Hearing it hurt her as well, but Nell sounded reassuring as she patted her daughter. "We'll pray, sugar; and if there's a chance, we'll help."

"I want to help and pray too," Ronni chimed, even though she'd only recently begun to pray. However, she felt it necessary. She also remembered what her onetime roommate Beau had told her about his life as a child. Thus, she couldn't bear to think that Thomas' life had been similar. Ronni pitied the sad boy-man who was now Beau's half-brother.

"Did y'all find out," Nell pondered aloud, "what Momma Dearest wants?"

"She wants what most people want," Ronni stated. She had seen the greed in Ophelia's eyes. "She wants money, and its provisions."

"Well then," Nell Moore said and shook her head. "There's no telling how far she'll go to get it."

Ronni revealed her theory. "That woman," Ophelia, "twistedly believes that what's Beau's should be hers, because she bore him. I really don't think she's to be underestimated."

"Then God help her," Nell uttered, feeling a surge of anger, "because when a person messes with others, things get messy for them."

"Talk about karma."

"Ronni, that reminds me," Kismet used her napkin. "Grandma Lacey—God rest her soul—used to tell a story." Nell's mother had often summarized an account from the Bible's book of *Esther*:

There had been a king. He'd married a woman named Esther. The king's right hand man didn't like the Queen, Esther. Right hand man's name was Haman. Haman also despised the queen's uncle because uncle would not bow to him. Therefore, Haman wanted the uncle put to death.

At the suggestion of his friends, the king's right hand man had a gallows built. "Now a gallows is an execution device, for hanging criminals," Kismet explained. She said Haman planned to hang the queen's uncle on the gallows. "Haman planned to kill Queen Esther, too." Then, Haman, further decided, he might as well get rid of the whole diaspora to which the queen and her uncle had been born.

"Since Haman wanted these things for no good reason, he created a lie. He claimed 'those people' didn't abide by the laws of the land. "Well, in conclusion," Kismet sighed, "Haman's evil backfired." His plan was uncovered and the king learned about the gallows that Haman had built. "Then the king, Queen Esther's husband, ordered his right hand man to be hanged—on that very device."

Lost in thought, Nell sighed. After a few moments, she called out. "KissGirl, maybe you should share that story with my sister-in-the-law."

The younger mother snorted, "Like Ophelia would listen to *me*. That woman hates me. It was obvious today."

"She might hear you," Nell teased, "if you say what your grandmamma used to say. Nell and Kismet spoke in unison. *"If you're gonna dig one ditch, then you had better dig two."*

Sleepily, Ronni nodded, "Yep; one for your victim, and the other one for you."

Chapter 21

KISS and Lyle were going to be parents, again. However, this time they were expecting their biological child. Valeria and Fabian were the first to know. Well, behind Aunt Nell and Beau. *Wow*, the IndiAfricAmerican woman thought, a new baby would be darling. It would be lovely if she were expecting too, Valeria mused and longed for the day.

"Game's on," Fabian called over a shoulder. He headed for his man cave, which was more a cozy male room.

Valeria nodded. The sooner her husband left, the sooner she could query her friend. What did it feel like to be so far along? Nevertheless, Valeria had to wait, because Lyle, who would join Fabian, had not yet left. Bent over Kismet, he placed a hand on her stomach and kissed her.

Okay. Lyle's big hand had been placed with such tenderness and pride that Valeria had to look away. She blinked back tears because she and Fabian had not yet shared their own similar moment.

Watching Lyle depart, Valeria realized something. Lyle and her longtime friend now shared a more authentic intimacy. That was another something Valeria wanted to experience with Fabian.

Unaware, Kismet rose from a kitchen chair. She said if Val didn't mind, she would just stretch out in the comfy, cream-colored den.

Valeria nodded and guessed her questions could wait. She knew Kiss had to be tired. Already the mother of two, a rambunctious little pair, Kismet was also expecting. God bless her, Valeria thought, lifting her friend's feet to an ottoman. "You want a blanket, Kiss?"

"No, I'm fine." The earthy rounder woman grinned. "Actually, it's just nice to lie here, *in the quiet*."

"You do that," Valeria coaxed. Walking away, she called, "Holler if you need me."

"I will." Kismet's lids drooped, but with concerted effort, she opened her eyes. "Val?"

"Yes, honey."

Kismet's eyelids fluttered. "Thank you."

"Anytime." In her bedroom, Valeria climbed up on the big bed that she shared with her husband. She crossed her legs yoga style and in a golden pool of May sunshine, she allowed herself to mentally drift. She remembered her own pregnancies. They had always ended before term. She had never progressed to the point of giving birth. Hmmm...

Never would she forget that very first go 'round, when the little white plastic had indicated she was pregnant. How excited she had been! Fabian, who was less excitable, had been a bit dazzled too.

Morning sickness had set in, and Valeria recalled being unable to eat or even stomach the smell of food, especially cooked meats. For three months, however, she'd rubbed her still flat tummy, while telling her baby it was okay. She told baby she could deal with the sick because so badly did she want him or her.

Then her baby came...but the wrong way. It had been a Saturday morning. Valeria had been lying in bed, watching a home purchasing channel. The jewelry was astounding, and she vowed to ask Fabian for a ring when their baby was born. She wanted to wear their offspring's birthstone on her right hand, to remind her of the miracle. Always.

However, there had been no miracle, just soft sucking, a sickening sound. Valeria remembered that before she'd heard it, she'd muted the TV because outside, Fabian spoke with a neighbor. Without rising from bed, she'd tried to pinpoint the older male with whom her husband spoke. That was when she'd heard the near gasp, coming from the apex between her thighs. Her eyes had widened, and she'd stayed very still. Then she'd felt the kiss. It had been wet, a sticky, bloody kiss that simultaneously licked both her inner thighs. She'd seen color on the white beneath her. She stared, horrified, as red seeped outward beneath her. The stain attempted to destroy her beautiful eyelet sheet.

The soft gasping continued, and there were additions to the initial seeping redness. These were more like blobs and globs, messy and dark. They were crimson and near purple, and so unlike anything that Valeria René had ever wanted to see, especially when she was expecting.

Oh God! She'd stifled panicked cries. However, she had not known what to do! She'd wanted to place her hands between her legs and hold things together. She'd wanted to gently re-pack herself because she *wanted her baby*! But she wanted baby months from then, at the *right* time. The right way.

Valeria remembered her tears. Hot and acrid, they too had oozed from orifices in her body. She'd wanted to cry out, to call through the open window to Fabian—but suddenly, she'd felt shame. The bed, she thought, if he rushed up, he would see it, stained with the life she had not been able to contain.

It had been then that she experienced her *initial* sense of failure. She had felt so un-womanly. Aware that she had failed, Valeria rose from the bed. She pulled the ruined sheet with her. She held it between her legs to catch the warm remains of what should have been growing inside her.

She eased into the bathroom, and there, alone, she'd cried. Then she showered. Beneath the water, that ran red with blood, she'd washed away evidence of her failure. When she was dressed, she stuffed the sheet and its mate into a trash bag. Prettily, she re-made the bed, although what had transpired there had been so ugly.

Later, in the kitchen, she'd told her husband. With her back to him, she'd sounded far away. She gave no details, despite still feeling the bleed. Clenching a feminine napkin tight between her thighs, the wife refused to recount the event, not even when her husband pressed. She only said she'd miscarried. Then she wiped away useless tears.

Fabian claimed he understood. He had tried to hug her too, but Valeria froze. How could he understand? Life had not left *his* body.

When months later, Mrs. Sinclair became pregnant again, her husband did not muster excitement. He simply said they would see. That had become their cycle. Getting pregnant and waiting to see.

So far, Valeria René Sinclair had *failed*, every single time.

Although she didn't want to, she thought about the incident last year, where she had been sick to her stomach, again. That time she'd had pain, in her back, sort of near where she guessed her kidneys would be. Her stomach hadn't felt right either. It had hurt, in a strange new way, but she had not seen a doctor. She had been too busy. However, Valeria had been aware that she had been expecting, alone; Fabian had adopted another wait and see attitude. He'd removed himself from the equation, from the inevitable sorrow, should she fail again.

Then it happened. Valeria told her husband she was going to the doctor because of the pain. That fateful day Fabian went to work. His wife had insisted, saying, "I'm sure this'll all be routine. So let's save time off for when we need it," for the day when she became a success.

At the doctor's office, the technician juggled and fit her in for an unscheduled sonogram. When the gel was squeezed onto her stomach, and the computer mouse-like thingy was rolled on her abdomen, Valeria told herself to breathe and forget the cold gel. She admonished herself to calm down because this time, things would be different.

Then the ultrasound technician wanted her feet in the stirrups. With the wand inside her, Valeria noticed. The technician's girlish face appeared pinched. Then Valeria found it hard not to hyperventilate.

The patient was asked to get dressed after a sponge off. She was asked to meet her doctor in the pastel office. Never would Valeria forget the nurses' faces as she passed them in the hallway. They looked sorrowful, and one appeared to have seen a ghost. Never would she forget either, that her doctor asked if her husband could be reached.

The doctor dialed the number that Valeria recited. The doctor pressed 'speaker,' and Fabian came on the line. The doctor announced she was with Mrs. Sinclair. The doctor said there was no way to soften the blow. Fabian's wife would be rushed to the hospital via ambulance. Why? – Because her fertilized egg had not traveled from the fallopian tube to the uterus, where it would have begun growing properly.

Fabian was told, "Your wife's is an Ectopic Pregnancy." The couple would be given literature, later. "But," the doctor stated, "this is why your wife has pain." It was explained; there was no way the fertilized egg could be transferred to the uterus, and there was grave danger. Fabian's wife could hemorrhage, if her body tried to rid itself of the aberration. Then she could bleed to death.

"Thus the precautions," the doctor explained. She said the offending fallopian tube would most likely have to be cauterized. It would be removed, due to the damage, and the sheer size of the embryo. The doctor said the operation was, by no means, to be considered routine. Then after everything, she divulged, the same type of pregnancy could occur again.

"However," the doctor briskly stated, "Mrs. Sinclair's surgeon can insert a light-transmitting telescope through her navel, to view her internally." The procedure was called laparoscopy. It was relatively simple, and other female parts would be saved, if possible.

Seated on her bed, Valeria remembered. It had *not* been simple. She'd had scar tissue, inside, from a painful operation performed when she'd been a twenty-something. Therefore, the surgeon had to scrap the laparoscopy and cut her, nearly from hip to hip.

Valeria had not recovered quickly.

Now, something was happening, *again*, inside her uncooperative body. She dared not think what it could be. Frightened, sad, and feeling so alone, Valeria René refused to ponder it. Not yet, anyway.

Chapter 22

RONNI took sick. For weeks, her condition had slowly been worsening, and her T cell count lowering.

Knowing this, her family of friends became alarmed, although they tried not to show it. Nevertheless, Ronni knew they worried because she knew *them*. She saw the anxiety on their faces when they thought she didn't. She saw it when they visited her at home or at the hospital. Although they brought flowers and tried to joke, they couldn't quite mask the pain. Then she wondered, why did they care? On the other hand, she marveled at being so blessed. She had people who cared.

Sure, she knew one of 'these times' as she'd taken to calling her emergencies, would be 'it.' Then she wouldn't return, so she tried to make Kiss and Val understand. She said it was okay. Ronni talked incessantly to Beau. She informed all her family members that back when she had initially found out she was HIV positive, she had been afraid. She hadn't wanted to die.

Then God had sent Keesa, and Keesa Louise Foster had died. Ronni had been there, and though she'd been horribly hurt, because she had been the one left, she had seen that dying wasn't so bad. In fact, she almost looked forward to it now. She tried to get this across to her family, although it seemed they could not, or would not, hear.

Therefore, it was becoming hard. Nowadays, sometimes Ronni even felt like her big, extended, multi-cultural quilt of a family was bringing her down. Similarly, she found things hard, because she believed she loved everyone more than they did her. The truth was her peops were all *she* had, but they had each other, and others. For some inexplicable reason, lately, that had become a problem.

Ever-present, Val and Fabian had driven Ronni to her apartment. They'd done so when she'd been discharged from the hospital this last time. Then quick as she could, Ronni had waved the Sinclairs off. Val had wanted to feed Ronni, to make sure Ronni needed nothing, but Ronni had her excuse ready. She'd sighed and said she only needed rest. When Val and Fabian had gone, Ronni had asked God to forgive her, for lying.

Sure, she was tired, but her time was coming, and soon. Heck, Ronni didn't need that much rest. She'd get plenty of it in the grave.

However, Ronni had feigned tiredness because Val and Fabian made her sick. Ronni didn't know when it began, but now she couldn't stand seeing the Sinclairs together, even though they were husband 'n wife.

Ronni guessed the couple's shared presence was just a painful reminder; *she* had no one…even though Curtis Hurst kept turning up.

In her lonely apartment, Ronni closed her eyes and tried not to think about the life she would never lead. She tried not to recall that Kismet was engaged. Independent, headstrong, Kiss would be married. She and the chocolate hunk—that luscious, looking-like-a-rugby player—Lyle, had sent out Afro-centric invitations. In a couple of months, they would have a broom jumping ceremony.

Ronni remembered the rolled parchment paper announcement that had been wrapped in raffia. So what, Kiss's sister was being a pain in the neck, trying to take over? That was Farai's way. At least Kiss was getting to do things that Ronni would not.

Thinking further, Ronni was aware of Beau. His relationship, if it could be called that, with skanky Scandal had been cut short. Yay! Still, Beau had choices. He met men everywhere, at *Cannes*, in Rio, and Tuscany. Valeria's co-worker, fellow optician Saavion, was also feeling Beau. In time, Beau would surely go out with the super-sexy maker and seller of optical goods, and gosh darn it! Going out was another thing Ronni wouldn't get to do, this side of Jordan, as Aunt Nell often said.

Ronni's eyes widened as Ezmerelda the cat sauntered by. Dang, Ronni remembered, even Kismet's *mother*, sixty-something *Nell* had prospects! How, Ronni wondered, had she forgotten the older gent, Claude Bevere? Retired from the New York City Police Department, he'd become sweet on Nell. An upstanding deacon at Mount Hebron, the family church, the laid-back man couldn't keep his eyes off saucy, buxom, Arnell Moore. With his muscular body, and close-cut gray hair, the church deacon often smelled of some clean, old-timey men's cologne, and boy. Boy, did he seem perfect for the sweet older woman.

Ronni shrugged, everybody had somebody, but her. They were all progressing, while, it seemed, she was regressing, degenerating even.

Oh, Lord. Pink-cheeked, brunette Amy had Harvey, Keesa's father, tall driven Dr. Foster, and Kiss' bossy, wealthy, half-sister Farai had that African prince of a man, Okaru. Not to mention Val's sisters. All of them were married or engaged. Well, Val's sister Sonji was supposed to be divorcing. However, Ronni bitterly thought, Sonji probably had a jump-off waiting, some big, fine, coal-black, sweet as sugar, honey of a man.

Closing her eyes because she was hurt, Ronni swiped at tears and longed to die. She wondered; for what was her ticker waiting. She was always in pain; she couldn't make plans, so *why* did she keep living?

Struggling up, Ronni stepped into slip-ons. She would get out of doors for a few minutes. Then maybe she could re-focus. Ronni knew she would never be able to walk far. Her joints ached, and even the blood that coursed through her veins stung mightily. Still, maybe a little outside air would do her some good, and who knew? If she got lucky, a car or truck might hit her, and *blamo*! Done.

"Shame on you, Veronica," she scolded as her phone rang. Ronni didn't want to speak with anyone, yet she eyed her caller ID. *Curtis Hurst.* She thought about letting voicemail pick up, but then again… The butter-yellow woman snatched up the receiver. "Hello?" she breathed. She listened before she said, "Curt, you don't have to apologize, and you're not bothering me. As a matter of fact, I was just going to take a walk, maybe to the park across the street."

She burst out laughing, something she hadn't done in a while. Her smile emitted in her voice. "If I *wasn't* going out and you said you were downstairs, I might have deemed you a stalker, but since I'd already planned on it, okay." She smoothed her hair.

Then Ronni caught herself. No. She could not become giddy like a girl. She was too old and *too sick* to simper and primp. However, she did long to be like her sista-friends. Ronni too wanted someone to love.

"Oh, forget it," she waved. Pulling on a sweater, she stepped into the outer hallway, remembering. Once upon a time, she'd had so many men. Suddenly she felt hot shame, because of all of the men she'd laid 'n played with, not one could be considered someone who cared. Worse, all those who currently did care belonged to other people. Fabian belonged to Val. Lyle belonged to Kiss, and Claude Bevere, the church deacon wanted to belong to Nell. Dr. Foster belonged to Amy, and Beau; he belonged to everyone in their family of friends.

Gingerly descending the steps, Ronni nearly burst out crying, because now that she was a bit older and a tad wiser, she wanted *more*. However,

134

she didn't have time. Had Ronni time, though, she would need the brass ring, like Kiss and Val. She, Veronica Marie Brown, would have wanted marriage, a honeymoon, and the day-to-day accoutrements of commitment; although in the past, she'd thought she was happy being footloose and fancy-free.

That knowledge brought Ronni to the crux of things. *She was jealous.* She had never been so in the past; she'd had no reason to be. Life had seemed right. Now though, Ronni wanted her life to be longer. It would be cut short, though. Therefore, Ronni envied her two best friends.

Out of doors, it was summery, and Ronni told herself to focus on the beautiful June evening. It was perfect for walking, with the man who'd parked so that he might accompany her. How sweet.

Ronni smiled up at Curtis. She also revealed she had a question.

"Ask away," Her supervisor advised. He stuck his hands in the pockets of his long denim shorts.

"How could you," Ronni began, "a man in his right mind, want to find yourself anywhere near *me*?"

She and he were both well aware that she was in the throes of full-blown AIDS, so Curtis spoke the truth. "You intrigue me," *and I think I love you*, he longed to say.

The pair crossed the street, and Ronni cajoled, "Come off it, Curtis."

"I'm serious, Ron. You're battling this thing, yet you spend your days educating college seminar halls and high school auditoriums full of people on the prevention of it. Don't think I'm not also aware that you spend your nights, well, some of them anyway, furthering your research on the latest technological miracles now offered to those that suffer."

Curtis shook his head and aided Ronni onto the sidewalk. "Lady, you amaze me, so much, until at dawn *and* at dusk you come to mind."

Ronni's throat constricted as she and Curtis stepped onto the path. In the park, a jogger and his dog trotted by as Ronni advised, "Curt, don't."

"What?" He blocked her. "Don't contemplate us in a relationship?"

Ronni tugged down her sweater sleeves, despite it being warm out. "Just let things be, okay? For both our sakes."

"Why should I?" Curtis insisted. "Is there someone else?"

Yes! Ronni nodded. That was it! She would allow Curtis to think she was involved. Then she could save him, from her.

"Do I know him?" Curtis asked, feeling his insides crumble.

"No," Ronni shook her head, feeling cold. "But he's good to me, and I'd never be untrue." She was lying, again—through her teeth! However, she had to, to save Curtis from the most fatal mistake of his life.

Her supervisor knew that workplace romances were a no-go. Still, he appeared determined. "So, what's this good-to-you man like?"

Swiftly, mentally, Ronni scrolled through all the men she knew, until she came upon just one. She spoke as she pictured him. "Well, he's tall and athletic. He's decent and he loves me." She walked as her conscience pricked because she'd forgotten to mention that Mr. Perfect was gay.

Walking alongside Ronni, Curtis inquired, "May I ask his name?"

"DeVeaux," Ronni blurted. Then she could have kicked herself when Curtis began to laugh. Pulling her up and into a sweet embrace, his lips were inches from hers when teasingly he spoke. "I like that guy too, but I gotta tell you. Lady, he's really not for you."

Aw, darn. Ronni remembered. She'd introduced Curtis and Beau at different silly work functions, a few times. She should have pictured her doctor instead. With his honey brown skin and sexy lips, Ashik Gupta was a cutie, inside and out. *His* name Curtis would not have known.

Suddenly, tears assailed Ronni, when she should have been amused. She told Curtis, "Let me down." She no longer wanted to walk. She said she was cold and ached all over. It was the truth. She limped back the way she and her supervisor had come. Ronni put out a foot, to step into the street. Curtis attempted to aid her, but she pulled away. "Go, okay? Please, Curt..." Ronni turned, nearly breathless with threatening sobs. If they erupted and Curtis saw, she'd be mortified. "Go," she croaked.

Curtis' eyes said he didn't understand. He'd thought they'd been having fun. However, Ronni knew, their good times could never last. Therefore, she hobbled toward her building. She called out, "It's not you, Curt. Believe me. It's me." She pushed on the lobby door as he stood watching. "See you Monday at work." Mightily aching, she disappeared.

Up in the apartment that had been called The Cohort Quarters because some years back, she'd shared it with her Cohorts Beau and Val, Ronni felt sad. Without removing her shoes, she fell onto her white camelback sofa, to have a good cry. Life was so unfair! As the first few tears fell, Ronni turned her head, because what was that?

Oh, the door. Who was it, *now*? Ronni swiped a cheek as she called, "It's open."

Face beaming, Amy Foster stood across the threshold. She held crockery in two oven mitt-covered hands. "Hello, my dear."

Brown curls bouncing, Amy entered the apartment. It was stifling hot, and old smelling, because it had been closed up for so long. "My sweet, would you like a hot meal?"

Ronni burst out crying. "Ay-meee..."

"Oh my!" Keesa's mother appeared flustered. She rushed her pot to the kitchen and deposited her grocery bag. Returning without her oven mitts, she sat and took Ronni in her arms. "Dear, dear." Amy attempted to lift Ronni's head. "Why do you cry so? Tell me about it."

Unable to speak, Ronni cried on, and Amy held her, as Nell had once held Amy. When Ronni ceased crying, Amy rose. When she returned, she offered a steaming bowl of chicken stew, a buttery biscuit, and homemade lemonade. Facing the windows as Ronni ate, Amy suggested opening the place up a bit, "To get you some air."

Ronni, who'd not realized she was hungry, nodded. "Ames, you keep cooking like this, and you can do anything you want."

Amy pivoted. "You like my dumplings? That's Zola Mae's recipe."

"So good," Ronni chomped. She recalled the African-American woman who'd taken care of Amy when Amy was a girl. Ronni said the stew and the biscuits were excellent, nothing like the bland hospital food she abhorred.

"Well, you're home now, dear. Home is where you get good stuff." Standing back, Amy admired the sheer panels that blew in the breeze. She thought it was nice that Val had left them when she'd married. "Oh, my darling," Amy called, forgetting Ronni's Cohort. "If you want, this evening, I can be your caretaker. Just tell me what you need."

"I need...a friend," Ronni said and again burst into tears.

"Oh, my." Amy sounded flustered as she attempted to comfort Ronni. "You just cry it all out, okay dear, because sometimes crying is good."

Ronni laughed through her tears. "I told *you* that, the Sunday you cried in church." And Kismet had said it to Ronni, in this very apartment.

With arms around her daughter-friend, Amy chuckled. "I know you said it, and see what good advice it was? I'm all the better for it now."

Ronni snuggled up to Amy. Pressing her face to alabaster skin, Ronni noticed the scent of lilies before she moaned, "I'm all alone, Amy."

"You are not," the socialite refuted. "I'm here, and what about my Harvey? He appears when he can. You've got sweet Nellie, and Kismet."

With her voice muffled, Ronni clarified, "But I got no man."

Amy claimed, "You do. There's tall, handsome Beau. Then there's Curtis Hurst—hey, why not call him?" Amy liked that idea. "Curtis would love to hear from you. You know he *is* sweet on you."

Ronni decided not to mention that she'd just sent the man away. Subsequently, she did say that perhaps she would try him later.

Amy was amenable, and as the evening wore on, Ronni noticed that due to Amy's presence, she felt a lot better. However, again, Ronni's heart was pricked, and things appeared dismal when Amy announced her intent. She would give Kismet a trip to *Los Cabos*.

"I thought it could be Harvey and my gift to the newlyweds." While soothingly knitting, Amy mentioned the classic island resort she'd picked. "Kiss and Lyle will enjoy fine restaurants, beach *palapas*, and hideaways. You know, so they can have uninterrupted time together, before the new baby gets here."

Ronni looked away because she'd forgotten about the baby! That was another thing she'd never have, but not because of illness. She had been told eons ago, after a couple of abortions, that the jig was up. She would never give birth. Now, that hurt too.

"I think your trip will give the lovebirds something more to look forward to," Ronni finally stated. "That's a great thing to give someone, Amy."

Ronni swallowed anguish, because the script of her life was so cruel and unfair. Oh well, she forced herself to internally admit, that was just how things were.

Furthermore, Ronni realized, she had genuinely meant what she'd said about the trip. She only wished *she too* had something to look forward to, other than ...death.

Chapter 23

VALERIA René bit her lip because, for weeks, she'd missed her period. She'd said nothing to Fabian, nor had she tested herself. She had been too afraid. Now, late in June, she looked at the plastic wand, her second in two days, and sighed. "This reads *pregnant.* Well, Mysti," she spoke to her feline friend, "guess I'll make an appointment..." And pray that this time would not be like the others.

ON a Saturday in July, Valeria informed her husband, she was expecting. On the same day, she was to meet her longtime friend Kismet Staar. As she drove to Delightful Desserts, the curly-locked one remembered the night that had started this, the spring evening that Fabian had shown up at her parent's home. After a heart-to-heart, they'd ridden home in his SUV. Per his suggestion, she'd stripped while he drove. She'd unzipped his pants, and bending while he steered, she'd taken him into her mouth.

Fisting a hand in her hair, he'd made her laugh because he'd sworn and stamped the brake several times. "Quit, or you'll make me hit my head on the wheel," she'd pronounced. He'd jerked to a stop in their garage. With the key still in the ignition, he'd shoved her against the passenger door. Pushing her legs apart, he opened her with his thumbs. He'd licked and teased her clit. When he trailed kisses up her belly, to her plump breasts, she'd unlatched her door. Nearly falling out of the vehicle, naked, she realized. She didn't have her key. Not caring, Fabian scrambled after her and hoisted her up against the door that led to their kitchen. Without preamble, he thrust into her. Digging her fingernails into his flesh, she wrapped him with her legs. She gasped as he'd bit at her breasts and fingered her anus, all while pumping her witless.

Now at the dessert place, Valeria would tell Kiss that baby Sinclair was due next year, in late February or March, if all went well. And to think, Valeria and Fabian had stopped trying. They'd just started sexing—oiled up or not, standing, sitting, bent over, lying down, in the tub, on a table, on chairs, in the grass, in her car, at the beach, in public restrooms—anywhere. They'd squeezed, hunched, and moaned. The couple had done so for pure pleasure, and look what happened.

LYLE drove his wife-to-be to the dessert factory, where Kismet hoisted herself down from his sport utility vehicle. "Bye, KissGirl," their small daughter called from her seat in the rear.

Both Lyle, and Valeria, who stood watching, chuckled. Kismet was not amused. "Déja, I am *Momma*," to you. Why, curvaceous Kismet wondered, did her child insist on addressing her as her mother did?

Settling into their seats in the confection house seemingly ripped from the pages of a fairy tale, Valeria grinned and spilled her beans.

Simultaneously both women screamed, delirious with happiness and hope, as others glanced over. With arms around her longtime friend, Kismet was all inquiries. "So when are you due? When did you find out? How do you feel? Everything's okay, right?"

"Baby's due near the spring of next year," Valeria happily announced. "Near Ronni's birthday and all is well...so far. And Kiss, I have to tell you, the sex is amazing!"

"Oh I know. Stay positive," Kismet advised. "And we'll keep praying," Kismet then appeared pensive as she mentioned her level two ultrasound. "It showed an infant girl."

"A girl, Kiss?" Valeria was thrilled for her friend. "I love it!"

"Lyle and I aren't telling anyone else the baby's sex. Not yet," Kismet revealed, "because I think there are two. The doctor claims there is one, but I've heard about a baby hiding behind the other. I even read about synchronal behavior patterns in twins, and about simultaneous fetal heart rates." Kismet bit her lip. "I feel like that's the case with me."

Valeria's eyes rounded. "Twins, Kiss, now that would be something!"

"I'm just looking for healthy," Kismet announced. "Still, this is a strange feeling I have right now; hopefully, it'll go away."

The topic became less exuberant. If only they could get a miracle for their beloved Ronni.

Valeria sighed and announced, "The night I just missed you at the hospital, Ronni's plight became a bit too much." Valeria said Amy appeared that evening, as she often did, "And seeing Amy, I just fell apart. I guess because I wonder *why Ronni?*"

Valeria said Amy assisted her from Ronni's room. Amy whispered, "We must be strong. Our girl mustn't worry about herself and us, too."

140

Fidgeting with her fork, Valeria couldn't meet Kismet's eyes. "Ronni is in *so* much pain these days, although she tries to conceal it. Kiss, she can't possibly continue like this. She barely sleeps."

A thought struck, and Kismet said she would speak with Lyle, and Farai." Her sister had tried to wrestle all wedding arrangements away from her. Kismet, nodded. "I think I need an earlier ceremony date."

Valeria appeared skeptical. "But the invites have already gone out."

Unintentionally, the curvier woman whined, as her daughter often did. "I know. However, I *need* Brownie to be there, and since Farai wants to help, she'll have to do this for me. Somehow..."

"**O**H, come on." Nell followed her daughter to the living room, where the expectant mother eased into a comfortable chair. "Call your sister back, KissGirl. She wants to speak to you tonight. It won't take long. I had a nice talk with her earlier."

Kismet gestured toward her child. "Why is she not in bed?"

"She screamed and stomped and hit at me, so her Nannie spanked her bottom. Then I said, 'Get up there.' She did, and fell asleep while I chatted with Pastor." Nell crossed her ankles. "Sometimes, nothing puts a wayward child to sleep like a good paddling."

Kismet sounded pensive. "What is wrong with my pumpkin lately?"

"The same thing that's going on with *you.*" Nell pulled herself up. Then lifting her grandchild, she puffed and blew.

Kismet spoke. "Ma, I'm expecting. Dé is four, she's not."

Nell cut her eyes. "KissGirl, she is. That's her problem."

Kismet appeared dumbfounded. "Ma, she was fine with this, before."

"Well, reality is setting in," Nell explained. "This child is imbibing some of yo' feelings, too. You got a lot going on. Mind you now, Déja has her own feelings. Some she can't yet fully explain, so she acts out."

Kismet clucked, "My poor girl. I feel sorry for her."

"Feel sorry for *me,*" Nell huffed. "I'm carrying her heavy behind. Just keep talking to her." Nell left the African motif living room with its lovely dried flower arrangements. "Oh, and ring your sister," she called over a shoulder, "or I'll be forced to use my strap on *your* bottom."

After a relaxing shower, Kismet dialed and was regaled with half an hour of her sister's plans.

"Kiss-met, you do remember that *awful* conversation about my Brosnan, don't you?" Farai inquired. "Well, despite you causing me angst, I pulled it together." In her East 60's, panoramic, Manhattan penthouse, the publisher admitted, "Your words galvanized me. They made me see that I need to spend time with Brosnan. Therefore," Farai gushed, "I've set aside two weeks in the late summer just for him!"

"You'll take Kiddo to church?" Kismet asked. Her theory, garnered from Nell, was that parents needed to provide spiritual guidance.

"My word, Kiss-met, if you don't sound like Mama. Yes, we'll attend services. Oh, and I have spoken with my Brosnan, various times, and get this! I have yet to hear from the academy that he has misbehaved!"

"Well, look at that," Kismet marveled. With her sister winding down, she figured it was time to present her dilemma. "Farai, you offered to help with my wedding, any way you can. Well," Kismet bit her lip and rushed on. "I need something from you."

"What can I do, dahling?"

"Help me hold the ceremony sooner."

"Oh no, Kiss-met Staar." Farai sounded disappointed. "We cannot."

"What do you mean, 'Oh no' and 'we cannot?'"

"Well, Sweetums, changing wedding dates, at the last minute, and expecting others to adhere is tacky—*trés tackay*. It is not done. For crying aloud, Kiss-met, it is July, already."

Although she longed to snatch her sister through the phone, Kismet breathed. Then patiently, she explained why she needed the change.

Pacing her 3,000 square foot, elegant home decorated in shades of bronze and ecru, Farai sighed. "I applaud your loyalty, Kiss-met. I really do. Yet to do as you've suggested would be tacky, and ghetto, as I said."

"Then *you* must cause it to be otherwise," Kismet demanded. "You live like a baller. You're boss, a power player. You've got pull. Help me get a different venue on short notice. I need this wedding put together, the *right* way." Kismet knew that last would untie her sister's hands.

Farai's cultured voice rose an octave, "Kiss-met, I am thinking... What if *I* host your wedding at my *house*! I can see crystal flutes and—"

The younger sister was flabbergasted. Although the sentiment was superb, the home in question was out of state. "Farai, my wedding needs to be here, in New York."

The elder sister would not hear of it. Although her Manhattan penthouse featured a library, walk-in bar, two wood-burning fireplaces, and quarters for the help, it was impractical. "Sweetums," the magazine's founding editor called, "Although my 25-foot balcony here is perfect for entertaining, it will never do, for *your* occasion." Magisterially, Farai waved. "This place is for more intimate gatherings."

"We've only invited about forty people," Kismet reminded her sister.

"Dahling, you've proved my point. We'll need more room. You'll need a few nannies, so you can enjoy your day. With the imported help, the event planner, and others, this place just will not do. Understand, Kiss-met, your wedding can be held in Nevada. It is beautiful in the cooler months. Now shush Sweetums, we'll fly everyone out."

"What?!" Kismet knew Farai had lost it. "I'm not made of money, sis, and I doubt Lyle wants to spend his that way."

"Oh, but *I* don't mind. I can spend on *you*, my sweet. You so seldom allow me to do a thing for you. You're like my Okaru." Farai chuckled. "You sure you're not a proud African diplomat? Oh Kiss-met, I *so* want to do this! Let me charter a flight for your guests."

Kismet was as frustrated as she had known she would be before she'd called. "Where will my guests stay?"

Farai spoke like a schoolgirl on speed, "Leave everything to me. I'll put them up in lovely hotels. They'll be fed, entertained, and everything. Kiss-met, I will cater the main event. I'll call in a photographer friend too, *the* best. Only the crème de la crème for you, dearest. I may even finagle a wedding spread featuring you, Sweetums, in one of next year's issues. Oh, I can't wait!" Farai squealed with a manicured hand to her face. "My sweet, you must understand, your way would have been...um, 'cute,' but now it'll be so much better!"

Yeah, because it would be Farai's way, Kismet thought. "Well," the expecting mother said and felt relieved, somehow. "If you'd handle it..."

"Oh, I don't *handle* Sweetums, I design, I create; I bring to fruition!"

"Okay." Kismet then advised, tantamount to relinquishing control, "instead of February, I need December—or even November."

"November of this year, it is!" Farai summoned her houseman. "Kiss-met, Rainier is about to bring me one of Mama's pink gins, to get my creative juices flowing. Don't worry either, dahling; I shall keep you abreast of everything. Ah, and soon we'll purchase your gown."

"I've got one," Kismet protested.

Her sister sounded horrified, "Like whatever *rag* you own will fit you in four months! Kiss-met, please. If this is to be a *Farai Lorelai*

Production, then you will be outfitted as befitting such! Oh-oh." The elder sister sounded distracted. "My other phone rings. Tsk-tsk, but business knows no time of day. We'll chat soon, dahling. Cuddles."

Yeah, yeah, "To you too," Kismet said and felt as though her head spun as she knocked. She entered the room with the mahogany chest of drawers. Easing onto a comfy chair, she told her mother all.

"Somehow I thought you'd be more upset," Nell revealed. Scantily clad and lying on her patchwork quilt, Nell enjoyed air conditioning on her round body. "KissGirl, you've always hated it when your sister took your things and ran with them. So you allowing her to do this is...new."

A sigh escaped, and exhausted after that call, Kismet placed a hand over her swollen belly. "I'm fine with it, Mama. Really."

"You are?" Nell's eyes widened.

"I am." Kismet divulged that she'd earnestly listened. "Mama, I know my sister. Farai is no slouch, she ain't cheap, and she's not selfish."

Nell agreed. "She's just a little self-*centered* at times."

"Well, if I'd lived my first thirteen years like royalty, I might be too," Kismet reasoned. "Anyway, I told her I'd discuss everything with Lyle and call her. She said whatever I can dream of, she can make happen."

Nell smiled because such was life. Kismet Staar worked on making *Ronni's* dream come true, so why shouldn't someone do the same for her? It was how the Lord worked.

Kismet admitted she would not get in Farai's way. "I don't need to micro-manage everything," like her sister, who insisted she would see to every detail. "Mama, you know Farai is extravagant, where I'm not, but whatever she wants to do," Kismet grinned, "I'm down. I won't argue."

"Why, you little *piglet*!" Nell clapped rose nail polished hands. Nearly choking with laughter, she leaned forward to whisper. "Honeybunch, after speaking with Ms. in Charge earlier this evening, I'm going along, too."

Kismet pulled herself up and kissed her mom good night.

"God, please bless both my girls." Nell quietly prayed as Kismet exited the room. "Oh, and Father?" Nell amended, "don't forget about my son—or his brother." Beau, and Thomas, Ophelia's other unfortunate offspring. "Those boys of mine need you, too."

Chapter 24

BEAU'S phone rang. Rolling over in bed, he eyed the clock on the nightstand. *Three a.m.* Who on earth? He reached for the receiver. "Hullo?"

"Beau," the voice was familiar. "This ya mama."

"Who?" he asked, highly annoyed at being dragged from sleep.

The woman sounded exasperated. "It's Ophelia."

Beau felt instant aggravation. "What do you want?"

"I wanna talk."

Beau nearly yelled. "At three o'clock in the friggin' morning? Look," he sighed. "This had better be good; I gotta be up in an hour."

"Look, yourself," Ophelia tossed back. "It ain't like I can catch you in the daytime; some weeks you're not home at all—*or* you don't answer your phone—so I gotta git in where I fit in."

"Ophelia," Beau near-growled. "What do you want?"

"Well..." she shillyshallied. "I needs a few thangs."

When she did not continue, Beau became fed up. "Look, either spit it out or get off my phone."

"You really turned into a tough cookie," Ophelia marveled, "because Beauregard, I gotta say: you were a real pussy-boy, back in the day."

"Yeah?" Beau hoped the insinuation would make Ophelia angry; "Well, my A'nt and uncle toughened me up."

Ophelia screamed because she had always despised the woman who'd 'stolen' her son. "I'on't wanna hear nothing 'bout fat-ass Nellie! Talk about *me*! If you got balls, they from *me*—not yo' daddy's people."

"Yo, you can go on a devilish tirade if you want," Beau growled, "but do it off my phone. Ain't nobody got time for this."

Knowing he was about to hang up, Ophelia hollered, "Wait!" She didn't dawdle. "I need money."

Loudly, Beau laughed. He sneered, "Don't we all?" From the moment she'd said her name, he had known what the woman was after.

"Well..." Ophelia thought she sounded sweet, "Since you're my son 'n all—"

"No. Stop right there." Beau cut his biological mother short. "Let me inform you, since you don't seem to understand. I am no longer your son. *You* made that decision, years back."

Incensed, Ophelia screeched, "I don't care about you—or decisions! But," she said, her voice deadly low, "you would *want* to do what I say."

"Piss. Off." Beau disconnected. He pulled the warm coverlet over his head and thought, trying to shake him down. The nerve of that woman. If she pushed, he might consider offing her. Beau thought it as his phone rang again, as he'd known it would. Thus, he reached out and silenced it.

IT was six fifty-two a.m. Monday morning, and Kismet Staar Moore, Client Managing Director of Global Accounts, answered her office phone. "Hey Diddle Diddle," she sang, as discreetly she shut her door.

Her cousin informed her that he was at LaGuardia Airport, about to board a plane and didn't have a lot of time, but, "*She* called."

Ophelia. Kismet's eyebrow winged up. "Did the old hag? When?"

"At three this morning."

"What?"

"Yeah." Looking like a male model in a leather jacket, a tee, jeans, and boots, Beau stood, because his and the surrounding rows would soon board. He hoisted his carry-on. "The old crone said she needs money."

"Don't we all," Kismet scoffed.

Beau's thunderous laughter caused two unsuspecting women before him to flinch. Heedless, he said, "Those were my exact words."

Kismet rose from comfortable leather. From her picture window, she gazed at Manhattan awakening. "So how'd she take being rebuffed?"

"I'on't know." Approaching the ticket agent, Beau shrugged. He said he'd hung up. "She called back, though, and got voicemail."

Kismet burst out laughing, as her cousin said, "Ol' hagarina went on a rant. Left five messages saying she'll ruin me."

"Where you headed?" Kismet called, raising her coffee cup. She was barely able to hear due to a voice blaring through airport speakers.

"L.A.!" Beau near-shouted into the receiver. "I gotta go."

"How long?" his cousin quickly inquired.

"A week, two the most." Beau sounded preoccupied, "Business—call you when I get there!"

146

Disconnected, Kismet pondered her cousin's biological mother, even as her hand went to her head because she would shortly see...

There was wild hair woman, and the clown, again, both from her prior vision. *Why* did the woman look so familiar? Kismet wondered, as again the pair appeared to be plotting. Uh-oh. Scene change. Wild hair woman and the clown were—

Oh, Lord! Bloated and floating face*down* in a muddy river.

BEAU flew high above the clouds, as a man and woman walked dusty streets in one of the worst parts of Brooklyn. There was no pretty park. There were no rooftop gardens, cafés, or boutiques. There was no hint of gentrification. There was only the shadow of the bridge.

Unbeknownst to the pair walking, another man followed. Not far behind, he kept an eye out.

The man and woman, who seemed a most unlikely pair, discussed a mutual 'friend.' They laughed too, both sounding harsh and hollow. They exchanged information, each with ill intent barely concealed. They parted.

The red-haired man with the big fake watch went his way.

The woman with the wild hair took a different path.

The man who'd followed dipped, still unseen, into a doorway. Having made a decision, that man fingered his cell phone.

Lighting a cigarette, he called, and thought it for the best. He waited while a recorded message played. It said his party was unavailable.

He left a message of his own. Then he hoped his phone would ring, soon.

Chapter 25

VALERIA René lost her baby. Everything was fine until her eighth month. Then she noticed; there was no movement. She realized she'd felt strange, for two days. It dawned on her. Her baby hadn't moved or disturbed her sleep. Alarmed, she had Fabian rush her to the doctor.

Everything afterward seemed a blur. All except for the sadness in the doctor's voice when gently, doc broke the news. The Sinclair baby no longer lived. However, for a reason—that Valeria had not heard, through waves of grief—now she had to carry the dead infant inside her for a while longer.

Horrified, she screamed, and screamed.

"Huh?" Fabian opened his eyes. "Val. Val." He sat up and tried to stop the flailing. "Babe, wake up." He shook her. "Valeria René!"

"Oh." Cognition dawned as she squinted at the light. "My God."

Turning from the lamp, cocoa-skinned Fabian took his wife in muscular arms. "That must have been some dream."

Panicked, Valeria nodded, because okay, that had been a *dream*. Still, it had been horrible! With her heart fluttering, she locked her arms around Fabian, her eyes darting around their berry-colored boudoir.

Valeria remembered. She was nowhere near eight months along. Thus, she would forget all she had seen, heard, and felt in that awful dream. Silently though, she prayed, for her rattled nerves, *and* for the baby that yet lived, inside her. She prayed for her family and friends because something was most likely wrong with someone, somewhere.

"You want to talk about it?" Fabian inquired.

Not a chance. Valeria shook her head. No sense in upsetting him too. Therefore, she extricated herself. "I need water." She tossed back the comforter, and Fabian rose with her. Reaching for her robe, Valeria said she would go downstairs. She wore her worn bunny slippers. In the dimly lit kitchen, she noted there was no sunlight trying to ease through the curtains. As Mystical wound his furry self around her legs, Valeria mentally pontificated all she had to do, and the calls she would need to make. Longing for bright, invasive sunlight, she accepted a glass.

148

Oh, her water.

"Ready to go back up?" Fabian asked.

His wife nodded, but it wasn't true. She didn't want to sleep, or lie down. Never again did she want to experience what she had in that dream, but she was no coward. Therefore, she went upstairs, ahead of Fabian. She followed Mystical, who leaped onto the bed where his mistress would stay awake, hoping for the moment she could call her doctor for an appointment. Valeria desperately needed good news.

Awaiting sunlight Fabian's wife also realized. She and the family ladies needed to trek up to see about Ronni. They needed to make sure she was okay.

VALERIA made calls. Although it was a bright sunny workday, she reached everyone but Beau. She left him a message. Profusely, she also thanked God because her doctor had a cancellation. She was told to appear at a specific time.

When she was checked, she found out.

She had not failed again. Not yet, anyway.

THAT evening, when she pulled onto Kismet's driveway, she sighed. Watching her sista-friend, big with her pregnancy, Valeria was relieved to finally be moving. The sooner they saw Ronni, the sooner she would relinquish remaining tension.

"Hey, honey." Nell patted the driver's hand. "You're looking mighty pretty this evening."

As she eased into the rear of her friend's vehicle, Kismet heard Valeria say, "Thank you, and thank cosmeticians for makeup." The curly-locked one glanced in the mirror. She'd nearly concealed all the sleep-deprived darkness beneath her eyes. She forgot her eyes. Backing out of the cute cul-de-sac, she told her loved ones about her dream.

"Oh, my," Nell's hand went to her throat. "That is frightening, but lil' Val, I believe you done right, alerting everyone. We need to check on our girl; most likely, she needs us." Nell peered through the window. "This morning, when I spoke to her, she tried to say she was okay, but I knew better, so I added an extra prayer to my dailies, just for her."

Chapter 26

RONNI was home! Kismet Staar didn't know how long the wafer-thin, butter-yellow woman would be, so she decided. Then she called Valeria René and Beau. Ronni wanted her Nile Soiree, but it had been planned for the next year. However, that wouldn't keep Kismet and her 'helpers' from throwing a different party this year.

Ronni, who loved themed events, had given her Cohorts the idea a few years back. She'd mentioned a Seventies Bash. Therefore, the Cohorts would host one, to chase away Ronni's doldrums, and theirs.

Beau was to unearth Afro wigs, platform shoes, dashikis, and bellbottom pants in ghastly polyester. Valeria had to procure big psychedelic swirl lollipops because she had already completed her major assignation. She'd stumbled upon a rental hall, replete with shag-carpeted walls and a disco ball suspended over a scuffed wooden floor.

Kismet's job had been to obtain music. She'd called Déja's other godfather, a part-time deejay. "Barry, I need a tight mix from the 1970s. It should include the jams, and some Dionne 'n stuff for Mama's crowd."

With Lyle's help, an excellent West Indian caterer been secured.

Thus, finally, the Seventies Smash came together. On a late-summer evening, the Cohorts, along with family and friends, excitedly congregated. It was Ronni Brown's biggest bash yet.

In the smoke-filled ladies' lounge, Kismet wet paper towel. She dabbed her face as her biggest baby looked on.

Raising both small hands, Déja, placed them on her mother's protruding belly. "Momma, what you doing?"

"I'm cooling off, pumpkin."

The door opened. The sound of disco diva Donna Summer's *Last Dance* could be heard. Then the door thumped shut. Entering the darkly tiled lounge, Valeria smiled at Déja, who scrubbed her small face with wet paper. With lengthy cornrows on either side of her face, the God-mommy patted her Afro wig. It sat on the back of her head. "Kiss," she called, "you said my look is cute and I love these

150

braids, but this 'fro is hot as—" Eyeing small Déja, Valeria caught herself, "Heck."

Curvaceous Kismet appeared amused as the ladies' room door opened again. This time a snippet of Anita Ward's *Ring My Bell* wafted in.

Slowly, Ronni entered the women's enclave. She wore a silver lamé jumpsuit that a few years before, would have fit like a second skin. An enormous platinum Afro wig wreathed her face. Although her eyes were glazed from various medications, she yet attempted to girlishly squeal.

"I'm having so much fun!"

"We hoped you'd love it," Kismet admitted, squeezing Ronni's arm.

Before the mirror, Valeria forgot her wig. "Then we should get back to our party."

The sista-friends agreed, glad that they were all together, once again.

Out in the great room, music pumped, people bumped, some hustled, and others freestyled on the waxed floor.

Aside, Curtis Hurst awaited Ronni.

Seated with her date, Deacon Claude Bevere, who heartily ate, Nell smiled and daintily picked at jerk chicken.

"May I sit on this side of you?" a familiar voice inquired.

Looking up, Nell smiled and took in the cutest tangerine, bell-bottom pantsuit. "Chitra!" Nell grinned, noting the upswept genie ponytail, and large hoop earrings. "You look like a *girl*!"

Mock insulted, Chitra said, "I *am*," before she and Nell chuckled.

"OK we're all girls inside," Nell smirked, "even broke down old me."

"Stop that," Chitra fussed as Amy Fox-trotted up. She was on the arm of Valeria's husband, Fabian.

"Hello Deacon," pink-cheeked Amy called. She wore an A-line floral-printed sheath. "Ladies, isn't this fun?"

"Yes, Lord!" Nell agreed over the BeeGees *Night Fever*. "The great thing," she added as Amy sat, "is that our girl is enjoying herself."

Amy nodded. "Kiss and the others outdid themselves."

Chitra agreed, watching her husband, who claimed he was no dancer.

Suddenly people yelped, "Ahhh yeah!" and "Bring it on Mr. Dee Jaaay!" as for their pleasure, he spun Al Green's *Let's Stay Together*.

The three mothers watched with undisguised glee as beneath the flashing disco ball, Kismet and Lyle appeared.

"They're wearing matching dashikis!" Amy shrieked.

Hunching her date, Nell called out, "Deac, look at my grandbaby."

With two large puffs of hair at each ear, Déja led her own entourage. Her small brother and Valeria's nieces and nephew. Among the children was the daughter of Ronni's supervisor.

"Nellie," Chitra called out when the DJ spun The Staples' *Let's Do It Again.* "I must say something." Chitra rose. "After this song."

"Good." Nell pulled herself up as well. "My old hips can only handle one song, and this is it—by that sanging sister Mavis!" Nell spoke to the man who assisted her. "It's you and me now, Deacon."

Across the room, Beau laughed. Wearing bell-bottoms, he stood at the bar with Valeria's co-worker, Saavion. Beau realized he was actually having a good time, when lately he'd felt bogged down. Ophelia had been dogging Beau, like a bloodhound, and Sandal had crawled back out of the woodwork. Both had endlessly pestered Beau, with Sandal moaning about togetherness, and Ophelia barking about money. Therefore, Beau hadn't believed he could forget long enough to enjoy himself. Nevertheless, here he was, having a good time, with Saavion.

Glancing down at ridiculously tight polyester, Beau gestured. "These pants are hugging me so, until I've nearly lost all circulation in my thighs." Beau attempted to walk, stiff-legged, and Saavion guffawed.

"Pull your shirt out, B. Maybe then no one will notice."

"Yeah, until I keel over. Speaking of shirts..." Beau gestured at Saavion's attire. "I don't think old Polly 'n Esther become you, either."

Beneath the flashing silver ball, Valeria danced, until Sonji cut in. The younger sister told Fabian she wanted to steal his wife for a sec. Out of earshot, Sonji said, "Val, I wanna do something for you."

Her curiosity piqued, mocha-skinned Valeria yelled over KC & The Sunshine Band's *Get Down Tonight*, "What you got in mind?"

"Well," Sonji smiled. "I spoke to Darren, and if you and Fabian agree, I can give you something you've wanted for a long time. Oh—tell you in a sec." Watching her angry husband dart up, Sonji turned.

The disc jockey slowed the momentum with Barry White's *Can't Get Enough*, and he made an appeal. "All the lovers in the house, meet your baby, your shorty, your wifey, or big poppa, on the dance floor."

Seated, Amy watched Ronni's supervisor Curtis gently cajole, until Ronni gave in. Joining other couples that danced close, intimately, Curtis whispered in Ronni's ear. Suddenly feeling a bit dejected, Amy glanced

152

away. Looking toward the door, she reminded herself. She would not be sad on this evening. She squinted. It couldn't be. She whispered, "Harvey?" As a man approached, Amy appeared perplexed. "Harvey!"

Surprised, she offered her hands. "Oh Harv, I saw a distinguished gentleman in the doorway, but I'd never have dreamed it would be you."

"Well *surprise*." Dr. Foster kissed the woman who asked if he was on call. "I am, but I'd love to dance with you." He looked toward the crowd on the floor. "I might ask Ronni, too, if my wife doesn't object."

As Marvin Gaye's *Let's Get It On* slowly spun, Amy knew Harvey felt similar to the way she had, upon initially meeting Ronni. He believed that somehow with Ronni, they could make up for their horrible inaction during Keesa's last year. However, Amy no longer felt the same way. Having requested Heavenly forgiveness, she had grown to love Ronni for simply being Ronni, but daily; Amy had to work on forgiving Amy.

Aglow, Amy moved to the music. Again, she was aware of how much she had always loved Dr. Foster. She'd loved him long before she and her childhood friend Gini had sneaked from her parents' huge house to hide in the bushes on a nearby road...

Teenaged bronze Gini had stood guard as young doctor Foster went to check on farmer Cromwell. When Gini deemed the coast clear, sixteen-year-old Amy ran forward. She poured sugar in the doctor's gas tank. Dancing in her husband's arms, Amy remembered racing back down the lane. At her parents' colossal house, she and Gini nervously sat on a metal porch glider. Aware that the dreamy young doctor's car wouldn't get far, they'd giggled. Remembering all, Amy did so in the present.

"You're twittering," Dr. Foster stated, his chin atop his wife's head.

"Oh, I was just thinking...about the sugar incident."

"That," Dr. Foster recalled, amused, "was entrapment."

"Oh pshaw!" Amy waved, as an up-tempo tune began. "Surely you jest, because my scheme saved you from freckled-y Magnolia Pharr."

Across the room teeming with family and friends, again Sonji approached her sister. As Thelma Houston belted out *Don't Leave Me This Way*, Sonji spoke before her brother-in-law Fabian could head off. "I told Val I wanted to give her something. It's for you, too."

"You never said what," Valeria stated and noticed Beau, whose pants were way too tight. Near the bar, he bent and did The Robot. Like those surrounding him, Valeria chuckled. However, she quickly refocused on her sister. "So what's up? What's the surprise?"

"We want to give you," Sonji spoke hesitantly, "well, you *and* Fabian, a baby." Sonji babbled, "I mean, if your baby—well, if it doesn't survive." The younger sister waved. "I'm not saying this right, but I would be your surrogate, should you need one."

Valeria immediately felt deflated, when moments prior, she'd been so happy. She had to appear crestfallen because Fabian's hands tightened protectively at her waist. Stiffly, he excused them. Unable to speak, Valeria wondered. Did what felt like a grimace to her, appear similar to a smile? Firmly, she affixed it as her brother-in-law sauntered up.

Appearing angry, once more, Sonji's husband stalked away. He had done the same thing the last time he'd approached the sisters.

"What is *with* that guy?" Fabian mumbled as Sonji explained.

"We just want y'all to have the baby you've always wanted." Hastily, on platform sandals, Sonji scuttled after her husband.

"Do you *believe* her?" Valeria hissed.

Fabian understood, his wife was upset.

"And stupid Darren! Darting up here. Fabe, I could slap him!"

Holding Valeria tightly, Fabian walked her off the dance floor. "Let it go, babe." He didn't want her upset. It would only cause their baby upset. Therefore, he said, "Don't think about it, Val. We'll talk later."

Valeria took the offered seat, just as Kismet and Ronni appeared. The mocha-skinned woman stared away. Moments later, she glanced at Kismet, who calmly ate brown stew fish, plantains, and salad. She also glimpsed Ronni, who serenely sipped from a clear cup.

Instinctively Fabian rose, but expressed he would return.

Licking a giant colorful, swirl lollipop, sticky-faced, Déja appeared. However, sensing her friend's need to speak, Kismet said, "Momma's talking right now, baby; grown folks." She pointed. "Go to daddy."

Valeria watched the little girl run off, and with hurt uppermost in her voice, she told her two best friends what happened. "That simple Sonji," she yowled. "She made me feel like a gotdurn *failure!*" Again.

Wiping her hands, Kismet beseeched the other woman not to be upset. "Oh, it's stupid for me to say that," she admitted, pushing her plate aside. "Heck, if I were in your shoes, I'd want to fight." Kismet appeared pensive. "You want me to go sock Sonji in the face?"

Valeria chuckled, despite her feelings. Then she admitted, "Her simple behind made me so angry. Now I can barely breathe." Valeria exhaled. "I wonder if you two understand."

"I do," Ronni admitted, a tad slurred. "Here you were, thinking you were about to get something you wanted. Then it got snatched away."

Ronni allowed her semi-glazed eyes to move from her friend to her boss, Curtis Hurst, who stood not far off. Noting the longing in his eyes, hurriedly, Ronni winked and tore her eyes away. "Val, now you know," Ronni slowly announced, "how *I* feel, every – single – day."

"Oh my God," Kismet Staar cried out.

Valeria looked semi-shocked. "What do you mean?" she asked, stupefied. "Please Ron," the curly-locked one pled, horrified, "don't say you feel this rotten all the time."

Ronni shook her platinum wigged head. "I didn't mean to get into it," she divulged, and especially not on the one night where she'd been having fun. This night she'd almost felt like life could last.

"Well..." Ronni sighed because she had never kept much from the other two. "The truth is I feel bad, lots of times because *I want to live*."

"Oh honey..." tears stung Kismet's eyes. Immediately she felt sad. "I want the same thing, Ron. For you and for us. We want you here."

"Don't make me cry, Kiss," Ronni advised, seeing the shimmer of tears in her friend's eyes. "Just listen. I want to live, but I won't, not for long. So, when I see you two really living, getting pregnant and married, and even fighting with family, sometimes I feel like *I've* been robbed. I want my piece of the pie too," Ronni moaned, "but I'll never get it."

Gloria Gaynor's *I Will Survive* triumphantly blared, and hearing it, Ronni tried to smile. "Sometimes I do remember," she said and caused inadvertent laughter, "that I got a *bite* of pie."

"Oh Boo," Valeria cooed, "I love you, and I'm *so* sorry for sniveling, and for your plight. I mean here you are, really going *thru*, and here I am, dealing with nothing of the sort, and I was coming apart. Reality check."

Ronni glanced toward the dance floor where a Soul Train line had begun. Patting her platinum wig, she said, "Don't sweat it, Val. Tonight, we're supposed to be getting our swerve on."

As the women tiptoed toward the fun, Kismet gently squeezed Ronni's hand. Holding the butter-yellow woman's other hand; Valeria thanked Ronni, "For keeping me grounded."

Chapter 27

BEAU was back in California, but he called Kismet Staar to say that Ophelia was threatening him again, via voicemail.

His cousin sardonically asked, "Is that how it's done, now?"

"I guess, and I have to ask: what'd I do to deserve her?" He fingered his dog tags as he admitted, "I've got so much going on, until I don't need this foolishness." Beau also mentioned another call, from a man who had given him a heads-up.

"Previously, when Ophelia talked about ruining me," Beau divulged, "I passed it off as idle talk. After listening to this man, I wonder..."

Hearing others in the background with Beau, Kismet felt uneasy. Yet she asked, "Can you tell me what the man said?"

"He's got proof that Oph's trying to out me. It seems she's already contacted the tabloids, to say I'm gay. She supposedly knows my gay lover, who—get this—has AIDS...which is news to me."

Kismet was stuck on "The tabloids!"

"Yeah, it seems that's part of why the paparazzi has been relentlessly chasing me, even out here."

Heated, Kismet felt that woman had no right! If indeed she was doing this, she could be held liable. Yet Kismet tried another angle, "Diddley, maybe photogs are just hyped because of your new movie. I hear it's pretty controversial."

"It's not just that, Kiss. The caller said compromising photos were promised, to go along with the dirt that's about to be slung."

"How awful," Kismet groaned, feeling growing hatred for the woman who had caused her son nothing but trouble, from day one.

Beau snapped a salacious 'news' mag shut and apprised his confidant of the fact that he had just read a story, untrue, "About guess who?" He said there was even a photo of him leaving an upscale eatery. "That was taken my last time here in L.A. when I met with my producers."

Beau mentioned a journalist who was currently wooing him. "She's interested in my recent documentary too, so," he sighed, "I guess now's as good a time as any to tell my side of my story."

That didn't sound right. His cousin asked, "What do you mean?"

"Well, I've been informed that my 'mother' and a crony are looking to get paid off selling my story. I figure I'll call my journalist associate and grant her a tell-all. That should take the wind out of O's sails."

"You'd delve into personal stuff in an interview, Diddley?"

"Yes, but with stipulations," Beau revealed. "Actually, I'm riding right now with Jah-YAY." Jayé was Beau's agent. "She and I will lunch with Mycah," Beau's publicist, "to discuss angles I'd like to take."

"But why go there? You're a private person."

"Babe," Beau sighed, "in my line of work, very little is private. Anyway, if I don't release my story, my way, Ophelia—or somebody—will, and add his or her own spin. Although," Beau thought aloud, "Publicity *is* publicity..."

"Do you trust this man? The one that called you."

"Yes," Beau answered. He debated as to whether he should say more.

Kismet heard the voices around Beau grow louder. Hurriedly, she advised, "Go. Call me, later. Don't forget."

"I won't. Love you. Bye." Beau got out of the luxury car. Semi-shielded from dazzling flashbulbs he walked with petite Jayé, Mycah, and security. Following both into the restaurant where others waited, he fingered his dog tags. He had not told his cousin everything. He would have to, and soon, if he really expected to do the TV interview. He would have to apprise his family of his caller's identity.

The man was his half-brother, Thomas. Moreover, Beau would truthfully say that earlier in October, he had been compelled to meet Thomas at Battery Park...

Beau and Thomas had walked the esplanade. During Indian summer, the area offered tourists spectacular New York skyline and harbor views. Therefore, because it had been nice out, and because he had seen himself in Thomas' eyes, Beau asked the younger man to take a jaunt with him.

Arriving at Bowling Green, they entered a popular bistro. They slid into a leather booth beside an exposed brick wall. There, Beau fed his brother, despite discreet glances at Thomas' attire and dirty footwear.

Ordering a classic French bouillabaisse, the house salad, and a ramekin of cassoulet, Beau advised Thomas to knock himself out.

The younger man did, ordering a table full of food.

A bit later, Beau asked, "Why're you telling me this?" His brother had apprised him of things of which he'd had no prior knowledge.

Thomas' answer was simple, guileless, "Because you my brother. Brothers supposed to stick t-together."

Beau was astounded, because from where could Thomas have learned that? Certainly not from Ophelia, who only stuck it to others.

"So...she beat you too," Beau repeated as his brother euphorically enjoyed *coq au vin*. Beau wondered if he should allow Thomas to eat so much; the man could wind up sick—but what the heck? Thomas was enjoying himself, probably for the first time in who knew how long.

Thomas nodded. "Yup, Muh beat me; made me keep it secret."

Sickened, Beau recalled having been through the same.

"She even made me do her."

Beau was stunned as sparkling water exited his nose. Cautious, and using his cloth napkin, he asked Thomas to explain.

"What's to s-say?" The younger man shrugged. "She used to trade me for drugs or m-money." Sampling Duck Terrine, Thomas looked up. "You know, for sex, when I was a little kid. When I turned eleven, *she* started doing things to m-me. Then she made me do stuff to her. The f-first time, she put my bird in her m-mouth."

Beau appeared puzzled, although he had an idea. "Your bird?"

"My thing," Thomas clarified and Beau knew the younger man was unaware of the clinical name for his penis. "She put her mouth on my peter; said she was getting me ready to do her."

"You knew that was wrong, right?" Beau asked, horrified, partially because had Ophelia not run off when she did, *his* story might have been the same.

Thomas scooped up poached salmon. "I knew," he said as innocently as a child would have. "But what could I do? Where was I gon' go? Everybody we knew was l-like her. If I'd run, they'd have done me worse. Thought about *you*," Thomas admitted. He'd been told he had an older brother. "Some days I wished you'd come get me, s-save me."

Poor *baby*, Beau thought with his heart aching because he'd wished the same about his father who'd died. Then his aunt had come. Suddenly Beau wished he and the fam had known about his brother sooner. Had they, Beau knew they'd have done all they could have, to save Thomas.

Intently Beau watched the boy-man who seemed nearly incapable of harboring bitter emotions. "You don't dislike her?" Beau inquired, astonished, "for all the things she's done to you?"

"Yup." Thomas continued to heartily eat. "Sometimes, I h-hate her, but 'til I do something else, what I'm gon' do—k-kill her?"

Beau leaned forward, in an attempt to understand. "Thomas. Do you want out? I mean what would you do if you weren't with her? How would you make money? How would you make a living?"

Thomas smiled, and looked to Beau like an angel, so sweet and bright, like sunshine. "I'd *read*," the younger one said enthusiastically.

Beau was intrigued. "You'd read what?"

Thomas gestured with his fork and chewed. "Um, b-books, newspapers, m-maps, cereal b-boxes, whatever."

"What would you *do*, though?" Beau reiterated, "To earn a living."

"I'on't wanna keep slinging shit for M-Muh. I know that."

Beau wouldn't want to continue small-time drug peddling for Ophelia, either. "Well, Thomas, what else would you do?"

"Work, with my h-hands."

"Drawing, painting, sawing, what?" Beau was curious.

"I f-fix things." Thomas sampled a bite of Bismarck herring. "Wood stuff. If a step breaks, or a wall needs smoothing, I fix it, good as n-new."

Beau felt proud, for some reason. "Really? You can do those things?"

Thomas nodded, and started on a decadent dessert. "Learned from a m-man Muh left me with for a wh-while."

Done eating, Beau forgot hating on Ophelia. He focused on wanting to help the younger man before him. He was aware that Thomas was smart, but a bit slow, and childlike. However, Beau attributed that to a lack of proper socialization. It wasn't like his mother would have made sure he went to school, and she could never have taught him etiquette.

Suddenly Beau longed to do for Thomas what his Aunt Nell and his beloved Uncle Brantley had done for him. He longed to give his brother dignity. Beau wanted to save the younger man, even though it seemed a bit late. "Thomas," he called.

"I'm Thom, okay?" The younger man's eyes pled. "N-nobody calls me Thom, but I always thought if I'd m-meet you, you'd call m-me that, and it would be like we're c-close. You know?"

Beau's eyes filled, due to the innocence of the mistreated man. "Then Thom it is," he nodded. "Now *Thom*, I want to see about getting you into a trade school, so you can fix things." Beau didn't want to make decisions without Thomas' consent, because that would be unfair, and too much like what Ophelia would have done. Therefore, Beau asked, "Thom would you *like* to learn how to get money for fixing things?"

Thomas eagerly nodded, demolishing a parfait. "I w-would."

Beau felt overjoyed, for the first time in a long time. "Well, you and I will make that happen—"

Wild-eyed, Thomas interrupted, waving. "You can't t-tell Muh, or she won't l-let me! She'll try t-to hurt you—her and that skinny guy, the one w-with the clown c-colored h-hair."

Thomas was literally frightened. Beau could tell. With his spine tingling, softly he inquired. "What skinny guy, Thom?"

"The one who said you his f-friend. He's a girl. We seen him at the m-mall. The day we seen you. I think he lies. He got s-spots on his face."

Spots on his face? Clown-colored hair? Clowns often had *red* hair. And skinny? Could Thomas have seen *Sandal*? Beau wondered. Had Thomas meant *that* red-haired, freckled, or spot-dotted slender man?

Kiss' vision! Hadn't she seen a wild-haired woman and a clown? Now that, Beau thought, was uncanny how accurate she'd been. Ophelia had wild hair, and Sandal definitely acted the clown, on occasion. Kiss had even seen a big fake pocket watch. Beau knew Sandal wore an ostentatious faux designer watch.

Beau's aunt always said it was amazing how God showed people things; how He would never leave one unwarned, *if* they put their trust in Him. So now, Beau would just have to inform his cousin and aunt.

Uh, Kiss had said something else; the woman and the clown had appeared to be plotting. Well, from what Thomas had unwittingly implied, perhaps they were. Gazing at his brother, Beau strove for nonchalance. "So Thom, how'd you meet this spot-faced guy?"

"I din. Muh d-did, at the m-mall, when you-'n-them left." Thomas appeared to ponder something. "Brother, can your cousin be my cousin? I want a whole f-family too, and friends, like a r-real person."

OMG. Beau nodded, suddenly wanting to take the other man in his arms. He desperately wanted to erase all the evil that had been done to Thomas, by the one person who should have cared for him. "Yes Thom,"

Beau said. He'd sounded sage, like his aunt. "We'll get you a whole family, and friends too," even if Beau had to pay people.

The older brother cleared his throat. He tamped down surging emotion, while Thomas stretched. He'd eaten more than he ever had in his life and appeared supremely happy. "Guess what, b-brother?"

"What, brother?"

"I got me a f-friend. I'd d-do anything for my friend."

Beau glanced at the check. "What's your friend's name?"

Thomas lowered his eyes as shyly he said, "Yours."

Beau was puzzled as Thomas giggled. "What's that, Thom?"

Thomas held his stomach, merrily gasping, like a child. "*Your* name."

"Ohhh..." Beau laughed too, from deep inside, and Thomas laughed harder. Leaning across the table, Beau attempted to ruffle Thomas's hair. "It's okay," he had to tell the man whose eyes became wary. Beau reassured the younger man who attempted to bury his chin in his chest.

"Thom," Beau gently called. "Look at me. Yes, look up. That's it."

Thomas raised frightened eyes.

"I only want to touch your hair." Beau opened his hand. "Let me?"

Thomas' eyes filled. Rapidly, he blinked and hoped his brother would not hurt him. "O-okay," he agreed, his voice small.

"See?" Beau ruffled the wooly, lint-speckled mass. "Nothing bad."

Thomas grinned. Again the sunshine burst forth as he repeated, "See? Not b-bad." He leaned forward. With both hands, he touched Beau's close-cropped hair. "Nice." Thomas didn't seem to know what to do with his hands, so he placed them around Beau's shoulders. With his head on Beau, he pressed his face to Beau's neck and murmured. "I knew I'd l-love you brother. All the t-time Muh said I wouldn't, but I knew. You like m-me too." Thomas sighed. "You smell n-nice. *My* brother."

Tears filled Beau's eyes. His vision blurred. The guarded doors of his heart flew wide open. Despite the curious glances of remaining lunch patrons, Beau hugged Thomas who patted him. Unashamed, Beau rubbed Thomas' back, as Nell would have rubbed his. Feeling most protective, Beau knew. He had to help this man who had so innocently tried to help him. This man who had looked a lifetime *for him.* The notion nearly caused Beau to erupt into buckets of tears. Here was another someone who had looked for him, someone who had loved *him*, just because. Here was someone he had not known, but someone he would never give up. This someone was a gift. His precious brother.

Chapter 28

KISMET Staar sighed because the second to the last day in November had finally arrived. Her sister had done everything to make it memorable. Kismet had to admit, things were more spectacular than she, the younger sister, had ever dreamed.

Relaxing in one of five bedroom suites, Kismet was grateful. She gazed around her own personal wing, done in crisp, new grass green, and ivory. She saw the crema Marfil fireplace and could not believe Farai. Seated on the palest green, roll-arm sofa, Kismet's gaze left marble to fall on antique white, a wood and glass table. She eyed fresh flowers in an emerald green cut glass vase. She gazed at the framed splendor of African-American artist Elizabeth Catlett, lit by a brass *torchiere*. There were ceiling-to-floor, heavy, cream-colored drapes with tassel tiebacks, and an ivory carpet with huge, pale green leaf inlays. Kismet realized. Farai had spared no expense in giving her the wedding of which she had never dreamed.

First off, Farai had jetted Nell, Kismet, and the children to Vegas. Then Farai sent her driver. Seated and wearing beautiful lace undergarments beneath a silk robe, the younger sister recalled the ride to the house. Called Twilight Links, the structure was set on a hill. Situated in the Nevada's Prominence Knoll country club community, Farai resided in a stunning Tuscan Villa. With its outside multileveled decks, massive lanai, soothing waterfall, resort-style landscaping, and gardens full of tropical flowers, the place was astounding.

A businessperson like her sister, Kismet had never made the time to visit Farai in Nevada. Nell had flown out several times. However, walking through the place, again, older Nell had been awed.

Sipping mint tea to calm her nervous stomach, Kismet remembered. Silhouetted in her home's dramatic entryway, Farai had worn a silk Kimono. Her wrought iron, circular staircase had been a backdrop, as standing beneath a colossal chandelier, the homeowner beamed.

"Welcome, Mama!" She'd sang and air-kissed Nell. Farai had then hugged Kismet. "Welcome to *you* too, Sweetums. How about a hug for

162

princess Déja?" Obscurely Farai waved at her houseman, wordlessly instructing him to take all luggage to the upper level. "Kiss-met, I am overjoyed to see you! I am aware too that Lyle must run his business, so we will apprise him of all things when he arrives." Farai spoke as her heeled slippers clicked on magnificent marble. "Follow me, and by all means, Kiss-met, do lay that heavy baby down."

Kismet remembered touring the home where her wedding would be held. Farai narrated as she clicked along, "As you can see, every window has a view." Panoramic each was, of the pool, the garden, the golf course, and the famed Las Vegas Strip, off in the distance. Walking, Farai announced that come evening, when The Strip was awash with color and light, she would point out the famed hotel where their guests would stay. "Then, on your day, we'll have them shuttled here."

Kismet remembered touring the house that had been designed for large-scale entertaining. She'd been impressed with the chef's kitchen and the wet bar; with numerous fireplaces, sumptuous bedroom suites and baths, the powder rooms were formidable. There was a theatre with two-level seating, a library, several plush offices, and an elevator. There was more, including the six-car garage with its RV/Limousine bay.

"So you see," Farai nodded, accepting a Martini, extra dirty, from her houseman, "We have 15,000 square feet of living space." That did not include the sauna, steam rooms, or the refrigerated wine cellar. "Now, Kiss-met, you know why I wanted to host your event here, and not at my Manhattan workweek place." Farai raised her cocktail glass, "So again, welcome Sweetums, to my itty-bitty gem in the desert."

Seated in her lovely suite, Kismet recalled Farai admonishing her to rest. "I know you need to, after that flight. Then, when you and Mama have freshened up, ring me. I'll send Anna up to the children. You know she's been with me since Brosnan was born. Her presence is soothing, like Mama. It's why I keep her on; I just can't bear her to go. The truth is this is more her home than mine because I'm so seldom here. Anyhoo, my sweet Anna will bathe, feed, and adore my niece and nephew. That is if you don't object, and we shall discuss your nuptials."

Discuss, they did. That evening, Kismet found out that she, her mother, and Farai had spa appointments that included intensive facial treatments. "Ladies, we must glow," Farai opined. "On Kiss-met's day, we want nary an imperfection. We only want silk-finished skin, which we will achieve via my makeup *artiste*."

Farai mentioned decorations and fresh juniper wreaths covered with merry berries and sleek gold bows. Winter roses were being flown in for enchanting snowflake splendor. Farai said the bride's bouquet would contain the roses, snapdragons, and oriental lilies. On each reception table, a crystal vase containing the same flowers would stand. "In addition to candlelight, the crystal will make our gala shimmer. Oh, and as you suggested," Farai gushed, "The vases will become party favors, Kiss-met. No cheap plastic crap for your guests, like at some affairs."

Farai revealed they would have a huge tree, decorated for Christmas, "Since it *is* after Thanksgiving already. The tree is really for my Brosnan because he'll be home. It'll be in the library for him and his cousins."

Nell chuckled. "Then we had better get presents to go under it."

Having left the food entirely up to her capable sister, Kismet was pleased to hear the menu, which included delicately smoked salmon. "Only the best, from the clear cold waters of the Pacific." Farai announced that silver trays would bear sliced ham and roast beef. "Oh, and champagne! We'll serve a Rose *Noir* Reserve, along with golden dessert wines containing clear notes of nectar."

Seated in her suite on the pale green, lovely sofa, Kismet shook her head because it had all seemed so grand. Now, in less than an hour, the proceedings would be underway.

Hearing a discreet knock on French doors, she called, "Come in."

With kinky ringlets bouncing, Déja entered. Kismet smiled. "Thanks, Anna. Yes, we're fine." To her daughter, who wore crimson velvet, and matching dress slippers, Kismet declared, "You look perfect, pumpkin!"

Déja smiled and leaned on Kismet's knee. Appearing perplexed, she asked *why* Mommy and Daddy wanted to jump over a *broom*.

Shaking with laughter, Kismet patted the sofa. She wanted to explain. It was a tradition begun by African slaves in the American south and the Caribbean. She wanted to say that since Africans have lovely rituals for each rite of passage, and since they had been carried as slaves to another world, they'd had to create new rituals. These mirrored those of their ancestors. Kismet's desire was to make her four-year-old understand that in North America, African slaves had not been permitted to legally marry, thus the creation of the broom-jumping ritual.

Kismet vowed to explain to her glowing daughter that the world's darker-skinned peoples currently jumped the broom to honor those gone on before, their ancestors. She'd add that the broom was also jumped to honor a couple's commitment to one another, and to their loved ones.

Thinking she could summarize it enough for a small person to digest, Kismet began. "Momma and Daddy will jump the broom, pumpkin, because people in our family, who are older than your Nannie, weren't always able to get married."

"Like you will today?" the child inquired.

"Yes, Déja. Those people, like Nannie, are our *ancestors*. They jumped over a broom. Therefore, Momma and Daddy will do it too. We'll do it to honor our ancestors, and to remember them. We'll jump because Momma and Daddy love each other, and you."

"Then me too," Déja innocently insisted. "I jump too."

"Okay..." Kismet chuckled and rose from the pale green sofa. She knew the unscheduled change would make Farai crazy. Hearing a new knock, the Momma forgot her sister to call out, "Come in."

Lyle entered, and saw his wife-to-be standing. With her robe aside, curvaceous wore a lace undergarment and a garter belt attached to sheer, lace-top stockings, all the color of a banana-inside. Turning from the full-length cheval mirror, Kismet noted the way Lyle's eyes slowly traveled over her exposed breast tops, her midsection, and beyond.

With a wink for Déja and her doll, the tall, broad-shouldered man strode over. Wearing tuxedo pants and a dress shirt, he took the Momma in his arms. He yearned to peel all that lovely lace away. He wanted to lie with her, to open-mouth kiss and lick her, to caress all her swollen parts, before ultimately; he merged his large body with hers. "My bride," he whispered. "Woman, you are gorgeous." Lyle stepped back, his amorous gaze roaming her. He loved seeing her this way, rounding more each day with his child. "Pregnancy becomes you."

Before Kismet could respond, she heard another voice. On the pale sofa with short legs sticking out beneath crimson velvet, Déja turned too.

"Uh Lyle-kins, what are you doing, in here?" Farai inquired, noticing the heated embrace. In the doorframe, she said, "Dahling, don't you know? It is bad luck for the groom to see the bride before the wedding."

"Leaving," Lyle grumbled. Passing Farai, he offered, "And I don't believe in luck." He felt as though he'd been taking orders from her for weeks. Sure, she was unspeakably generous, and funny-ish, in her way, yet Lyle wanted no more. He simply wanted his wife to himself.

Sensing his frustration, Farai called, "It won't be long now." Shutting double doors behind Lyle, gracefully, Farai whirled. Clasping manicured hands, she gushed, "Kiss-met! Isn't this *the* most fun?" Looking at her niece, she asked, "Aren't you a doll? Are you having fun, princess?"

Déja nodded, pulling a comb through her naked brown doll's hair. To the Momma, the Auntie spoke. "Sweetums, just wait till you see this place! Wow. I hardly know it, and it's my house!"

Kismet chuckled because Farai's joy was infectious. "What little I did see was beautiful." Uh-oh. Her eyes filled. Durn! The crying syndrome.

"Ooh dahling, don't do that," the slender woman in the silk lounging ensemble gasped. "Sweetums, if you become emotional..." Farai pulled the dressing table chair, "then what will become of us, and my princess? Look, she's frightened."

Kismet beckoned her daughter over as she sat. Snatching a tissue, she dabbed her eyes while Farai stood behind. Locking eyes in the mirror, the elder sister ran her hands over the younger's exposed shoulders. Softly, Farai advised that neither could afford tears, "Or precious Dante's work on these oh-so-glamorous faces of ours will all have been for naught. Sister, you must agree."

Kismet laughed because Farai was *so* over the top. As was the three-strand, classically elegant choker of diamonds and rare pearls that graced Kismet's neck. Gazing at it in the mirror, Kismet recalled it being the latest extravagant gift presented by her sister, just that morning.

Appearing puzzled, Farai revealed, "I cannot wait until this baby is born Kiss-met, because you're such a changeling. *Now* you're chuckling, when a moment ago, you nearly had us all blubbering."

"Farai, I was thinking," the younger sister explained, "that you are extra—but in a good way. You've done so much for me, and—"

"Don't," Farai commanded, "because I *cannot* cry. You hold that thought and let me ring Mama. We must immediately get you into that stunning gown, and I've got to get into my own fabulous attire."

Kismet grabbed both her sister's hands. "Listen, Farai." Doggedly, Kismet admitted her reluctance to release the pulling off of her ceremony. "But you've given me everything, and spared no expense—"

166

"Do stop," the wedding coordinator immodestly begged, although she did love flattery. "Not another word Kiss-met, because I know."

Farai then looked like she would indeed cry. "Lil sis, you must understand. *You are my best friend.* You have always been, ever since we were teensy girls residing in separate homes." It was true. Farai divulged that those who worked for her feared her. Others despised her for being independently wealthy, and for her relentless pursuit of perfection. "Even my select-few friends are fair-weather fowl, unlike you, my sister."

Kismet stared, some of those things her sister had never said before.

"Sweetums, just know: I *had* to do this;" especially, Farai thought but did not say, since Kismet's wise counsel had given Farai and her son a better relationship. At that moment, Brosnan, the young usher, was downstairs feeling important as he greeted guests. "Now, upsy daisy."

At a new knock, the host turned. "Mama. You look lovely."

The dressmaker entered afterward, and loudly, Farai clapped. "Lisette, I was about to— Oh, never mind; just flurries and fanfare everyone. Flutter, flutter. It is time!"

At four fifty-seven p.m., heavy with child, Kismet Staar looked breathlessly radiant. Silently, she appeared on the Twilight Links curved, wide, marble staircase. Amid softly played African instruments, she descended. At five p.m., the bride stopped under a glittering chandelier.

Standing, her guests murmured appreciatively, as decadently fragrant, she passed, *en route* to the altar. Wearing an elegant, low-cut gown of gossamer and gold, Kismet did not see most people. At that moment, she could only see Lyle.

Before a gleaming wall of windows he stood, with hand outstretched. Mirroring a curtain, his long locs draped his shoulders. Handsome, he wore winter white, as did the best man, Lyle's engineering firm partner.

Look at my baby, was all Lyle could think as he took Kismet's elegant hand. Kissing it, aloud, he recalled the long wait he had endured to get here. Bowing low before his bride, he shared other thoughts, before he revealed, "Now, I am simply and sincerely honored."

Approving murmurs rippled through those in the grand foyer.

Following a prayer and the exchange of vows, the new Mr. and Mrs. Lyle Manfred kissed. The small flower girl raced forward. To the amusement of all, Déja wrapped petite shapely arms about both her parents' legs. Then the expecting couple, joined by their daughter, 'jumped' over a miniature straw broom, the handle of which was beribboned. All in attendance cheered.

Massive, double doors were thrown wide. Mr. and Mrs. Manfred exited, and momentarily, Kismet's breath eluded her. With a manicured hand at her chest, she marveled at the grand stairway, and the sand-hued walk, lined with porcelain pots. Each pot contained a crimson holiday Amaryllis. With unfurled, large blooms, the exotic Christmas flowers were striking against the backdrop of freshly mown grass and sand-colored pathways. Thinking there must have been hundreds, Kismet smiled because her sister had seen to everything. How she would aptly thank Farai, Kismet honestly did not know.

Out of doors, it was a breezy sixty-seven degrees with sun and passing clouds. Standing with the scrolled iron and glass doors behind them, the bride and groom happily greeted all who exited.

Overjoyed, Kismet saw that Ronni had indeed made it. Having spoken before the chartered flight for her guests, Kismet knew that Ronni, who wore a layered georgette sheath, had not been feeling well.

"I'm so glad you could accompany her," Kismet told Curtis Hurst when he offered congratulations. Looking into his eyes, Kismet also murmured, "I want you two to have fun this evening, together."

"Well then," Curtis chuckled and nodded at Ronni. "I guess we'll have to oblige because nobody wants an unhappy bride."

UNDERWAY, the Manfred reception boasted a tempting array of appetizers. All were served on the lavishly appointed deck and the massive lanai with its soothing waterfall and sparkling pool.

Later, in the dining room, dinner was served. All doors were opened, and big band ballads wafted in from musicians situated on a lower deck. Balancing drinks and edibles, people spilled out and into the starry eve.

Moving gracefully among everyone, Kismet noticed people strolling the tropical gardens below. Upon hearing a woman admire her sister's resort-style landscaping and lighting, Kismet smiled. She stopped at the table where Valeria's parents sat. Without her husband Darren, Valeria's sister, Sonji, had made the all-expenses-paid trip.

"Thank you, Ms. Chitra, your gift is beautiful." Secretive, Kismet's eyes twinkled. To the woman who looked ravishing in topstitched turquoise silk, Kismet whispered. "I'm actually wearing it right now..."

"My dear Kismet." In brocade and gemstones, Amy spoke as the bride turned to hug her. "Everything is divine!"

Receiving a kiss from Amy's husband, Kismet admitted, "Dr. Foster, I am delighted that you made this trip."

He winked. "I would not have missed it for the world."

"Or he would have had to answer to me," Amy revealed.

Out on the main deck, Beau spoke with Kismet's longtime friend. He laughed with Abigail's companion, famed pop music mogul, Joseph Forrester. Sampling shrimp creole, Abigail mentioned how radiant her friend appeared. Beau raised his brandy balloon. "Yep. Here's to love— it'll make one radiant. Love *and* money," he added, and caused the couple to chuckle. When his cell phone vibrated, Beau excused himself. Wending his way through dancing couples, he hissed. "What is it *now*?"

Indoors, Kismet passed Curtis and Ronni, whose hand she squeezed.

With a bevy of edibles before her, Ronni motioned to her plate. "This is all so delicious, especially the kimchee."

Ahhh, the spicy fermented cabbage; Kismet was happy that Ronni ate, because too often, lately, Ronni had to be coaxed to do so.

"Kiss," Valeria called as Fabian returned to the buffet, "come."

Running a hand down Ronni's arm, Kismet turned. She took Fabian's seat. Glad to be off her feet, she nodded. "Val, you look lovely."

The matron of honor patted her stylish chignon. At her nape, it was secured with a rhinestone pin. She gestured at her fitted crimson satin, its square neckline offering a glimpse of bosom. "Why, this old thing..."

Chuckling with her silly friend, Kismet admitted she was starting to feel beat. "And boy, does my back hurt."

"You need to sneak upstairs and lie down," Valeria suggested, just as Twilight Links' owner appeared.

"Ms. Vee Ree-nay, you are a woman after my own heart," the hostess declared. Farai's sleek one-shoulder gown was the rich color of eggplant. "I told my sister that, not five minutes ago. With these babies coming, you and she must take it easy." Her neck laden with diamonds, Farai pivoted. "Sweetums, look at your nephew, and my niece."

Turning, the women watched small Déja and her older cousin Brosnan. Handling her as if she was porcelain, the thirteen-year-old walked the little girl round and round, as tightly, she grasped his hands. Squealing, small Déja thought 'dancing' with her velvet slippers atop Brosnan's shoes was the most fun.

Fabian returned with roast beef and whipped potatoes. Kismet struggled up, despite him admonishing her to remain seated. "I'm going to find my husband," she stated and grinned. "I like that; *my* husband."

Kismet found Lyle. *Sans* jacket, the groom was engrossed in politics with his father, brother, best man, and his new brother-in-law, Okaru. Requesting to 'borrow' him for a moment, Kismet whispered that she would go lie down. Absently, she rubbed her massive belly. "Tell Mama, okay; she's got Chance, and Anna will watch Dé."

Lyle appeared concerned. "Want me to come up too?"

Kismet touched his long hair. "No. I need some time alone."

Lyle watched his wife gracefully ascended the curved staircase. He found Nell. She enjoyed music and dessert with the Deacon. As Lyle relayed his wife's message, Nell handed over her sleepy grandson.

Beau re-entered the dining room and saw his aunt. In a camel-colored knit ensemble with fabulous faux fur, she exited, to cross the marble foyer. In her sensible shoes, where was she headed? Beau wondered. He had seen her give Kismet's toddler, Chance, to a nanny, so perhaps he should follow. If he did, Beau knew, he would come upon Kiss, who had also disappeared. Then, Beau thought, he could tell both women about the strange call he'd received from his manager. That had been moments before he'd received another call, from Thomas.

Seated with Curtis, who admitted he normally abhorred weddings, Ronni laughed. "Why?" she asked. "They're magic and full of promise."

Curtis revealed he often felt *he* hadn't been promised anything.

Ronni knew the man wanted more, from her, and from their relationship, if that's what it was. Closing her eyes, she tried to extricate her hand. She didn't need Curtis reading more into the handholding than there was, so she sighed. "Curt, I can't make promises. You know that."

"You're protecting me," he whispered, "but not this way, Ron..."

Movement caught Ronni's eye, and she watched Valeria and Fabian ease past the dining room doors. Ronni observed that on the deck, flickering with the light of floating candles, the couple slowly danced.

Possessively, Fabian pulled his wife close. Despising jealousy, Ronni watched her friend's dangling ruby and diamond earrings catch flame light. Ronni told herself not to envy the beautiful wedding set ablaze on Val's slender finger. Yet Ronni did. She also fought depression because

170

the bud of her friend's pregnancy was apparent. Suddenly, Ronni turned to Curtis. Suggesting a walk in the moonlight, she grabbed her shawl. She let him lead her from the room where many things hurt her feelings.

Slow dancing in the arms of her beloved, pink-cheeked Amy noticed Ronni. She left with the young man who was so right for her.

Flitting about, Farai, the attentive host, noticed that sister of Valeria's. Farai tried to recall the chick's name, as out of doors, sister-girl rudely cut in on Val as she danced with her handsome husband.

What did Sonji want *now*? Valeria wondered. This was the third time she'd cut in, and the older sister was sick of it. With clenched teeth, Valeria hoped the flicker she'd seen, as Sonji's eyes passed too slowly over Fabian, had been flame light, or else!

"Arnell," Chitra began, taking the empty seat aside. "I wanted to thank you. You helped me manage grief over my LorRen. I can honestly say, it is now dissipating. Somewhat."

Kismet's mother recalled Valeria's baby sister. Their dear girl had suddenly died of Lupus. Rhetorically Nell inquired, "Well, Chee, honey, what's a friend for?"

In turquoise silk, Chitra smiled. "Last Thanksgiving, I meant to thank you. Then in August of this year, at Ronni's Seventies Smash, I wanted to say something, but we all got to dancing."

"Oh yes, to Mavis Staples. Well, sugar pie, you are welcome." Nell then clucked as Déja, wearied of 'dancing,' made her way over.

"She is precious." Chitra caressed the child's upswept kinky hair.

Déja hoisted herself onto her grandmother's lap as Nell revealed, "Her Momma don't think so, not when this baby calls her 'KissGirl.' "

Valeria's mother wickedly cackled. "Now, Nannie that is *your* fault."

Moments later, Ronni and Curtis re-entered the room. Following them, Kismet reappeared, looking refreshed. Nell glanced up at her daughter, the curvaceous bride. "Honey pie, our guests will soon be shuttled back to their hotel."

"I know, and what a day!" Nell's daughter exclaimed.

"I must agree," Chitra nodded. "This has truly been a lovely affair."

Standing aside, Beau realized. He too would have agreed, a couple of hours ago, before all the phone calls.

Chapter 29

KISMET Staar and Farai bid most of their guest adieu. "This was heaven," someone whispered, caught in the bride's fragrant embrace.

"We should do it again," another teased, "and soon, too."

When, at long last, only the bride, the groom, the mother of the bride, the Deacon, and the first cousin remained, the host sighed. Then smiling because she had an idea, Farai caught her husband's eye. "Okaru, love, you and I should dance."

Okaru's African accent became apparent. "Cleaning is taking place."

"As well it should," Farai magisterially stated. "It is what people have been paid to do." She took Okaru's hand. "Come." She headed for the balustrade beyond the dining room. "Our musicians have another fifteen minutes. Therefore, we mustn't allow these moments to waste."

Gracefully, to the familiar big band tune, Farai and her African prince began to whirl. Watching, Kismet felt Lyle slip his arms around her from behind. Nell, her Deacon, and Beau watched as well. Older Nell spoke with admiration apparent. "Now who'd have thought those two would be so light on their feet?"

Beau chuckled, aware of precisely what his aunt meant. Okaru was reserved, quite stiff even; 'the colonel,' his wife, so often barked out orders, until this was a side of both that was rarely seen.

Farai pivoted, Okaru dipped, and Kismet laughed.

When her younger daughter continued, Nell turned. "You're not getting hysterical on us, are you, sugar?"

"No, Ma," Kismet waved, "but seeing Farai like this is funny."

"Oh, you haven't seen anything yet," the older sister proposed, as loudly, she clapped and leaned over the balustrade. Softly she spoke with the musicians on the lower deck. After casting an appreciative glance over her beautifully lit gardens, Farai dramatically faced those in the room.

Seconds later, she and Okaru Tangoed to sultry guitar strumming. "Ahhh, you guys know nothing of this," he called; sounding stilted as lively, he stepped with his wife whose hair came un-pinned.

Kismet wanted to stop laughing as wildly Farai whirled. However, the mother-to-be could not, despite her sides and back aching. With her sister raucously ad-libbing, Kismet found herself tremendously tickled.

"Sit," Nell instructed. "Uh Farai," Nell called over the applause of Beau and workers who'd watched. "You and Okaru come sit too."

When her pirouetting daughter plopped down beside her, Nell winked. "Farai Lorelai, your little show was wonderful."

Near breathless and fanning herself, Farai admitted to being grateful. "I tell you Deacon, if Mama hadn't stopped us when she did—whew! In a minute, I'd have had a heart attack!"

"Stop," Kismet moaned, wanting mirth to dissipate.

"Come." Farai rose and beckoned. Forgetting that she'd made her sister laugh until she'd cried, the elder re-pinned her hair. "On to the library," she announced, "where we shall relax."

The little procession was made. All entered the large but inviting room. The walls were caramel-colored, as were the plush leather Paloma chairs. Other traditionally elegant, comfortable furniture pieces were arranged in groups. Pride of place, an upholstered, chenille sofa was the color of a sienna sunset. Lamps cast their cozy glow on artwork, and creating the fabulous foundation for all was an Indo-Persian rug. On it stood a majestic Douglas fir, decorated for Christmas. Warding off the evening chill, split logs blazed in the fireplace.

Seated, Kismet gazed at a lit hurricane lamp on the cocktail table, softly, she began. She told her sister how she had not believed it could be done. "I didn't believe my wedding could be so lovely, and on such short notice. You only had four months, but Farai, you outdid yourself. Saying thank you doesn't seem like enough. Still, I do thank you."

"Oh, Sweetums, I would do anything for you. For me, this was nothing—if not pure fun. 'Anything for family' is what I always say."

Seated aside, Beau would have smiled, but he pondered other things.

Nell nodded. "Farai Lorelai, I am proud of what you accomplished here this weekend."

"So you've said, Mama."

"Be that as it may," Nell waved. "I am proud of both you girls for working together and not fighting. Everyone had a lovely time."

"I hope so," Farai gushed. "Oh, and I want to thank my sister."

"Me?" Kismet's eyes widened. "For what?"

"For always allowing me to be me." Farai sat on the caramel-colored leather Paloma chair nearest her sister. "See my dahlings," Farai offered, "People often think that I, and my lifestyle, are some kind of act."

As those in the room burrowed deep to listen, Farai explained; while in silence, her houseman served those who desired, coffee, or *eau de vie*.

Farai said one day, she'd come to terms with who she really was. Then she'd vowed to live genuinely, on her own terms. She said by then, she had learned to ignore the scrutiny of those who wanted her to be less, so that they might feel comfortable. "I had to be authentic."

Aware that he too had to live in truth, Beau raised his hand. "Farai, I'm with you. *I* had to learn to be my true self, as well. We all should."

"I agree, and in learning those things," Farai continued, "dahlings, I scraped and scrapped." The publisher nodded at Nell, Kismet, and Beau. "You three know I worked in a fishery. You know I handed out towels in that uptown-club bathroom, and fetched for that rich older woman. I was a dog-walker, a dog groomer, and a pooper-scooper."

Most of Farai's guests chuckled before she acknowledged that she'd met many people who had tried to wear her down. On jobs, others had poked fun at her. "They tried to demean me by saying I spoke funny. Still, in my heart, I knew I was meant for more. I think a few of those who ridiculed me knew it too. Nevertheless, I was like the kid who waits tables to put herself through film or law school. I became resolute about good grades. I was determined to become somebody." Farai said her determination was born of knowing. "Back then, I knew that education was my ticket to the life I would live.

"I believed *this* was my destiny," the founding editor somberly stated. "Not to create and run the magazine or live in my many fine homes, but to do my real work, to help others…" Farai glanced at those around her. "You all know about my charities. You know I make sure many are clothed, fed, and housed. Most of all, though, I fund *education*; because with that, a woman can do anything for herself, and others."

"Why'd you work so many jobs?" Lyle asked because this side of his sister-in-law he had never known, yet he found it intriguing.

174

"Mama told me to," Farai simply stated. She smiled at Nell. "Mama never bullshit me. When I went to live with her and my father, she told me I was a trust-fund baby. No one had ever been as honest before. Full disclosure: my great grandfather invented a type of shoe sole and tongues. Now they're mass-produced, but my family maintains the patents and rights. Anyway, Mama said, 'Farai Lorelai, you will one day have more than most people can even dream of.' Mama said there was nothing wrong with that. She said lots of people would gladly trade places with me. Mama said some people would try to use me, or worse. She said they would try to tear me down, to weaken my spirit. Thus, over the years, Mama taught me to understand people. She taught me how to treat them too, because back then, I was...well, a bit hoity-toity."

Kismet laughed. "And you aren't now?"

Farai waved, "Oh, Kiss-met. You know that coming from where I did, I saw most people as the help. Still, Mama squashed all that. She taught me that money shouldn't make me. Mama said I should make it, and use it, to live as I choose. She advised me to help others. And Sweet Mama," Farai gazed adoringly at Nell, "I have tried to do just that."

"I know, honeybunch." Nell patted Farai's knee. "You are alright."

"Well..." Farai sighed. "Those are the reasons I don't make excuses for my life now. Those reasons are why I could do this wedding fanfare, and do it again, if my sister wanted—no offense to you Lyle—because I know that unlike others, my sister truly loves me."

Farai discreetly dabbed an eye. She whispered, "Kiss-met sees me. I love her for that. She sees past all the 'stuff.' I get on her nerves, and she cusses me the hell out—sorry Mama, but Kiss-met Staar truly loves *me*. I know my sister is not jealous, either. She just wants the best for me."

Nell squeezed her elder daughter's hand, aware that for Farai, it had taken considerable effort to discuss her true feelings. Nell then turned to Beau and seemingly digressed. "Farai Lorelai may have been born with possessions, but you, Puppy, were born with the voice of an angel."

"Ain't that the truth," someone agreed. "His solo was wonderful."

Sheepishly Beau smiled, and immediately the women in his life sensed that something was amiss.

Kismet, heavy with the child she would deliver the following month, leaned forward. "Diddley, something we don't know about, happened?"

"Cousin," Farai's eyes narrowed, "what are you not telling?"

Beau got up. Behind the richly appointed bar, he refilled his brandy snifter. To the Deacon, to Okaru, and to Lyle, he spoke. "These three should have been detectives."

Okaru's laughter thundered out, as Lyle agreed. "Tell me about it."

"Beauregard, are you going to talk to us?" Nell asked, concerned.

Beau gulped spirits. "It's nothing, a'ight?"

"Then why are you upset?"

"I'm upset; Kiss," Beau angrily barked, "because I wanted to have fun today! I wanted to be free of that bitch," he snarled, "for one day! But no! She had to call and leave her usual threatening messages."

Kismet became livid, as did Lyle, who rubbed her aching back.

"Diddley," Farai called. "That Ophy woman threatens you?"

Beau sipped, shrugged, and said he could handle it.

"Still–"

Stifling his elder cousin, Beau admitted, "I got a call from Thomas, too." Beau's brother warned him of something that would soon take place. "Then my manager called. That's why I kept going out during the ceremony. My cell was blowing up."

"Oh my," Farai eyes widened as a hand inched to her throat. "I was being facetious when I said you should have worn a diaper. I apologize."

Beau shrugged. "Now, you know cuz. The restroom wasn't calling."

"Puppy." Nell sounded calm, despite churning anger directed at Ophelia. "What did your manager say? Anything you can share?"

Beau shook his head. "Doug was all questions. He said he fielded calls from 'some woman' who wants to ruin me. Mycah," Beau's publicist "called too. Mycah said he told me, in the past, to stop screwing the on-set caterer and masseuse. He was trying to lighten the mood."

"If only it were that simple," Kismet mumbled.

"Anyway," Beau wryly continued. "It seems this dang woman has threatened to go to the supermarket rags. Doug said O told him that soon we'd see me splattered all over them lying enquiring mags. That is if Doug doesn't set up a meeting with 'his client' and with Ophelia."

"The client is you," Nell's Deacon knowingly interjected.

"Right." Beau nodded and said his manager repeated what the woman said. "She's got career-damaging info, ready to hit the airwaves."

If *only*, Kismet thought, she was not pregnant, for just twenty-four hours! She and Beau would hop a flight. Back in New York, they would find Ophelia—because that's who 'the woman' was, although Beau's manager didn't know. Kismet would then beat the old reptile down, to the ground. Kismet's hand flew to her face as cognizance dawned.

"What is it?" Lyle asked, hoping the baby wasn't coming, not just yet, and not while they were so far from home and Kismet's doctor.

"My vision..."

Aloud, Nell recalled, "Kiss-Girl, you saw a wild-haired woman."

"You told me about a clown, too," Farai added.

Okaru wondered. "Who could the two be?"

"The wild-haired woman is most likely Ophelia," Nell sagely stated, setting her pink gin aside. "Up to her old tricks again."

"And the clown—"

"With the big fake pocket watch," Lyle added for his bride.

"The clown will show up," Nell stated, unaware that Beau already knew the clown's identity. Sandal. Beau's ex. "But, the woman," Nell opined, "has got to be Ophelia."

"She's doing this shit now?" Farai inquired incensed. "When she disappeared for decades, without a trace?"

Nell nodded. "That about sums it up."

"Well, in my home country," Okaru shrugged, "such people are easily disposed of." He looked over at his wife. She only had to ask.

"In this country, my prince," Farai shot back, her mind matriculating. "That trollop can also easily disappear."

"Not so fast." Beau was nearly amused at the way his family quickly rose to defend him, against his mother. "The truth is..." The tall attractive actor stated, as he swirled liquid gold, "I *want* to know what Ophelia has up her sleeve."

Kismet appeared astonished. "You want her to play her hand?"

"You mean *tip* her hand," Nell scoffed.

"Tip or play," Okaru's accented voice emitted clipped and stern, "However, one says it, there are ways this can be dealt with. *That*, we must all remember."

Chapter 30

V ALERIA René left her motor baby in the driveway because the day was lovely. Later, she would pull into the garage, but right now, she would enter her home.

Was that *a woman's voice* she heard? Who?! Quietly removing her shoes, Valeria crept, like her little gray Mystical, on silent cat feet. Reaching her kitchen, Valeria could have flown in Kamikaze style because that hussy had her hands on Fabian! Despite his advice that she remove them.

Valeria made her presence known. With narrowed eyes, she asked, "Why you look startled, Sonji, to see me in my own home?"

Valeria turned to question her husband, and Sonji spoke. Conversely, Fabian cut her off. Yeah, Sonji had grown up with Val, but she didn't know adult Val as he did. Soft-spoken, that no-nonsense tone she'd just used? It meant one thing. Someone was about to be ripped a new one if things weren't quickly clarified. That was the reason Fabian explained to his livid wife that her sister had stopped by, *unannounced*.

"Sonji claimed she wanted to talk to me, alone, to not upset you..." Nevertheless, even to him, it sounded fishy. Fabian knew he should never have let his sister-in-law in.

"Kiiisss..." Valeria hissed. "I had to keep telling myself that I was carrying this here, baby." Valeria rubbed her little bump. "Had I not, I would have whupped Sonji's simple, scheming ass!"

Kismet chuckled. "So, what did you do?"

"I told that heifer to get outta my house. I told her to never return."

"Good for you."

Valeria's eyes narrowed. "I know why I threw her out, Kiss, but why are you applauding me?"

"Your sister is conniving." Kismet had never been anything but truthful. "I mean why she got to push up on *yo'* man? There are millions of men in the world. Why seek yours?"

"Okay, you're feeling me, but Kiss, I don't like thinking—"

"Stop." Kismet raised a swollen hand. "Ask yourself one thing. *What was Sonji doing at your house*? She knew you wouldn't be there. She knows when you get home from work. So ask yourself, why'd she carr' her rusty behind over there, knowing that only your husband would be home? What did she hope to accomplish, a quick romp, if he would?"

Valeria hadn't wanted to think the worst. Therefore, she said, "Well, you know Sonji and her husband *have* been going thru..."

"Don't make excuses," Kismet advised. "She and Darren are fighting. Just say it, because she did some stupid sh—*stunt* to cause the upheaval."

"Okay, Kiss," Valeria began because she loved her sister; "I'm aware that Sonji and Darren aren't getting along. I know their marriage is a sham, one she claims is mainly for the sake of their son, but—"

Again, Kismet interrupted, "So since she fell out with *her* man, she should make a play for *yours*? Open your eyes, Val. I saw her at my wedding. She was pushin' up on Fabian then, with you there. She's counting on you, the older sister, to hide from facts."

It certainly seemed that way. Suddenly, Valeria was grateful for a friend like Kismet Staar. The mocha-skinned woman was glad too that she didn't have to spell things out, or worse, defend her own actions. "Things are getting complicated," Valeria complained, appearing to digress, "and the foul part is: I knew this would happen."

Kismet appeared puzzled. "You knew Darren would leave?"

"No. Yes. Well, the truth is: Darren wanted an excuse to bounce, and Sonji gave him that when she cast herself as surrogate for me."

In Kismet's Afro-Centric living room, where the winter sun shone bright, Valeria mentioned her brother-in-law's argument with his wife. "Darren told Sonji that people get paid for carrying babies for others." Valeria placed her small hands protectively over her protruding belly. "Then that Negro called me late one night, yelling about how all Sonji would get out of this would be pain and suffering. He said she'd get stretched out of shape too, and for what—a simple 'thank you?'

"Kiss, I told him the truth. I never asked Sonji for a thing."

Valeria sighed. "But back to the day she was at my house when I wasn't there. Fabian said Sonji asked him to help her. She asked Fabe to visit, and take lil Darren out. She claimed her boy needs a man around."

"Well, Val, Sonji should'a thought of that 'fore she ran her man off."

Valeria leaned forward. "Kiss, my *sister* even said—to *my husband*—that if I don't carry this baby to term, she'll help, but then she would need him more. Sonji mentioned doctor visits, back massages, and hand-holding during delivery since it *would be* Fabian's baby."

Kismet's eyes narrowed. "I'm honestly marveling at your ability to remain calm, because in your shoes, I'd have beat her butt, twice."

Valeria laughed, despite feeling quite perturbed.

"Val, you ever see *Swim Fan*? Your sister seems demented, like the lead in that movie."

"I know," the curly-locked one sighed. "Now, I wonder. What if Sonji *was* my surrogate—if I needed one? She's proving to be so rotten selfish; she probably wouldn't want to give my baby up after delivery, even if it started out as *my* egg and Fabian's sperm."

Kismet could only shake her head. "Forget that mess."

Although it pained Valeria to think about it, she admitted she had to discuss these things, once, and no more, with her trusted sista-friend. "I thought about breastfeeding too, Kiss. A surrogate would have milk..."

"And you wouldn't."

"I wouldn't be able to feed my own child, naturally."

"Val, breastfeeding also creates a bond."

"One that would make it even harder for Sonji to release my baby. If we had to go that route." Valeria shook her head while staring at the wedding set that never left her hand. "Now you see what I've been wrestling with. I don't want to seem ungrateful, but—"

"But nothing. We're not talking about this," Kismet stated. "It is pointless. You're expecting now. You're farther along in this pregnancy than you've been in a long time, yet you keep thinking about the past—about how you lost." Kismet no longer reclined. "Val, you have fears. They're why you ask yourself if you'll one day need a surrogate."

Valeria could have wept because Kismet understood. Kismet was aware that her former college dorm mate was exhausted. Kismet knew that since her friend felt as though she'd been such a failure in the past, awful memories often overshadowed Valeria's current joy.

Valeria thought about how much she wanted a baby, born of her own body. This baby. The one that she carried. Heaven knew it too, but what if it didn't happen, again? What if she wound up needing Sonji, to do what she couldn't?

180

The truth was Valeria would be torn up inside. She couldn't watch Fabian watch another woman grow round with his seed. Never would Valeria be able to stomach another woman breastfeeding the baby that she would only be able to *bottle*-feed. Suddenly, with tears apparent, Valeria almost wished she'd done as Kismet had years ago. Why hadn't she too exercised the adoption option?

"Val…" Kismet called, watching the woman who appeared highly disturbed as she paced back and forth. "Val, I'm going to need you to speak to your sister if you haven't already. I need you to have a real come-to-the-altar meeting with her. And forget being nice. She's not nice. Forget she's your sister, and remember one thing. Sonji is *a woman* who is slyly attempting to steal your man.

"Oh," Kismet added, "and since you *are* going to have *this* baby—the one you're carrying, forget Sonji. That sister of yours can't be trusted. Kira and Magi said they would willingly carry for you, if need be, so if you choose to go that route, after this baby, speak with them, not Sonji."

Valeria nodded. "Okay Kiss, but I keep thinking if I fail, this time, the surrogate will get all the attention."

"I know," Kismet sympathetically interjected. "You feel like the surrogate will get the attention that *you*, the new mother, should get."

"You know I love you, right?" Valeria admitted she did, partially because Kismet Staar understood. "Other people act like I'm an ingrate. When I mention Sonji's revolting actions, people seem to think I should be grateful that my sister is willing to aid me. They say that maybe I should make concessions for her. You, Kismet Staar, are the only one acknowledging *my* feelings, and that Sonji might have ulterior motives."

Softly Kismet reminded her friend, "That's because I know you, Valeria René. I know your sister too. She's always been this person."

Valeria sighed and agreed. "Sonji has always been conniving, jealous, and in a rivalry with me. My aunts used to say she was just trying to be like her big sister, but my Nenna said no, 'Vee Reenay, keep your eyes open and your back arched.' She said, "Stay ready to hiss and claw.""

Kismet grinned. "I knew I loved your jazzy grandma."

Feeling immensely better, Valeria revealed that she and Fabian had revised their birth plan. "Only he, and you, will be present."

"What about your mom, Ms. Chitra?" Kismet inquired.

"She'll arrive later, with my dad, who thinks waiting rooms are for men, not birthing rooms."

"Kiss, Fabian and I are starting Lamaze soon—and that's another thing. Sonji wants to be my coach, when that's *my husband's* job! The day I threw her out, Fabian said he couldn't fathom what her problem is. He said he doesn't care either, he just doesn't want her near us anymore."

"I knew I liked your husband, too." Kismet nodded, "And he's right. The fewer people involved in your affairs, the less drama."

Valeria smirked and admitted that had she not known Kismet Staar as well as she did, she, Valeria, might have been offended, "But I'm grateful for your candor, Kiss."

The mocha-skinned woman shook her head. "I just can't believe it's my *sister* who's trying to betray me.

"To tell you the truth," Valeria René said and sat on the sofa next to her longtime friend; "I'm not proud of this. However, I always thought if anyone betrayed me, that person would be Ronni."

"I know." Kismet nodded. "We both thought that because of how she was—or rather, how we *thought* she was."

The women sat in silence for a moment.

Then Kismet grinned. "I've got a secret."

"Tell me."

Kismet winked. "Then it wouldn't be a secret."

"Kismet Staar, come on," Valeria yowled. "Tell me!"

"Well...your mom told me and Mama that if ever the time came, *she* would gladly carry her grandchild for you."

Valeria was flabbergasted. "Ma-Ma said that?"

"Yep, Ms. Chitra wants this that badly for you...but Valeria René?"

The curly-locked one's eyes were wide. "Yes?"

"You are going to deliver *this* baby." Kismet took her friend's hand and gently squeezed, "Oh, and since this baby will be born healthy and whole, you did not hear any of what your mother said, not from me."

182

Chapter 31

TWO weeks before Christmas, Kismet Staar went into labor.

"You've got a little girl," her doctor announced. He did so after hours of his patient wishing she had never become pregnant.

Elated, Lyle Manfred kissed his wife's perspiring forehead, just as she squeezed his hand. Her grip was so tight that in pain, he winced. Lyle heard his wife groan, in what sounded like sheer agony. Peering at her, he wondered, *why* did she appear to be enduring another contraction?

Moments later, Kismet wearily leaned back. Perspiration beaded on her forehead. Alarmed, Lyle asked, "Babe, what is it?"

"Oh, oh," the nurse spoke to no one in particular. "Looks like we're going 'round again..."

"Around—*what*?" Lyle asked, confused.

Kismet braced herself for another contraction. Through clenched teeth, she hissed. "I told you *two*." Stupid! Lyle had not listened when she'd insisted there were two babies. In the throes of another contraction, she gritted her teeth.

The doctor tried not to smirk, but he had seen it before; two babies with synchronized heartbeats, when only one had been seen and expected. He had also seen many a mother's tears and agony. The doctor had seen poor fathers too, appearing lost and helpless. What he had seen most, however, was the look on Kismet's face. It was one he'd seen during delivery when a weary mother deemed her mate insensitive, idiotic, or merely the cause of all her misery and pain.

The longtime physician knew his patient currently wished she had never met the man who attempted to coach her. The doctor knew the feeling would pass. Soon enough, Kismet's tears of exhaustion would become those of joy. Therefore, the doctor encouraged her. "You're doing great, Mother," he said and meant it.

WELL, they say mother knows best," Nell smiled. Through the nursery window, she cooed at the two newest additions to the family.

"Twins. Can you believe it?" Lyle asked his mother-in-law.

"Sugar, your wife *did* say she felt there were two babies." Nell waved at her granddaughter, Belize, and at her grandson, Bonaire [Bo-NAR]. Both had been named for the places their father loved most. One was the home of his birth. The other was the place where he'd spent many holidays with his grandparents. Often, Lyle had spoken of the great festival dances. Hearing about Bonaire's traditional Simadan Festival, Kismet had been intrigued. She loved Lyle's stories of Bonairean culture.

"But how did she know?" the new father asked, feeling incredible pride. "I mean this is Kismet's first go 'round at having a baby."

"Like I said sugar, sometimes a mother knows." Nell patted her son-in-law's arm. "That's something you might want to remember."

NELL bent to kiss and ask how her daughter felt.

Kismet whispered one word. "Exhausted."

With a chuckle, Nell patted the younger mother's hand and acknowledged, "As well, you should."

"Five pounds, each," Kismet softly marveled, feeling wrung out and tremulous. "And they both came out of *me...*"

Nell smiled. "They sure did, sugar pie." Then noticing that her daughter had drifted off to sleep, Nell lovingly repeated herself. "They sure did, Mama's baby."

AT home, Nell had laid down the law; there was to be quiet. Still, Kismet felt out of sorts. She didn't want company, well-wishers, or neighbors dropping by. She wanted no visiting co-workers. All she wanted was to get out of what felt like a chaotic spin.

Hearing it again, Nell said she understood. Soothingly she also acknowledged that her daughter had every right to feel that way. "Your body's undergone massive changes, sugar. Only time will help you regain your sense of self. Oh, and a little help won't hurt."

Although she was aware that it would soon be time to feed the twins, Kismet enjoyed the feel of her mother rubbing her back, and a lump rose in her throat. She hated that she had become emotional, again. However, Kismet was grateful because what would she have done had Nell been in California? Silently, she prayed, God, please bless my mama because the short, round, gray-haired woman meant the world to her. Kismet also wondered at being a waterspout. The babies were here, so why the tears?

"KISS-GIRL, I've said all along that I'd have to go back to San Diego." Nell stood in the oak and white kitchen. She handed her daughter a cup of coffee. "Don't stare blankly, sugar. This cup's only half-full. You can drink a little of this now."

Absently, Kismet reached for the mug. "But I don't *want* you to go."

"I know, sugar," Nell conceded. "If it weren't necessary, I'd stay." Retired from Juvenile Corrections, Nell had been in New York for months. It was implausible to think she wouldn't have loose ends to tie.

"I got used to you being here." Kismet wanted to appear rational. Nevertheless, her mother was going, to her own home, her own life.

Nell sipped fragrant coffee, "I'll return, ten days, tops."

Ten days! Kismet wanted to scream. How would she manage for that long? "Is this house too small?" Maybe if she'd gotten her lazy self up, at Lyle's suggestion, before she'd gotten big with the twins, perhaps if they'd found another house, Belize and Bonaire's Nannie wouldn't be leaving. "It's too loud around here, with the crying, that's it, right?"

"KissGirl, I *had* a baby. I've raised chirren, so ain't a thing too much or too loud." Truthfully, Nell admitted, "I've just got things to tend."

When her daughter dejectedly bent her head, Nell hugged Kismet and rubbed Kismet's back through her terry robe. Nell knew her daughter was afraid, but Nell would not become a crutch. "Sugar, when I had you, your Grandma Lacey was with me. I was fine, until she packed her things. Then in that way she had, she said, 'Arnell Aretha, Mama's been wit'cha long enough.' Mama told me it was time she went. She up 'n left, too. She didn't return either until you were thirteen months old."

Scared witless, Kismet looked up, "So you're doing that to me?"

"No, sugar." Nell continued rubbing. "I'll return, Lord's will. I just mentioned your Grandmama, so you would know I know how you feel. Honey pie, when Mama left, I didn't know what to do. Suddenly, you, my little baby, became a stranger to me."

Kismet looked up. "You never told me this before."

"Kismet Staar, I was ashamed and embarrassed."

Back in the bedroom, one of the tiny twins began to whine. Panicked, Kismet looked up at her mother. *What* would she do—all by herself?

Holding her daughter, Nell murmured. "You've got your husband here, and Ms. Martha's coming. She's your friend Abigail's mother-in-the-law. Such a pretty thang, that Abigail."

"Ms. Martha Dora is Abigail's *sister's* in-law," Kismet sulked.

"Well, whatever." Nell waved. "Martha Dora's capable, a good sturdy Christian woman. She's coming from upstate to look after you."

With folded arms, Kismet got up to go check on the twins. As she went, sullenly she mumbled, "But she's not *you*, Mama."

NELL packed, and Kismet pretended Nell was already gone. It was a trial run. "Déja, wait," was what the younger mother found herself saying time and again. She knew lil' mama wanted to help, but the kid was becoming a nuisance. Seated on her rumpled bed, Kismet tried to breastfeed. Déja tugged at the suckling baby. "Hi Leez," the kid incessantly cooed and placed her big head in the way. She kissed tiny Belize. At least Déja wasn't jealous, Kismet thought. That was a plus.

Baby Bonaire began making see-about-me-too noises, and Kismet's eyes filled. Her toddler, Chance, babbled, "Ma Ma, Nah's ky-eeng." Yes, Bonaire and Momma would both be bawling soon, because how was she supposed to do this? And would a kid always be fastened to her tit?

Kismet dabbed her eyes with her knit shirt. She had to come together. Still, with the warm baby lying on her and pushing at her, boy was she hot! And why was she still experiencing crying jags? Kismet took a deep breath. She reminded herself that she needed to speak with Lyle. She would do so when she didn't have a kid hanging off her, after she'd made the bed and tidied up. But when would that be? These days, she couldn't get a thing done. She was too tired, and hungry. When she finally pulled the covers up, it would be time to fall back into bed.

The Momma forgot all that. She needed to refocus on her husband. He was sweet and doing his best. He helped before he left for work. He got up at night and brought the babies to her. He even occasionally left semi-folded clothes in the basket. He mopped the kitchen and bathroom floors. He did all the unobtrusive things that he always had, *but* he had mentioned moving. Again. He'd even mentioned getting a pet.

Kismet recalled losing it. She'd griped that they couldn't *move*! Who had *the time*? With a baby in her arms, she'd eked, who would house-hunt, and choose schools? Who'd supervise the move, and unpack? Who would get Dé and Chance re-enrolled? Who would re-establish a routine for the twins, when their current one was being tweaked? And who the fu—*fig* would walk a dog, or scoop cat poop?

Kismet forgot those things to pat her smallest daughter's back. Seeing her baby's drooping eyelids, the Momma wished for sleep too. Sure, the twins were beautiful little brown things, but wouldn't it be great if she'd wake and they were seven months old, instead of seven weeks? Kismet finally gave in and let Déja hold her infant sister. The Momma scooted off the bed and realized. She had other needs.

She wanted sex. Good, skanky, messy sex! Sometimes when Lyle was near, Kismet grew wet and wanted to be impaled. She wanted her husband's greedy mouth and hands on her big tits and ample booty. She wanted to lie open, or ride Lyle like he was a randy stallion. She wanted every delicious inch of him. She wanted to drip with sweat and skeet, but she couldn't. Exhausted, she cradled her infant son and wondered. How was she, the Momma, to get what *she* needed when there was always a baby stuck to her, and other kids to care for? Truly, was she depressed?

NELL was gone too long, but Kismet got the hang of the mommy-of-four thing. However, one night in bed, she tossed and turned. She tried not to wake Lyle, but he sat up. Turning on a lamp, he peered curiously at her. He put a finger beneath her chin. "What's wrong, Momma?"

Kismet blurted that she was afraid.

Gazing at his big sexy wife, Lyle appeared puzzled. "Afraid of what?

"Losing."

"Losing what, Kiss?"

"You. Our family." Kismet gestured, "What we have."

Lyle wanted to know, "Why would we lose anything?"

"I don't know," Kismet sounded exasperated. "Well, okay, I do know. Things are becoming good again, at least in my opinion, but I keep thinking. What if this isn't what *you* want? You could leave."

Lyle was confused as wearing old b-ball shorts and a tank, he got out of bed. "Why would I leave, Kiss?" he inquired, returning with his infant daughter. "This is the life I've always wanted, with you."

Kismet bared a full breast. "Men leave all the time."

Seeing all that smooth brown skin, Lyle felt uber horny, so he tore his eyes away, and suddenly he understood. "Ah." For some reason, his wife was having a bout with her way too independent self. The self he'd dueled with to get her to marry him, and he sighed. "Look, I'm staying."

"That's just it," the wife jibed as the baby suckled and kneaded. "Who plans to leave? People one day realize they want out, when in the beginning, they thought they wanted forever."

"Kiss, there is no forever. Shit ends. Death sees to that."

"I know." Again, she felt the hurt. "My daddy left. Death took him."

"So you're torturing yourself with that. You're also wondering what if something happens to me." Lyle looked into his wife's eyes, knowing she carried the pain of losing her father. He knew she carried hurt over slowly losing Ronni too. Although Mama Nell had said she'd return, her being gone was another small hurt to carry. Therefore, Lyle said, "Kiss, stop looking for reasons to be sad. Think about what we have, and enjoy it. Live in the now. And for Heaven's sake, love, depend on me."

Lyle said he knew his wife believed dependence would make her less capable, "But cross that bridge already. You depend on me, and I on you." Through thin fabric, Lyle open-mouth kissed Kismet's unoccupied breast. "Shush." He spoke with his face against her. "Trust that I'm man enough to say what I need. And I need some of this;" he fondled her. "Trust that our situation is good, Kiss. It's chaotic, but it's ours. If it needs re-working, I'll say so. Or you can." Again, he kissed her breast.

With a sigh, Kismet realized. She tended to make the little big. She ran a hand over Lyle's locs. "Forget I said anything."

He lifted his head. "No. If you can't come to me, your man, with stuff, we've got problems. If something bothers you, tell me." He squeezed both her and the baby. "I can't fix everything, but I'll know."

Kismet smiled because Lyle really was right for her. Sure, their lives weren't that perfect, fairyland stuff that movies were made of, but it was real. Déja's clothes were on top of the hamper, where they'd been left after her bath. The diaper genie in the kid's room always needing emptying, and household staples were ever depleting, but their family was blessed. Each child was healthy, the house was warm, and they had income. It was also nice to be at home with her children, Kismet realized. Furthermore, it was nice to have someone who also found the kids' antics funny. It was even okay when she and Lyle were so tired they couldn't see straight, because they were together.

Kismet actually *liked* being in the trenches with Lyle. They made meals, brushed teeth, changed diapers, combed hair, doled out medicine, carpooled, and fought to administer eardrops. Hey, she, the Momma, wasn't even crying as much. Perhaps that was because Lyle made most things, even doctor visits, a bit more bearable.

Kismet handed baby Belize to her daddy while feeling like this wee morning feeding hadn't turned out so bad. As she put her other nipple in the suckling mouth of the half-sleeping boy baby, Kismet offered advice. "Lyle, you need to cover your shoulder."

With a scoff, he sat his daughter on his knee. He placed a large hand on her chest. The baby's tiny chin rested on the web between her father's thumb and forefinger. With his other hand, he gently patted her back. "Yo, you're talking to a pro," he told Kismet, intending to induce a burp. "I don't need wuss contraptions."

"Okay." Suddenly Kismet laughed because Belize opened her little mouth and dribbled onto Lyle's big hand.

After he'd cleaned up and put the baby down, he nuzzled his wife's neck, his hands roaming her lush, warm body.

She murmured, "Don't start nothing…"

Allowing her to feel *him*, he whispered that he sure wished he were in tiny Bonaire's place—or even beneath the Momma, or behind her.

Gazing down at the suckling baby, Kismet became conscious of desire. Feeling it unfurl, she whispered, "Maybe I'll give you some. I want it skanky though," because that was what *she* needed.

Lyle grinned. "The nastier, the better."

"Only if you burp him." Kismet handed baby Bonaire over. "Oh, and you'd better catch me before I fall asleep."

Lyle quickly signaled. "Gimme my boy—and you, woman, get undressed."

Chapter 32

THE four of them trooped up to the hospital to visit Ronni Marie Brown. Kismet, Valeria, Amy, and Nell, all went on a cold but sunny Saturday. Dressed as men, they appeared, and Ronni smiled. "This is nice," she said, touching the parcel of food that her family had brought. It included Nell's delicious Brown Betty. "Now I can eat," Ronni stated; although her family of friends knew she really couldn't. Often, she was fed intravenously. However, for the gesture, Ronni was grateful.

Valeria pointed. "Look at Amy, She's got a mustache."

"Yep, she looks like Charlie Chaplain," Kismet offered.

"Well, look at you." Wanly, Ronni smiled. "You look like *Earth, Wind & Fire* with your big wig and psychedelic colors, Kiss."

"This mess was left over from *your* seventies bash."

Ronni's visitors laughed, and she joined them. She endured a severe bout of coughing as a result. With reddened eyes and Amy rubbing her back, the sickly woman finally managed to whisper. "I can't believe y'all did this, for me. Even though you're the ugliest things..."

Before the visit, the women had hesitantly concluded that Ronni might not get to the all-male bash that she'd long desired. Therefore, they'd dressed like men to fulfill her request, and to make her laugh.

Looking like a chuffy man, Nell adjusted her bosom; as holding Amy's hand, Ronni turned to a less exuberant topic. Looking at each woman, Ronni said she needed someone to care for Ezmerelda. "I know some of you are feeding her now and cleaning her litter pan, but she will need a home, soon...one where she won't be mistreated."

Amy volunteered, murmuring, "Poor kitty's been shuffled about."

Sighing with relief, Ronni lay back. "Now I won't worry."

LATER that evening, on the phone, Kismet said, "Val, I'm glad Amy's taking Ezmerelda." Kismet then threw in, as if it was no big deal, "You know, since Amy's been feeding that cat, it knows her. It knows you too because you feed it when Amy can't."

"Furry Ezmerelda knows you too, Kiss," Valeria pointed out. "You clean Ronni's place 'n stuff, and you love cats. You love my little Mystical. You could have taken Ronni's cat if Amy hadn't offered."

"No." Kismet sounded indignant. "I could not have."

Having heard the vehemence and something more, gingerly, Valeria probed. "Kiss...what do you think is wrong with Ezmerelda?"

Kismet remained silent. When her friend did too, the curvier woman blurted, "Okay! I don't want that cat because everybody she belonged to, died! First, the old lady, then Keesa, and now Ronni..."

Valeria spoke softly. "Kiss, we're all going to go someday. So tell me, do you think the cat is an omen?"

"I didn't say all that," Kismet huffed, not wanting to get into it. "I just have too much to live for."

Valeria was shocked. Then she became incensed. "And Ronni doesn't? Look, Kiss, you'd better not say that to anyone else, or they'll take it wrong. They might not understand."

Yo, who was judgy Val trying to reprimand? Kismet fumed as she stated, "I don't give a damn how anybody takes anything."

Valeria was curt. "Well, okay. She flatly told the woman of whom she was ashamed. "I gotta go,"

"Whatever." Angrily, Kismet clicked off. Moments later, though, she was filled with regret, and she re-dialed. "Val... Hey. I'm sorry."

"Kiss, I know. I understand. I apologize too; I was judgmental."

A day later, Nell informed her daughter that although Amy had offered to take Ronni's cat, Amy called, with an issue.

"Nellie, I spoke too soon," Amy had moaned. "I didn't take my Harvey's allergies into account." Amy further admitted that when she took the cat in her house, it had been terrible. "Arnell, you should have seen Harvey going out of here, all swollen, with slits for eyes."

Nell chuckled, and joining her, Amy was thankful that while she'd lived, Keesa hadn't inherited her dad's allergies. "So Nellie, what to do?"

"Oh, something will work out," Nell promised.

After realizing she had been silly, Kismet cornered Lyle. Almost begrudgingly, she told him, "You wanted a pet. Now I know of a cat that needs a home." Kismet shrugged, "All you have to do is go get her."

Unbeknownst to his wife, Lyle had already been made privy to the goings-on. Earlier, his mother-in-law had innocently relayed Amy's tale. Therefore, he listened in silence as Kismet called.

"Hi Amy. We're good, and you? Nice. Well, Lyle is willing to swing by tonight to pick up Ezmerelda—if that's okay. Sure. How's eight?"

"That's purr-fect!" Amy gushed, "But I can do better. I'd like to see the kiddies, and Nellie, so if it's not a problem, I'll head that way."

That evening when Amy brought Ezmerelda over, Déja and Chance were ecstatic. Carefully watching, to make sure the squealers didn't pull the wary cat's tail or injure her, Kismet realized she had done right.

"We got the cat, now when can I bring my dog up in here," Lyle teased later that night. Behind his wife, he positioned himself.

"Ooh, if he's big, bring him now," she advised sultry and low. "Ohhh. Yes," she gasped, feeling Lyle glide inside. When he squeezed her plump rump, Kismet purred. "That's a good dawg."

ONE midweek evening, the female foursome again trooped up to the hospital to check on Ronni. Looking up at Valeria, who'd blossomed with pregnancy, the sickly woman spoke from her bed.

"Girl, pray that baby is born after April 19th."

The mother-to-be frowned. "Why?"

"So your little bugger won't be me." Ronni sounded like she believed it. "You know, it's always been said that when somebody in a family dies, someone else is born. And honestly? I don't think y'all could handle another me. Not so soon, anyway."

Kismet was visibly upset when she spoke to the woman who shivered beneath a thin hospital blanket. "I wish you wouldn't talk like that."

Ronni gazed at curvaceous, to ascertain whether or not she was playing. Realizing Kiss was not, Ronni turned her lower lip down. "Poor Kissy pooh, you just don't want to face it, but I really am leaving."

Disturbed as well, Amy turned away. Aware that Ronni had only spoken of the inevitable; Amy went to stand before the window. With her back to the others, she hated that they were losing Ronni by degrees. She'd tried to brace herself, yet she'd wept many times. Now Amy wondered. Why did Ronni have to speak of her demise in jest?

Amid jumbled emotions, Amy heard Valeria ask the nurse for an additional blanket. Facing away, Amy also heard Ronni speak.

"Kiss, just tell yourself, Brownie's going on a long trip." Ronni forced out a raspy chuckle. "It's one I'm dying to take. Get it?"

Moments later, Ronni had to be soothed due to the scraping cough that ever threatened to tear her asunder. Watery, red-eyed, and physically depleted, she also struggled to breathe.

As Valeria covered butter-yellow Ronni Brown with the requested blanket, Kismet admitted to being salty.

"See Brownie," the curvy woman began through clenched teeth, "none of this is funny. You hear me?" Kismet got in Ronni's face. "Neither your jokes, nor this;" Kismet indicated the hospital bed, the room, the failing flowers, and the machinery; "none of this is funny! This predicament that we're all in is not funny!"

Shaking with emotion, Kismet attempted to calm down, while the others remained silent. Unable to pretend any longer, she broke down and cried. "Dang Ronni," the twin's mother tearfully wheezed, while feeling helpless, "you play too much! We love you..." Kismet sniffled, wanting to stop crying. "So, your dumb jokes hurt." Tearfully Kismet wiped her nose with tissue from Nell. "I don't know about anybody else," Kismet sniffled and swept out a hand, "but to me, all of this is hurtful." Suddenly she bent and silently wept.

After a few moments where Nell rubbed her back, Kismet found her voice. Looking into the others' tear-bright eyes, the Momma announced Ronni was unfair to those who'd be left behind. "You'll be gone," Kismet pointed out. "You'll be light and life, but we'll be here trying to get over you, for God only knows how long. So do me a favor, Veronica Marie; nix the stupid shit. Or," Kismet growled at the woman she loved like a sister, "I'll kick yo' lil yella ass—as a 'going away' present!"

Nell couldn't help it. She laughed out loud, as did Amy, through her tears. Dabbing a pink cheek, Amy also asked, "Well, how about that?"

Valeria sighed; glad the air had been cleared. She nodded at her friend in the rumpled bed. "Don't look surprised, Ron. You started this."

Appearing sheepish, Ronni apologized. "Forgive me, Kiss. Everybody else, please forgive me, too. That was in bad taste," Ronni recanted. "But what I said is true." Ronni needed her family of friends to understand. "I am miserable y'all. I can't wait to be out." Looking directly at Kismet, Ronni slowly affirmed, "You love me, now understand, I – am – tired. My *soul* is tired. I am worn; Kiss, from fighting this thing. I've battled pneumonia, shingles, and stuff I'd previously never heard of, so I need everybody to understand. Understanding is what I had to offer Keesa. I had to let go." Ronni sniffled. "I had to let her go... I told her she could go in pece without worrying about me. Now I need you all to do the same thing, for me."

"We know, baby." Nell hugged Amy, who openly sobbed. "We will."

Despite Amy's tears, Ronni nearly sounded excited. "A'nt Nell, when you were back in Cali, Amy and I kept going to church. We missed seeing you in your beautiful hats, but I did something. I accepted the Lord into my heart. It's why I have peace, now, with all of this. So now, you don't have to worry. Now you know where I'll spend eternity."

Nell bent to gently hug her 'niece.' "That is great, honey pie. You should've come on sooner. Maybe then you'd have had more fun."

Clasping her hands together, Amy serenely smiled. Returning to her window, she spoke, and her voice carried. "Ronni, dear, I want you and Keesa...to take care of each other." Amy sounded far away. "I also need you to promise me one thing."

"Anything," Ronni breathed, fading, fast.

"Promise me that you'll tell my Keesa...that I loved you, just like I loved her. Tell her that I was stupid...Tell my beautiful girl that Mama was scared." Amy's voice broke on a sob. "Tell my Keesa Louise that despite all that, I never stopped loving her, or you, and I never will."

Hearing a knock at the door, Valeria dabbed her eyes as a nurse advised them of the time.

"Guess we'll have to leave in a few," Nell said, collecting her outerwear, "but I've got a joke. Kiss got it in email."

Kismet groaned, while although weak, Ronni wanted to hear. Both Amy and Valeria appeared interested as well.

Pulling on her coat and wool scarf, short, stocky Nell began. "A man—let's call him Don—drank, and got sloshed in his apartment one Friday night. When he started on beer number six, somebody knocked on his door. Don stumbled over, and there stood a six-foot-tall cockroach."

A couple of the women snickered as Nell announced, "That giant creature punched Don in the face, and walked away." Amid more chuckles, Nell said the next evening, Saturday, Don got his drink on. "Demolished four beers before the knock came, from guess who?"

"That giant cockroach," someone interjected, "again."

"This time," Nell stated, "Roach kneed Don in the groin and elbowed him in the head-back before walking away." Nell said the following evening, Don didn't drink, yet there was a knock, so Don was cautious."

"Don't say he opened the door. Again," Amy moaned.

"You know he did," Nell shrugged. "Roach beat the tar out of Don."

"On a Sunday night," Valeria chuckled.

"Listen y'all," Nell called amid louder snickers. "The following day, Don sat in the doctor's office, asking what he could do. The doctor looked over his spectacles." Nell looked over her own as she stated, "The doctor said, 'Well Don, there's not much you can do. This thing's gotta run its course. It's just a nasty bug going around.'"

The women, with the exclusion of Kismet, screamed with laughter.

Noticing all, Ronni beckoned her friend. Butter yellow whispered. "Kiss, if you guys were morbid, I couldn't take it. So lighten up. Okay?"

As the women threw kisses and turned to go, Ronni mocked Kismet's sister Farai by calling out, "Oh, Kiss-met! Dahling, if you guys don't have my party, the real thing when I'm gone, I'll be forced to hang around and scare you."

Kismet squeezed Ronni's fingertips as the nurse again peered in.

"Kiss," Ronni rasped and reached for her friend who'd pivoted.

Kismet turned back, their fingertips barely touching. "Brownie?"

"Even though you'll have to do it without me, make it nice, okay? It can even be different from what I said. Okay?"

Kismet's eyes filled, and she could barely speak. "Okay."

"You'll have fun?" Ronni asked just to be sure. "And it'll be grand?"

"It'll be the grandest of them all," Kismet eked over searing heartache. She blew her sista-friend a kiss. "I love you, Brownie."

Lying back down, Ronni smiled with closed eyes. She whispered, "I know..." It was one of the only things she had left to hold onto.

Chapter 33

ONE evening, Kismet came in from work. Nell watched her toe-off her high-heeled shoes. Heedless of her elegantly tailored pantsuit, the young mother happily scooped up a twin in each arm. She also listened as her older children babbled about their day. As they, and Ezmerelda the cat, followed her from room to room, Kismet asked questions.

When Nell finally heard the Momma running water for the older children's bath, gray-haired Nell wondered how to begin. Busy in the kitchen, she pondered how to bring up doing something to honor Ronni's memory, when Ronni finally left them.

The frail little woman's deteriorating condition was steadily worsening. Nell had known when it was the same with her love Brantley but she hadn't wanted to face it. Now, Ronni would soon transition.

Passing the master suite, Nell saw the chubby twins lying on their mother's bed, while nearby Kismet changed. The Momma advised Déja to bring her notebook and she told toddling Chance it was tub time.

In her own room with *The Golden Girls*, Nell was aware that she had to broach Ronni's touchy subject. First, because Kismet had not accepted that she would lose her friend. KissGirl kept hoping for a miracle. Secondly, Nell needed to bring it up, but tread lightly, because, to discuss a memorial, she'd need KissGirl to face reality.

Good-byes were said and the door closed behind Ms. Fannie, the woman who helped during the day. When all the children were asleep, Nell began. "KissGirl, you think it would be nice to do something?"

Wearing a velour jogging suit, Kismet instantly became irritable because she knew her mother was plotting. "Something like what, Mama?" Not allowing Nell to reply, Kismet groused that she had enough to do. Headed toward her oak and white kitchen, and the meal that awaited her, Kismet tumbled into a frustrated diatribe. She'd had to shorten her maternity leave, brass' orders, "Because the company can't seem to function without me. Then with house hunting, because Lyle got himself approved, and told me: get my butt in gear, Ma, I'm exhausted."

Nell spooned up dinner while her daughter spoke of rising early to pump breast milk. She mentioned taking Déja to school, and leaving work to get and take her to dance. There was grocery shopping, and the cleaners and the pharmacy, before again picking the child up, and heading home to start her real job. Nell set the plate down as her daughter continued. "If Lyle didn't get Chance, and occasionally run the twins to the doctor, I'd probably lose my mind. Oh, durn..." Kismet touched her forehead. "I forgot that three-day conference, dang." She stared at her food. "Jeez Ma, no, I don't want to 'do something.'"

The Momma couldn't say she hadn't been warned. While expecting, people had predicted that sometimes Kismet would be so tired her eyes would cross. They had been right. Thank God Nell helped, and Ms. Fannie, the day lady. Amy lent assistance too, as did others, but at the moment, feeling aggravated, Kismet could not express gratitude.

"Well," Nell sighed. She knew she would seem insensitive, making her request after all her daughter had said. Still, it was now or never. Nell took a deep breath. "KissGirl, why don't we have people over for a small repast? You know, following the services for Ronni."

Kismet's voice became shrill. "What services, Ma?!" Although she didn't say it, Nell's daughter just knew they weren't speaking of Ronni's demise, not now. It was too soon!

"You know what service, KissGirl," Nell gently articulated. She honestly didn't want to hurt her daughter. Nevertheless, the younger woman had to face facts. Ronni Marie Brown was going to leave them.

"If you're talking about Brownie," Kismet's voice hardened, "Then no. I don't want people from her funeral to come here."

"Why not?" Appalled, Nell followed the woman who stalked from the kitchen. "Git," the grandmother told Ezmerelda, whose white paws she had nearly tripped over. "KissGirl, Ronni's your friend—your sister."

"There's your answer," the Momma shot back, tumbling onto her plush, cocoa-colored sofa. "*She's* my friend, not the people who'll show up crying 'n carrying on like they loved her so much. Right now—" Kismet nearly burst out crying, "Not one of them can be found!"

Knowing her daughter needed to express a few things, Nell remained silent. Lowering her voice, Kismet spoke again. "I'm sorry, Ma, for yelling, but right 'long in here, I'm not feeling friendly. Furthermore, I don't know most of the people who will show up—after Ronni's gone, and I don't want to know them."

Nell tried her best to explain. "KissGirl, there will be your first cousin, Beau, and Val and Fabian, and Val's family." Nell said her own good friend Amy, and Dr. Foster, and Ronni's family would need looking after. "Those are the people I'm talking about."

Kismet sighed. "Mount Hebron serves a repast after every funeral, Ma. You and I both know that. Oh, and when you mentioned Brownie's family, you lost me. She's got nobody—outside of us. Cliff, Jr., her trifling brother disappeared and been out the picture for years. He's got a wife that he cheats on and controls; she wants to, but she can't visit. And Brownie's parents are dead. Oh," Kismet became sarcastic, "but we can't forget Aunt Calista. Brownie ain't seen that bitch in years, even though the saints know Brownie's tried. So with that family, I can't."

Noticing her elder son in the hallway, fingering his pull-up, Kismet stood. After taking Chance to potty and back to bed, she re-entered the living room. Regarding the people last mentioned, Kismet declared, "I don't want their bad energy in here. I have small children and babies. As their Momma, I take providing a peaceful home and a protective environment seriously. I'll never waiver on that, so all them sometimey folk, or others like them, will never be invited to traipse through here."

Nell understood. Her daughter claimed she was guarding her children, but she was also shielding herself. The knowledge didn't banish Nell's disappointment.

Kismet looked away. "Mama, I need you to understand."

Quietly Nell said, "We'll allow the church to fix the meal for the family of the deceased."

Suddenly Kismet bolted forward, no longer resting her head on the sofa back. In anguish, she screamed, "I hate that word—*deceased*!"

Small, startled attempts at crying could be heard. They emitted through the baby monitor on the cocktail table.

Nodding at Lyle who appeared, Nell told him, "It's alright. Maybe you want to check on them, though." Nell indicated the monitor.

The man of the house looked at his wife, who stared at the floor. "Babe," he called, as rivulets raced down her cheeks. "You need me?"

Dabbing her eyes with a fingertip, Kismet shook her head no.

"That dang 'deceased' mess," she choked out as Lyle walked away. "That's how they referred to Daddy. Like that means a person is less dead." Kismet spat, "Deceased, passed, transitioned, dead—or whatever, it means the same thing. Our loved ones will never come back!"

Lyle was about to walk Bonaire into the kitchen, but seeing dad and baby, Kismet held out her arms. "I'll take him."

When the baby lay against her, she kissed his soft little face. Rocking, she held him to her chest. Through his yellow sleeper, she patted his diapered backside. Trying to get at her nipple, despite her clothing, the baby moved his head, and Kismet chuckled, yet her face crumpled. Her bottom lip quivered, as immensely hurt, she tried not to cry. However, thoughts of her tiny, now-frail, sista-friend Ronni, who hung onto her hand every chance she got, caused Kismet Staar to sob.

Again, she heard Ronni's raspy whisper. It echoed from the dreams that lately plagued Kismet. 'Don't let me go, Kiss, hold on to me...'

Rocking her baby, Kismet cried harder, because in her waking hours, the real Ronni said, every chance she got, that she wanted her Nile soiree. She wanted it even when she was gone. She just wanted her friends to have fun, together, she never failed to say.

"Let me take lil bit," Nell offered, pulling herself up from her chair.

"I've got him," Kismet eked. She rocked and patted her small son, whose plastic diaper softly rustled.

Watching as her crying daughter buried her face in the baby's sweet chubby neck, Nell nodded. Then ambling over, she rubbed the Momma's back. She rubbed Lyle's back too because he reappeared. Looking up, Nell informed him, "Lil' Momma just needs to get it out, you know?"

Lyle did know, and so he said.

"I hate being a wuss," Kismet hiccupped, "but I'm just tired, y'all."

"We know, bae," Lyle offered, squatting next to his wife's chair. As his cat brushed against him, Lyle knew Kiss was as depressed as he had once been. He'd watched his beloved Gran slip away, over one long year in Bonaire, previously his happy place. But one day the sun returned.

Short and stocky, Nell softly admitted that her life had never been as complicated as her daughter's life. "Honies, I didn't birth twins. I didn't have two bigger babies already, and I still struggle with the internet." Her voice became more robust, "But I did have to make funeral arrangements, like you've been drafted to do, KissGirl. I have loved and lost some of those dearest to me, like you have, Lyle. And I'll tell you both, sometimes it got so hard until I just wanted to lie down and sleep away from here."

Kismet's head jerked up. Nell patted her shoulder. "I'm okay now, sugar, but let me say this. KissGirl, I'm no Rhodes Scholar, but I *can* help you through this. Tell me what you need," Nell patted her daughter's shoulder, "and I'm on it; our lovely Lyle will be, too."

Despite his wife's sadness, Lyle nearly chuckled when Nell winked up at him. Turning to leave the couple, she said she would brew coffee.

"Yours'll be half whiskey, KissGirl." From the hallway, Nell waved. "Oh pish-posh, I'll just make 'em all mostly liquor. Heck, we need it."

The broad-shouldered man tossed his long locs. "Bless you, Mama Nell," he said, just as the phone rang.

Kismet reached for it. Cradling her infant son, wearily, she answered. "Hey Farai. How are you?"

Lyle could only hear Kismet's end of the conversation. "Yep, that's about how I feel," she admitted.

"Nooo. No girl, I couldn't let you. No. No, Farai." Suddenly Kismet laughed through her tears. "You're a lovely pest. I guess I could talk him into it..." She winked at Lyle, her eyes beginning to shimmer.

"Okay. Call you when we get there." She dropped the phone. "We're going out," she told Lyle. "For all night—Mama!" Kismet hollered before her husband could pummel her with questions. "Ma, help, please."

Nell appeared with a mug in each hand. "What'cha need, sugar?"

"Will you look in on the children? Farai's gotten Lyle and me a suite at the Helmsley Palace tonight, with champagne and other goodies."

Nell threw her head back and laughed. "Well isn't that nice?" The grandmother waved. "Y'all go. Ask God while you drive, to bless my other girl. Lord knows she can always be sunshine after a heavy rain."

200

Chapter 34

Y OU two don't know how relieved I am to see you."

"I got in the car, Amy, as soon as you and I disconnected."

"Kiss called me on the way." Valeria followed Amy and Kismet into the somber, sparsely furnished apartment. Valeria rubbed her baby bump. "Kiss scared me so, barking that I should come outside—clothed or naked—pronto, until I almost went into labor."

"I apologized, Val, but we needed to get here." After rubbing her friend's arm, Kismet laid her sweater aside. In hushed tones, she asked, "So Amy...how is she?"

"She awake?" Valeria inquired, although it was after midnight.

"She just fell asleep again," Amy confided, her voice low. "Our girl won't sleep long, and I...well, I just knew you two should be here."

About to agree, Kismet turned. "Who on earth?" More mobile than either of the other two women, Kismet sprinted to the buzzer. Silencing it, she hoped Ronni hadn't been alarmed. "Who-ooh?" she whispered.

Amy looked quizzical, as Valeria crossed arms over her hard belly.

"Diddley." Valeria acknowledged the tall, buff, brown man when he stepped into the apartment. "Curtis—hi."

Beau embraced the women. He revealed, "Kiss called, so I thought I should be here. I met Curtis downstairs."

Amy looked up. "He's been here. Curt dear, did you get some air?"

Wearily, Curtis nodded. He kissed the two younger women's cheeks. "I don't know why," he told them, "but when Amy called, I knew I had to be here, too."

"Oh dear," Amy wrung her hands. "I didn't know what else to do. Earlier, Chitra, your mom Val, and Nellie, and I shared the sacrament with Ronni." Amy saw it again in the eye of her mind. Nell held the broken bread, then the wine to Ronni's lips. Nell had even whispered a passage of scripture, paraphrased, from the Bible's book of Isaiah.

"May our Savior give you *beauty for ashes*, and may he bless us all with *the oil of joy for mourning*. May he give you, Veronica Marie Brown, the *garment of praise for the spirit of heaviness*."

With her head cradled in Nell's lap, Ronni had wanly implored all the women to rejoice, "Because," she'd whispered, "I'm going home." At last. Ronni had never really had a home on earth, other than the one she'd shared with her Cohorts, Val and Beau, for a short time. However, Ronni knew she would soon be received joyfully in her real home, her permanent home, where Keesa now resided.

With tears glistening, Amy shook herself to say to those standing about, "Nellie, Chitra, and I did those things in remembrance of our Lord, and to aid our dear in passing over. Then I made calls. I guess because in the south, didn't matter what time it was, we held vigils. I even called Gini." Amy recalled her bronze childhood friend, whom she had also told about Keesa, months prior.

To the overly nervous woman who had become a loving mother to Ronni, Kismet spoke. "You did right, Amy, and we thank you."

Quietly, Ronni's condition was explained to Beau, since for Curtis, Amy's frantic, late evening phone call had said it all.

"I need to see her," Kismet announced, pivoting and heading down the bedroom hallway. Valeria followed. Appearing doubtful, Amy hung back, near the kitchen. Twisting a dishtowel in two hands, she whispered after them. "You'll be quiet?"

Beau thought to distract Amy because she had worried, alone, for long enough. For days, she had been with Ronni, although others had dropped by. Beau knew that dread and waiting, and aiding hospice, had taken a toll. So raising his head, he sniffed. "That you cooking, Ames?"

Nodding, she tried a smile, one that didn't quite reach her sorrowful eyes. "I do it when upset. Zola Mae's recipes, you know…for comfort."

"Well, let's see what you've got." Beau made the suggestion like it was a decent dinner hour. He looked over at Curtis.

With sleep-deprived haunted eyes, the man sat forlornly on the edge of Ronni's white, camelback sofa. The sofa that Beau had lounged on when he'd lived with Ronni and Valeria René in the same apartment, come to think of it. Back then, they had all been so young and playful. Never had disease or death truly crossed their minds. Back then, they'd referred to this, their home, as The Cohort Quarters. They'd called themselves and Kismet Staar The Cohorts. Now, only one Cohort inhabited the place, and that wouldn't be for much longer. Beau shook himself because he didn't want to think about such things.

"Curtis, you should come too," the actor suggested, turning to the kitchen. Beau said so because he hated to see the other man so lonely and worn. Beau had noticed, Curtis hadn't shaved, possibly for a couple of days, although somehow he'd managed to pull on un-ironed clothing.

"You go on, bruh," Curtis waved. "I'm a'ight." He said it, although there was no earthly way he could be. Yet on the sofa's edge, Curtis wondered. How had it come to this? How could Ronni—*his* Ronni—be in the other room, dying? When he and she hadn't gotten to...

Wearily Curtis scrubbed hands over his stubbly face as the realization hit him afresh. There were so many things he and Ronni hadn't gotten to do! Now they never would. He and Ronni would never get to Coney Island together, something she'd wanted. Under a hazy afternoon sky, in stupendous heat, they would never stroll the famed boardwalk. They wouldn't eat hotdogs, with voices, color, and a carnival atmosphere all around. They would never visit Niagara Falls, or San Francisco in spring. Together they wouldn't get to Greece, France, or a piazza in Italy.

With hurt lodged in his chest as he fingered the tiny box in his pocket, Curtis knew that now he would never convince Ronni. Damn it, he'd just needed a few more days, and he could have persuaded her to become Mrs. Hurst. It would not have mattered if she were his wife for a day, a year, or a decade. Curtis simply wanted the pleasure of giving Ronni, and himself, that gift. Now it would never happen.

Curtis tried to breathe shallowly. He did so because the ache he felt was like a blade slicing through his heart each time he breathed. Desperate, hurt, and confused, he tried to latch onto Beau and Amy's muted voices. In the kitchen, the pair marveled at the dishes she'd made. They uncovered others, too, delivered earlier by Chitra, Nell, and others.

Easing into another aching breath, Curtis tried to focus on the white candles. He'd seen Valeria light them. He was unaware that she'd done so to illuminate Ronni's path when Ronni transitioned. All the same, Curtis attempted to focus on the flames so that he might forget.

Breathing shallowly, through the pain that seemed to be killing him too, Ronni's supervisor told himself to forget that it was nearly over. He reasoned that 'over' would be a good thing, for Ronni. She would be free, finally, from screaming pain and delirium. She would be beautiful again, and she would soar. That, Curtis would hold onto. Therefore, with great effort, he got up and walked to the large living room window.

Staring out into the dark of the park, he ordered himself not to feel like his life was nearly over. But without the possibility of Ronni, wasn't it?

In the kitchen, Kismet spoke. Sounding weary, Amy replied. "Oh, that's nice." She raised tired eyes. "It's good of Valeria to sit bedside. Just in case, Ronni wakes. Our girl won't feel alone."

With a toss of her curly brunette head, Amy tried to forget that she'd left her daughter, Keesa, alone at the end. However, Amy remembered, and bit her lip, Keesa had not been alone. She'd had Ronni. So God bless Ronni, Amy prayed as on her lip she felt sluggishly oozing blood.

Again, Beau sat in the living room. It had once been beautiful. He held a plate of food. Greedily, he'd have forked in on any other occasion. Forgetting that, he pondered the room that had once been a mystical showplace. Back when he'd lived at The Quarters, foliage had graced the place, so had objects d'art acquired on his and Valeria's sojourns. There had been music in the background, and he and Ronni had fought weekly. They'd managed to laugh too. Back then, neither of them had had any inkling that they would face...*this*.

Movement caught Beau's eye. He was jogged back to the present. Fabian was there, handing his wife, heavy with child, a glass half-filled. When had Val's husband arrived? Where too, Beau wondered, was Kiss?

Seated on the bed, Kismet's weight comfortably pulled the bedclothes tight around Ronni. Dear God, Ronni realized, she had been so miserably cold all before, despite the many comforters piled atop her.

Kismet held the thin yellow hand. "Let me get Val," she suggested, as tears streamed from her eyes.

"No, Kiss," Ronni softly rasped. "I spoke to her. This is for you... I love you. Before Amy came, you were a big sister and mama to me. You fought for me. You fought with me too, but I always knew. You love me. Kiss—" Ronni coughed, something for which she had no strength.

"I'm okay," she managed to lie. Her eyes were dull, her skin was waxen, and her breathing was labored. "Kiss, I gotta say this. I spent the best years I had with you...and Val and Diddley. Never forget that."

Kismet swiped her nose and tried not to sob.

"Kiss, you won't let everybody see me, will you?"

"No, baby. Hush," Kismet managed as her heart threatened to tear painfully through her chest. "I've got all your wishes written down. No one but Val and I—oh, and those here, will see you."

Ronni reached out a shaky skeletal hand. "You'll explain to Amy?"

Kismet gently squeezed the frigid hand that was now mostly bone. "I already have, baby girl, and she understands."

"Make me look pretty, Kiss...like I used to. I want to wear a spring color, maybe a nice bright green, so Keesa won't see me looking bad. At the church, let the choir sing and y'all be happy for me..."

Although she didn't want to, Kismet sobbed aloud, and the sound hurriedly lifted Curtis, in the living room, off the sofa.

Just as he got to the bedroom door, he felt a blast from the small space heater. He also felt...lost, suddenly, because Ronni turned her head. She smiled at him. Then her eyes changed.

Brown, and no longer filled with pain, those eyes became unseeing.

In that instant, Kismet knew. Tearfully, she leaned to hug and kiss her dear sister-friend. Noting the time, Curtis knew, too.

Ronni had transitioned.

Amy and Beau, who appeared, knew as well. They could feel it.

"I love you, girl," Kismet sobbed and pulled Ronni up. Kismet's throat felt raw as she held her friend's warm skeletal remains. "I always will. Veronica... Oh God," Kismet moaned and rocked. Through tears, she peered down into the emaciated face. "Brownieee... Oh, God."

Anguished, Kismet closed Ronni's eyes. Then she screamed, her voice becoming raw and ragged. The sound seared her throat and rang in everyone but Ronni's ears. "Oh God—Ohhh GODDD!"

Curtis felt Kismet Staar had spoken for him. In the stiflingly hot room, he bent. Gently he set a glittering solitaire, in its open blue velvet box, atop the bedside table.

It was an engagement ring, the one he had longed to see on Ronni's finger.

Chapter 35

KISMET Staar could not believe how dizzying her life was, and to think, it used to be so serene, when she'd lived alone. Sometimes she thought about those days. She, Valeria René, and Ronni had attended Clark-Atlanta. At the HBCU, they'd been inseparable. Upon graduating from the university in Georgia, Kismet returned to New York and got a place of her own. Val, a native New Yorker too, and Floridian, Ronni, had roomed across town. They'd welcomed Beau into their Astoria apartment. The four of them had been thick as thieves.

Now, look at the turns their lives had taken. Kismet thought it as she drove. Ronni had been violently ill, unto death. Val, who'd had all kinds of trouble conceiving, currently carried a healthy baby. Beau was now a recognized actor and producer, and here *she* was, Kismet recalled, a businessperson, a bona fide Momma, and a wife.

As she drove, Kismet tried to think of any and everything but what she was about to do. Peering through rain, she thought about her twins. Thanks to nursing them, she'd lost more weight than she'd gained. However, she didn't think she'd make it to the six-month mark. My Lord, Kismet suddenly thought, Valentine's Day had come and gone.

Using her signal indicator, at the rain-slicked corner, she carefully turned. She again wondered. What kind of mother was she? Was she bad for wanting her babies quickly weaned? She sure hoped not. She simply wanted the freedom of a bottle-fed baby mama. Then she could go out with her bigger children and her husband without worrying about drips. Kismet shut off her car's ignition. With a sigh, she bowed her head.

She could no longer occupy her mind with other things. She had to get down to business. She got out of her car. In the soggy parking lot, she stood staring at the stone front of Mt Hebron African Methodist Episcopal. It was the Church to which her family of friends belonged. Kismet scolded herself and murmured, "Get a move on, girl." She pulled on gloves. In drizzling rain and cold, she walked. She wanted to go home, but she forgot that. Kismet reminded herself. On this particular Friday evening, she had tasks.

Entering the sanctuary, she felt a hush, one she'd never before noticed. She rubbed her coat sleeves with gloved hands to stave off the chill that threatened to envelop her.

Then aloof Anna Spivey, the too tall, bony-faced, Mt. Hebron church member, and mortician, passed.

Kismet returned the woman's nod and entered the chapel. Slowly, she walked down the long, carpeted center aisle.

Perhaps she would sit on the first row's cushioned pew. From there, she could face Ronni. Kismet could gaze at the other woman's form, in the open, rose-colored casket.

Spotting a chair aside, Kismet pulled it up before her friend who lay in a slumber from which she would physically rise no more. Dabbing at tears, Kismet whispered, "I love you, girl. I only hope you knew how much." She sighed and recalled that during Ronni's lifetime, so many hurdles had been overcome. Shaking her head, Kismet whispered, "You could always make me laugh." Then realizing that Ronni would never again do so, Kismet moaned. "Brownie, why'd you have to go, so soon?"

As Ronni lay, looking powdery and nothing like she once had, Kismet brought a fist down on her thigh. "Why couldn't you have waited? Why'd you have to be so dag-blame fast Brownie, all the time?"

Thinking back to when she, Ronni, and Valeria had all been girl-women in college, Kismet wept. Back then, Ronni had been daringly promiscuous. "Why'd you have to be so stupid?" Kismet inquired, her face in her hands.

Yet she recalled, there had been joy. Thus, she asked through tears, "With you gone, who's gonna give me 'n Val license to clown?" Kismet's eyes scanned Ronni's remains. "Who am I gonna tell to quit talking with their mouth full? Who am I gonna tell: be nice."

Kismet leaned forward. Gazing at her friend, she absorbed every detail so that Ronni's image wouldn't fade in years to come. Like Kismet's father, Brantley's image had.

Eyes roaming, Kismet realized. Ronni looked nothing like she had in the past. Where Ronni had once had a softly rounded face, and the most beautiful, short, dark, naturally wavy hair, now there were only jutting, lifeless, skeletal angles. Ronni's skin was powdered, but back in the day, she had been supple, so glamorous, and shapely! Ronni Brown had always been exquisitely poured into stylish clothing. Dang! Kismet miserably thought, how she wanted so many things to be different.

She wished Ronni had never had that long, tumultuous battle with Acquired Immune Deficiency Syndrome. Kismet wished she could have made Ronni better, sort of like she did with Déja when the child scraped her knee. A little antiseptic, a bandage, a hug, and her eldest daughter was good as new.

With a sigh, Kismet spoke aloud. She hoped she had been the best friend to Ronni that she could have been. Kismet prayed she had done all for Ronni that she could have. Mentally then, she scanned a phalanx of moments, those that she and Ronni had spent together, and Kismet felt peace. She knew she had done her best. Attempting to stifle a yawn, Kismet willed Ronni, wherever she was, to hear.

"Brownie, you're not in pain anymore. Now you can be as cute as you ever were. You and Keesa. Hug little blue eyes for me."

As she sat, Kismet remembered her sista-friend's words. On her last day in the hospital, Ronni had grasped her hand.

"Kiss, make me look as pretty as possible," Ronni had implored. "Bury me in a nice spring color, but don't let anyone other than Val look at me. I don't want anybody to remember me like this." Ronni's bony grip had tightened. "You'll do that for me, won't you, Kiss?

"You have my list of songs too? Make it a celebration, Kiss, because Keesa's waiting. I feel her around me. I've even heard your Grandma Lacey's voice, and I'm not scared anymore. I simply feel like I'm finally going...home, someplace where I'll be wanted, and safe."

Seated in the warm sanctuary, Kismet shrugged out of her coat. With folded arms, she rocked back and forth. She also pondered a collage of mental images. Suddenly she realized, there were still so many things she needed to say to Ronni. It was strange, though, because while Ronni lived, Kismet had believed she'd said everything.

While she sat, Kismet felt as though she transmitted some of her feelings to her beloved friend. Kismet began to relax. Then after what seemed an eternity, her mind drifted. She remembered her husband, whom she would call. She would tell Lyle she loved him because times like these caused one to remember what was most important.

Kismet remembered her father too. Big and brawny, he had been the best. She thought about her mother, as she eyed her wedding set. Nell's daughter recalled that love never really left if it was rooted deep enough. Then Kismet's eyes darted right and left because she heard... creaking.

With breath caught in her throat, she realized, that creaking—there it was again—came from in front of her. But only *Ronni* was before her.

Slowly, Kismet raised her eyes to see Ronni...sitting up...in the rose-colored coffin, when moments ago, she had been lying down!

Oh, Jeezis! Kismet stared, as with eyes sewed or glued shut, Ronni's jaw dropped, and a wail emitted from her open mouth.

Horrified and frightened beyond belief, Kismet wanted to hop up. She wanted to run from Ronni, whose emaciated little head swiveled on her thin neck as she continued to wail. OMG! Ronni looked dead, but she was howling, eerily, like she was alive, and in pain! But it couldn't be!

With a thud, Kismet's chair hit the carpeted chapel floor. Mightily scrambling, she attempted to get over it, tangling herself in the upright legs. With a sob caught in her throat, Kismet had to get out of there before Lord only knew what would happen—to her!

Up the center aisle, she ran, full speed, bosom heaving as tightly she clutched her purse. The aisle hadn't seemed as long when she'd strode down it half an hour ago. Kismet knew pure terror as running, she wondered, what to do? She dashed through the vestibule door and felt icy grasping hands. She screamed and swung.

"Kiss! Hey! It's me. Stop!"

Valeria dodged Kismet's balled fists. "Calm...down, it's me." The mocha-skinned woman's voice became soothing because she could see that something had happened. "Honey..." she pulled Kismet into an embrace. "You bolted from the chapel, but you can't be out here without your coat." Valeria looked into Kismet's eyes and wondered, why did curvaceous look as if she'd seen death incarnate? "What happened?"

The mother of four could barely speak. "I, I—don't know."

"Kiss, breathe. Start at the beginning. How long were you here?"

Aware of the cold drizzle, Kismet shivered. Gulping air, she allowed Valeria to pull her into the vestibule. Jerkily, Kismet apprised Valeria of all that had taken place. Trembling, Kismet pointed back the way she'd come. She said it was stupid, "I know it, but Brownie was crying."

Valeria didn't believe she'd heard correctly. "Huh?"

"Inside," Kismet moaned, unwilling to allow the other woman to steer her past the vestibule doors. "Ronni's crying—and sitting up!"

"Oh, my Lord," Valeria whined as her palms went damp. She had no idea what was going on, but it wasn't right. Making matters worse, the spindly mortician, Anna Spivey, floated drearily past.

Striving for sanity, the mocha-skinned expectant mother exhaled. "Come back with me," she coaxed, her eyes on her girlfriend. "Spivey just came from there. She looks fine—well, for her, anyway."

Kismet shivered and opened her purse. "Spivey would look the same if she 'n Satan fought. I'm going home. Where are my keys?"

"Probably in your coat pocket. Please Kiss, go with me," Valeria begged. "There's gotta be an explanation." Valeria tried another tack. "If you're really not staying...you need your coat."

The mother of four moaned, "Val, I can't."

"Okay, just stand and watch me; don't run off either," because what if she needed somebody to witness what would happen to her, Valeria mused. "This is crazy," the braver woman whispered and inhaled for courage. "Kiss, I'll go down front." Valeria peered at her watch. "People should soon start arriving, and Spivey will want to close...the casket."

"Hurry," Kismet pled. Then without warning, her maternal side kicked in; "But if Brownie is crying, we need to know why—right?"

"Good girl," Valeria nodded, and stepped forward, as her friend still stood at the sanctuary door, appearing dubious and ready to run.

Sure-footed, Valeria started down the carpeted aisle. "All seems to be in order," she called, as she neared the coffin. "Kiss, your chair is knocked over." Valeria righted it and grasped Kismet's puddled coat.

When Kismet stood a few feet behind her, Valeria turned. Having retrieved the fallen coat, she noticed slight puffiness. Sure, it was around Kiss's eyes, because she had been crying, but her face had that other look. The one Valeria had seen many times. "Kiss," Valeria softly called handing over the garment. "Is it possible that...you fell asleep?" She knew her friend was exhausted.

Donning her coat, Kismet didn't raise her eyes. "I may have, I guess." That would explain a lot, like why Ronni now appeared serene.

"You were sitting there, right?" Valeria René indicated the chair that Anna Spivey removed. "You cried, and then maybe you slept and dreamed."

Kismet nodded because it was plausible. "Okay," she said, accepting that she had most likely dreamed that horrible scene.

Valeria noticed the mortician. The woman stood nearby, ready to abide by orders given prior. "Mrs. Spivey, I need a few minutes." Seeing others who'd begun to gather in the vestibule, Valeria promised, "I won't be long."

Bending over Ronni's remains, the curly-locked one noted her own falling tears. With her heart aching, she kissed her fingertips and placed them on the lips that now felt like refrigerated clay. Yet she whispered, "I love you, Ron, forever."

Dabbing tears, she nodded at the mortician who discreetly walked over. Spivey then closed and shielded Ronni from prying eyes, as had been Ronni's wish.

Sliding onto his wooden bench, softly, the organist began to play *Nearer My God to Thee*.

To her dear sister-friend, Valeria offered a hand. "Let's go, honey. We gotta fix your face."

With bowed heads, the women walked. Hand-in-hand, slowly, they trod up the carpeted aisle, tears falling as they went.

Kismet spoke softly. "All that seemed so real, Val. I wonder why?"

Sounding choked up, although her answer was simple, Valeria nodded, "Because in our hearts Kiss, we really want Ronni to be alive and well. Not gone."

Chapter 36

SATURDAY morning turned out to be miserable. It was a cold, wet spring day, and though it had been tedious, the Moore-Manfred family managed to get out on time. Kismet Staar remembered...

The rain had been slashing down the windows. Angrily, it had also pelted the roof. She'd wanted to burrow deeper under cozy bedclothes. Yet she dragged herself out to shower. She did hair and makeup while hubby sleepily padded in, carrying Chance. The two males soaped up beneath shower spray as Ezmerelda sat aside, licking a white paw.

Near-dressed, Kismet sponged off the sleeping twins. She also blessed her mother for a mug of steaming decaf. "Is that you frying bacon?" the daughter asked, aware that she would never be able to eat.

Nell nodded. "Got eggs, toast, and fruit, too, for all who want it."

Dressed and seated in the rocker, pulling Chance's socks up, Lyle wanted. "I want too," the toddler sleepily croaked, parroting his father.

"On to the kitchen then," Nell crowed, thinking of how muddy it would be at the gravesite. "Oh, I got missy up," Nell spoke of her oldest granddaughter. Re-belting her robe, she stood in the warm nursery, staring out at the rain. As Kismet dressed small Belize, Nell revealed, "Déja's eating, but we already pulled on her undies and tights. When she's done, I'll finish dressing her. She and I will ride with Deacon."

Nell said the retired police officer, also a pallbearer, would shortly arrive. "I have to pull on my suit, but KissGirl, if you have baby Leez ready by the time Deac gets here, I'll carr' her with me too."

"Thank you, Mama." Kismet had concentrated on getting the twins ready. Dreading the day, she'd kissed the head of her infant daughter. Buttoning Belize up, Kismet had laid baby aside. Readying her brother, the Momma had hated that on this day, she would say goodbye to Ronni, for the last time...until they met again, in the great beyond.

ACROSS town, Valeria René dabbed concealer beneath her eyes. She looked critically at herself. Shooing furry gray Mystical to the other sink, she washed her hands. "Well, Mysti," the mother-to-be said, as lazily the plumed tail swished, "guess that's the best I can do."

In the cozy, lamp-lit bedroom where his wife reached for her purse, Fabian fastened a cuff link. Noticing the cat tiptoeing around her, he said, "Babe, with your hair back, you look great. Unlike this awful day."

Valeria stood on the carpeted staircase landing, gazing through the window. "Fabe, we might get soaked, graveside, if this keeps up."

IN another New York home, this one palatial and near a Long Island vineyard, a man entered from the garage. In the dimly lit kitchen, he called out. "Amy..." He brushed lint from his suit. "The car's started."

Up in her suite of rooms, Dr. Foster's impeccably dressed wife knew he meant get a move on. "I'm coming Harvey, I just need my hankie."

ON the Cross Island Parkway, Beau rode in a luxury rental. He had no music or talk radio going, yet he barely heard the tires hissing along on wet tarmac. Turning down the heat of his leather seat, Beau realized. Never had he thought it would come to *this*. He had never believed that Ronni would actually go, not when she had been so spirited.

Well, his feisty little friend had not gone without a formidable fight. That, Beau would always remember.

UNDER the darkened, sobbing sky, Horace touched his wife's arm. "Chee, let me pull up in front. You can get out there, then I'll park."

Chitra faced her husband. In a pinstriped suit, how handsome Valeria René's father appeared, after all they had endured. "Horace, love, I'll stay and we'll walk together."

"No, pretty girl." Horace squeezed Chitra's hand. "You get door-to-door service. Now out; I got a line of angry mourners back there."

Huddled against the wind, at the same time, they all hurried up the wet walk. Standing outside the façade of the gray stone church, clothing flapped, fingertips wiggled, and small hands were clasped. Greetings were solemn and straightforward, as chill winds blew. People fought with upturned umbrellas, they chased hats, and others slammed car doors. Beneath sodden clouds, small inconveniences were forgotten as arms were opened, and hugs were tight. Cold rain pelted heads and faces, but no one seemed to care, as precipitation commingled with salty tears.

FINALLY, for her Homegoing Service, Ronni's family of friends, and others, were tucked into the hallowed halls of Mount Hebron African Methodist Episcopal Church.

With Fabian holding her hand, Valeria half-heartedly listened as the massive choir sang *I'll Fly Away*. She noticed Cliff, Jr., Ronni's brother. He ignored his wife. Natalie was out of her seat, again. Valeria wondered, where had Cliff Jr. *been* all these years? Why hadn't he stopped by or called? Ronni had so longed to see him and to re-connect.

Again, Valeria noticed Natalie. Since everyone had entered the church, Ronni's sister-in-law had chased her toddler. Natalie had done so even while the bereaved filed into the pews closest to the altar. However, not once had the child's father, Ronni's brother, intervened.

Casting *her* eye in that direction, Kismet recalled Ronni saying she had a nephew. Ronni's sister-in-law had let her know when the child had been born. Then nothing. Ronni had moaned about not getting to spoil her nephew. She'd hated that she'd never seen him, not even in a photo.

Valeria dabbed her eyes and thought it was strange. Ronni's brother didn't even glance at his child. Valeria wondered if Cliff, who slouched, would have preferred to be out, cavorting. She'd heard that was his way, like his and Ronni's father. Poor Natalie, Valeria thought. She'd noticed the rings of fatigue beneath Ronni's sister-in-law's eyes.

Seated with Déja on her lap, Kismet too felt for Natalie. She knew Ronni would have loved the woman, had Ronni's brother ever allowed the two to spend time together. Boy, did Cliff, Jr. turn out just like his and Ronni's father. The Momma glanced at her own husband. Seated on her right, Lyle was a different kind of man, evidenced by how he cradled his boys, the toddler and the infant, one on each arm. Forgetting Cliff, the brother whom Ronni knew was like her abusive, philandering father, Kismet watched as Amy walked forward.

In memoriam, pink-cheeked Amy tearfully announced that she had lost a second daughter. Briefly, she informed all present of how Ronni had become incredibly dear to her, just like Ronni had been to her daughter, Keesa Louise Foster.

When Dr. Foster headed toward the altar, with his heart heavy, he surprised everyone. He offered simple but sincere words. He also revealed that Ronni had helped him, and his wife, regain lost joy.

Next, Chitra stood before those congregated. In her melodic and lisping voice, she recounted how she, too, had loved Ronni. Pinching her sari, Chitra gazed at the closed rose-colored coffin as reverently she spoke. "Ronni, love, may all of Heaven now be warmed by your wit and infectious charm."

Seated, buxom Nell appeared saintly in white. She rocked baby Belize and felt Chitra touch her shoulder, in passing.

Although Chitra could not say it right then, ever shy, she had been grateful for Nell's gentle nod of encouragement.

Trembling, Valeria patted her chignon and focused on A'nt Nell. The older woman's smile said, 'Go on little Val, you can do this.' Buoyed by the knowledge, Valeria thanked Ronni for the memories. Valeria announced that they would remain in her heart, even though she and Ronni had come to the end of their rainbow, for now. Blinded by tears, the expectant mother stumbled back to her seat, and into Fabian's waiting arms.

Someone nodded, indicating Kismet should have words, following Curtis Hurst, who currently spoke. Kismet looked away. She had said what she needed, to her beloved friend. There was no one else to impress. With her gaze lofty, the Momma attempted to forgive, because most of those present had not seen Brownie in years. Only the family of friends had been there for Ronni, Kismet recalled. And *she* had been there too, for nearly twenty-one years...

Despite the insistent ache that threatened to tear her asunder, Kismet almost smiled as she recalled meeting Ronni. They had both been eighteen, two wild girls away at college. Now Kismet was thirty-nine, the same age that Ronni would have been, in just days. Yep, Kismet mused despite silent tears, she and that lil yella girl had had a good run.

Beau, the last person to offer words, recalled how he and Ronni had met. The terms had not been the best, he admitted. He also divulged that down through the years, he and Ronni had many skirmishes. "But," the tall man offered amid chuckles, "Ronni and I managed—miraculously—to laugh more than we clashed. Our good times," Beau said, his clear tenor voice reverberating in the beatific sanctuary, "by far, outweighed the bad." Looking over at the box that housed his one-time roommate's remains, Beau's eyes filled.

As someone in the congregation sympathetically murmured, Beau raised a hand, in an attempt to regain his composure. "I learned one thing about my friend," he finally managed. "Like many of us, Veronica Marie Brown didn't do everything right, yet I know this; a lot of what she did was in the sincere search for family and love."

Hearing the elegant man speak candidly about his sister, Cliff Jr. felt uneasy. He wanted to run. That, he did best. It was what Cliff had done since he and Ronni had fled their parent's tumultuous home. He'd never stopped. Still, why, Cliff suddenly wondered, hadn't he run by to see his baby sister, every now and again while she'd lived? She'd been funny and brash, and a real softie inside. Cliff guessed he'd thought lil Ronni would always be there. Now he knew, she would not. That hurt, a lot.

Someone in the audience stifled a cry as Beau continued speaking, this time only to Ronni. "Little girl, now you'll get all the love you ever needed." Severely choked up, the attractive actor returned to his seat. Beside his aunt, he felt comforted as in the stillness, Nell patted his hand.

With her robe softly rustling, the auburn-haired Shanrae Price-Owens, soloist par excellent, stepped from the choir loft. With her voice angelic and soaring, she sang the Thomas Dorsey hymn, *Precious Lord.*

As The Cohorts bitterly wept, Shanrae trilled, *"Take my hand..."*

Unrestrained the melody spiraled on, and red-faced and tearful, Amy could barely contain herself. Sobbing into her starched handkerchief, she clung to Dr. Foster, as grieved also; he tried to be of support.

"Through the storm," the soloist wailed, while Valeria extricated her hand from Fabian's. Excusing herself, slowly, the mother-to-be trod to the ladies' room, where she dissolved in tears.

Upon her return, followed by her mom, Valeria and Chitra noticed that the presiding female reverend had begun the eulogy. The women also saw a small-framed yellow woman who appeared to be an older version of Ronni. Kneeling beside the casket, the woman wept.

When Reverend Tonya McDowell eloquently closed, she addressed all gathered. "Our dear sister has gone on, but I know, of a surety, that she made peace with her maker. So, brothers and sisters, the question now is: where – will – you – spend eternity?"

Kismet's eyes widened, and in their father's capable arms, her sleeping sons jumped. Unmoved by the loud caterwaul, Lyle's big hands closed protectively around his boys. Soothingly, Lyle rocked, until sleepily, again, the toddler and the baby both nestled against him.

What the devil? Kismet's eyes widened as another howl rent the air. Raising herself slightly, she shifted fatigued Déja, sprawled on her lap. Kismet wondered, was that bawling real, or had she fallen asleep, again? The same way she had last evening.

"Who *is* that?" Lyle asked through clenched teeth. Then his wife knew. She was awake.

The howling became so loud that while offering prayer, the reverend could barely be heard. Down beside the casket, the woman with skin and wavy hair so like Ronni's, continued to disturb all.

Calmly, Nell handed baby Belize to her nephew. In a sweater outfit, the baby continued to sleep. Settling her, Beau smiled as the cherub suckled, in her dreams. Nell, however, strode to the church front. Discreetly she motioned at concerned ushers. "One moment, please."

Again, the woman on the floor ominously wailed. "Ronneee, oh!"

Nell bent slightly. Quietly she ordered, "Shut – this – down. Now."

The wailing heightened, and Nell called the woman's name. "Calista. Calista, stop this mess." Feeling the eyes of many on her back, Nell diplomatically kept her voice low, as on the floor beside Ronni's casket, the woman writhed. "Calista, help us get you up." As she bent nearer, Nell smelled the liquor. Then she said, grabbing hold and beckoning the ushers to do the same; "Get up, now, or I will kick you black 'n blue."

Without a word, Calista complied, as Nell issued a command. "Move, and keep it quiet." As she, the slender woman, and the ushers, marched past a sea of curious eyes, dignified and solemn, Nell held the intoxicated woman's elbow.

Pushing Ronni's aunt into the women's lounge, Nell forced her onto a seat. Nell informed the ushers that she would only be a moment. Bending, the stocky older woman advised, "Calista, do not pull that stunt again. It was not cute at the wake last night, and it's even uglier today."

Turning her head, Ronni's aunt nervously fumbled with her clothing.

"You heard me." Nell was resolute. "When we go back out here, if you feel overwhelmed, or whatever, you deal with it, *quietly*.

"Another thing," Nell just had to say. "You ain't fooling a soul, because if you cared, like you making out, you'd have called that child. While she suffered, you'd have visited. For crying aloud—you live ten minutes from where she did! And she tried with you, for years."

Nell turned to go. "I'm ashamed of you, Calista, for many things, but most of all, for embarrassing that girl's memory. You disgraced your sister's memory too, her mama, by cuttin' the fool up in here." Nell pulled on the ladies' room door. Thanking the ushers, she shocked them by calling out, "Remember Calista: cut up again, 'n I'll force my foot so far up yo' behind, you will gag on my toes."

EN ROUTE to the cemetery in one of the limousines, Kismet turned to her cousin. "You believe that little performance at the church?"

"You mean Ronnie's aunt?" Beau appeared cynical, "Such stupidity."

Kismet stared out the window. "Wonder what Mama said to her."

Seated across from his wife and her cousin, Lyle chuckled. "She threatened her, I'm sure." Lyle's wife and her mother were good at that.

Thinking of Ronni's aunt Calista, Ronni's wayward brother, his tired little wife, and their unruly kid, Kismet shook her head. Those were just *a few* of the people Nell had suggested entertaining, at Kismet's home.

THE family of friends stood graveside, shivering, while with the babies and other children, Lyle remained warm and dry in a limo.

Beneath the darkened sky, wearing a winter coat, Valeria huddled closer to Fabian. He held an umbrella that did little to shield them from torrents of rain. Folding hands across her protruding midsection, she whispered, "Beau, I can't remember a more miserable spring Saturday."

With a nod, he peered at his feet. He stifled a chuckle too, because quick-lipped, Ronni would have said he was a fool, for wearing Italian leather instead of boots. She would also have laughed heartily, if she had seen him slipping in the mud, inching closer to her newly dug grave.

"It is miserable," Amy nodded. She and Dr. Foster stood behind the mother-to-be. Holding to the physician, Amy prayed not to slip and fall.

After Reverend McDowell solemnly called, "Ashes to ashes, dust to dust…" the family of friends bent to place flowers on Ronni's casket.

All watched as the gleaming box was lowered, then people pivoted. Fighting blowing clothing and umbrellas, they hastened away, yet Amy did not leave. When the doctor prompted her, she sighed. She wondered too whether her husband's face glistened with precipitation or tears.

Feeling a surge of emotion, she turned face-first into whipping wind. With rain pelting her, Amy triumphantly screamed. *"Love never dies!"*

Chapter 37

BEAU wheeled onto his cousin's tree-lined street. There, all was in bloom. Pulling onto her sun-dappled driveway, he felt like he'd gotten run over by a bus. This spring, Beau had been busy. Amid his booming career, he'd had to go to the Brooklyn house of detention. He'd contacted a lawyer and had gone to court. Then Beau had gone to a penal facility, when Thomas was transported there.

Now here Beau was, wondering how to tell the fam. He also wondered, why did he care about what had happened to Ophelia? After all the evil she had dispensed to him and his brother.

Making sure he had his envelope; Beau got out of the rental. At the front door, he smelled the Brown Betty. He knew it was for him. His aunt hadn't said so, but while speaking earlier, she'd said he didn't sound right. He'd kind of lied, so as not to worry her. She wasn't that young anymore, and he wouldn't do anything to shave off any of her years. Now, however, smelling the baked pudding, he was momentarily again a tall, lanky kid. Back then, his aunt had mixed apples, sugar, and spices just for him. She'd done so when he'd felt bad, like when someone had stolen his favorite baseball mitt.

When the actor entered the oak and white kitchen, all the attention made him laugh. "Not you too, Amy," he chuckled, embracing her.

"My stars, Beau! Your TV interview was wonderful." She gushed, "It was so candid! Now everyone will feel as though they know you."

Beau smiled down at Amy, glad the tell-all had gone so well. To think, he'd been pushed into doing it, by Ophelia, and Sandal, perhaps.

"Sit with Amy and Kiss-Girl," Nell suggested. Beau acquiesced as his aunt left the sun-filled room. He noticed the coffeemaker gurgling away. In the hall, Nell called out, "Be back in a jiff!"

Huffing and blowing, the round woman returned. She carried a beautifully wrapped, flat, rectangular box. This she handed to Amy.

"For me?" Amy mirrored a surprised child, "But isn't this Kismet Staar's impromptu shower, since we hadn't had time to give her one?"

Nell waved. "Ames, honey, just open it."

Quickly, Amy tore wrapping paper and lifted the lid. "My gloves!" she exclaimed, her cheeks pink. "Arnell Aretha, you got me my gloves!"

"Just like your Zola Mae wore when she ushered, back at the little church of your past," Nell nodded.

Amy hugged her friend. "All these years, I've wanted a pair..."

"They're the long-sleeved kind," Nell revealed, aware that Amy could have easily bought the gloves, but it would not have been the same.

"I'll wear them to my ladies' tea." Again, Amy reached for a hug.

"Well, since we're giving," Beau said, "here." He handed over an envelope. Seated aside and softly humming, Amy pulled on her gloves.

"Sit up a minute, pumpkin." Kismet eased Déja forward on her lap. Extricating a department store gift certificate from Beau's envelope, the Momma leaned in for a kiss. "Thanks, Diddley."

"Go, lil girl. *The Proud Family* is on." Nell sent Déja away with chocolate milk. "Lyle honey," the grandmother called, as Kismet handed out coffee cups. "Please get that raspberry swirl from the fridge."

Gloved, Amy smiled. "Beau you get a cheesecake, from Val."

Nell set a glass dish mid the table, "You get a Brown Betty, too."

"What about me?" Kismet teased. "It's my shower—small that it is."

"I'll get that," Beau offered because the doorbell chimed. However, already on his way, Lyle waved. "Sit bruh, eat."

The front door creaked, and Fabian's *basso profundo* could be heard when he laughed. Re-entering the room with Valeria's husband in tow, Lyle saw that his mother-in-law had spooned up sweets.

"Hey Fabian," Nell lifted her face for a smooch. "Have a treat."

"Thanks, Miz Nellie." Fabian gave Beau a pound and looked over. "Hi Ms. Amy. Hey Kiss. Hope you don't mind, but I saw my wife baking that cheesecake, and I had to follow it over here."

Everyone laughed. "I thought you were here to get the goodies we packed for her," Kismet revealed, eating.

Fabian offered his gift bag. "Val sent this for the twins."

Amy looked up from smoothing her gloves back into their box. "How's our soon-to-be-mommy?"

Noticing the tiredness and the sorrow still in Amy's eyes, although it had diminished some, Fabian replied. "Okay; she's got swollen feet and legs, though."

"I spoke to her this morning," Kismet admitted. "She wanted to come, but I told her now's not the time to gallivant."

Fabian received the lowball glass into which Lyle poured. "That's enough," Fabian instructed. "I'm on baby alert, remember?"

"Right, right," Lyle nodded. Concentrating on his glass, he said he hadn't forgotten. "I know what it's like, you gotta stay ready."

"Okay listen," Beau called out eating Brown Betty. "I know this is supposed to be an impromptu co-ed shower for Kiss, but—"

"Diddley, we don't need anything else," the Momma said and received a twin from Lyle. "You should see all the stuff Farai sent."

"Boy, can my oldest girl spend money!" Nell chortled. "Your family too, Lyle. In this race, it seems they and Farai are neck-and-neck."

Squeezing baby Belize's chubby leg as she contentedly gazed up at her father, Valeria's husband marveled. "Dang, she's getting big." He gazed at the sleeping boy baby. "They're cute."

"That's what you're going to have, and soon too," Amy predicted, a spoonful of dessert at her lips.

Fabian nodded. "Looking forward to it. Maybe even next week."

"Next week?" Kismet scoffed. "Sooner. Mark my words."

"Well, Val has had false labor," Fabian admitted, attacking his wife's cheesecake. Suddenly he thought of licking some off her nipples.

Over the din, Beau called out. "Ophelia's in the hospital..."

Everyone quieted as he added, "Things look bleak, too."

"Oh dear," Amy dithered, her dessert forgotten. "What happened?"

Silent, but with a raised eyebrow, Kismet could only think one thing. The old crone had had it coming.

Following a gulp of hot coffee, Beau said he would start at the beginning. Adding heavy cream, he admitted to answering an unknown number. He'd heard Thomas, but Thomas had sounded like he was crying. The younger man said he was at the men's house of detention in Brooklyn. He said he was scheduled for transfer to a facility in Queens. So that was where Beau had visited his brother.

Beau apprised his family of having sat in one of the penal institute's ugly, utilitarian rooms. There, he'd asked where Ophelia was. In monotone, Thomas had replied, "She in the hospital."

"What's wrong with her?" Beau had asked, not caring.

Thomas wiped his nose on his shirtsleeve. "All her h-hell done c-caught up with her."

"What, Thom?" Beau had been confused. "What's that mean?"

"Muh told me she was gon' get r-rich, off you. She was glad about her l-lil p-plan with the t-telltale p-papers. She 'n that guy with the clown colored h-hair h-hatched the p-plan. They was gon tell the p-papers that you a h-homo. They was 'posed to get big p-pay for f-photos of you."

Beau had been surprised, almost. "Well, did they go to the paper?"

Thomas sighed. "Naw. When Muh was on huh w-way, N-Ninja, Carlos' boy, took huh down."

"What do you mean, 'Ninja took her down?' Why did this 'Ninja' do that?" Needing clarity, Beau leaned forward, "And who is Carlos?"

"That's when the C O barked at me." Beau mimicked the man, "Too close. You're too close. Separate."

"The sea oh?" Amy appeared puzzled.

Retired from Juvenile Corrections, Nell nodded. "Correctional officer, honey."

Resuming his tale, Beau said that seated across from Thomas; he was told that Carlos and Ninja had been Thom's drug suppliers. "They ain't killed muh," Thomas revealed, "b-but they might as well h-have."

"Why?" Beau inquired. He'd felt like he was extracting teeth instead of information. "What did Ninja 'n them do to your mother?"

"Muh s-started it," Thomas whined. "She m-mouthed off, like usual."

Thomas said Ophelia had not been aware that *he* had called the drug lords. "I used a phone c-card, to block m-my cell n-nimba. I pretended I was somebody different. I made myself sound like a white guy. I said, *'that Tom guy is stealing product.'* I said *'Tom is using too.'*"

"I had to laugh," Beau told his family as they stared at him. "I mean, Thom might be slow, but he's nobody's fool. He didn't even stutter when he called Ninja and Carlos. Didn't either when he used his white man voice. Anyway, Thom said Ninja and Carlos raced over."

"Muh got in it," Thomas stated, "when she was 'p-posed to be gone." Thomas said Ninja 'n Carlos hit him a few times. Then Ophelia followed them.

Beau had asked, "That how you got the black eye, Thom?"

Thomas had shrugged, and said an older man had appeared, ranting about how he was sick of the commotion, all the time. Ignoring the neighbor, Ophelia followed Carlos and Ninja, who had only wanted out by then. As was her way, she put her hands on one of them.

Attempting to vacate the cramped, dark building, the thug shoved the older woman. "Look," he'd snarled, "stay outta this!"

Yet Ophelia had hung onto him, attempting to get in a few jabs. Therefore, the thug punched her several times.

Ophelia's youngest son saw and heard her head snap backward, as blood and teeth flew. Thomas said it all happened so fast; in the frayed hall carpet, Ophelia's heel caught and her ankle twisted. She lost balance and tumbled downward. Moments later, the two darkly clad youths raced down the same narrow stairwell. With no regard for Ophelia, both scrambled over her. In the sunlight, they took the crumbling front steps, two at a time. In their loud, expensive car, they sped away.

Racing into his apartment, the angry neighbor said he would call the authorities. When he returned, he tried to comfort Thomas who'd slid down. In a dank corner of the upstairs hallway, Thomas hugged his knees. He didn't tell the neighbor that he'd seen Crack Jack.

However, Thomas told Beau that while Ophelia had lain in a crumpled heap, the thieving addict had stealthily entered the premises. He noticed Ophelia's oddly tangled limbs. Dismissing her moans, Jack placed dirty tennis shoes on either side of her. Bending, the addict wrangled away the onyx ring she'd recently retrieved from the pawnbroker. Crack Jack grabbed Ophelia's gold chain. Paying no mind to oozing blood or her moans, he'd fingered her wig. He must have realized he couldn't get much for the matted hair because he left it, askew, on Ophelia's head. Jack disappeared, and Thomas used his cell phone again. He reported himself to the police. Looking up, he told Beau he'd wanted the blue uniforms to get him, take him out of that hellhole.

Thomas said when the blues arrived; he was afraid, but he had let them find drugs on him. Thomas said he'd done so because he needed safety from further attacks by Carlos, Ninja, and their minions. "But mostly, I just wanted away from M-Muh," Thomas revealed.

"So," Beau finished, "Ophelia is in the hospital, and Thom is behind bars, moaning about how it's all his fault." In Kismet's kitchen, Beau stood. He admitted, "I know why Thomas did what he did, and I don't hold any of it against him." In the quiet kitchen, the older brother revealed, "I just hope one day, he'll be able to forgive himself."

"So, how is *she*?" Amy dared to ask.

Beau used Thomas' words, "Probably go'n die."

"Will you go see her?" Amy wanted to know, as Nell stood aside, a hand at her bosom. "I mean, if you haven't already?"

"I think not!" Kismet blurted, despising the idea. "That woman's administered nothing but misery to both Diddley and Thom."

"Oh honey..." Nell's point of view differed, as her eyes found her nephew. "Puppy, you have to let your heart lead you."

Suddenly Fabian's phone rang, and he raised his banded hand. To those gathered, he mouthed, 'Val.' "Hey babe," he said into his cell.

"Hey babe," his silly family mimicked, and called out, "Hi honey!"

Fabian quickly stood. With his legs, he pushed his chair back. "Be right there." To those with upturned faces, he shrugged. "Here we go again." Hurriedly he scooped up the last of his cheesecake.

At the door, Kismet advised, "Don't forget this." She shook the large gift sack. "Call me," she yelled as her friend's husband jogged to his sport utility vehicle. "This time, it might be for real!"

In the kitchen with clasped hands, Amy murmured, "How exciting."

With car keys in hand and baby Belize in the crook of his arm, Lyle announced that he too had to go. "I'll lock the front door, Kiss."

Over Amy's head, Lyle kissed his wife, a couple of times. Then smoothly, he transferred the baby from his arm to hers. The wee one bunched her fists and made tiny upset noises. Raising Belize to her shoulder, Kismet gently rubbed the small back. She also explained to Amy, who appeared perplexed, "It is big boss' Saturday to work. It's just for a few hours. Shush Leez," she cooed. "Shush-shush..."

When both Lyle and Fabian were gone, Beau remained to tell the ladies more. Beau said that during another call from Thomas, he learned that Thom had wanted to be like him, ever since the day they'd met at the mall. "Thom said that for a good while, he'd been tired of living as he had. Thom said he didn't want to stay in the gutter, on drugs, and fighting off Ophelia's dirty demands."

Kismet's eyes narrowed. "What – dirty – demands, Diddley?"

"Well," Beau sighed, as both Amy and Nell looked on in alarm. "If Thom was still a child, and if his mother had been caught, she'd have been prosecuted for...molestation."

Angered beyond belief, Kismet shook her head, while Amy murmured, "That poor, poor young man."

224

Beau continued, his voice devoid of emotion. "Whenever Thom refused, his mother threatened him with eviction."

"That's why he looked so sad," Kismet half-whispered. "Didn't I tell you Ma? I said we had no idea the horrors he'd endured."

Nell appeared stricken. "You said that, KissGirl."

With her eyes on peacefully sleeping baby Bonaire, pink-cheeked Amy concluded, "Well, the poor fellow just got fed-up."

Beau's lips twisted. "Funny that you should choose those words."

"Ooh, and I almost felt sorry for her," Kismet spat. "Now, I feel she got what she deserved. Don't eye me, Ma." Kismet faced Beau. "The truth is: Ophelia wanted to leave *you* in a crumpled heap, but isn't it strange? That's just how *she* was left."

Nell remembered the words spoken when Ronni had been alive. If *you're going to dig one ditch, then you had better dig two.*

With her chubby baby daughter at a shoulder, Kismet turned from the table, just as the house phone rang.

BEAU told his first cousin to go on in; he would park and meet her.

On the ward with the shiny tiled floor, Kismet exited the elevator and was very nearly knocked aside, by Valeria's sister.

Looking down the hospital hallway, Kismet called after the woman whom she had angrily shoved. "Try that again, Sonji, and I swear—I'll punch you in the face." She would gladly do so, Kismet mused as gently she knocked, because Sonji was another woman who needed her comeuppance, just like Ophelia had needed hers. Forgetting Sonji, the Momma pushed open the birthing room door. Inside, she softly spoke. "Hey, Ma-Ma..."

"Hey, you," Valeria responded.

Kismet kissed the older woman who sat aside. "Hi, Ms. Chitra."

"Hello, Kismet Staar." Valeria's mother rose. "We'll chat in a bit." She collected her purse, "But I'm off to find Gramps."

"He's downstairs." Kismet removed her purse strap from a shoulder, as she revealed, "I just saw Mr. Horace out front."

"Smoking, no doubt," Valeria said of her father. She knew her mother exited to give her and her sister-friend uninterrupted time.

Taking the seat next to the bed, Kismet looked around. She noticed that the inviting birthing suite and its kitchenette were decorated in lovely coral and aqua. It appeared soothing. Vast seascapes on canvas lined the walls. The late afternoon sun peered in and made slats on the tiled floor, mirroring those of the blinds at the windows. Serenely glowing vanilla candles lent scent, and Indian music gently wafted from small speakers strategically placed throughout the suite.

Kismet smiled, knowing the candles and music were Valeria's doing, through her husband, no doubt.

DOWNSTAIRS, Beau stood with the men in the late afternoon sunshine. He listened as Horace, Valeria's father, and Fabian, the new daddy, traded childbirth 'war stories.' Fabian's brother chuckled with amusement, while Beau recalled that at Kismet's home, when Fabian had hurriedly exited, Beau had thought, today is Val's day.

Then not long after Fabian had left, perhaps an hour later, Fabian had telephoned back. Nell picked up the phone. Excitedly, she'd yipped, "This is it—the real thing! Fabian says Val's giving birth!"

Kismet had apologized for cutting things short, "But I want to—"

"Oh, go, girl," Amy waved. "Hug the new mommy for me, and I'll be here with Nellie. We'll watch the kiddiewinks." Amy cooed at Belize, who, unlike her sleeping brother, stared inquisitively. "Right, princess?"

"Go!" Nell shooed Kismet away. "Hug lil' Val for me, too." Turning, Nell grinned. "Now, Ames, honey, we'll get to do things our way."

"Hallelujah!" Amy crowed, clapping the baby's small chubby hands.

While the older women made silly we-get-to-be-in-charge noises, Kismet asked Beau to drive her to the hospital. He'd wondered, why did she seem more nervous than when it had been her turn?

"Gimme a minute," she'd pled. "I need to freshen up."

Beau knew that meant he had time. Catching her keys mid-air when she tossed them, he headed for the door. Jumping in Kismet's car, he'd called out, letting his curious aunt know he'd be right back.

Now, outside with the men, Beau recalled having raced into the large pharmacy/sundry store just streets from his cousin's abode. He'd dashed down the right aisle. Then he'd waited, impatiently, to pay for his items.

Back outside, and seated before Kismet's home, he'd placed cigars in a felt-lined humidor. He had done so while thinking that Fabian could not possibly have had time to purchase smokes. The man would need a few to pass out when his kid was born.

Thus, when he stood on hospital ground, in a cloud of cigar smoke, Beau felt proud as people trod or were wheeled by. He felt like he had done his bit, and Fabian had been happy to receive the decorative box.

Uh-oh. Ms. Chitra's voice pulled Beau from the reverie. Scolding her husband, she said he was corrupting the younger men with smokes. Still, Mr. Horace winked at Beau, because they both knew. Val's mom would never believe her sweet Beau had been the culprit, this time.

As the men joked and laughed, Beau informed Fabian that he needed to speak with him, aside. When they stood mere feet from the others, Beau again congratulated Fabian. Then he said, "I gotta be frank. I saw that sister-in-law of yours—the crazy one with the blazing angry eyes—upstairs. Yo, she's dangling bruh. She's on insanity's edge."

Fabian chuckled, and dramatically blew cigar smoke. "I know."

"It sounds funny," Beau admitted, "but it ain't," Beau revealed that no one knew better than he did how family would do one harm. "Beat Sonji down, if you have to," Beau admonished, "woman or not, because sure as the sun rises, she's up to something. It's foul. I know it."

Beau did not mention Sonji's look, which mirrored the look he had often seen in Ophelia's eyes, just before she had done him evil.

Unaware, Fabian thanked Beau. He also revealed that he'd been warned twice, the first time by his mother. "She was a nurse in a mental ward for more than twenty years, so you know she knows the signs. Anyway, she told me the same thing you did. Mom said, 'your sister-in-law's headed for a breakdown.' She said, 'Just don't allow it to involve you or yours.' So I'll keep watch," the new dad informed Beau. Fabian added, "If you want, you can join the watch brigade. I'd appreciate all the help I can get."

UP in the birthing suite, Kismet wanted to know how her friend fared.

"I'm okay. I think." Not looking like she had recently experienced childbirth, Valeria leaned back. Wearing no makeup, her riotously curly hair was piled atop her head. A few tresses had fallen to frame her face and neck; undoubtedly, they had been plastered there with sweat, a little while ago. At present, however, her mocha-colored skin appeared dewy, and she wore a lovely gown and robe.

Kismet recognized both as two of the gifts that she and her mother had given Fabian before he'd polished off a good portion of the cheesecake that his wife had baked.

With a slender hand, Valeria indicated the side of her bed.

Rising, Kismet walked around it and saw the bassinet. "Ohhh," she softly gasped. She bent to have a closer look. "She's beee-yootiful!"

Valeria beamed. "I think so. Her name is VerRia. Cherish."

"The name Fabian chose. VerRia Cherish. Such a beautiful name, for a beautiful baby—and Val, I am not just saying that. It's true."

"Pick her up, Kiss, so you can look at her."

Kismet turned. "First, let me wash up." When she exited the suite's restroom, smelling of soap, Kismet wore a hospital smock.

"Oh." Valeria closed her eyes a moment. "I was going to mention that, but you've done this before, so you know."

"I do." Gently Kismet lifted the seven-pound bundle. Cooing, she unwrapped the pink blanket and noted the little raven-haired beauty.

"Oh, Val," Kismet whispered, "this baby is a living doll." The infant was the spit and image of her mother. Tiny VerRia had her mother's pout and an elfin cap of dark shiny curls.

Kismet fingered a teensy hand as she sat, cradling the newbie. "You've checked her?" she asked, referring to the newest Sinclair.

Valeria wanted to laugh, but her insides felt off-kilter, so she nodded. "I did. Fabian's mom, Mrs. Sinclair, did too, and so did MaMa. Baby's got all ten fingers and toes, and she's smooth as butter."

Kismet laughed. "I guess it's what mothers do." She gazed at the baby. "Val, I said it before, but I'll repeat it. This baby's perfect. I mean, I love mine, but they didn't look like this at first. They looked puckered like they'd been in water."

Valeria did laugh, despite the pain. "Well, Kiss, they had been in water, your amniotic sac, for nine months, and the twins are gorgeous."

Chuckling, Kismet felt pride as she re-wrapped her new niece. "Yes, they are. Now." Rocking, she asked, "Did you have a hard time?"

Valeria shook her head. "I didn't." The new mom remembered sweating profusely during the actual birth, "But Kiss, it seemed like MaMa, and I were at home one minute, and speeding here the next. I kept feeling like I wanted to push, and before I knew it, my doula was saying 'baby's coming.' Kiss..." Valeria's voice teemed with awe as she whispered, "I can't believe it, you know? She's here. She's fine, and she's mine. *I* gave birth to her. *I didn't fail*...and Fabian got here, just before my baby came. He got to see her come into the world. That's all I wanted. I can hardly believe it."

"I know, and after all you've been through, isn't God good?"

"All the time," Valeria nodded. Leaning back into her pillows, she closed her eyes and turned to a less exuberant topic. "Sonji's here."

"I saw her. I almost kicked her butt out in that hallway, too. She raced by, trying to knock me down. What'd I ever do to her?"

"Oh, Kiss, you always would fight." Valeria smiled as she rested her eyelids. "You did nothing. You're just my friend."

Kismet refused to say that Sonji had evil intent written all over her. Now was not the time to reiterate that precautions were needed. She didn't even ask what the devil was Sonji doing at the hospital when the plan had been for her to stay away. Kismet simply placed the newborn back in her bassinet. As she did, the curvier woman vowed to speak to the one who, more so than Val, needed to be vigilant.

"Kiss," Valeria spoke with her eyes shut. "She hates me."

"Your sister is a sick individual," Kismet offered. "Face that, Val. Then you'll stop feeling like you can fix what's wrong between you."

Hearing the door open, Kismet looked up and saw Fabian. "Hi, Daddy." The mother of four turned to her girlfriend, aware that curly-locks had to be exhausted. "I'm going, Val." Curvaceous shed the hospital gown as she spoke. "You get some rest. I'll be back tomorrow."

Kismet planted a kiss on the new mommy's cheek, and then beckoned Fabian over. "Walk with me a minute?"

Squeezing his wife's fingertips, Fabian followed. With hands in his jeans pockets and an unlit cigar behind one ear, he rocked on his heels.

"What's up, Kiss?"

"You know her sister is a loon, right?"

"Sonji?" Fabian nodded. "No doubt."

"Well, I want you to be careful with your wife and your daughter. Let Drew watch too," Fabian's brother.

"It's covered, hon." Fabian admitted that he and Beau had had a heart to heart while she and his wife visited. "Cuzzo told me the same thing, so I won't be lax."

"Good." Kismet hugged him. "God bless you—and your girls."

"My girls." Fabian beamed. "I like the sound of that." As she walked away, he thought about the woman who was more of a sister to his wife than one of her own. "My girls," Fabian repeated as the elevator whisked Kismet away. "I've finally got both of them."

THE jasmine scent of her, mingled with the sweet of the roses nearby, caused Fabian to realize. Despite the turmoil of the months prior, he had fallen in love, again, with the woman he'd married.

As his erect penis throbbed, Fabian also realized that it had been far too long since he and his wife had made love. Looking at his new daughter, lying skin-to-skin on her mom, he understood some things would have to wait. The truth was, he didn't mind, that much.

SONJI peered out of the en suite bathroom. With a hand at her mouth, she nearly giggled, because she was too smart! Here she was, in the very room that no one wanted her in, and it had been so easy. She'd sauntered in while Fabian walked Kismet big-stuff to the elevator.

Sonji had made sure MaMa was gone. When she'd seen Chitra go in search of Horace, her Dad, Sonji waited until Fabian's family dispersed.

Then Sonji had stopped feeling cheerful. She'd reminded herself of how everyone was acting as if this was some kind of holiday. It was sickening! And Val, she had nerve, telling Sonji to stay away. The coward had issued 'her command' over the phone and not face to face.

Peering unnoticed, from the bathroom, Sonji scowled. Now Val was propped up in bed, like Queen Somebody. Well, people often overthrew queens, and dethroning day had arrived! Sonji thought it as she willed herself not to scream because that bitch held the baby that rightfully belonged to *her*. Why didn't anyone know it? With narrowed eyes, Sonji hated Val for acting like the man was hers, too. But it didn't matter, because all would soon be made right. Sonji would see to it.

The younger sister peered out into the pretty suite as Valeria raised the baby to her shoulder. Rubbing the tiny back, she asked that traitor Fabian, "Isn't she gorgeous?"

Sonji watched, and her heart ached because her baby was more beautiful than she'd expected. All those days and nights spent softly singing while in the rocker. Sonji had yearned for baby, and now baby was here. But the baby needed to be in her real mama's arms, not Val's.

Wait—was Fabian leaving? As Sonji watched, a small voice whispered, *you have to give her up.* No! Sonji nearly shouted. Never! Sonji would never give up her miniature companion. Why, the very idea caused her bitter tears. However, with the back of her hand, she dashed them away.

She was brave and smart. Sonji would fight back. Then she would have what was rightfully hers—both the baby and the man. Oh, and the house too, the one that sat regally up on the hill.

Just bow out gracefully, the small voice whispered.

Standing in the darkened bathroom, Sonji wished the voice had a body. She would have ripped that body to shreds.

Oh, man! Sonji bent because suddenly, she felt as though she might suffocate. With her head down, she could still see Val holding her baby.

Sonji felt rage ratchet up another notch when her thieving cunt of a sister murmured, "My baby...I've waited my whole life for you."

That was when Sonji realized. Val had always taken everything from her, but no more! Val was alone now, and she was weak after having brought Fabian's baby into the world. That was what *Sonji* was supposed to have done. Oh well, it didn't matter. She and Fabian would make other babies. She just had one task to perform, and the time had come.

Sonji would kill Val. To do so, she had brought just the right tool.

Chapter 38

LEAVING the Pietro brother's gym, Beau carried canvas grocery bags. Walking with one in each hand, he just wanted to get home. There he would stretch his cramped fingers. He recalled that as an actor and producer, he could have help, yet some things liked doing himself. That was the New York way.

Desperate to unwind, Beau thought about removing his shoes. Upstairs, he would also wash his hands. Then he'd put his groceries away. He would pour himself a glass of smooth, too. Feeling blue, he would play a little *Nina Simone*, maybe even a little *Miles Davis*. Then while he lounged, he would contemplate why.

Why did he care that Ophelia had died? Why didn't Thomas care that he was imprisoned? Why was he, Beau, yet so hurt that Ronni had passed? She'd made it known she was ready to go. And why the eff was Sandal still hounding him? Was the man cray?

That little red clown had walked alongside him on Fifth Avenue. Looking sallow-skinned and slack-eyed, Sandal had loudly demanded to know why he'd been tossed aside, like a sack of trash.

Beau rolled his eyes because Red was melodramatic. Wearing leather thong sandals, Beau had not replied. He'd just kept it moving, with thoughts of home at the forefront of his mind. Beau turned to enter his building, and his doorman greeted him. Then Tad had dissuaded Sandal. It was what Tad had done for weeks. Beau owed his doorman.

Then Sandal had done what he did best. He'd ranted and raved. He'd thrashed about like some mad thing. Suddenly Beau had become grateful for Boulder. Beau had nearly chuckled too because a while ago, he'd told his manager he didn't need security. However, Beau had given it a try. Now he saw that heavily tattooed Boulder, his bodyguard who had once been army—special forces—had come in handy, a few times. Therefore, Beau guessed, he probably really did need security.

On his way upstairs though, Beau had no idea that he had been watched...

SANDAL had been unaware that he, too, was being watched. Had he known, he'd have been afraid. Rodrick, whom Sandal called Rodrigo, had been meticulously tracking slender Red's every move, for days.

Had Sandal known, he'd have known that Rodrick was angry; then Sandal would have been even more frightened, especially had he realized. The stockier man felt he was being cheated on. Rodrick had had the feeling for a while. Snide remarks and sniggering had triggered it. Whispers that he was being duped had made matters worse. Then, Rodrick vowed, he would find Sandal's other guy. At that time, he would decide what measures to take.

Thus, he'd followed Sandal, again. Possessive, Rodrick had ridden the train with Sandal, but unobtrusively. Standing in a different car, Rodrick kept an eye on little Red. Inconspicuously, Rodrick had exited the train when Sandal did. Above ground, in the full light of day, Rodrick saw the other man, Sandal's love interest. Roderick lost his breath. The other man was tall and unimaginably good-looking.

Hey, Rodrick thought, that man was on TV!

With narrowed eyes, Rodrick watched as hurriedly Sandal scampered along behind the man on TV. With his baseball cap pulled low, stocky Rodrick skulked along, unnoticed, as Sandal tried to talk to the man who looked better alive than on screen. As usual, Sandal made a fool of himself, but TV man didn't seem to care, nor did he appear interested. When Sandal managed to touch him, TV shrugged Sandal off.

Rodrick stopped short as the man who was on TV turned into a building. Rodrick looked up. The place was nothing like anywhere that Rodrick had ever lived. It was for the rich, with a glass entryway. There were potted, live, green trees inside and out. The flooring was dark marble, and there was carpet *outside*, beneath a swanky, lettered awning. Rodrick made himself stop gawking. He needed to eye the mountain. That dude was a wrestling Smackdown look alike.

Sure, Rodrick looked powerful, but what people didn't know was that his bulk was hard fat. Smackdown? He was pure muscle. That, Roderick could clearly see. Now that Rodrick thought about it, Smack had been walking near the TV man all the time. They had even spoken, perhaps about disposing of Sandal.

Quickly, and still unseen, Rodrick crossed the busy Manhattan street, in front of several yellow taxis and limousines. Unaware, stupid Sandal kept following the man from TV.

Rodrick watched as the door attendant threw shade at Sandal. Then Smack, bald and fair-skinned—probably the product of a bi-racial union—effortlessly escorted Sandal from the premises, as TV man disappeared.

Rodrick was glad big Smack wasn't handling him. Hell, The Rock's evil twin did not appear friendly; even the back of his baldhead looked mean with that huge dragon tattoo on it, and his arms looked like granite.

Standing just across from The Pierre Hotel, Roderick stroked his goatee. Doing so, the forklift driver got the picture. Mr. TV was whom Sandal was trying to trade up for, huh? Rodrick watched downtrodden Sandal. He always tried squeezing into places he didn't belong, like a rat.

Sandal turned away, and from his stance across the street, Rodrick wished his little queen had seen him. Then red-hair would have noticed Roderick's sneer. Perhaps then Red would have felt like an idiot, because when would he get it? People like them weren't meant to have more. They just needed to be grateful that life was what it was for them.

Rodrick walked, past the famed green lawn of Central Park, and past a horse-drawn carriage. Leaving Sandal behind, Rodrick passed people who could probably buy and sell him. Furiously, the forklift driver thought. Which measures would he use to punish Sandal? Because he needed to make Sandal think, and remember.

Sandal was not going anywhere. That, Rodrick would never allow.

IN his posh apartment, Beau drank a glass of *Beaujolais*. He pan-seared fish, and thought, how strange life was. Gingerly, he turned the flaky, browned filets, and reminded himself that he would soon see Thomas, who had been convicted. Dang. Thom was going away, for at least three years, due to drug charges. From their lawyer, Beau had heard that Thom could get less time for good behavior.

Beau plated crisp green asparagus with his fish, and thought of Thom. Upstate. With hardened, decades-long real criminals. Beau nearly cringed because his brother was entirely too childlike. Hell, Thom could wind up severely taken advantage of...or worse.

SOME time later, Beau visited Thomas. Although the trip was arduous, Nell accompanied him, saying, "That young man needs family."

During the visit, Beau and his aunt found Thomas happy—of all things! Thomas had long dreamed of being away from Ophelia, and now he was. He'd been almost gleeful when he said he had been learning.

On the ride home, Nell patted Beau's hand. "You're proud Puppy, that Thom will get his GED and learn a trade. I know you are."

At home, Beau showered. Then barefoot and shirtless, he stood in his darkened living room before his picture window. With the night sky appearing near black, and with the lights of Manhattan gloriously golden, Beau did what he should have, months ago. He made that call.

Saavion Kennings answered on the second ring, and Beau was ecstatic. The other man wasn't even peeved with that Beau hadn't called sooner. Not since they had both attended Ronni's seventies bash.

Saavion said his co-worker, new mom Val, had apprised him that Beau had a lot going on. Saavion mentioned Beau's television interview that would re-air later that week.

Feeling a bit excited, Beau admonished himself to calm down. Then he quickly fell into conversation. Beau told Saavion that although he hadn't known it while recording, the interview had somehow freed him. Beau was no longer afraid of someone telling his story and adding his or her spin. He'd told his story, his way.

Saavion was a good listener. Therefore, Beau wound up speaking about his brother, who was finally free and happy, although imprisoned. "Go figure."

Beau summarily briefed Saavion on Ophelia, too. In Brooklyn, at King's County Hospital, she'd suffered. "She had injuries—resulting from a punch and fall."

Saavion tried not to chuckle, but the way Beau phrased things.

Beau relayed his tale and said, "After all the malingering, she died. As her next of kin," Beau divulged, "I had her cremated." He recounted receiving her ashes, "Which I promptly flushed...down several public toilets. Now she's in the sewer." He shrugged, "Where she belongs."

Saavion laughed, hard. "Ah Sukey, I'm sorry," he said. Guffawing, he choked out, "But I can't help it—that is funny! You are a riot!"

Beau laughed too, for the first time in a long time.

When he and Saavion settled down, Beau admitted he'd been petty and mean, "But darn if I don't feel good." He said he felt as though he'd finally received a modicum of closure and peace.

Again, Beau made Saavion laugh. He spoke of Thomas' new friend, Goon. "Most inmates steer clear of that dude. Now they avoid Thom, too." Beau said that from Thom's letter, he'd learned more. Goon has a small son, on the outside. Thom wrote, "I remind Goon of his boy."

Beau shared with Saavion that his Aunt Nell had alluded to Thomas getting an education. She'd said, "This won't be wasted time for Thom." While lighting candles in his posh apartment, Beau felt comfortable enough to divulge that now he had a pup. Cradling the phone and adjusting the drawstring pants that rode low on his hips, Beau admitted he would look after Thomas, the way his peops had looked after him.

"That's quite a progression," Saavion said, impressed.

"I guess it is," Beau agreed. He liked the notion. He was doing something that meant something.

When he and Saavion hung up, Beau gazed at candlelight. He realized that he had previously pondered stupid stuff—things like having more money than he could wisely ever spend. Now, outside of seeing to his aunt, and his children's charities, Beau had another cause. He had Thomas, along with his work. Beau had a purpose. He sipped from the glass at hand. Maybe when his brother got sprung, Beau would get Thom a dog. He would teach Thom to love the dog, to look in its eyes, and see the canine trust. That was what Beau had loved about his little dog, Pal, the trust. His aunt had given him his best little Pal, all those years ago.

Beau would also explain, as many times as he needed to, that neither he nor Thomas wanted to be like Ophelia, an abuser of trust. Suddenly feeling overwhelmed, Beau realized how much he loved his brother, a man he had not known for years.

Beau recognized that speaking with Saavion had crystallized something more. Beau actually liked Val's co-worker. Therefore, Beau would indeed call the optician again. If things continued to fall into place, Beau could see himself inviting Saavion out.

Beau would do so because the man seemed different. Saavion was sexy, about five feet eleven, slim, with sunlit, kinky brown hair, and sand-colored skin. Saavion was intelligent. Suddenly, Beau could see why the man and Val were more than co-workers. They were good friends. Beau could even envision himself getting to know the man who would become godfather to Val's new daughter.

Beau could even imagine *that day*. The one where he would slowly undress and caress Saavion…before they joined hard bodies.

However, that wasn't all he wanted, the actor realized. Beau wanted to *create a life* with someone who had morals, standards, and goals, a man who knew that family was important.

Beau wanted a man who didn't run around seeking anonymous partners to ride, bareback. He wanted a man who was often busy because that man had his own life. It might even be cool, Beau mused, to merge their two lives, one day. Maybe they'd even have a dog, or two.

Beau could now easily envision the life he wanted. It would involve him and his man simply sitting, sometimes, and enjoying each other's company. Beau and his man could do so, maybe after they'd entertained others on a Saturday evening. Beau thought it because he liked having people over. He wanted music in the background while he poured good wine. He liked making fondue, and serving fresh seafood. The actor liked telling jokes and hearing his guests laugh.

Then on Sunday, he and his man could read the paper while sipping hot, creamy coffee. Beau wondered if Saavion had a sweet tooth. Maybe Saav would want a pastry with their java. If it was a rainy day, they could just lie in, listen to jazz, and take it slow and easy.

Seated in candle glow, Beau tapped his heart and admitted one thing. His go-round with Sandal had not been all bad. It had helped reveal what Beau really wanted out of life. He wanted someone of his own to love. Beau desired an honest to goodness, real, man, whom drama did not follow. He wanted someone who would love him like his uncle had loved his aunt, whole-heartedly.

Therefore, Beau crossed his fingers, because…just *maybe* he had found that man.

Chapter 39

ONE sunny Saturday morning, while out running errands, Kismet parked. She and Nell then climbed down out of Lyle's SUV. In a buzzing, bright shopping district, companionably, the women walked. They admired potted plants hanging, or standing proud, just outside of each prettily attired shop.

"The geraniums are my favorite," Kismet remarked, eyeing floral faces alive with color.

"Well, look-a-here, look-a-here," Nell jovially stated and halted.

Kismet sounded surprised too. "*Curtis*...fancy meeting you here." She raised her sunglasses to see him better. "How are you?"

"I'm good." He nodded, "You?"

"I'm fine too." Kismet noticed that Curtis appeared much better than he had a few months back. Now he looked neat. Gone was the stubble, and some of the bleakness that had haunted his eyes. Looking trés male chic, as Farai would say, he wore flowing well-cut linen pants and a white designer tee. Chivalrously, he bowed. "Miz Nellie, how are you?"

"Honey," she waved, "I'm as fine as I'm gonna be, at this age."

"Well, you look great," Curtis truthfully offered. "Got your toenails done." He stage-whispered, "I've got a foot fetish, you know."

Nell felt twenty again. "Why, young man, are you flirting with me?"

"I might be." Curtis winked, "But don't tell the Deacon."

Heartily Nell laughed, and Curtis continued. "You look extra too, Kiss." He liked her lengthy v-neck dress. The watercolors complimented her beautiful brown skin, and the straps crisscrossed in the back were eye-catching, as were her strappy sandals.

Curtis tried to keep his eyes from straying to where Kismet's dress dipped in front. Nevertheless, he did catch a glimpse of her magnificent cleavage. Turning to Kismet's mother, Curtis teased, "Miz Nell, this one thinks she's hot, but who can hold a candle to you?"

Fingering her jonquil-yellow tunic and matching pants, Nell girlishly giggled. Adjusting the gold bangles on her chubby arm, she glanced around the busy upscale shopping plaza. "I'm off to the perfumery, you two." She gestured them out of the way as a motorist parked alongside. Flouncing away, she announced she would also spend time in the bookstore. "So Curtis, honey..." Nell squinted because the sun blazed behind him. "Have a wonderful weekend. Don't be a stranger, either. You come on by the house any Sunday; get you something good to eat. Lyle would welcome you to watch a game with him."

"Yes, Ma'am."

With a nod, Nell bustled away, and Curtis flashed his pearly whites.

"Kiss, your Mom is something else."

"That she is," the younger woman stated, aware that Nell was giving her time to confer with Curtis. Kismet had longed to do so ever since Ronni's funeral. Therefore, indicating a cappuccino café a few yards away, she asked, "Join me for a few minutes?"

"I can do that," he said and fell in step beside her.

At an umbrella-covered table, Curtis pulled out wrought iron chairs.

Ordering a frothy drink, Kismet sighed and removed her shades. Looking into her companion's eyes, she earnestly inquired, "Curtis, how *are* you, really?" Kismet admitted she asked because she and Curtis hadn't spoken at the repast following Ronni's interment, "So I'm curious."

A muscle throbbed in the man's square jaw, and his eyes misted. He looked heavenward.

Kismet placed an elegant hand over his. "I apologize if I'm pushing."

Curtis shook his head. "You're not. You loved her." He couldn't speak Ronni's name. "And you and your peops took to me because I was with her."

Having regained his composure, Curtis nodded, "Thank you."

Their server appeared, juggling drinks, and what Curtis thought of as her own oversized jugs. He laughed upon realizing that watching him, Kismet was amused.

Unable to take his eyes off the woman, Curtis remarked. "I suppose she's good for business."

"Looks like she is," Kismet chuckled. "It also looks like you've got a fetish for more than feet." Ronni's friend was glad to see that Curtis wasn't yet visibly pining for love lost.

Curtis nodded. "I might revisit this café, just to watch our server 'juggle.'" Then the man caught Kismet off guard, as with unexpected strain, he asked, "Does the pain ever go away?" He needed to know, he said, because he had not lost anyone before. "I mean...nobody like her."

Aware that Curtis spoke of her dear departed sister-friend, Kismet's eyes filled. "Curtis," she softly called, "Brownie was one of a kind." Swallowing salty tears, Kismet added, "I'm sorry to have to tell you this, but the pain never fully goes away."

Curtis appeared shocked. "Whu-what?"

"Oh, it lessens," Kismet assured him, "as time passes, but any lil thing can bring the hurt dashing back." She sipped iced coffee and froth. "Listen. My dad used to wear one cologne. He passed when I was young, so I thought I'd become okay with that. Then one day, about a year ago, I had lunch with one of my company's older male clients. He wore the same cologne. Lord, did that scent bring back memories..."

Curtis appeared concerned. "I'm sorry."

Red-faced and a bit teary, Kismet shook her head. "No, don't be, because although memories flooded back, they were good. I could laugh, even though I cried—a little—because my dad is still gone."

Kismet then touched Curtis's hand. "All I'm saying is: one day you'll laugh again too. You know?"

The man nodded, and softly he divulged, "I miss her. Every day. Like crazy."

Kismet did too. Not a day passed that she didn't think of her late, bubbly, ever pulled together friend. "I know." The Momma admitted that others who'd been close to Ronni had also voiced feeling the same way.

"Kismet Staar," Curtis called and bit his lip because he just had to say it. "Kiss, I would have loved her..."

"You did—you *do*, love her," Kismet acknowledged.

"No, not like I could have," Curtis clarified. "I keep thinking if I'd persevered, despite the walls she threw up, maybe she'd still be here."

"Oh Curtis," Kismet's eyes clouded. "She would have been gone, regardless, due to circumstances that transpired long before you or I ever met her. So don't blame yourself. Brownie *had* to go, *it was time*. I hate to face it, but losing her, and others, is part of life."

"Yeah, but it's hard as hell." Curtis revealed that back at the seventies bash, he had been hurting. He said he'd wanted to race to the table where Ronni had been seated with her girlfriends. "I ain't no sucker, but I

240

wanted to beg her to stop the pain," of unrequited love. Curtis added that now, he repeatedly re-lived the wee morning that Ronni died.

Kismet nodded because she often did as well.

Curtis reminded Kismet that he had been at Ronni's before Kismet and Val arrived. He divulged that he'd held Ronni, and told her things that he had previously only kept inside.

"I told her I loved her, that I'd loved her for five long years, ever since she started at Gay Men's."

Searching Kismet's eyes, Curtis quietly inquired, "Do you know what it's like to love someone who doesn't even know you exist?"

Understanding the question was rhetorical, she remained silent.

Curtis said that for a good while, Ronni hadn't been aware of him. "I was just her supervisor, and for me, that was akin to...being dead."

He apologized for the analogy.

Kismet was unfazed and said so. "Curtis, I know Brownie loved you. As a matter of fact, that's one of the reasons I wanted this time with you." Pushing her drink aside, Kismet dug in her large purse. Within seconds, she produced a pastel envelope, "Been carrying this around."

"Brownie ordered me to give this to you—after some time had passed." Along with the envelope, Kismet pressed a small familiar felt box into Curtis' hand. "She told me to tell you: *don't argue.*"

Seeing her mother, carrying a perfumery purchase, and a bookstore tote, Kismet planted a kiss on the man. Rising, she stepped from beneath their canvas umbrella. With the sun breathing warmly on her nearly bare back, she reached for her drink. "Like my mama said, don't be a stranger."

Curtis fingered his new envelope. "I won't. I promise."

As Kismet walked away, Curtis handled the lavender envelope. It was the color of aromatherapy items he'd given Ronni during her last days, to help her sleep. She'd remembered, even now.

Curtis got in his sporty little convertible. He wondered why he felt nervous. With fumbling fingers, he used his car key to slit the envelope. Involuntarily, his breath caught because...on lined paper, he saw *her* handwriting. Reminding himself to breathe, he began to read.

She drove away with her mother beside her. As she did, Kismet could not know that the card she'd handed over stated that indeed Ronni had loved Curtis Hurst.

Written in her own inimitable style, Ronni also asked, *Curt, do you know the measure of love it takes — to let someone go?*

With you, I learned. Now, for me, please do the same. Oh, and I asked Kiss to return my engagement ring. To you.

Curtis recalled that he had not gotten to give Ronni the ring while she lived, so how had she known that he'd even bought it?

I knew, Ronni wrote, as though she'd read his mind, *because I know YOU. Anyway it was all in your eyes. You were powerless in the face of all this — all my 'lush-shee-oss-it-tee' — All my luscious-ness. (I think I made up those words).* ☺

Throwing his head back, Curtis exploded with laughter, because even now she could bring him joy. From beyond, she could still make him laugh. With a shake of his head, he fondly thought, *that girl…*

Ronni had further written, *Curt, give my ring to the right woman. I will forever watch over you. Not when you guys do it - - I do NOT want to see THAT - - especially since you and I didn't get to do it. I had lots of dreams of what we could have done though. Man I would have turned you out! You just don't know.*

More laughter rumbled from Curtis. *Oh well, perhaps in another lifetime - - one free of illness. Anyway I'll be around. If your new woman is good you guys will have peace. If she's not I will haunt her ass! I will drive her stark - barking- mad. For real.*

I must go now.

Remember Curt: You helped make my last days some of my best.

Until we meet again…

With all my love,

Veronica Marie Brown

a. k. a.

~ R o n n i ~

Curtis fingered her name as tears ran unchecked down his cheeks. He also realized. Kiss had been right. Already, remembering didn't stab, jab, and hiss and sting as it once had.

Pressing his lips to Ronni's handwriting, Curtis felt freer than he had in a long time.

"Thank you, girl," he whispered, grateful for having known Ronni.

Laying the letter aside, Curtis Hurst slipped on his sunglasses. With his key in the ignition, he let his convertible top ease back and down.

Gunning his coupe's performance engine, suddenly his heart raced at the prospect of a wind-chased ride. Releasing the clutch, he engaged the accelerator. Beneath blue sky and golden sun, Curtis zoomed off.

With a whoop, he grinned. Headed for Montauk Highway, he would just bet... Veronica Marie Brown wouldn't have it any other way!

Chapter 40

IT was late October, a chilly windy evening. Excitement filled the air. With Halloween approaching and all the joyous holidays to follow, it was no wonder.

Scores of family and friends arrived. Some alighted from motor vehicles. Others searched for parking, while people made use of valet parking.

Pulling into the lit lot, Valeria excitedly waved at her parents. It was their anniversary. Aside, in the passenger seat, Fabian turned to check on their beautiful girl. Now six months old, she was nestled in the rear.

Across the parking lot, Deacon Bevere parked his car. He placed a hand on Nell's arm. He made her laugh when he told her to wait for him, "Forget that uniformed kid in the thin jacket. *I* give good service."

Fallen russet-red leaves crackled underfoot as beneath the night sky; all took a short walk. They felt rushing wind. It hinted at an early frost. Crazily, crackly yellow leaves skittered across both street and sidewalk. Looking up, all saw golden light. It poured from the stately edifice that would soon house their autumnal anniversary fete.

With the wind whipping, women hurried upward. Some clutched at lovely wraps, while others pulled evening coats close to ward off the evening chill. Men were attired in savvy suits, some boasted tails, and all wore their good shoes. Under street lamps, every one hastened to beat the cold. Little girls skipped in velvet and tights, while their small male counterparts scampered in sturdy wool or corduroy.

Up a short flight of steps, people gathered under a dazzling and decorative light. Beneath its many extended branches, they hugged, laughed, and kissed. In the impressive receiving room, color swirled, voices called, and glorious scent hung in the air.

Out of doors, Horace, Valeria's dad, stood sentinel. Beneath the glittering catering hall canopy, the older gent smoked his usual cheroot. Stoically, as was his way, he greeted all who appeared.

"Happy Anniversary!" people called out because it was the October eve of Horace and Chitra's forty-fifth.

Presenting embossed invitations that asked each guest to dine and dance with the happy couple, all were graciously ushered about. Children were lead one way, while their parents were led another.

In the Jacquard Room, on glossy parquet, there was a central open bar. Stationed around the room were tables laden with hors d'oeuvres. Flickering wall sconces and chic vases of fresh herbs lent the space an intimate, inviting feel. With jazz man Terence Blanchard's rendition of *Let's Get Lost* softly playing in the background, people quickly caught up.

When The Duke's *A Train* began to play, dapper as always, Beau stood with a tapas plate in hand. Saavion stood alongside. Sampling seafood, the sandy-skinned optician asked about Beau's brother.

Raising his stemmed glass, Beau drank and replied. "Surprisingly, Thom is doing a lot better than I expected."

Glancing around the decadent room, Saavion also inquired about 'that other guy.' His nemesis, he didn't say. As Beau stabbed something on his plate, Saavion clarified, "The one you used to kick it with." The cat then slipped from the bag. "Val said he's freckled," among other things.

"So she told you about Sandal, huh?" Beau sounded amused as Nora Jones crooned. "As a matter of fact," Beau began, "I saw ol' boy the other day..."

Saavion wasn't so sure he would like what he was about to hear.

"I was down in The Village," Beau began, "and who did I see?"

"Your boy," Saavion dryly interjected.

Beau nodded, "He's all broken up. Somebody *beat* – his – ass."

Nursing pale ale, Saavion's interest was piqued. "Say what now?"

Beau noticed Amy in sequins. She entered with distinguished Dr. Foster, resplendent in a tuxedo. "It looked like Sandal had gotten the crap beat outta him. So needing to know what happened, I crossed Eighth Street. I called him several times, and he knew it, but he ran from me."

"He ran?" Saavion was interested and feeling jokey. "Why?"

In the glittering Jacquard Room, as people passed with nods, smiles, and small plates of enticing items, Beau nodded back. "I didn't know," he admitted, "but Sandal was hobbling, fast, on crutches. Don't clutch the pearls yet; listen. When I approached, he shook his head—that was bandaged. Sandal even tried, with all his might, to scram. Guess he didn't want to see me, *or* he didn't want me to see the stitches. Above his lip and eye."

"Who got stitches?" Kismet asked. Wearing a sexy, sapphire duster and matching slinky dress, she steered Valeria over as well.

Beau noticed the mocha-skinned new mommy's hair, a mass of curls atop her head. Wearing an emerald green backless concoction, naughtily, she grinned, "Yeah, Diddley, who got stitches?"

Briefly, he began again. "Somebody beat the snap out of Sandal."

"Who would do that—to Juwanna man?" Valeria wondered, wide-eyed, and her friends chuckled.

"I needed to find out," Beau admitted. "Doubtless, his ass deserved it, but I wanted Sandal to shed some light. He didn't. Instead, he launched into hysterics. He yelled that I should get away from him."

As Saavion guffawed, Beau smirked. "The boy screeched that his condition was *my* fault." In imitation, Beau's voice rose an octave. "I've been in the hospital, because of you, so...*stay away*—from me!" Still doing his Sandal impression, Beau squawked, "Don't come any closer. *Please!*"

Kismet laughed. "You sound like Erica Kane."

"From All My Children." Valeria agreed. "Saav, remember that soap opera, from back in the day?"

"That's who Sandal sounded like," Beau insisted. "He was teary-eyed, and kept looking around, all frantic like somebody was after him."

As his friends chuckled, Beau could not have known that Sandal feared another beat down administered by Rodrick. Sandal believed the stocky forklift driver was most likely on the stalk, again. On crutches and trembling all over, Sandal would not soon forget that the overly possessive man had flown into a rage. Clouting Sandal everywhere, Roderick had spilled out all he'd seen and heard. The stocky man had grunted and punched until he landed his little red lover in the hospital.

"Well good, if he didn't want to talk to you," Kismet stated, unaware of Sandal's subsequent butt whupping and hospital stay; "because at one point, *you* couldn't shake *him*."

Valeria agreed. "How many times you told *him* to leave *you* alone?"

Glad the little scarecrow had left the field open for him, Saavion had one thought. What a pleasant evening this would be...

ACROSS the mirrored room, Chitra and Nell discussed Sonji's hospitalization. Chitra admitted that since her youth, Valeria's sister had

246

been mentally unstable. As an adult, suffering her second miscarriage, Sonji had spiraled downward, beginning with depression.

"Her poor husband," Chitra voiced. "He's been through many things with her. Although this last..." Sonji's attempt to slit Valeria's throat, with a paring knife, "was too much, and right after Val gave birth."

Nell nodded and spoke candidly. "Here we all were, thinking Darren was the one who was off. Oh, my Lord."

Sonji's mother sighed as Ella Fitzgerald inscrutably scatted in the background. "I don't doubt it. For a while, Sonji even had Horace and I believing Darren was ill. I figure it all became too much for him when my child decided to become the surrogate for Valeria René."

Chitra shuddered and revealed there were other incidents, before the attempt-to-kill. "Those should have alerted us to Sonji's true state." Shaking her head, Chitra wondered aloud, "How did I miss the signs? I'm her mother, Nellie; now I nearly feel incompetent, somehow."

Nell patted the younger mother's hand. "Honey, there are times when we are not responsible for others' actions, not even our children. What's important is that your lil' Sonji is getting help now."

Chitra nodded. "I suggested counseling for Darren, too, because he was my daughter's enabler in a lot of ways."

"Is that why you now have Sonji's child?" Nell asked.

"Yes, and Horace and I will have my grandson indefinitely."

JUST before the dinner hour, heavily bejeweled, Farai found her sister and Valeria. "Come, ladies." Kismet's sister set her martini aside. Lovely in crepe-back satin, Farai advised, "Let's take a peek at what-all we've caused to come about."

With a smirk for Kismet, Valeria was lead down a short Aubusson carpeted hallway. They entered a room more decadent than the one prior. Looking around, Valeria was pleased. Through a large window, she stared at the creamy full moon. "Isn't it beautiful?"

Kismet agreed. "Farai Lorelai, you outdid yourself again."

"I didn't," Farai waved. "*We* did."

Kismet decided not to argue. Instead, she smirked. Noticing that she did, Valeria nearly laughed aloud. Both were aware that amid planning the celebration for Valeria's parents, using ideas from Ronni's Nile soiree, Farai had strong-armed her way in, and thereby wrestled the whole project away from the sister-friends.

Turning in a semi-circle, Farai spread her arms. "Ladies, how is this for intimate?" She indicated the mirrored, silk-papered walls. In the elegant space, a quartet softly tuned up. The vintage jazz trickled and tumbled like a clear waterfall, and Valeria felt it enhanced the stunning surroundings. "This will be great," she stated, "and Ronni would have loved it."

"Your parents will too," Kismet acknowledged, viewing linen-covered tables.

In flickering flame light, Farai hugged herself, while murmuring. "I must tell François that his choice of settings has again proved impeccable."

When the women returned to the Jacquard Room, where people were yet mingling, Farai called out. "Kiss-met, and Val, dahling; upon entering that other room, the three of us will need to station ourselves where we may greet our guests as good hostesses should."

Seeing her husband across the populated room, Kismet dismissively waved. "You do it. I'm gonna eat 'n make merry."

Catching up, Valeria looked from sputtering Farai to the woman who drank from her husband's low-ball glass. "Kiss," Valeria caught the curvier woman's arm. "You're not going to do what Farai said?"

"No. I am not. Let her boss her *son* around. I am gonna enjoy myself." Kismet suddenly broke out in a grin. "Since she took over..."

Valeria laughed and agreed, *sotto voce*. "She did." Therefore, now, Valeria would also allow Farai to handle things, for better or for worse.

WHEN the dinner hour approached, all were ushered to the Venetian Room. Many marveled at the wait staff who wore finery from the time of the Egyptian pharaohs. A roving photographer, a jolly-faced man, weaved among those attempting to find their seats. As they did, he got his specialty, candid shots. Many he would digitally compile, for the anniversary couple.

On the arms of both her son-in-law Okaru, and his son Brosnan, Nell smirked as she called out. "Aren't *I* just the lucky gal?"

"You are the cat's meow. Oh-oh," Amy pinked-up as she whispered, "Nellie, better get rid of these two. I just saw your main man."

Nell beamed and called out, "Yoo-hoo! Deac, Mama's here."

248

All gathered laughed, especially when Okaru's wife moaned that she didn't have one male escort, thanks to her mother, who now had three.

"Well, you're busy hosting, honey."

Farai moaned, "I too want to enjoy myself."

Nell waved. "Then quit holding up the wall. Come on in here. These people can do their jobs without you." Releasing Farai's menfolk, Nell took the arm of Deacon Bevere. However, before heading off, she turned her face up to receive a kiss from her handsome, now fourteen-year-old grandson. "Brosnan, come back later, okay? You and I will dance."

"A'ight Nannie." Grinning, he dashed through pocket doors.

HALFWAY through the second course, Kismet looked up. She noticed. Her friend appeared a bit disheveled. "I thought," the Momma began, "maybe you 'n handsome there, took off for the night."

Valeria smiled, noticing her parent's soiree was well underway. Fluffing her napkin, she barely moved her lips. "We had a quickie."

Kismet stared. Then she laughed and mock-scolded, "Why, you two nasties!" Kismet lowered her voice. "Where'd you go?"

"Down the hall." Valeria sipped water while remembering.

"Hurry," she'd coaxed Fabian, who'd locked the sitting-room door. In the dimness, she'd pulled his arms around her, while pressing her body to his. Feeling the heat of his lips on her exposed neck, shoulders, and breast tops, she gave a little gasp of pleasure.

With hands roaming her, Fabian nearly gasped himself as he realized. His wife wasn't wearing a thing beneath her emerald green gown! Hastily pushing the garment up and spreading Valeria's legs, Fabian had been mad with need for her.

Purring with pleasure, she'd wrapped him with her legs. Valeria had also used her touching feet, behind Fabian, to lock him to her.

Recalling the throbbing heat that she and Fabian had generated, Valeria remarked. "Kiss, there's a cute little room down the hall. It has a sofa and a couple of club chairs, but you'll have to lock the door. People kept trying the knob while Fabe and I were in there."

Kismet laughed again.

"Go," Valeria ordered, "or we just might. Again."

Kismet shook her head and quietly revealed, "I'm laughing because Lyle and I did it in the elevator. After we dropped off the kids."

Valeria squealed, causing others to turn. "Fabe." Pulling at him, she whispered, "They're the reason we couldn't stake out other floors."

Fabian nodded approvingly at Lyle, as Kismet informed Valeria, "Lyle stopped the elevator." Kismet didn't say that with her slinky dress bunched, and Lyle's ravenous mouth trailing from her immense breasts to her navel, she'd moaned. With his lips traveling further downward, he'd parted her with two hands. Then looking up, before he commenced tonguing her well, he'd softly announced, "I love eating out."

"The alarm went off while we were in there," Kismet revealed. "Then a man talked to us, through that little speaker thingy." She said the man stopped speaking at one point, and they heard him snicker. Kismet guessed he'd done so because he'd listened to their grunts and moans.

Valeria nearly choked as she asked, "Fabe, don't elevators have cameras?"

"Most do, nowadays," Fabian nodded and guffawed.

"Well, that man got an eye-full." Kismet felt naughty as she adjusted her girlz. With her nipples pearling, she leaned to whisper, "Lyle, Momma needs a lick. Ready for act two?"

DURING the main course, The Venetian Room was filled with Jazz, expertly played by a quartet that shared the small stage with a woman. In her fifties, midnight dark, the sultry singer's smoky voice meshed with the keyboard, sax, bass, and the rat-a-tat-tat of the drummer's hi-hat.

Seated not far from the songstress, Amy remarked, and Dr. Foster agreed. Brosnan was indeed an exceptional young man. Watching Farai's son, Amy encouraged her husband to note how the fourteen-year-old delighted the younger children, now present.

"He reminds me of someone else," Dr. Foster said, suddenly stoic.

"Doesn't he?" Amy asked because every single day she missed or thought of her beloved Keesa. And Ronni.

The chanteuse sang on, and Amy changed tracks to ask, "Isn't it wonderful Harvey, how we've garnered such a lovely new family of friends?" When for so long, Amy had felt sequestered and alone.

"Keesa led us to them, Harv. I know it, and I often think of her, and about our life. We have so much, our health and each other. Despite our pain, we truly have been blessed."

Taking his wife's hand, Dr. Foster admitted that he too thought about their life. "It's why I now promise to spend more time with you."

Amy was speechless, as she gazed at the man who eyed their joined hands. "I've already informed my staff. I intend to work fewer hours." Dr. Foster kissed his wife. "You deserve it, Amy Louisa Foster."

"No." She became emphatic, "We—you and I both—deserve it."

THERE was a saxophone solo. The woman on stage swayed, as did others, and in the near dark, Lyle repeatedly kissed Kismet's neck.

"Okay, that's enough," Valeria teased and tried not to shake with laughter. "Hey. You dirty doggies need a room."

Touching her healthy hair, Kismet kept her voice low. "That's just how we did it." She'd insisted, not wanting her short coif squashed.

Valeria softly sang out. "TMI Momma. Too much information."

Again, Kismet touched her 'do. "Val, why are we acting like we never get out?" Kismet caught Lyle's big hand as it inched up her torso. "Girl, we're all acting like horny teenagers."

Mrs. Fabian Sinclair stared. "It must be that dreamy full moon."

RESPLENDENT in gray silk and diamonds, Chitra gazed at her husband as he held their newest granddaughter. Drinking her favorite, a paradisimo, with ruby red grapefruit for garnish, Valeria's mom thought, what a beautiful baby. Just like the baby's mother had been, at mere months old. Horace looked much like he had back then too, when he'd held this baby's mother, their first daughter, Valeria René.

At that moment, Chitra fell, all over again, for the man with whom she had laughed, cried, fought, and made love. Once more, she tumbled, for the man she'd married, the one for whom she had borne six children. Again she plummeted, for the man that her parents had said was no good for her because he was not of her race. As she tumbled headlong into love again, she recalled.

Many times, down through the years, her parents had apologized. They'd had to admit how wrong they had been, because, said they, Horace was a man among men, one of the best anywhere. And watching him with his and her granddaughter, again, Chitra had to agree. Her Horace was the best.

DEACON Claude Bevere peeked at a twin, in that small chair-like thingy. He smiled too as buxom earthy Nell patted his hand.

"When this baby wakes," she teased, "I'ma let you hold him because you seem concerned."

The Deacon turned his hand up and clasped Nell's. He had to ask her tonight. There could be no more waiting. Therefore leaning close, he revealed, "Arnell Aretha Moore, I'm scared you might go back to California. You've said you wouldn't, but to make sure, I'm asking you to marry me." He held out a dazzling ring, her birthstone nestled among diamonds. "Stay Arnell. I love you. I know you love me. Agree to become my lover, my wife..." share my life.

Kismet looked over when loudly her mother whooped.

Then when she and Farai stood over the fervently hugging couple, Beau strode up. Appearing puzzled, he asked, "What's up?"

"Deac wants me to marry him!" Nell yipped, "Old lady me!"

Beau leaned to clasp the Deacon's hand. "She said yes, right?"

With Beau's hand clasped in his big paw, the Deacon nodded. "You bet she did."

"Arnell Aretha *Bevere*." Kismet hugged Nell. "That sounds nice."

NELL'S grandson didn't understand all the fuss. All he knew was now, when he went to his Aunt Kiss's house, that man, the Deacon would probably be there, taking up all his Nannie's time. Wait—that big old cop might make even Nannie move away, with him!

Sulking, Brosnan didn't like that Okaru, his father, leaned to shake the gray-haired man's hand. Getting married was no big deal—unless his mother Farai had something to do with it. Then it would be crazy, Brosnan knew, because Mom made everything a big deal.

Uh-oh, he heard his Mom whisper. Why should *he* say something?

Standing ramrod straight, Brosnan mumbled. "Better take care of my Nannie—or I'll hurt you." Red in the face, the teenager giggled when his grandmother pulled him down to mash his face into her bosoms.

With his face hidden in the fragrant, pillow-like softness, Brosnan laughed as he was tickled, while Nell whispered. "Your Nannie will always love you, Broz, and you can always come to see me too, wherever I may be. Now stand up, young man." Nell became firm, as she straightened her grandson's jacket. "Show some happiness for me. You may start by apologizing to my Deacon—because you were rude."

Brosnan apologized before Farai dragged him off. Ugh! Who foxtrotted with their mother? How embarrassing.

LYLE crossed the room carrying his boy twin. Bonaire furiously kicked because he wanted to toddle. Letting the child slide down, Lyle was surprised at the revealing conversation he'd had with his brother-in-law. Lyle could hardly wait to tell his wife. Kiss would be flummoxed.

Okaru and Farai were adopting a small African boy. It seemed they and their son Brosnan were already taken with the little guy. Lyle believed Okaru had said the child's name was Entebbe.

Okaru said he and Farai couldn't wait to bring the child home. They'd already submitted reams of paperwork.

Lyle swung back his long locs and grabbed Bonaire's chubby hand before the small boy got away from him. Wouldn't Kiss be surprised? Yep, since Farai had once told Kiss to get rid of 'those adopted kids.' Back when Farai said it, Lyle had also felt riled up, upon hearing that about his and Kismet's older children.

Now, look at how the tables had turned.

SHED of his jacket, Fabian made faces for his infant daughter.

Merrily VerRia laughed, a lovely sound. The baby claimed her fair share of attention as nearby, people oohed and ah-ed. Daddy kissed his sweet little curly-headed girl, the one who looked just like Mommy.

ON the dance floor, Beau waltzed with his Aunt. Admiringly she spoke of Saavion, the optician. "I do believe he's a nice young man."

"Yep," Beau winked, "and so is yours."

"How do you like that, Puppy?" Nell squeezed the man she'd raised as her son. "I got *me* a man, after all these years." Suddenly her eyes filled. "I wonder what my sweet Brantley would say? God rest his soul."

Beau held Nell tight. "Uncle Brant would say be happy." Grasping her hand, Beau rested his chin on his Aunt's head. "Enjoy it...Mama."

WHAT happened?" Beau asked as he ran a gentle hand over VerRia's raven hair. As Saavion explained, Beau also thought, damn if that baby didn't look just like Val.

Saavion said he'd been walking the halls with Kismet's older children when he saw a couple. "They shall remain nameless," the optician chuckled, "but this couple inched out of a coatroom, and the woman's dress was unzipped."

Those at the table laughed, including the culprits.

A man slapped Fabian on the back. "You sly devil."

"Wasn't me, not this time," Valeria's husband declared because she was MIA. Fabian dipped his head in Farai and Okaru's direction.

Both appeared sheepish. "Oh, hush everyone," Kismet's sister advised. She inconspicuously checked her zipper. "Listen too, because Mr. Horace just dedicated a song to his wife."

BILLY Eckstein's *A Sunday Kind of Love* diverted everyone's attention. All turned to watch the handsome couple mid the floor.

After being with Horace for forty-five years, Chitra no longer expected him to dance. Still, the way he held her and swayed was nice.

Murmuring, Horace revealed something he knew. His wife had dreamed that when they got 'here,' they'd celebrate with *all* their kids. "But it looks like we're right where we started. It's just you 'n me, lady."

"That's fine." Chitra's hand was in Horace's, "Because I love *you*. I married you before there ever were any children for us."

The dark imposing-looking man squeezed his wife as their song ended. "Ditto for me, my girl. Now let's go cut this cake."

Horace and Chitra's guests drew near as the couple stood behind a table. On it, a vast, decorous confection rested. With the jazz quartet softly playing behind him, Horace spoke, and someone clinked a spoon against a glass.

"I remember the drill," Valeria's father called out. He leaned to touch his lips to Chitra's. Horace also advised, "Now you with that spoon, stop it, or else, because my doll 'n I have got to cut this cake."

Chitra chuckled as she sliced, while her man stood nearby. When she was done, Horace asked, "Chee, how about we go another forty-five?"

Licking cake from her fingertips, she replied. "I wouldn't go without you."

Those gathered cheered, and someone yelled, "Speech!"

Bowing out, Horace informed Chitra that this one was hers.

Sighing audibly, the anniversary woman smiled meekly at her guests. Then clasping both hands together, she announced, "I'll make this brief.

"Many people ask how Horace and I have remained committed for so long. Well, I love him, and he loves me—madly, but it has not always been easy. Things worth having seldom are."

254

"Go Horace!" a longtime friend cheered.

"I'm not one for a lot of talk," Chitra admitted, her East Indian lisp apparent. "However, I will say, my Horace and I could not have made it without our faith. Our deep abiding trust in a source greater than ourselves has pulled us through many things. That is why I'll remind you. In life and love, the grace of a higher power is often needed."

Suddenly Chitra felt her courage fail. Then her eyes fell on Nell, who nodded. Therefore Chitra said, "We thank you for coming. Now let's eat sweet!"

MOMENTS later, at the table where she and Kismet had giggled like schoolgirls, Valeria admitted, "It would have been nice to have had Brownie here tonight."

Kismet fussed over her biggest babies. "I know. I thought that too, several times."

"Oh, Kiss-met!" Farai glided up. "I want to say goodnight, Sweetums."

Kismet beamed at her sister, the woman she'd learned to love.

Farai dispensed air kisses. "I've had a talk with my Brosnan, and he will behave and do his schoolwork. I've sent you his teacher's email, and a list of other contacts, so God willing, I will see you next Sunday."

Farai glanced over. "Oh, and Ms. Valer-Ree-uh, I heard your good news. Congratulations on your next baby." Farai pirouetted away. "*Ciao*, ladies!"

"Chow to you too," Kismet murmured.

Gazing at her sleeping daughter, Valeria chuckled. "Kiss, Farai seems…happy. She's no longer that snobby thing I met years ago."

"She is happier, and notice… she's *leaving*, when she lectured us on her 'good hostess' mess."

Valeria laughed, as did the Momma, who sighed. "Guess I'd better get my brood home."

The newer mommy agreed, "Me too."

The Chanteuse began the last song of the set, *Sunny Side of the Street*. "*Life can be so sweet,*" she sang as the sister-friends-turned-mothers wended their way through those standing nearby. They passed others still seated, enjoying coffee, dessert, and conversation.

Melodically the songstress' words followed them and Valeria thought they rang true; there had been a time when she'd lived her life in shade.

However, she was no longer afraid. Despite its unpredictability, life now seemed incomparably sweet. Therefore, from here forth, Valeria vowed, she would always try to live on the sunlit side of the street.

OUT of doors, beneath the autumn night's sky, Beau leaned on Saavion's coupe. With crossed ankles, Beau shared his first cigarette in years, since he had long ago quit. Watching family members old and new exit the building, the actor admitted, "Saav, our particular lifestyle can sometimes offer crazy, but I want more than that."

Saavion faced Beau. "I'm not following. Can you explain?"

"Well," the actor exhaled, and smoke billowed. "Sometimes, it's hard for us as gay men to find real relationships, but Saav; I'm tired of the superficial." Beau revealed his desire to progress in something monogamous and real. "I'm no longer willing to be some man's sponsor. Nor do I want another somebody climbing all over me, just to get his jollies. At this stage in my life, I'm ready for so much more." Beau hoped the other man was too.

Crushing out the remains of their cigarette, Saavion nodded. "Sounds like you're looking for something similar to what Val's parents have."

Beau turned because the man had sounded so sage. In the moonlight, Beau *saw* Saavion then, perhaps for the first time.

Feeling a door inside himself creak further open, Beau leaned in. Saavion did too, and they bumped shoulders.

Then leaning further over, because it was time, Beau allowed his lips to meet Saavion's. It became bliss. Sinking further into the kiss, both explored the other's mouth, and within them, something ignited, and roared to life.

Yet engaged in the kiss, Beau silently prayed, for *progression*.

When he could at last release Saavion, Beau took the other man's hand. He held it to his lips. In the chilly night, beneath a thousand stars, the men continued to watch people trickle from the beautiful building.

Squeezing the other man's hand, Beau asked, "How about you and I take a walk?"

Saavion's smile spread, slow and easy, "A nice long one?"

With leaves skittering in the promising night, Beau turned and took Saavion into his arms. With finesse, he again pressed his lips to the other

256

man's lips. Sinking once more into a blissful kiss, Beau ground himself against Saavion, whose arms eagerly slid to enfold him.

When their lips parted, just a bit breathless, Beau feathered kisses across the sand-hued brow. Beau then allowed Saavion to feel *him*, that substantial erect part of him, as he said, "Saav, answer me this. Is there anything other than a nice – long – one?"

After years of wishing, hoping, praying, sending messages, and waiting, the optician replied. "You know, Beauregard, I don't think there is, at least not for you or me…"

If you've enjoyed

Progression

Book II of **The** Cohort Trilogy,

Then meet the friends again in:

Iniquities

Book III

In the closer, The Cohort Trilogy's third novel, learn how beautiful, buff Beauregard DeVeaux and the women in his life became forever friends.

Take a peek into his closeted world; see his sexcapades, his lifestyle, his loves, *and* his longings. Join him, and those he loves, on the ride that *just might* finally tear his fragile family of friends apart…

April Alisa Marquette

Photo: Tina Dennis©

As an author, editor, and freelance writer,
April Alisa Marquette
pens fiction as well as non-fiction.
A lover of art and literature, she is committed to creating beautifully
detailed works about people of color, and others.
Ever working on something,
she is currently tweaking one of the exciting novels in her
Sea Isles Series.
Visit her at www.aprilalisamarquette.net